Miami Twilight

Also by Tom Coffey

The Serpent Club

published by Pocket Books

Miami Twilight

TOM COFFEY

POCKET BOOKS
New York   London   Toronto   Sydney   Singapore

POCKET BOOKS, a division of Simon & Schuster, Inc.
1230 Avenue of the Americas, New York, NY 10020

Library of Congress Cataloging-in-Publication Data

Coffey, Tom, 1958–
    Miami twilight / Tom Coffey.
        p.   cm.
    ISBN 0-671-02829-4
    1. Private investigators—Florida—Miami—Fiction. 2. Cuban Americans—Fiction. 3. Miami (Fla.)—Fiction. I. Title.

PS3553.O365 M5 2001
813'.54—dc21   2001021374

First Pocket Books hardcover printing August 2001

10   9   8   7   6   5   4   3   2   1

POCKET and colophon are registered trademarks of Simon & Schuster, Inc.

Designed by Kris Tobiassen

Printed in the U.S.A.

To Skyler and her mom

"To spend time in Miami is to acquire a certain fluency in cognitive dissonance."

—*Joan Didion, Miami*

Miami
Twilight

PROLOGUE

*W*here does betrayal begin? Does it start with an action? With a thought? Can it begin with something even more nebulous—a desire that always remains unspoken, a vague feeling of dissatisfaction with your circumstances?

I have had time to consider these questions. I sit amid the debris that is my life, staring from a one-room apartment, and all I do is think. Occasionally I conjure a scientist mapping out every micron of the human body, helping to tear away what few mysteries remain in life. I imagine this scientist isolating a hitherto-unmapped gene. The story will be reported in the appropriate technical journals before being disseminated to newspapers, magazines and television. The story will say—pending peer review and the verification of the relevant data—that a new explanation can be given for one of the most puzzling aspects of human behavior. The scientist will say, in qualified language, subject to change after a rigorous challenge, that he has discovered a piece of biological wiring that disposes us toward either loyalty or duplicity.

The scientist will emphasize that he is not a determinist. He will stress that environmental factors play an important role in our behavior. They always have.

But in the last twenty years, it seems to me, the thrust of science has been this: The Calvinists were right. Our destinies are preordained. There's nothing we can do to alter them. Free will does not exist.

Magdalena made me think this way—the small, dark, beautiful woman who entered my life in a peripheral way on a nondescript evening in Miami as the brief twilight vanished.

1

ONE

I slipped into the party and admired the view of Biscayne Bay and nodded to my boss to make sure he knew I'd shown up. I had not wanted to attend and my impression was of an evening as dull as all the others. My company kept renting nice rooms in nice hotels, and the same nice people kept attending.

I got a beer and made small talk with some of our current and prospective clients. I also tried to avoid looking at my watch, although it was difficult to stop thinking about the Yankee game that started at seven-thirty.

My back was to the door when I heard a sharp *whoosh* behind me, as if the outer edge of a hurricane had just blown in from the Atlantic. I felt a surge of tension and excitement, the buzz of kinetic energy. My boss hurried past, almost knocking the beer out of my hand, and I heard him say, "He's here, he's here," in the tones of a six-year-old whose father has just returned from a business trip.

I turned to look. So did everyone else.

I saw a man surrounded by acolytes and sycophants. He was about six feet tall, with graying hair and a thick, dark mustache. He had handsome features and I pegged him at around sixty but there was more to him than looks; he had an aura that inspired fear and deference.

I suspected that I was supposed to know who he was.

He shook hands and smiled a lot while joking in Spanish with people who made a lot more than I did.

When I returned to the bar for my second beer I told myself I was reaching the limit. My plan was to drink slowly and circulate awhile before returning to a house that still had more boxes than furniture.

As I pulled away from the bar I nearly bumped into the distinguished-looking man whose name I should have known. I mumbled an apology in my imperfect Spanish.

"Don't worry about it," he said.

I was surprised to see him there. I figured that if he wanted a drink, somebody would get it for him. Perhaps he just wanted to get away from the crowd.

I tried to step away. He asked if I was in a hurry. I looked at my watch and decided to tell him the truth. He looked like a man who heard it rarely.

"Actually, I'm hoping to catch the Yankee game on ESPN," I said. And then I grinned.

"El Duque is pitching tonight."

"I know," I said. "I love to watch him."

It turned out the man was a huge Yankee fan and by the time I finished my beer the short twilight had turned dark and we were leaning against the bar, talking about the current team and favorite players from the past and memories of the best games we'd ever seen.

At the end, as I was about to leave, after I'd had one beer too many, I gave him my card.

My boss called me into his office as soon as I got to work.

"You were busy as a beaver last night," he said.

I shook my head in an "aw shucks" manner and asked what he meant.

"Ernesto Rodriguez. We all saw you buttering him up. Like he was freaking popcorn."

I resisted the urge to tell him he meant "friggin'."

"He called us today. Said he wanted to do business with us. Asked for you specifically. Said you were the cream of the crop. That's what he said: 'the cream of the crop.'"

I nodded.

"We've been trying to do business with him for a long time. A long, long time. So call him up. He's expecting you."

My first inclination was to do some research and find out who this man was and what he did and why everybody seemed so interested in working with him. But my boss was the type who'd check ten minutes later to see if I'd made the call. So I phoned Ernesto Rodriguez's office and hoped I would get away with leaving a message.

I gave my name and the company I worked for. I had booted my computer and accessed the Web and was ready to launch a global search for Ernesto Rodriguez as soon as I was told he wasn't in.

"Wasn't El Duque magnificent last night?" asked a voice that was becoming familiar.

I had to agree.

Ernesto Rodriguez worked out of a storefront in the middle of a non-descript commercial stretch in Hialeah. No sign on the door or in the windows said what the name of the company was, and an enormous over-hang blocked almost every trace of sunlight from reaching the building.

The door was locked, so I rang the bell. After a few seconds, some-body inside buzzed me through.

I had only a moment to look around the large square room, which was filled with women who were tethered to their desks and speaking urgent Spanglish into their headsets. A door opened on the other side of the room and Ernesto Rodriguez came toward me with his arms out-stretched, as if we were best friends who had been separated for years. He put both his hands on my shoulders. Not knowing what else to do, I returned the gesture. For a second I thought we were about to engage in sumo wrestling. "Mr. Doherty," he said, pronouncing my surname in the anglicized way I abhorred. I decided to let it pass and then he asked if I wanted coffee and I said I did. As he guided me across the room he issued a soft-spoken order for *cafés con leche*, and the woman outside his door began rushing about.

Like the offices of many Cuban exiles, Ernesto's was furnished in a util-itarian manner, as if he didn't want to spend too much on his surroundings because he thought they were temporary. The only personal touch was a wall calendar that showed scenes of Havana, pre-1959. I was surprised by the lack of photographs of wife and children and grandkids.

We talked a little about El Duque and Derek Jeter and how dominant a reliever Mariano Rivera had become. The coffee arrived, and it was excellent. I suspected the beans were freshly ground.

"Señor Rodriguez," I said at last.

"Ernesto. *Por favor.*"

"What's on your mind?"

He leaned close to me and lowered his voice, as if he were afraid his own office was bugged.

"My project," he said.

I nodded.

"It's big," he said. "Huge. The biggest thing I've ever done."

I nodded again. I still had no idea what he did for a living.

"I want you to help me," he said. "To handle the publicity."

"That sounds good."

"It's agreed, then."

"There's just one thing."

"And what is that?"

"Publicity for what?"

Ernesto Rodriguez looked startled, as if I were joking about the only matter in the world he regarded as sacred.

"They did not tell you?" he asked.

I shook my head and grinned. "Nobody ever tells me anything."

He reached into his desk and took out a huge key chain.

"Come with me."

I followed him to the rear of the building, which led into an alley that separated his office from a Laundromat. He pointed out a fleet of vans he had leased for his company—the firm was growing; he had to be able to send his people out—before guiding me by the elbow to a new Cadillac.

As we headed west, Ernesto asked if I had any children and I said no and he told me I should get started; a man is not complete until he's a

father. He asked why I had moved to Miami and I said I'd been transferred from New York. My wife and I had lived in South Florida for
more than a year and were beginning to like it.

"Yes," he said. "It's like that. This place can be seductive."

We reached the turnpike and went south on wide smooth concrete,
so unlike the potholed streets of home. I told him how I started rooting
for the Yankees while I was a kid in the seventies, in love with the
brawling teams of Munson and Reggie and Billy Martin, and Ernesto
nodded and said those players had a certain panache and seemed to
enjoy themselves. Today's young men take things far too seriously.

When we got off the turnpike, Ernesto turned west again and drove
through piney scrubland. We passed trailer parks and shacklike mom-
and-pop stores and even a couple of barns that seemed to be in danger
of falling over.

Finally I asked, in what I hoped was a pleasant tone, "Where are we
going, Ernesto?"

It was his turn to grin. "We're almost there, my friend."

We stopped in the middle of a vast flat field. In the distance I saw
dark vegetation that I assumed was the Everglades. Helen and I kept
talking about going there, but so far we hadn't gotten around to it.

Ernesto wrapped his right arm around me and began making broad
gestures with his left. I imagined Ponce de León doing the same thing
to his first mate that fateful Easter morning.

"The whole expanse," he said. "Imagine it. Can you imagine?"

"I'm trying to."

"Three-thousand-square-foot homes. At the least. Some as large as
six. We'll have several models for customers to choose from. The archi-
tects are drawing up the plans."

The field was muddy. I tried to avoid looking at my shoes.

Ernesto described a gated community that would contain more than
five thousand houses, a golf course designed by Jack Nicklaus and a six-
hundred-acre park with a duck pond and the largest playground in
Miami-Dade. The streets would curve gently and be flanked with palms
and jacaranda.

"Magnificence," he said. "Every home has a built-in swimming pool. Every one. No amenity will be spared. Sub-Zero refrigerators in every kitchen. Every one. Plus built-in microwaves over the stove. I will spare nothing."

"Sounds nice."

"There will be video cameras on every block. Every one. For security."

Over the next few days Ernesto and I had several conversations in which he told me that his main concern was dealing with *The Herald*. Like many prominent Cuban exiles, my client had a problematic relationship with Miami's leading newspaper, which he regarded as a leftist, pro-Castro rag. But he needed good publicity for his project, which he had named Tierra Grande.

"That is where you come in, my friend," he said. "You are someone new to the scene. Fresh. With a different perspective. I hope you can talk to them."

I told him I had a good relationship with a number of editors at *The Herald*.

"I know," he said. "I've asked about you. The reports are excellent."

I had done asking of my own. Ernesto Rodriguez had arrived in Miami as a teenager in 1960 and immediately volunteered for the force that blundered ashore at the Bay of Pigs. After he was released to the United States, he went into business for himself. Military ventures aside, Ernesto Rodriguez was not the type of man who liked to work for other people. He made his first fortune battling tropical insects in the years before anyone took the environment seriously. But in the seventies and early eighties, his business was ruined by inflation and recession and eco-freaks. Ernesto Rodriguez declared bankruptcy and faded from sight. In a "Where Are They Now?" article in 1984, *The Herald* had reported that Ernesto Rodriguez was working as a janitor in a run-down hotel in Miami Beach and living in a three-bedroom house in Little Havana with his wife, Luisa, their four children, and both sets of grandparents.

But there are second acts in American business, although never in exactly the same line of work. Ernesto bought that hotel, the Orlando, for a price he never divulged publicly. He kicked out the tenants and renovated the place and sold it when the area began to take off. Since then, he had become one of South Florida's leading real estate developers.

There were rumors about drug money.

As I entered the pastel-laced restaurant with my wife, Ernesto Rodriguez jumped up to embrace me. I tried to return his gesture with suitable enthusiasm before introducing him to Helen. Ernesto kissed her hand and murmured that it was a pleasure to meet her. You can tell a lot about a man by the woman he chooses and I had obviously chosen well. Helen smiled.

"This is good," Ernesto said as we took our seats. "It's good to see you outside of work. The pressures."

I agreed that it was good, and that we were both under pressure. The waiter handed Ernesto a wine list, from which he immediately ordered a Chilean merlot that proved excellent. When I asked where Luisa was, my client dismissed the question, and her, with the kind of wave one uses to shoo away a fly.

"Obligations," he said. "Children. She is what you would call a homebody. But business requires you to be social." He raised his glass.

As Ernesto and I talked about baseball, I caught Helen studying the wallpaper intently, as if she thought this pattern would be perfect for our still-unfinished living room.

"I am sorry," Ernesto said to her. "We're boring you."

Helen said she was the one who should apologize. Her mind was wandering.

"What would you like us to talk about?" Ernesto asked.

"Garry's told me about your project," she said. "It sounds interesting. Ambitious."

She smiled at him and I could tell Ernesto liked her. Almost every man I ever met liked Helen. She seemed open and sincere and totally without guile, and her short hair was highlighted in a way that made it seem as if she'd just walked out of the sun. She also had a husky voice that more than a few men told me they found sexy.

Ernesto talked about Tierra Grande, but most of it was stuff I already knew. Now it was my turn to zone out, and I wondered if Helen could really be serious about the wallpaper, which I found overbearing.

"Now your husband is getting bored," Ernesto said. He threw out his hands. "I don't know what to do. I can't keep both of you interested at the same time."

I grinned. "I am interested, Ernesto. I think Tierra Grande will be where everyone wants to live. Everyone who can afford it."

We all laughed. Politely, as I recall.

And then Helen raised a question I'd been wondering about, but had considered improper to pose. Coming from me, it would have sounded as if I were suspicious or had a hidden agenda. Coming from Helen, it sounded like genuine curiosity.

What my wife asked was this: "Where are you getting the money?"

Ernesto raised his wine to his lips. I noticed a cloud over his eyes, but then they brightened, as if he had just thought of the perfect answer.

"The money comes from many sources. I have access to lots of capital. As do you, I understand."

Helen smiled again and blushed a little. "It all depends," she said. "I deal with emerging markets. At least we hope they'll emerge someday."

Halfway through the bar, on our way to the parking lot, we all stopped when we heard a voice call out Ernesto's name. The voice was hard and flat and twanged, and it reminded me of cactus and tumbleweed.

Ernesto froze. I glanced at him and saw the side of his face for only a second but he looked like a man who had just unearthed something that he thought was buried forever.

He turned around and straightened and assumed a dignified mask.

We were approached by a man in his mid-forties. He was more than six feet tall, with salty hair that had once been blond. The crinkles around his eyes gave away a life spent outdoors.

"Ernesto Rodriguez. I thought it was you."

He put out his hand, which Ernesto accepted without enthusiasm.

Ernesto asked the man why he was in Miami.

"Bidness," he said. "The same as always. Bidness and opportunity."

Suddenly I stopped seeing him. Because a woman had come up beside. She was almost a foot shorter than he was and should have been overwhelmed but she had dark skin and darker eyes and long straight hair parted in the middle and she wore diamond earrings and a necklace with a crucifix and a simple black dress that showed a hint of cleavage.

I heard Ernesto murmur in Spanish how good it was to see her again and heard him say the name: Magdalena.

Soon there were introductions all around. I was pleased that Ernesto now pronounced my surname the way I preferred—*Dock-er-ty*, a set of syllables that rise from the mists of Gaelic. The man with the tumbleweed voice was Frank Hedges. He and Ernesto had been in bidness together a long time ago. The woman was Hedges' wife.

"I'm glad I found you, Ernesto," Hedges said. "There are some things I want to discuss. Bidness opportunities."

"Now is not the time or the place," Ernesto said.

"Then I'll call you tomorrow. Bright and early."

TWO

"You have to check these guys out," my boss said the day Winston and Evan Copley walked into our office.

The Copleys were overweight but bore no resemblance otherwise. Evan was older and shorter, with thinning hair and psoriasis. He kept glancing around nervously, as if he were afraid an IRS agent was about to leap out of the closet and threaten an audit, and his voice tended to quaver, like that of a man who was unsure of just about everything.

Winston the younger had the booming tones often found in second children who grow up struggling to make themselves heard. His shirt seemed about to burst and whenever he removed his jacket, it was hard to ignore the stains under his armpits.

I asked for a short biography but they gave me the long one. We all need something to believe in, and the Copley brothers believed in real estate. They told me they grew up in Saugus, Massachusetts, where their father worked for the phone company. They thought they'd work there too, but the government broke up AT&T and all the divisions were spun off and nothing was secure anymore. The Copley brothers had not been anticipating a world full of risk. They hadn't thought it was necessary to go to college, but in the breakup's aftermath they began attending Salem State at night. That was when they started to dabble in commercial properties.

"It was a revelation," Winston said. "A goddamn revelation. Like Moses on Mount fucking Sinai."

"Winston, your language."

"I'm sorry. I'm just trying to convey the excitement I felt."

I told him I understood.

"I knew you would," Winston said. "From the moment we met you. Isn't that right, Evan?"

"It is. It is, indeed."

"Because real estate has risks. It can fluctuate."

"It can. It can, indeed."

"But commercial property always produces revenue."

"It does."

"That's why it's so much better than residential. In the long run, you can't lose money. We started out by putting our money into strip malls."

"We did."

"A lot of people disparage strip malls. But we don't. And do you know why?"

I didn't have a chance to shake my head.

"They're a gold mine. A goddamn gold mine."

"Winston, your language."

Without meaning to, the Copley brothers had pioneered REITs on the North Shore of Boston. It didn't take long for larger companies to extract even more money from the Copley formula. The brothers felt squeezed and wound up selling to a big firm for far less money than they felt they deserved.

"They played hardball with us," Winston Copley said.

"They did," Evan said. "They did, indeed."

A couple of vacations in Florida had convinced them of where they should relocate. Sure, there had been falling markets in the past, downward cycles—*troughs*, if you will—but the magic of the Sunshine State was that it always recovered. And do you know why? Winston asked. I wasn't even through shrugging before he said it was because people *wanted* to come here. Florida had sun and surf and palm trees, and you could play golf year-round. Yes, there had been a hurricane last year. Yes, it had caused a lot of damage. But that only created more opportunity.

"Why do you need me?" I asked.

"Publicity," Winston said. "We want to get into *The Herald*."

"We do," Evan said. "We do, indeed."

I prepared four-color brochures on glossy paper and called the business journals and radio stations and rented a conference room at a Marriott downtown for an information seminar on an exciting investment opportunity. I said that Winston and Evan Copley had made a fortune doing this in Boston, and they now promised to bring their expertise to Miami. Three days before the session I called Victor DeLuca, the business editor at *The Herald*, and gave him my spiel. He said he doubted he'd be able to send anyone. Lots of people were selling things in Miami and he had only a limited amount of space and you had to do something unusual to warrant coverage in the paper.

Only half the seats in the conference room were filled, mostly with retirees who were killing time before bingo. Evan Copley blew into the microphone and identified himself and said the investment opportunity they were about to present was the closest thing in the world to a guarantee of high yield and low risk. He said this with the enthusiasm of a dentist emphasizing how important it is to floss twice a day. Evan introduced his brother by saying, "Winston is the talker in the family."

I heard the shuffling of feet and of papers. People shifted their weight in their seats.

In front of a crowd, Winston acquired his brother's tendency to mumble, and the sweat under his armpits seeped through his jacket. Instead of the Elmer Gantry–like performance I was expecting, Winston Copley made the prospect of future riches sound as enticing as a call to eat more broccoli.

I looked out the door, hoping that if I gazed hard enough I'd make a reporter from *The Herald* appear.

* * *

Sometimes I wonder if just thinking about something can lead to the outcome you desire. Make a wish, but take no action, and see if the Fates reward you.

The Copleys' seminars kept moving to progressively smaller hotel conference rooms all over Miami-Dade and Broward Counties, and my handling of their publicity became increasingly apathetic. One day I was standing in the back of an out-of-the-way room on the second floor of a Days Inn in Miramar with my arms folded across my chest and my thoughts turning toward sexual fantasies involving a woman I had met only once and briefly.

I heard heels clicking quickly and loudly on a cold tiled floor.

I turned toward the sound and did not believe what I was seeing.

Magdalena was smoking a slim cigar in defiance of the no-smoking ordinances, and her Donna Karan dress was the only pale thing about her. She leaned her head inside the door as she scribbled notes on a yellow legal pad, then withdrew and paced and smoked.

I walked to the door.

"Are you going to tell me to stop smoking?" she asked.

I hadn't had a chance to say anything.

"Because if you are, I'm going to leave right now. I can understand why they don't want it in the room, but banning it everywhere—it's like a dictatorship."

"We've met," I said.

"*Yo sé.* You were with Ernesto. And your wife."

I asked if she wanted to come inside. I told her she might be missing something.

"I can hear enough."

"What do you think?"

She shrugged, then took a long puff on her cigar before poking her head back in. Winston Copley was explaining how the revenue stream from their commercial properties guaranteed a return on investment, even when the real estate market was falling.

Magdalena withdrew her head from the room and turned to me.

"It sounds so . . ."

Another puff. She exhaled.

"Safe."

After the seminar was over I saw her sitting alone in the hotel coffee shop. She was smoking another cigar and reading *The Wall Street Journal*.

"You didn't stay till the end," I said.

"I'd heard enough."

I sat opposite her. She folded the paper and pushed it aside.

"Why were you there?" I asked.

"My husband asked me. We have some money to invest."

I told her I could set up a meeting with the Copleys and gave her my card and wrote down my cell phone number. I told her to call anytime.

Frank Hedges rang the next day and asked if I was free for lunch. He had bidness to discuss. I had no plans but pretended I needed to cancel a reservation with a couple of clients. Hedges said he appreciated what I was doing.

I waited for him in the lobby and after fifteen minutes he walked in with a state trooper's stride. I extended my hand and he took it and I could tell immediately that he was one of those guys who regards a bone-crushing shake as a sign of manhood. He asked if I'd ever ridden in a Karmann Ghia. I shook my head. He smiled and said, "It's the balls."

The car coughed and sputtered as we lurched down Biscayne Boulevard. Hedges wore wraparound shades that would have looked cool if he were ten years younger. We drove toward Coconut Grove and on the way Hedges pointed out a couple of buildings in which he was trying to acquire an interest.

We stopped at a Jamaican restaurant. Hedges asked if the jerk chicken was good today and the waitress said it was. He placed an order and asked for a Red Stripe. When I told her I wanted iced tea, Hedges looked at me as if I had violated an ancient and important protocol.

"What kind of Irishman drinks iced tea, for Christ's sake?" he asked.

"One who doesn't drink booze until dinner."

He laughed and said he wanted to talk bidness. I told him to go ahead.

Over the years, Frank Hedges said, he had been involved in many lines of work. Some of them, just between us, had been on the risky side. Occasionally he had skirted the edge of legality. When you live that way, you learn how to judge people instantly. Your life can depend on your ability to read people quickly and accurately.

"And so," Hedges said, "when I say that I like you, it really means something."

"Thanks, Frank. I appreciate it."

"How long have you known Ernesto?"

"We just started working together."

"What's he up to? What's the project?"

I had been hired to do publicity, so I told Frank Hedges about Tierra Grande. He nodded as our jerk chicken came and nodded some more as he asked the waitress for another Red Stripe.

"Sounds like Ernesto's doing pretty good for himself," Hedges said.

I said I wouldn't know. He lived in Coral Gables so I assumed he was doing all right but beyond that I knew nothing about the state of his finances or personal life. I hadn't even met his wife.

"Luisa's a nice woman," Hedges said.

"Then you probably have a better idea than I do. Sounds like you and Ernesto go way back."

Hedges shrugged. He said he and Ernesto had done bidness together in California in the eighties but the venture ended and the two of them drifted apart. Ernesto returned to Miami while Hedges went to Eastern Europe, the former Soviet Union, even the Middle East. "I like to be where the action is," he said. "Do you know what I mean?"

"I can imagine."

"But lately I've been thinking. I'm not getting any younger. Who the hell is?"

Both of us laughed.

"I like you, Garry. I really do. And I'm glad we could talk like this. Because here's what I'm looking for: one good deal. One really good deal where I could get enough to just walk away from everything. Go someplace nice and live off the interest."

"You could play the lottery."

We both forced some laughter as Hedges finished his Red Stripe and signaled for another. I sensed layers peeling away from him, like old coatings of varnish being scraped off a piece of furniture.

"Ernesto's project—is he looking for partners?"

"I don't know. Why don't you ask him?"

"I wouldn't feel comfortable. I'd like to use a third party."

I thought of this man's wife and imagined her walking toward me, wearing nothing but black lingerie.

I tried to shake my head clear and said, "I can ask him. There's no harm in it."

"No harm at all."

"But tell me something." I rubbed my hands together as if I were warming them over a fire. "You don't have to answer. In fact you can tell me to go to hell. But I get the sense that you and Ernesto didn't part under the best of circumstances."

"Go to hell."

My back straightened. Frank Hedges looked grim and dour and I suspected I had stepped over some kind of line. But then he laughed and punched me playfully on the arm, although his eyes conveyed no humor at all.

"It concerns my wife," he said.

I raised my eyebrows and made a motion with my hands that indicated he should keep going.

"Toward the end in California, he became very . . . solicitous. That's the word I'd use. Solicitous."

"I'm sure you had nothing to worry about. He's so much older than—"

Hedges cut me off. "That's not what I mean," he said. His voice was rising and I wondered if it was caused by anger or alcohol. "It was more like . . . father-daughter. He thought she needed something like that." Hedges shook his head, as if the idea was too ridiculous to think about.

She would have been younger then, a womanchild, perhaps not even twenty if I was guessing her age correctly. Ernesto may have felt that Frank Hedges was unsuitable for her, even if the two men were doing bidness together.

"What about now?" I asked. "What if Ernesto gets . . . solicitous?"

"I can handle it. We're all older now." He leaned close to me and I could tell he liked talking to people this way, as if he felt that engaging in a conspiracy was the best way to communicate. "There's something Ernesto doesn't understand about Maggie: She's an old soul. She's always had one."

He called her Maggie. I hated the harsh way it sounded, as if she were a bland-looking farm girl about to board the train to the big city.

I liked her full name. *Magdalena.* The way it rolled off my tongue.

As we walked back toward the Karmann Ghia I asked Hedges if his wife had said anything about the Copleys. He nodded and said she was unimpressed, although he had looked over their literature and thought there might be something to what they were doing.

"I'm not surprised at her reaction," I said. "They don't come across well in their presentation. But what they're selling is sound."

I leaned close to Hedges. It was my turn to act like a conspirator.

"I'd like to get a front man. Just to do the pitches. But they won't hear of it."

I sat in Ernesto's office, sipping Cuban coffee and watching him point to places that were only splotches of blue on a surveyor's map. I felt jazzed by the caffeine and my client's enthusiasm.

"We will start here," he said.

I nodded.

"Have you called *The Herald?*"

I told him I'd faxed some material to their business section. I was going to call Victor DeLuca as soon as I returned to my office.

Ernesto made a note on the back of one of his business cards while murmuring a few words of approval in Spanish. Groundbreaking on Tierra Grande was set to begin in less than a week.

"How's your wife?" he asked.

"Fine," I said. "Helen's fine. Thanks for asking."

Solicitous, I thought. *Ernesto is still solicitous.*

"No children yet?"

"We're thinking about getting a dog and working our way up."

Ernesto stared at the map for a few seconds, as if he was trying to will the development into existence. Then he rolled up the map, tied a rubber band around it and put it on top of a filing cabinet.

"Can I ask you a question?"

"Certainly, Garrett."

Ernesto liked to use my formal given name. I told him I had no preference.

"This is outside my purview, and you can tell me to get lost, but are you interested in taking on any partners?"

"It would depend on the partner."

"Frank Hedges would like to do it."

Ernesto raised his eyebrows in a manner that indicated he would rather become poor again.

"We had lunch together," I said quickly. "At his request. I said I'd ask."

"I heard you had lunch with him. I'm glad you told me."

I felt my spine stiffen involuntarily, as if some unseen Torquemada was turning the rack a couple of notches. I wondered if all my movements were being watched, if Ernesto had spies who kept track of everyone he did business with.

"I do not want Frank Hedges involved in this project. Please convey that information to him."

"I will."

I got up to leave but there was a question I wanted to ask. It was an issue that was best left unexamined, but the idea that Ernesto had me under some kind of surveillance made me feel as if I had a right to information that would normally be withheld.

"What kind of business were you in with him? If you don't mind me asking."

Ernesto looked away from me and down at the small cup that by now contained nothing but muddy grounds. He twirled the cup between his thumb and forefinger, as if the question I'd posed had several different answers that were all true in their own way.

"We were fighting the Communists," he said at last.

I resisted the urge to laugh. Ernesto seemed absolutely serious. Instead I said this, with incredulity inevitably seeping into my voice: "In California?"

"That was our base," he said. "Obviously, we didn't fight them there. Except in Berkeley, of course."

I chuckled, but as Ernesto looked into the dark brown heap at the bottom of his cup, he seemed to grow reflective. And from the look on his face and the tone he adopted, I could tell he wanted to try to make me understand something, even though he realized that the effort was most likely futile.

"There is only one left," he said. "One Communist. You know who I'm talking about."

I nodded.

"There is nothing I wouldn't do—nothing—to drive him from power. I know what Americans think. What you're probably thinking right now. That we should stop living in the past. Accept reality. Forgive and forget. But you don't know what it's like to have everything you love taken away from you—your property, your life, your country, the very air that you breathe. When you have all of that stolen from you, you are resolved to get it back. No matter how long it takes. By any means necessary."

After a few minutes of schmoozing, I asked Victor DeLuca if he'd received the material about Tierra Grande.

"Sure did. What is this—Ernesto's swan song?"

I said Ernesto had never indicated to me that he was thinking about retirement.

"I'm just guessing," DeLuca said. "But it looks like he's trying for a home run. Like this could be the capstone of his career."

"He regards this as his masterpiece. He's told me so himself."

"A masterpiece is something by Rembrandt, not a developer."

I told the man that he had a point. I also mentioned when the groundbreaking would occur and said we'd be delighted if *The Herald* could send a reporter and photographer.

"I guess we have to," DeLuca said. "I hate to do it. But it's so fucking big."

"Why do you hate to do it?"

"Because we're giving you free advertising."

"That's the whole point."

Helen slid open the back door and extended a gin and tonic. I sipped it and told her it was good. One of her best ever. I placed the drink beside the grill, then flipped the steak.

"It smells fattening," she said as she stepped fully outside. I asked how the corn and salad were doing and she said everything was ready, she had followed my instructions to the letter and now the side dishes awaited only the final touches from the master chef. I grinned. Helen said she liked it when I wore an apron. It made me look like a domesticated beast. I grinned again. She said there was something she had forgotten to do and disappeared into the house.

I flipped the steak as my cell phone rang. I picked it up, expecting a panicky call from the office or a client who needed extra stroking. I figured I'd return to the grill after a couple of quips.

"Is this Garrett?"

I knew who it was right away and the sound of her voice made my lips go dry and I could feel my heart trying to pound through the wall of my chest. I liked the way she rolled the *r*'s in my name and clipped the *t*'s and decided I did have a preference, at least with this woman—I did not want her to use my nickname.

"Magdalena. How are you?"

"Is this a bad time?"

"I'm cooking. A little barbecue. Nothing complicated. What can I do for you?"

She said she wanted to talk about the Copleys and I told her to go ahead. She said she had been talking to her husband, who was away on business. He had been doing some research into the brothers and he thought something was there that he wanted to pursue.

To be honest, she told me, she did not feel the same way.

In any event, she said, when he got back to town he would contact me to set up a meeting with the Copleys.

I thanked her for calling and said there was something I had to tell her husband. She asked if I wanted to tell her and I said it would be better if I delivered the news myself.

I also said I was delighted to hear from her. I said I had meant it when I'd told her to call anytime.

She said she had never doubted my word.

THREE

Traffic on 95 was worse than usual, and I arrived a half hour late at a gallery on Las Olas with gleaming black walls and cool, pale light. I took off my shades the second I stepped inside. From somewhere in back, a woman slipped soundlessly into the room.

"Are you Josette? Or Teresa?"

The former. She wore black pants and a shirt with pastels and her hair was short and spiky and bleached the color of bone. A diamond stud graced her left nostril.

"You're from New York," she said, as if she could tell everything about me from a glance. "I'm glad. I asked for somebody from New York. The learning curve is less steep."

The gallery was named Red White & Blew and its walls were lined with Disney animation cells, numerous reproductions of Jasper Johns' flag, and Norman Rockwell magazine covers. Mingled in were some works by Andy Warhol, who would have approved of the place.

"Who do you like?" Josette asked.

"De Kooning. After he got Alzheimer's."

"His work improved, didn't it?"

I asked why she wanted to talk to me and she told me to look around. We were the only two people in sight.

"I remember your firm from New York," she said. "You did some work for a friend of mine. Diego Montoya."

I smiled with the pleasure of fond reminiscence. "Lisa Shapiro handled that account," I said. "I helped her out. It was one of the first things I worked on."

Diego Montoya's SoHo gallery specialized in urban-themed works by minority artists, so it did virtually no business in its first six months. Then Lisa hit on the idea of spending a dollar to buy a bus that the City of New York was about to junk. After alerting the media, she had the bus towed to the vacant lot next to Diego's gallery, where a group of his artists went at it with blowtorches and cans of spray paint. Just as Lisa anticipated, the cops tried to stop them. Lisa had coached the artists on how to react, so when they were led away in handcuffs they cited freedom of expression and the First Amendment and police brutality and racial and ethnic discrimination. In Lisa's most inspired touch, Diego draped himself across the back of the paddy wagon as if he'd been crucified. The story went national and even made CNN. The next day there was a line to see the controversial bus, and Diego's gallery was overflowing.

Josette told me that she wanted an idea or event that would grab people's imagination, something that would get the trendoids up from SoBe. I suggested an art-in on Fort Lauderdale Beach, using topless German sunbathers as palettes.

"Too *Sports Illustrated*," Josette said.

I told her I'd try to come up with something better.

Ernesto Rodriguez stood between two bulldozers. He wore a hard hat—a touch I had insisted on—to contrast with his Versace suit and Bruno Magli shoes. I counted four TV crews, three still photographers and the all-important reporter from *The Herald*.

I mopped the sweat that was beading on my forehead and looked up at heavy clouds that seemed to grow darker every minute. Ernesto plunged a shovel into the ground. Cameras clicked and whirred. Ernesto mopped his face with a handkerchief.

I eased myself next to *The Herald's* reporter, a guy just out of Brown named Sebastian Overstreet, and wondered if he was serious about the bow tie he was wearing.

"Are you getting everything you need?" I asked.

He nodded.

"Because if you want any information—anything at all—I can go back to my Rover and get it for you."

He nodded again, thanked me and resumed looking at his notepad. But I noticed he wasn't writing anything down.

The unexpected sound of a car engine drawing closer forced me to turn and look. I saw a red Miata, its top open, pulling quickly to a stop as the dirt it had sent flying drifted back to the ground.

Magdalena got out. Her dress was a print, mostly black, and she wore open-toed shoes. Her nails were painted a pale shade of pink.

Ernesto smiled as she walked up to him. They embraced while I hovered a few feet away.

"Who are you?" one of the TV reporters called out.

Magdalena stepped away without replying. It looked to me as if she was trying to hide her face.

"Do you regard this as the most important thing you've ever done?" Overstreet asked Ernesto. The reporter's pen was poised over his notepad.

"The most important thing I ever did was land with the Freedom Brigade in 1961," Ernesto said. "I hope this will be more successful."

The crew from Telemundo asked Ernesto to repeat his comment in Spanish, which he did.

"Mr. Rodriguez." Overstreet again.

"Señor?"

"I'm wondering about the financing for your project."

"I'm not."

This generated laughter from everyone except the reporter.

"How much does the project cost?"

"I don't want to get into that." Ernesto smiled, although his mustache obscured his upper lip.

"I talked to one of your competitors this morning."

"Which one?"

"I'm not at liberty to say. The conversation was off the record."

Ernesto was muttering under his breath in Spanish and I hoped the crew from Telemundo could not pick him up. Even with my imperfect grasp of the language, I understood that my client was casting aspersions on the manhood of anyone who would talk about him and not admit it.

"This man said Tierra Grande would probably cost a hundred million dollars. And he was wondering where you got the money."

The look that passed over Ernesto's face was almost as dark as the clouds that were coming closer. I stepped up to his side and murmured that he should deflect the question with something other than "No comment." I also told him this would be the last question, that I would step between him and the media and say Señor Rodriguez was running late but he appreciated everybody turning out for the beginning of what promised to be a spectacular addition to the good life of South Florida.

"I don't have to discuss my financing in detail," Ernesto told the reporters. "That's one of the advantages of being privately held."

"But the banks—"

"The financing for Tierra Grande is more than adequate. You have my word."

I stepped in front of Ernesto to deliver the spiel I had promised. In my peripheral vision I noticed Ernesto talking to Magdalena and embracing her again before getting into his Cadillac.

"The banks."

I turned around. Overstreet was only a few feet away.

"What about them?"

"They have a fiduciary responsibility. To their depositors and shareholders." He'd probably learned that in a class somewhere.

Magdalena was walking toward her Miata.

"I've called a number of institutions and none of them have lent any money to—"

I looked directly into Overstreet's glasses, clapped him on the back and grinned.

"I'll ask Ernesto about this myself. For all I know, the money's coming from space aliens." I took Overstreet's card and promised to call or e-mail him as soon as I had an answer. Then I clapped him on the back again.

Magdalena was almost in her car. I went after her at a half-run and called out her name.

When she turned, something flashed in her eyes. I would have preferred a look of longing, or at least flirtation, but it was the kind of annoyed-with-yourself face that you acquire when you remember that the cable bill is overdue.

"Garrett," she said. "I'm glad you stopped me. There's something I have to tell you."

Anything. Tell me anything.

I gulped. Then grinned.

"My husband is back. He wants to set up a meeting with the Copleys. Do you think you could arrange it?"

"Of course. No problem. I'd be happy to do it." I started to walk toward my Rover and silently blessed the gods of sexual attraction when she fell in beside me. I wanted to prolong the conversation. I wanted to spend as many seconds with her as I could.

"What does he want to discuss?" I asked.

"He's being vague. But I think he has some kind of a partnership in mind."

I was afraid I was ruining her shoes.

"I don't know if they'd be interested in that."

"My husband can be a persuasive man."

It was then that we heard it: the boom of a thunderclap that sounded as if it were only a few feet above us, followed by the whoosh that indicated the imminent arrival of windswept rain. The dark clouds born over the Everglades were almost directly overhead.

As big fat drops crashed around us, Magdalena and I ran toward the Rover as quickly as the muddy ground would allow. I threw my jacket over her head and opened the door and helped her in. While I splashed around to the driver's side, the rain turned into drenching sheets that hit me sideways.

I jumped in and sat behind the wheel. The water had seeped through my clothes and skin before settling in my bones.

"Oh, shit," she said, "my car."

The Miata was barely visible, but its top was still down.

"I can drive over there and try to get the top up."

"You don't have to. You'll get wet."

"It doesn't matter. I'm soaked already."

She turned to look at me. And when she saw my disarray—hair matted, shoes scuffed, clothes hanging soggily off my body, an image-conscious professional suddenly devastated by nature's caprice—she put her hand over her mouth, as if she were trying to stop herself, but that only made her body shake more with unexpected laughter.

I asked if I looked that bad.

She said I looked worse.

I swore and she laughed harder and I started the Rover and headed toward her car and congratulated myself because, more than a year after its purchase, my SUV was finally doing some off-road driving.

Magdalena gave me her keys. It was still pouring but I told myself I didn't mind as I got out of the Rover and felt the mud squish over my ankles. I plopped in a seat where a puddle had already formed and started the car and raised the top. After I secured the roof I sat there a second and wiped my eyes with my sleeve. I thought about staying there until the rain stopped. But then I remembered her sitting beside me and how much I enjoyed hearing her laugh, even if it was at my expense.

I bolted for the Rover. The rain crashed so hard into my face I thought it would tear off my flesh. I sat behind the wheel and listened to my breath gradually return to normal.

Magdalena reached into her purse and took out one of her slim cigars.

"Do you mind?"

I did, but said I didn't.

"That was good. What you did before."

I asked what she was talking about.

"The way you helped out Ernesto. When that *idiota* was asking questions."

I shrugged. "That's what Ernesto pays me for."

I turned and looked around on the backseat. I was hoping that either Helen or I had left a beach towel there.

"Nice car," Magdalena said.

"It's not a car. It's an SUV."

"Whatever."

I found a towel and started wiping my face with it.

"You're right," I said. "It's a glorified car. Who am I trying to kid?"

The towel still smelled of sweat and sunscreen and I thought of how much I'd enjoy lying on the sand with the woman who was sitting next to me.

I went into a history of why I bought the Rover: After we moved to Miami, Helen and I needed vehicles. At first I thought I'd get something economical, perhaps a Toyota. But my boss shook his head and said if I wanted to be successful, I had to project a successful attitude: "Small isn't beautiful anymore. Bigger is better. And massive is best."

I was chattering, but I couldn't stop myself.

Magdalena asked what my wife drove.

"A minivan. Some kind of Ford." Helen hadn't wanted to. She thought they were ugly and wanted a sleek sedan but after only a few days of driving around in a rental she said she felt dwarfed by all these huge things on the road; they were intimidating and she couldn't see and she didn't feel safe.

That was important to my wife: feeling safe.

I had a flash of memory and reached below the passenger seat in back and took out a cooler filled with ice and fruit and bottled water. Helen had packed it for me. She said I'd be out for a long time and might need a snack.

I opened the cooler and asked Magdalena if she'd like anything. She took a half liter of water and an apple and thanked me for being generous.

The downpour slowed from torrential to moderate. The wind died down. Pieces of sky were visible over the Everglades.

"Why did you come here?" I asked.

"I know how much this means to Ernesto. I didn't mean to be late. Those fucking cameras. I hate having my picture taken."

"You've known Ernesto a long time."

"Since soon after I got together with Frank."

Solicitous, I thought. *Ernesto was solicitous.*

"That was in California?"

"I met Frank in Mexico."

"That's where you're from?"

She nodded, inhaled, blew smoke.

I formed an image of the way she must have been. A girl of seventeen or so, poor but intelligent and extraordinarily beautiful. The gringo Hedges, passing through on one of his adventures, must have known right away that she was too good to pass up. And she understood that he offered a way to a better life, or at least a more affluent one.

"What was he doing there? If you don't mind me asking."

"He was working for the government," she said. "Your government."

"Doing what?"

She looked straight at me.

"Whatever was necessary."

The tension running between us was electric. It was sexual tension, of course, but also the tension of a woman who didn't know how much to reveal.

"I asked Ernesto what kind of business he and Frank did in California. And he said, 'Fighting the Communists.' I almost keeled over."

"It was the eighties. A lot of people were fighting the Communists."

"What does Frank do now? The Cold War is over."

"Not in Miami."

The rain had almost stopped. Magdalena rolled down her window and leaned out and looked up at the lightening sky. She glanced at her watch and said she had to get going. I got out of the Rover and took the beach towel with me and ran it over the driver's seat in the Miata.

Magdalena got in. Mud splattered her toes and ankles. I thought about sliding her shoes off and rubbing the towel over her feet and then flicking my tongue against them before running it up her calves and thighs and then—

31

She thanked me again and looked directly into my eyes. I could tell she knew exactly what I was thinking.

"It's been hard for Frank," she said. "The past few years. He's a man of action and there isn't much these days."

"Peace is hell," I said.

"I don't mind it. Although I used to think I would."

As I flipped burgers in the backyard and contemplated asking Helen to make another gin and tonic, I found myself staring around at a place that still seemed more theoretical than real. When we moved to Miami we rented an apartment in South Beach and it was fun for a while but parking was a bitch and we had no place for our stuff and it was loud all the time. The worst part came when we did our taxes. Both of us gasped when we saw the bill but our accountant explained that we had no deductions. DINKs who rented had to pay. I told Helen that if we had any more years like this, I was going to start voting Republican.

We did something we had sworn we'd never do, but the logic of our situation was remorseless: we bought a three-bedroom house in a suburban development near a shopping mall. And suddenly, instead of too much stuff, we had too much space; every morning we faced an existence dominated by boxes and empty rooms.

We began to buy things: a wall unit and a DVD player and a wide-screen TV. We made plans: one bedroom would be ours, the second would become a guest room, and we'd turn the third into an office. Out back, we'd put in a deck with a built-in grill, and possibly even a swimming pool and Jacuzzi.

But our ideas remained ephemeral. It seemed as if Helen and I were waiting for some unidentified something to happen to our lives to force us into a state that might resemble permanence.

My cell phone went off and I snapped back into the moment, which at that point was dominated by grease and flames. I pinned the phone against my shoulder while wielding the spatula like a baton.

It was Magdalena. She asked if I was busy.

"I'm in the middle of— Christ!"

A burger landed the wrong way and tottered on the edge of the grill.

"Are you barbecuing again? That causes cancer."

"Everything causes cancer."

I nudged the burger over before it could fall to the ground. Magdalena said she wanted to talk about Ernesto but perhaps another time would be better. I told her I had an appointment with the Copleys at a downtown Starbucks in the morning, but after that I was free.

She said the timing was interesting. Her husband was talking with the Copleys at this very moment.

I grunted. I'd helped set up the meeting although I hadn't wanted to. I'd also given Hedges the bad news about Tierra Grande. He said "SHIT!" so loudly I thought the phone was going to explode.

Magdalena suggested we have lunch together.

My voice cracked as I agreed.

FOUR

While I wondered why I had ordered an extra large iced cappuccino, the Copleys considered splitting a blueberry muffin until Winston decided that what he really wanted was apple walnut.

"We met with that fellow you recommended," Winston Copley said. "Hedges."

"I didn't recommend him. I just thought you should meet."

"What that man suggested," Evan said. He shook his head in disbelief, as if Hedges had proposed that they give up pastries.

"What did he want? If you don't mind me asking."

"It was unacceptable and undesirable," Winston said. "Let's leave it at that."

It sounded to me as if Hedges had lowballed them. Like a lot of people who ran their own businesses, the Copleys had trouble distinguishing the personal from the commercial.

"I'm sorry," I said. "I didn't know what he had in mind. But to be honest—which is something I hate to do—"

I paused, waiting for a laugh or a chuckle or even a raised eyebrow. There was no response.

"To be honest," I said, "we're not making any progress, and I thought he might be able to help."

"We will make progress," Winston said, "once people understand."

I resisted the urge to roll my eyes. My clients were beginning to resemble the people in Hitler's bunker who thought the war could still be won.

"Strip malls are great investments," Winston Copley said. "Outstanding."

"The revenue streams are unbelievable," Evan said.

"Incredible," Winston said.

I told them that modern investors wanted something with a little glamour—software startups, multimedia firms, industrial combines in developing markets. A row of stores in Generica had a hard time competing.

"But strip malls are a sure thing," Winston said.

"Or close to it," Evan added.

"We need to get the word out."

"We need a stunt," I said. I was surprised these words escaped me. I was rarely this direct.

"We don't believe in stunts," Winston said.

"It was poor choice of words." I found myself feeling more confident. "We usually call it an event. Something out of the ordinary. To break through the clutter."

The brothers nodded. So far they were with me.

"We need a pitch, and I think I have it." I was getting excited. Perhaps the extra large iced cappuccino was working after all. "It's an idea, a slogan, a theme. It's so simple it's brilliant." I paused for dramatic effect, then leaned close to the brothers and dropped my voice as if I were about to impart a military secret.

"'Strip Malls Are Beautiful.'"

Winston and Evan stared at me.

"Think of it," I said. "We organize an event and send releases to all the media people. We hold it in the parking lot of a strip mall—one of the places you've invested in, the tackiest one we can find—except we say it's beautiful. We even make sure civic groups and environmentalists know about it."

"Why?" Evan asked. He sounded like a man who was quite certain that at least one person at the table had taken leave of his senses.

"So they can protest. It'll make great TV."

*   *   *

35

I noticed the red Miata in the parking lot and smiled to myself as I entered a restaurant that was dark and woody. The maître d' guided me to the table in back that Magdalena had already taken. She was wearing a dark blue sleeveless dress and her only jewelry was the gold band on her ring finger.

I imagined this woman with her legs spread apart, urging me to go harder, faster, deeper.

Magdalena said she was glad to see me. I opened the menu and asked what was good.

"Not much," she said. "But this place is out of the way."

It sounded like a recommendation for soup and salad.

"You wanted to talk about Ernesto."

"*Sí.*"

"Then let's talk about Ernesto."

She said she wasn't sure how to broach the topic. "Perhaps it's more accurate to say I want to discuss the situation between Ernesto and my husband. There's a history between them."

"I'm aware of that."

"I'm afraid Ernesto is letting that history get in the way of his judgment."

"How do you mean?"

I wanted her to keep talking. I liked listening to her voice. It was soft and low and I would have described it as seductive, except she had done nothing to seduce me.

She said Frank was intent on getting involved in Tierra Grande. He talked about it so much he was driving her loco.

I pointed out the obvious: It was Ernesto's project. If he didn't want Frank involved, that pretty much settled the issue.

Magdalena said it wasn't as simple as I thought. When her husband really wanted something, he was impossible to dissuade.

My lunch arrived. The lettuce looked wilted and the soup had almost congealed. I was tempted to send everything back until I remembered hearing about chefs who spat on the plates of customers who wanted their food redone.

"Ernesto must know that," I said. "It's a price, or a potential price, he's willing to pay."

"It would be so much easier if he'd just let Frank in."

"I already asked Ernesto about this—on behalf of your husband. Didn't he tell you?"

She nodded. Part of her face fell into shadow as she moved her head.

I said Ernesto's answer would be the same if I asked him again. In fact, I had the feeling that if I raised a point he believed was already settled, he might try to find another public relations man.

Magdalena gazed at her lunch. It looked worse than mine.

I remembered Lisa Shapiro ridiculing Ogilvie, her fellow vice president, as she kicked back behind her desk in one of the after-hours sessions she liked to call The Education of Garrett Doherty. "The guy hasn't had an idea in years, and he's proud of it," she said as she sipped neat whiskey and looked out the high arched window that somehow seemed to attract sunlight from three directions. "So he has no idea what the biggest part of your job is: suggesting the obvious. And being amazed that they didn't think of it themselves."

"Why don't you ask Ernesto yourself?" I said. "He's very fond of you."

Solicitous, I thought. *Ernesto was solicitous.*

Magdalena looked directly at me with eyes that were trying to open up, as if she were going to allow me a glimpse inside.

"It wouldn't be good," she said. "He'd try to . . ."

"Try to what?"

"To talk me into leaving my husband."

She took a long drink of water and tried to attack her lunch, as if energy would overcome how bad it was.

"I don't know where Ernesto is getting the money," she said at last.

"Neither do I. But he doesn't have to tell me. Or you. Or anybody."

"I've done some research. The numbers don't add up. Ernesto doesn't have the resources or the backing to pull off a hundred-million-dollar project."

"So that guy from *The Herald* wasn't such an *idiota* after all."

"He's still an idiot. He doesn't realize how good his questions were."

*   *   *

The dark-haired woman just inside the door at Red White & Blew asked if I was the publicity guy and I said I would be, if I could come up with any ideas to publicize. She looked at me as I had just started babbling in Mongolian and I asked if she was Teresa and she said she was. I stuck out my hand and introduced myself. Her grip was firm.

I apologized for being early but I had allowed extra time to drive up from Miami so of course 95 was clear. Teresa nodded vigorously. She said that no matter what you planned for, the opposite occurred.

I asked where Josette was. Teresa said she was probably still at lunch. They took their breaks separately to make sure someone was always at the gallery but there were so few customers the two of them could take three-hour siestas together at the beach. Maybe they'd finally get tan.

"You'd have to worry about melanoma," I said.

"I know. You have to worry about *everything*."

"You used to live in New York." I grinned. I couldn't think of anything else to say or do.

Teresa said she and Josette had lived together in a loft on Avenue A and run a gallery on Mercer Street but eventually city life grew to be too much. At least for her. Teresa said she wasn't sure about Josette. She seemed like such an urban creature.

"But you're not?"

She shook her head. "I like to ride." I must have looked puzzled, because she then added: "Horses."

Teresa said they had lots more living space now and the daily pace was more civilized and she went riding several times a week at a stable in Davie. It was a good life and she wanted to keep it.

Josette walked in. We engaged in cheek-kissing and pleasantries. I grinned a lot. She asked if I had any ideas and I tossed out a few that mostly involved barely dressed people parading with tchotchkes down Las Olas Boulevard. Josette and Teresa grunted a few times.

"Don't be discouraged," I said. "Sometimes it takes months to figure out the right approach."

"I don't know if we have months," Josette said.

"You do if the right idea comes along." I mentioned how much trouble I'd had with the Copleys until I came up with "Strip Malls Are Beautiful."

Josette's breath became short and quick, the way it does when the object of your affection tells you she loves you. She put ring-laden fingers on my wrist and said, "That's so kitschy, it's brilliant."

"Maybe we can play off it," I said. "Get the gallery involved somehow. Unite art and commerce."

"All of us are put on earth to learn one big thing," Josette said. "It varies from person to person. And the big thing I've learned is this . . ."

She paused, as if for dramatic effect. I imagined her studying with Stella Adler.

"Art *is* commerce."

The traffic was bad going back and I wound up stuck on 95 listening to Sarah MacLachlan proclaim that we were all born innocent. I had never heard something I disagreed with more strongly.

I called Ernesto on my cell phone. One of the women who worked for him answered with *"Hola."*

"Señor Rodriguez, *por favor."*

"Who's calling?"

I identified myself and a minute later I heard Ernesto's baritone and found myself admiring the dignified way he approached every conversation, even ones about the weather.

He asked if I had seen the story in *The Herald* and I said I had. The groundbreaking on Tierra Grande had been played on the front page of the business section.

"I did not like the tone of the article," Ernesto said.

"I have no control over the tone."

"They said I 'refused' to discuss the financing. 'Refused.' It makes it sound as if I have something to hide."

"They ran a picture. That's more important. People remember visuals, not words. And you looked great in the hard hat. I bet your family got a kick out of it."

Ernesto paused before saying, "They were quiet, as usual."

I knew what I wanted to say to him but I was unsure how to broach the topic so I decided to adopt an air of wondering-out-loud bantering, as if the idea had suddenly entered my head and was proceeding, unfiltered, to my mouth.

"You could probably get the tone of the articles to change if you told that kid more about the financing."

"It's none of his business."

"I know that. But the questions will persist. I feel I should point that out to you."

"I understand. Have you been talking to Frank Hedges?"

I waited a few seconds before answering. I was becoming more and more convinced that Ernesto had people everywhere who reported back on the activities of everyone who did business with him.

"I had lunch today with Magdalena."

"How is she?"

"Fine."

"She wants me to let him invest in Tierra Grande, doesn't she?"

"That's the gist of it."

"It's difficult for me to say no to Magdalena. But in this instance, I will have to. When you talk to her next, let her know."

"Why don't you tell her yourself?"

"Believe me, my friend, she will ask you about this before she asks me."

Traffic was at a dead halt near downtown Miami while I drummed my fingers on top of the steering wheel. I knew I was close to *The Herald* building, even though I couldn't see it from the highway. It made me think of Sebastian Overstreet and I decided to call him to convey my client's displeasure and tell him that Ernesto wasn't going to tell anyone, especially a reporter, the source of the money for Tierra Grande.

I got Overstreet's voicemail, but I didn't want to leave a message. So I hit the pound key and waited for a person to pick up. The phone went unanswered for twenty-six rings—I counted because I had nothing better to do—before an ennui-laden woman's voice said, "What is it?"

I said I was looking for Victor DeLuca.

"Who's this?"

The voice had more attitude than I'd ever heard in New York, and I was tempted to adopt a GoodFellas accent and say I'd better be put through to Mr. DeLuca before somebody got hurt.

"This is Garrett Doherty. I'm with Cooperman and Associates."

A pause as the phone was fumbled. I heard the woman call out, "Victor!" and then say, "Some flack on three." After another pause, she mispronounced my name.

"Garry, how are you?"

Victor DeLuca, sounding harried.

"Your people are a little slow in answering the phone today." It was a polite way of saying, *What kind of morons are working for you?*

"Haven't you heard? There's a labor shortage."

I told him that my client, Ernesto Rodriguez, did not like the tone of this morning's article about the groundbreaking for Tierra Grande.

"Not reverential enough?" Victor asked.

"He did not appreciate all the questions about the financing."

"It's a legitimate question. We're gonna keep asking until we get an answer."

"He's not gonna tell anyone."

"Then we'll have to find out some other way."

Lisa Shapiro entering my head. Bringing a shot glass to her lips and saying, "Sometimes you have to grovel a little."

"Look, Victor, I'm not telling you how to do your job. I have too much respect for you to do that. But Ernesto and *The Herald* have a long and painful history, and it seems to me that this is a chance to start a new chapter. Can't you cut my client some slack? If he says he has the money, he has the money."

"I'll let our reporter know. If he ever gets back here. We're on deadline and he's late and nobody's heard from him."

I said I'd be happy to talk to Sebastian Overstreet whenever he showed up. I said this was just a business story. We should keep politics out of it.

Victor DeLuca laughed loudly. "After you've lived here a while, Garry, you'll realize something: in Miami, politics is involved in *everything*."

A breeze off the Atlantic provided the first stirring of wind all day. Helen was discussing the pros and cons of investing in Brazil with Jorge Salazar, a man who called himself a venture capitalist from São Paulo.

Salazar leaned close to her as he spoke. Occasionally he glanced at her neckline.

I did not like the way this man was looking at my wife.

They talked about bond yields and currency rates and the potential for recession. They went on about diversification and corruption and the future of the rain forest. They surveyed untapped markets and the importance of the coffee crop and the beaches in Rio. Salazar was especially keen on promoting a container port near the mouth of the Amazon.

"The plans are magnificent," he said. "If you're available tomorrow, I'll bring them to your office."

Out in the distance a cruise ship steamed toward the Bahamas. I imagined old couples shuffling around on the deck to the tunes of their youth.

"Your wife tells me you're in public relations."

I hadn't expected to be involved in the conversation. Usually when I accompanied Helen on one of her business dinners, all I did was nod a lot. But when Helen went to one of my dinners, my clients were always . . . solicitous.

"That's right."

"Perhaps you'd like to promote my project."

"How viable is it?"

"Extremely viable, if your wife loans us the money."

I laughed and said Helen would make the decision with no regard for what I thought, which was probably just as well.

Salazar asked if I was working on anything interesting and I mentioned Tierra Grande. He nodded and said he had seen the story in *The Herald.* Of course he also knew Ernesto Rodriguez.

"You do?"

"You can't do business in Miami without knowing Ernesto."

"I've only met him recently. While working on this."

Salazar reached into his shirt pocket, took out a silver cigarette case and motioned to Helen and me. I wasn't sure if he was offering us one or asking if it was all right if he smoked, but in any event we both shook our heads and told him to go ahead.

He opened the case, revealing a neatly lined cache of cigarettes. He lit one and inhaled deeply.

"Ernesto is a good man," he said. "But he likes to keep things—as you Americans say—close to his vest."

"That's fine by me," I said. "But when you do something this high-profile, questions come up. Everybody wants to know where he's getting the money."

Salazar exhaled. "Ernesto always finds a way to finance his projects. And it's best for everybody if the questions are kept to a minimum."

FIVE

"The boss wants to see you."

Isabel's first words to me were announced loudly enough for everyone in our wing of the office to hear.

I grinned and hung up my jacket.

"He said, 'Right away.'"

I nodded, as if this was a summons I'd been expecting, and walked toward his office while telling myself it was important to project an attitude of nonchalance edging toward confidence.

But I had to wonder. It was easy to imagine a scenario in which Ogilvie had decided to eliminate the last of Lisa's guys, even if I was far removed from the center of corporate power.

My boss's door was open, but I knocked on it anyway.

"You wanted to talk?"

"Well, well, well. Look what the cat dragged in." He bounded from behind his desk and came over to greet me.

I wondered what kind of severance package he'd offer.

My boss closed the door, put his arm around my shoulder and said there was something we needed to discuss.

I wondered if counselors were waiting outside. "Outplacement" was the word management liked to use.

"I got a call from New York yesterday," my boss said. "They asked about you."

Perhaps it was time to go into business for myself, although I really didn't know what I would do.

"I said you were an ace. A heavy lifter. One of the guys who made the office function. Yadda yadda yadda."

I nodded and gulped a few times and grinned again.

"And they said they were pleased to hear that. Because frankly they had some concerns. Not about you. Not directly. I don't want you to think I'm gonna lower the boom or anything."

"It never crossed my mind."

"Great. Great. I'm glad we're on the same wavelength here. Or should I say bandwidth? Gotta keep up with the lingo, y'know."

"It's important. Cyberspeak."

"Cyberspeak. That's good. I'll have to remember it." He slapped me on the knee, as if I were a country wit who had just told a rib-tickler. "That's why we have to keep you around, Garry. Nobody else knows this shit."

He paused and looked around, as if he couldn't recall why he had wanted to talk to me in the first place.

"New York is concerned about one of your clients," he said at last. "Ernesto."

"I thought landing Ernesto was a coup."

"It was. Absolutely. That's what I tried to tell them. But you know the bean counters. All they can see is the bottom line."

"I'm not sure I follow you."

"They said"—and here he imitated the nasally but officious tone of the company's senior female clerk—"'Is he aware that this Rodriguez fellow owes the company thirty thousand dollars?' And I said, 'No, why should he be? He's not in Collections.' And this woman said, 'Everyone in this company has a responsibility for its financial success.'"

I tried to think of what I could say and realized I was looking at a discussion that required a script, so I started jotting down notes on a yellow legal pad under the heading "TALKING POINTS WITH ERNESTO."

My phone rang before I could finish. I looked up at Isabel but she was deep into a nail-polishing session and I knew she'd be content to let my voicemail take it.

If it was Ernesto, I wondered what I would say.

I picked it up on the fourth ring, figuring that whoever was on the other end was ready to talk to my machine and would be discombobulated by my actual voice.

"This is Garrett Doherty." I took care to pronounce my surname.

"Hello? Hello?"

The man on the other end was confused, as if he didn't know if he was talking to a real person.

I let a hint of impatience creep into my words. "This is Garrett Doherty. How can I help you?" Of course I did not sound helpful at all.

"Garry? Hi. It's Sebastian Overstreet." His voice kept catching, as if his bow tie was impinging on his vocal cords. He said he was sorry he wasn't in yesterday to take my call. He was supposed to be around but something had come up. He always preferred to hear complaints directly rather than have them filtered through an editor.

I said I understood. But I wanted to convey Señor Rodriguez's displeasure with the article. He did not feel the line of questioning about Tierra Grande's financing was appropriate. Ernesto Rodriguez was a legitimate, respectable businessman. If he said he had the money lined up, he did, and its source was nobody's business.

"He particularly objected to the word 'refused,'" I said. "That he 'refused' to discuss the financing. It's a harsh word and he thought he handled the situation politely."

"I wrote 'declined,'" Overstreet said. "But the copy editor changed it. It's a style thing." He coughed. I sensed he was uncomfortable and decided to let him keep talking. "I'd like to talk to Señor Rodriguez again. One-on-one this time. My editors want me to do something in-depth about his plans and his vision of the project. That sort of thing."

I mouthed a silent prayer of gratitude to the media gods and imagined a huge spread in the Sunday business section complete with charts and graphics and Ernesto looking serious in an office we'd probably have to rent.

I told Overstreet that I rarely set conditions for an interview, but in this case I'd have to insist beforehand that he ask no questions about Tierra Grande's financing.

"That won't be a problem. Somewhere in the story—and I'll bury it as deeply as I can—I'll have to note that he hasn't discussed the financing. But I won't bring it up in the interview."

I said I'd call Ernesto. Señor Rodriguez was a busy man but I was sure we could carve some time out of his schedule.

"I'm sorry I wasn't in yesterday."

Overstreet had already apologized and I didn't feel like listening to the same words but there was a confessional tone in his voice, as if he was about to tell me a secret that had haunted his family since it arrived on the *Mayflower*.

"Something came up," he said.

"You told me already." It was time to employ my GoodFellas accent. "Fuhgeddaboudit."

"My car was trashed."

"Excuse me?"

He said he was covering a press conference at the airport and when he returned to the parking garage his car—a new Infiniti, a gift from his parents after he graduated from college—had been wrecked by a person or persons unknown. The tires were cut to ribbons, the windshields and windows smashed, the doors banged in. But nothing had been stolen.

I expressed the sympathy that everyone in this country has perfected because we're all acquainted with victims. The authorities say crime has declined, but I don't know anyone who believes it.

I punched in a number and heard a ring that was followed by a click and hum. A woman's recorded voice said the number I had requested was no longer in service. I shook my head and told myself it was my own damn fault for not having Ernesto's office speed-dialed. I'd been meaning to do it for days.

I redialed, this time making sure I touched every digit precisely. The response was the same. I looked at the phone as if it were malfunctioning, then called Information. I listened as the number was repeated twice.

It was the same one I had tried before.

I left for Hialeah during the middle of the afternoon downpour. At times it came down so hard I had to turn on the Rover's high beams, but by the time I reached Ernesto's address the rain had slowed to a drizzle and shafts of sunlight were breaking through the clouds.

I pulled up to the storefront office and turned off my lights but kept the engine running. The interior of Ernesto's place of business was dark. I cut the engine and walked over wet pavement to the door, which was locked.

I took a few steps to the left, pressed my face to the glass, shielded my eyes and peered inside. The office was still filled with neatly arranged filing cabinets, as well as desks that were topped with computer monitors and printers. All the chairs had been slid in, as if the occupants had fastidiously closed up shop but expected to return soon.

The door to Ernesto's cubbyhole was closed and the nameplate that had adorned it was no longer there. Beside the door was a coatrack with a couple of women's sweaters.

I walked to the corner of the building and peered around. The vans that belonged to Ernesto's company were still parked in back. On the other side of the alley, a fluorescent glow was coming through the front window of a Laundromat.

I entered it slowly. In the rear was a Cuban woman of about sixty, her gray hair knotted behind her head, her arms both heavy and sagging from years of lifting baskets of other people's clothes.

"Buenas tardes, señor."

"Hola."

"What do you want?"

I told her I was looking for the man who worked in the office next door—or at least used to work there. Señor Rodriguez. She nodded, as if the question did not surprise her, and asked if I was a friend of his. I said we were more like business associates. She asked if he owed me money.

"No," I said. "It's not like that." Then I grinned. "Well, maybe he owes me a little. But that's not the reason I'm here."

"Then why are you here?"

"I haven't been able to reach him. As I said, we do business together, and there are some matters I want to discuss with him—important matters."

The woman looked toward the ceiling, as if she wasn't sure she should believe me, before saying she had not seen Señor Rodriguez for days.

"Has anybody been in the office?" I asked.

She shook her head.

"Do you have any idea what happened to him? Or to any of them?"

She shook her head again. She said she had lived in Miami for many years, and the reason she had survived in Miami for many years was because she stayed out of trouble.

I used my cell phone to call Isabel, who picked up on the sixth ring. "What is it?"

"I hope you don't talk to clients that way."

"Clients always leave voicemail."

I asked her to look up Ernesto Rodriguez's home address in my Rolodex. She said looking in my Rolodex meant she'd have to get up from her desk. I said I needed the information. Isabel sighed before telling me it would take a few minutes.

As I sat behind the wheel, drumming my fingers on the dashboard, phone wedged between my ear and shoulder, a man walked up to the door of Ernesto's office. Years of living in New York had taught me to avoid eye contact with strangers and I tried not to look at him but as he jerked the knob and then turned away in what seemed to be frustration and disgust, I shifted my gaze from an indeterminate point between the windshield and the building and looked directly at him.

And he looked at me. He was in his early twenties, Latino of course, with slick hair swept back into a short ponytail. He seemed to be trying, with only partial success, to contain his rage.

He walked away from the building slowly, looking directly at me until he was out of my sight line.

Isabel came back on and said she'd had a hard time going through my Rolodex because I'd left it open at "B" but eventually she found Ernesto's address. I grunted. She gave me the number and I asked where that was and she sighed and said she'd have to look it up on a map to find it precisely but the street name sounded like it was in Coral Gables. I told her that was good enough.

I stopped in front of the number Isabel had given me, smack in the middle of a block lined with Mission-style colonials framed by willows.

I expected a darkened house, no car in the driveway, the lawn overgrown with weeds that also crawled up the walls. But all the lights inside were ablaze; two minivans consumed most of the driveway; the grass and garden reeked of a recent pesticide treatment.

I considered driving away. Obviously Ernesto was at home with his family. But then I wondered where his Cadillac was.

I got out of the Rover and walked up the driveway, careful to avoid the children's toys strewn around the grass and asphalt. From inside the house I heard shouts and high-pitched squeals.

I rang the bell and told myself I was out of my mind. In modern America, an uninvited walk to somebody's door can provoke a reaction that involves guns or attack dogs.

The ringing bell provoked a shushing sound followed by the uneasy quiet of children restraining themselves. I felt eyes peering out at me. A few of the lights were turned off.

The door opened, revealing a black man in his late thirties. I was so startled I didn't say anything.

"What do you want?" he asked.

I told him I was looking for Ernesto Rodriguez.

"Nobody here by that name," he said before stepping back from the door, which he started to close.

I reached into my pocket. The gesture froze him and he looked as if he were about to lunge at my hand to separate me from whatever weapon he was sure I was taking out.

It was the piece of paper on which I had written Ernesto's address. I read from it and asked if I had the right place. The man told me I did. I most certainly did. This was his house and he had lived in it for three years and he knew there was nobody named Ernesto in it. His voice was rising.

"I'm puzzled," I said.

"Puzzled about what? That an African-American can afford a house like this? In a neighborhood like this?"

"That's not it at all."

"I've worked hard for this. A place for myself and my wife and my children, and I don't have to take any nonsense from some racist—"

"I'm not a racist."

"—who doesn't believe I deserve it."

"I'm looking for Ernesto Rodriguez. He told me he lived here."

"Obviously he doesn't."

The man had a point.

"Now get off my property."

Helen bent over the stove, opening and closing the oven as if whatever was inside needed constant attention. She was wearing an apron I had bought for her as a joke. My wife had never tried to cook from scratch.

I asked what she was doing.

"What does it look like I'm doing?"

"If I didn't know any better, I'd say you were making dinner."

"This is no time for sarcasm, Garry."

Helen thrashed about, opening and closing doors and drawers with great fervor but little apparent result. Something boiled over and a pan clattered to the floor, followed by a cry of "Shit!" I saw Helen flapping her right hand in the classic manner of a person trying to wave away a burn. I asked if she was all right.

"I'm fine."

I asked if she needed help.

"I said I was fine."

I walked up to her forcefully and grabbed her by the shoulders and shouted: "All right, lady, what have you done with my wife?"

Helen laughed and fell into my arms. I felt her head against my chest and held her closely and ran my hands over her back and hips.

All the while, I was thinking of Magdalena.

SIX

"I think we've got a problem."

I said this casually to my boss, as if we were having trouble getting the site we wanted for the company picnic.

"Problem solving is why I'm here," he said. "Although I also believe in delegating responsibility. Do you know why?"

I shook my head.

"A manager who delegates responsibility has more time for golf."

I made sure my laughter was louder than his.

"What's up?" he asked after we had subsided to chuckles.

I said I wasn't sure. Perhaps that, in itself, was the problem. As I described in detail what had happened when I tried to reach Ernesto Rodriguez, my boss began glancing at his watch and looking out the window at the teal-colored water of Biscayne Bay. When I finished, he tilted back in his chair, laced his fingers together and looked up at the ceiling, as if he were hoping to find a solution in the off-white panels that looked like cardboard.

"I see where you're coming from," he said. "Thirty thousand dollars is nothing to sneeze at, but we need to low-key this. Maybe even sweep it under the rug."

"What do we tell New York?"

"For now, nothing. Ogilvie will hang both of us for this, if he feels like it."

"I'll keep trying to find Ernesto."

"It shouldn't be too difficult. A man like that doesn't just fall off the face of the earth." My boss clapped me on the back. It was a habitual gesture of his that I was growing to dislike. "I'm glad we have an old newshound like you to sic on this."

I shook my head. "I only did a little of that Woodward and Bernstein stuff."

"I bet you were good at it."

"I once nailed a city councilman for fixing his son's parking tickets. That's about it."

My boss clapped me on the back again. He said I was intrepid.

I didn't tell him that the councilman was quite popular, and his son was the quarterback of the city's best high school football team. After my story ran, hundreds of people canceled their subscriptions, dozens of businesses yanked their ads, and I was banished to covering three towns on the edge of the circulation area where cows outnumbered people by about fifty to one.

To my surprise, Evan answered the phone. Winston usually picked up, or else I got their machine. I figured Evan was phone-shy and so, before he could say more than three words, I began to enthuse about the strip-mall campaign and how I had found a gallery in Fort Lauderdale that could help with the artwork.

"We have a chance to do something different here," I said. "It'll be exciting. Fun."

"There's something we should tell you," Evan said.

"I'm all ears."

"We don't like your idea."

I remembered something Lisa once told me: "Always stay positive. Upbeat. Let your energy flow outward." She lit another cigar. "Never be anything less than pleasant. Even when you want to kill them."

"What's the problem, Evan? You don't like creativity?"

"We're not quite sure this is for us."

"Why is that?"

"The whole premise is so over the top. We're a bit more staid. You can take the boys out of New England, but . . . "

I silently mouthed a few obscenities before saying, in what I hoped was my most businesslike voice, "You hired me to do publicity for you, right?"

"That's correct."

"And I've come up with an idea that could get you a lot of publicity."

"It could."

"Tell me something, Evan—am I doing my job too well?"

"I think I explained our position," he said, his *chowdah* accent growing thicker with every sentence.

Lisa again, crashing into my consciousness, jabbing her cigar in the air as if she were trying to poke out Ogilvie's eye: "When you have a disagreement, or you just can't get them to do what's obviously in their best interest, get them onto your turf. And don't let them leave."

I suggested that the Copleys come to my office as soon as they could. I even promised to provide a box of Krispy Kremes.

As I approached the Rover I could tell it was sitting low and as I got closer I saw that all four tires were torn and shredded. The tire by the front passenger door was ripped all the way to the hub.

I wondered why the alarm hadn't gone off.

Most likely it did, but nobody had paid attention.

I looked to my left and right. No one was visible, but of course it was possible that whoever had done this was hiding behind a pillar or barricade, waiting for the owner to appear.

I turned all the way around. The only noise was my own breathing, as deep and heavy as the sound effects in a horror movie.

I walked up to the Rover and looked in, expecting to see signs of forced entry—the lock smashed open, wires pulled, the stereo and CD player gone.

But it all looked normal. I reached in and took out my cell phone. At home our machine kicked on, Helen's recorded voice giving our number and the please-leave-a-message shtick. I began to speak, but she picked up as soon as I said "slashed."

"I was getting ready for dinner," she said. "I figured it was a telemarketer."

"All four tires," I said. "Cut to ribbons."

"Are you all right?"

"Fine." I reconsidered. "A little shaken, actually."

"I don't blame you. Maybe you should get out of there."

I told her I thought I was safe and put the phone away and began to walk all the way around the Rover, trying to see if there was any damage I had overlooked. I saw nothing else I'd need to tell the insurance company, but I did see a piece of paper fluttering under the windshield wiper. I figured it was a circular from a local car wash and almost crumpled it up. But I noticed that whatever was written seemed to be hand-lettered, and so I smoothed out the paper and rested it on the engine hood.

In neat, cursive writing, the message was this: "Stop meddling in matters that do not concern you."

With rare hints of excitement and interest in her voice, Isabel said a police officer was waiting to see me. When I told her to send the gentleman in, she giggled a bit.

I rose the moment I heard footsteps outside my office and prepared myself for a beefy handshake followed by male banter that expressed equal concern about scumbag criminals and the Dolphins' chances of making the Super Bowl.

The uniformed officer had frizzy hair that brushed the shoulders, dark eyeliner that highlighted brown eyes, and lipstick a shade short of crimson. Her name tag said "Hurtado."

I leaned across my desk and smiled as I extended my hand.

"You're the 'gentleman,' huh?"

"I am."

"Shows what I know. Please, have a seat."

Our hands touched briefly in the perfunctory way men and women greet each other in a business setting. Police Officer Pilar Hurtado sat down, put her cap on my desk and pulled out a small notebook, which she flipped through with great deliberation.

"There was an incident yesterday," she said.

Correct.

"Could you describe it?"

I told her as much as I wanted to. She furrowed her brow while taking notes, as if my account didn't quite make sense, and asked if I was sure that nothing was taken from my vehicle. I told her I was.

"This is unusual," she said. "It makes me wonder."

"Wonder what?"

"Whether it was random."

I thought about giving her the note, which I had put in my briefcase along with other items that I thought might be important someday, like information on 401(k)s and HMOs. But something instinctive held me back. I had grown up in a neighborhood filled with cops whom I did not like or trust and I knew nothing about this woman and I was unsure what the note meant, or if it meant anything at all. The only thing I wanted from Police Officer Pilar Hurtado was a report that would satisfy my insurance company.

Josette was on the line, immediately expressing interest when I told her I was thinking of doing something sneaky. I described the Copleys' hesitation about the strip-mall campaign but said we might be able to win them over if we could find the right place.

"I'll go with you," Josette said. "Teresa thinks this whole idea is crazy."

"It is crazy," I said. "That's why it's so good."

An hour later I stopped in front of the gallery. Josette was looking anxiously out the window, reminding me of a high school girl who's not sure her date is going to show up. She seemed startled when I emerged from a red Taurus, which I'd rented while my dealer tried to find tires for the Rover.

"What's this?" she said as she walked onto the sidewalk.

I told her what had happened and she shook her head. She said she'd been looking forward to riding in the SUV and I said I knew what she meant. Down low to the ground in an ordinary sedan, I felt as if something bad could happen at any moment.

Josette got into the car and asked if I wanted gum. Wrigley's Spearmint. I declined and she unwrapped a stick for herself and said, "Teresa is such a bitch." Here Josette adopted a whiny howl. "'You get to go out while I have to stay cooped up here just in case a miracle happens and we get a customer.' So I said, 'Fine, you go. Or we'll both go. We can close for the afternoon.'" The fine whine returned. "'No, you go. It's all right. Just go.'" Josette shook her head. "Women. I don't know why men put up with us."

I had a list of the places in which the Copleys had invested. I handed it to Josette and she directed me toward some nearby locations. After a while they blurred into each other, boxy things on commercial strips filled with drugstores and Radio Shacks and fast-food joints.

"They're really ugly, aren't they?" I said.

"They're America," she replied. "Look at them at night, when the neon lights are on. They're beautiful in an artificial way. Kind of like Pamela Anderson."

We kept going south and eventually we crossed into Miami-Dade. Without saying anything to Josette, without even admitting it to myself, I aimed the Taurus toward Ernesto's office.

As we pulled up to the storefront, Josette said this place would never do. Its flavor was much too Latin.

I stepped into the humidity and looked up at the dark clouds starting to skim by. A fat drop of water landed on my forehead and I realized that the daily downpour would begin in thirty seconds so I moved under the overhang and pressed my face against the glass.

The room was empty. All the desks, chairs, cabinets and computers were gone.

Thunder cracked and boomed only a few feet above and behind me. I heard feet splashing and then Josette, too, pressed her face against the glass. Water seeped through her blouse, which was clinging to her black brassiere.

She said she enjoyed these storms. The violence of them.

I pressed my face harder against the glass. The door to what had once been Ernesto's office was closed.

"What is this place?" Josette asked.

"Ernesto Rodriguez's office. Another client of mine. He works here."

"Worked here."

I looked around the corner. The vans that belonged to Ernesto's company were gone, but the Laundromat was open.

"I love Laundromats," Josette said.

We walked in and saw the Cuban woman in back: eyes half-closed, gray hair pulled back.

"Buenas tardes," she said as we approached.

I asked if she remembered me.

"No."

I told her I'd been here a few days before and had asked about Ernesto. I jerked my thumb in the direction of the storefront Josette and I had just left.

"I don't remember. A lot of people come in here, señor."

I looked around. The Laundromat was empty except for the three of us and some clothes tumbling angrily in the dryers.

"Who owns these buildings? I'd like to talk to him."

"No sé."

"Then who owns this Laundromat?"

"A man. And his wife. That's what I've been told. I've never met them."

"Tell me this: Who pays you?"

"None of your business."

I kicked at the floor with my shoes and was happy to see them leave a few scuff marks.

Back outside we heard another crack of thunder, followed by rain that obscured the street. We ran until we stopped again in front of the office that had once been Ernesto's.

And then, like an apparition, a form appeared under the overhang at the edge of the building. Josette inched toward me, lightly brushing her fingers against my arm. As the form came toward us, I could tell it belonged to a man who was about my height. I could sense the rage coming from him and for a moment I was as afraid as I'd ever been. I've always believed that fights are won by whoever is angriest.

It was the guy I had seen the last time I was here: early twenties, ponytail, Latino. He came close and looked both of us up and down. Josette stepped behind me and he circled around us with his eyes locked into mine before glancing away. From behind Josette let out a low whistle of relief.

The guy strode toward the storefront door and put his hand on the knob but it refused to open. He stepped back and looked at us, as if we were responsible for what had happened or at least might have an explanation.

"It's all gone," I said. *"Todo están ido."*

Another crack of thunder that sounded only inches away. I felt as if I were about to become a modern Lear, raging bilingually against the elements.

"Everyone," I said. "Everything. *Ellos desaparecen.*"

He pressed his face to the glass.

"Fuck," he said.

I asked if he had any idea what had happened.

"There was stuff here yesterday," the man said. "They must have taken it out overnight. Fuck."

"Who took it out?" I asked.

"Whoever."

Josette peered around my shoulder. "It'd be nice to get inside," she said. "Just to look for ourselves. Maybe there's something behind that closed door."

The guy looked hard at her, as if he couldn't believe she was serious about an idea he had kept suppressed and unarticulated.

The rain was slowing down. In a few minutes shafts of sunlight would stream through breaks in the clouds.

"If we're going to do it," I said, "we'd better do it now."

The guy reached into his pocket and took out something that looked like a cross between a long hairpin and a shiv. Josette gave a little gasp as he stood there with his instrument and for a moment I thought he might thrust it right at my face. But then he turned and walked toward the door.

The rain was stopping. More cars were on the street and I could sense people stirring inside the buildings that surrounded us.

"It's open," he said.

He stood in the frame, his arm extended across the width of the door. Josette and I hurried toward him and slipped inside. It was dark and the dust made me sniffle.

"Don't turn on the light," Josette said.

"It's dark in here."

"Somebody might see us."

"I've been coming here every day for a week," the guy said. "The only thing I've ever seen is him."

We were walking as lightly as we could across the thin carpet, as if we were afraid someone in a passing car might hear our footsteps.

"If you never see anything," Josette asked, "why do you keep coming here?"

"The guy I work for. He wants me to check."

We reached the door to Ernesto's cubbyhole. It was locked of course. Josette and I turned to our newfound companion and looked at him the way children stare at a neighborhood magician who constantly pulls rabbits from a tall black hat. He tried the instrument he had used before but the door remained locked. After a couple of minutes he shrugged and rammed his shoulder against the frame. The door made a shattering noise as it flew off its hinges.

"I'm glad we kept so quiet before," Josette said.

"Are you trying to be funny?" the guy asked.

"It would never occur to me."

The room was stuffed from floor to ceiling with desks and chairs and office equipment stacked on top of each other. Through a crack between a couple of filing cabinets, I could see Ernesto's calendar still hanging on the wall.

"What the fuck does this mean?" the guy asked.

"It means they plan to come back," I said. "Ernesto probably figured this was cheaper than storage."

"They'll know somebody was here," Josette said.

I sensed that my companions were becoming nervous, as if they were afraid Ernesto and half his exile friends were about to march in and demand an explanation. Josette and the Latino began to back away toward the main door, but I stayed. I, too, was a bit afraid, but I also felt something pulling me in, as if the room contained a secret it was vital to find out.

But the secret was about Ernesto tangentially, if at all. What the room held was something that would connect me to Magdalena.

"Garry."

Josette's voice had a sense of urgency I'd never heard before.

"I think we better get out of here."

I looked around one last time. Down on the floor, wedged between two stacks of desks, was a business card that appeared to have some writing on the back. I bent down and scooped it up and put it in my pocket.

"Did you find something?" the guy asked.

I turned around slowly. Then I grinned and held out my hand.

"Just a dustball," I said. I blew on my hand and sneezed.

"It's disgusting in here," the guy said. "If there's one thing I can't stand, it's dust."

I was picturing Magdalena on the edge of a bed with her legs in the air while I stood between them, pumping into her, as she urged me on in Spanish.

"Watch out for that truck!"

I hit the brakes and felt the Taurus slow, then stop, only inches from a gasoline tanker. Josette asked if I was all right to drive.

"I think so. Why do you ask?"

"You seem preoccupied."

I stopped in front of Red White & Blew and cut the engine and looked over at Josette, expecting her to recognize that this was a signal to leave me alone so I could indulge in more sexual fantasies. But she stayed there, gazing at me the way a puppy looks at a person who's about to feed it, until finally she asked, "Aren't you going to look?"

"Look at what?"

She sighed and said, "The card. The one you picked up in that office. I saw you. That was a good move, talking about that dustball. You're slick, Garry."

I reached into my jacket and took out the card. It was one of Ernesto's and it was bent at the corners. I turned it over and put it on the dashboard so we could both see the writing on back:

Hedges
Orlando
7

Josette snapped back her head like someone inhaling a particularly potent line of cocaine. "What the hell does that mean?"

I kept my eyes focused on the card and said nothing. I didn't even look at her. I recognized the writing as Ernesto's.

"I've been to the Orlando," Josette said. "They don't need any landscaping. What kind of business was this guy in, anyway?"

I tore the card in pieces and told her it was a dead end.

I entered the lounge at the Orlando and slipped past a bored-looking teenage girl who was blowing out smoke from an inch-wide cigar. She wore a clingy white dress and had straight blond hair that stretched almost to her waist. I sat at the bar and after a few minutes a guy with aquamarine hair and six rings in each ear strolled over, tossed a napkin in front of me and asked if I wanted anything.

"Martini."

"Gin or vodka?"

"Gin. With a twist."

He shook his head. Everybody was drinking vodka these days.

I turned around on my stool and examined the room, which was awash in pink and lime-green pastels. The lights in the walls were hidden inside scalloped fixtures, but they illuminated every Deco detail, and I wondered if this was what Ernesto had seen, so many years ago, when the only people in South Beach were junkies and hookers and grandparents waiting to die.

"Here's your drink. Gin."

I swiveled around and grinned, pointed the glass toward the bartender in a mock salute and took a healthy sip. Then I blanched. The gin was a grade above antifreeze and he had put in only a drop of vermouth, I assumed as an act of protest.

He stood a few feet away from me with his back leaning against the cash register and his arms folded across his chest. His upper body had the chiseled look that comes from several hours a day at the gym, and I wondered if he worked out to impress men, women or himself.

I grinned again and told him I was looking for Frank Hedges. He shook his head and said he'd never heard of the man. I asked if he was sure and started to describe Magdalena's husband, but each piece of information prompted a more vigorous shake of the head as the bartender stated, with increasing amplitude if not conviction, that he did not know anyone like that.

"I heard he came here a lot."

"You must have heard badly."

I asked if he had ever met Ernesto Rodriguez. The bartender shook his head again and I started to doubt that he knew any other gestures. I said Ernesto had owned this hotel a number of years ago. The bartender asked why he should even be aware of a man like that. I might as well be asking about somebody who lived during the Dark Ages.

I asked him how much the drink was.

"Seven-fifty."

I rolled my eyes and put down a twenty. The bartender took the bill with a deep sigh, as if I'd just told him he should give up looking at himself in the mirror for Lent.

I sensed someone coming toward me and glanced over my shoulder, half expecting to see Frank Hedges with his hand out in a display of fake heartiness, or perhaps Ernesto, smiling in his dignified way and ready with an explanation for everything that had happened.

The blonde was walking as quickly as her dress would allow. The cigar was still in her mouth and in her hand were the remains of a large blue drink that had contained several pieces of fruit. She was five foot ten, could not have weighed more than one hundred twenty pounds and looked seventeen. I wondered what kind of ID she carried, or whether the bartender had bothered to check.

She blew a perfect circle of smoke while she sat next to me and put her drink on the bar. "It's empty," she said as she slid her drink across.

"He drinks gin," the bartender said as he slammed my change in front of me.

The girl shrugged. I asked what she was drinking and she described a complicated daiquiri that involved rum, triple sec, sugar, lime, pineapple chunks and banana slices. It was especially important to do the pineapple just right.

"You think you can make that?" I asked the bartender.

He glared at me, grabbed the girl's glass and took most of my change.

"I only asked because he fucked up my martini," I said to the girl, but loudly enough for him to hear.

"I like martinis," the girl said in a voice that tried to be world-weary but sounded only six months removed from the Galleria. "Gin, vodka, it doesn't matter. I'm just not in the mood today. I want something more . . ." She paused and for a second I thought I saw panic behind her eyes, as if she were afraid she'd just run out of conversation.

"Frivolous?" I said.

She tipped some of the cigar ash into a metal tray. "That's it," she said, the world-weariness returning.

I leaned back in my chair. The girl's eyes held steady with mine.

"So," I said.

"So."

"I'm looking for someone."

"Isn't everybody?"

"His name is Frank Hedges. I heard he comes here. It's strictly a business matter."

The girl's lips pursed as I described him and I took that as a sign she was thinking. "I know a guy who looks like that," she said at last. "He calls himself Bill."

"Tell me about him."

She said he came around once or twice a week and always had money and liked to greet as many people in the lobby and bar as he could—as if everyone was a potential business partner.

"Except he calls it 'bidness,'" I said.

"Yeah," she said, and I could almost see her brain churning. "Now that I think about it, he does."

The bartender put the girl's daiquiri in front of her. She bent over, swept her hair behind her right ear and wrapped her lips around the straw.

I said it sounded like the same guy, but wondered why he called himself Bill.

"He probably doesn't want his wife to find out."

"Find out what?"

"What do you think?"

"I know his wife. I can't understand why he'd go someplace else. No offense."

"None taken. It's 'bidness.'" She smiled and I did too. She said their transactions were straightforward: He'd buy her a couple of drinks and then they'd go up to a room. "Strictly oral," she said. "No intercourse. I'm saving myself. Interested?"

I shook my head but thanked her for the offer. She sipped her daiquiri again and made the same motion with her hair. It was sexy in a schoolgirlish way and I said perhaps we could do bidness some other time. She said there might not be another time. She was going to cut back once school began.

"When did you see him last?"

About a week ago. She couldn't remember exactly.

"Was he with somebody?" I remembered to grin. "Besides you, I mean?"

She looked at me with the gauzy eyes a woman displays when she's beginning to warm up to a man. Then she flashed a smile that I thought she meant. Her teeth were pearl white, straight and even, and I wondered how recently her braces had come off.

She said she'd been sitting at the table where I had first seen her. She was with Bill or Frank or whatever his name was and they were getting ready to go up to their usual room and he seemed particularly anxious because he kept telling her he was tense and on edge and needed a release. He'd had a rough day. Miami was a tough town for bidness.

An image of Magdalena came over me, more powerful than any I'd had before, and I saw her looking at me over her bare shoulder and telling me in Spanish to relax before she began to crawl up my body and brush her lips against my flesh.

"Hel-lo," the girl said in a singsong voice. "Are you with me?"

I grinned and apologized and told her she had reminded me of something so I'd zoned out for a second. She said she understood. She herself was forever making connections that she could never explain to anyone else.

"You were at the table with Bill or Frank."

"Whoever."

"Then what happened?"

She said a man walked in and looked around the room as if he was expecting to find someone. Her companion lowered himself in his chair, which surprised her because she had never seen him shrink from anything before. She asked if he knew the guy and he told her to shut up.

I asked her to describe the man.

She said he was really old—maybe in his fifties. He was still good-looking, although he should lose a few pounds. He had gray hair and a thick dark mustache and a bearing about him that was impressive, ramrod-straight posture that indicated he'd probably been in the military or something.

"Cuban?" I asked.

She rolled her eyes. "No, Martian."

I laughed as the girl leaned over and touched my wrist with a smooth but firm hand. "Tell me," she said in a voice growing full with a sudden rush of excitement, "are you, like, a private eye or something?"

I shook my head and grinned again and told her I was a businessman who was just trying to make sense out of some strange events. I asked her to describe what happened after the older man walked into the room.

She said he saw her with Bill or Frank or whatever his name was and started to walk directly toward their table. Her companion told her to stay where she was and intercepted the newcomer a few feet away.

She was disappointed. She wanted to meet him. She was always looking for new customers.

I asked what the two men talked about.

I heard you were here, the man with the mustache had said.

Can't this wait until tomorrow?

No. I am tired of this matter. We must resolve it now. I have plans and you are interfering.

I just wanna do bidness.

After that, she said, she couldn't hear clearly because they went over to the bar. But their conversation sounded extremely animated. They were almost in each other's faces. The older man kept saying, "Impossible. What you ask is impossible."

I pointed to the bartender and asked if he had been here that night.

She looked quickly at the guy as he leaned against the corner and glowered at us. The girl smiled at me and sipped the dregs of her drink, once again sweeping her hair back over her ear.

"I don't remember," she said. "Sorry." I sensed she wasn't telling the truth, but decided not to press.

She pointed to her drink and announced that it was empty again.

I pushed her glass across the bar. "Could you make another one?" I asked the bartender in a voice that was several decibels louder than necessary. "If it's not too much trouble?"

He snatched the glass and walked away. I heard the angry deployment of ice and utensils.

"How did it end up?" I asked the girl. "Did they get in a fight or anything?"

"I thought they might," she said. But finally the guy she was with stood up and said it wasn't over between them, he wasn't going to take no for an answer and he still had contacts who could make life difficult for the older man. At that point the man with the mustache stood up and walked quickly toward the patio that fronted Ocean Drive. He strode right past her. He looked angry and upset. Before he was entirely out of the room the man she'd been with called out: "And you just stay away from Maggie, you hear? I know you've been calling her. Just cut it out."

The older man turned at the veranda doors that the hotel kept open in the hopes of catching any air that stirred. He looked at Bill or Frank or whatever his name was and said, in a low voice dripping with contempt, "You do not deserve her."

The bartender put another drink before the blond girl. I took out a twenty and slid it toward him. He took the bill without saying a word.

For the first time since she'd sat down with me, the girl took her cigar and puffed on it. After a few attempts, the ash glowed red. She took a deep breath and let the smoke come out.

The bartender slapped my change in front of me. It sounded like a rifle shot echoing around a courtyard. I pushed the money toward the girl and told her to keep it.

Her eyes narrowed. She said she didn't want my pity.

"It's not pity," I replied, although she was exactly right. "You gave me your time and some information I've wanted badly. This is the least I can do."

I don't know if she believed me, but somehow she made all those bills disappear inside her dress.

I got up and walked through the doors Ernesto had used. Perhaps I half expected to find him on the patio, sipping cool rum and telling me he had new ideas for marketing Tierra Grande.

The brief twilight was over and I watched pedestrians parading under the glare of retro neon. A few people pointed at me, as if I had somehow become a piece of the local color.

Suddenly I sensed eyes behind me, boring into my back with laser-like intensity.

I turned around slowly.

She was alone in the corner, illuminated only by a flickering candle and smoking a slim cigar in a manner that bespoke extreme agitation.

Magdalena.

For a second I thought my mind was conjuring her, but then I told myself her presence was inevitable: everything I had discovered had led her, and me, to this point at this time, in the last summer of the millennium.

I stopped and stood above her. She continued to stare straight ahead, repeatedly bringing the cigar to her mouth.

There was something ritualistic in the way we were moving, as if we were unwitting participants in a form of Kabuki. Finally she raised her eyes and looked into mine.

"You too?"

"What are you talking about?"

"Her." Magdalena jerked her head toward the bar. "The girl. That *puta.*"

"If you were watching us—"

"I was."

"You noticed I didn't go anywhere with her."

I sat down and asked when she had started spying on me. Magdalena turned her head and exhaled.

"I wasn't looking for you. I was looking for Frank."

"Oh."

"He comes here a lot. Word gets around. I haven't heard from him in two days."

"And that displeases you?"

"He's disappeared before—sometimes for weeks. But he's always called me every day. Even if it's to say he can't tell me where he is or what he's doing."

"He was here a week ago. That's the last time the girl saw him. He got into an argument with Ernesto."

Magdalena tilted her head and looked up at the moon. My eyes traced the taut outline of her jaw and neck.

"I have a pretty good idea what they were talking about," I said. She did not respond so I decided to continue. "Tierra Grande—and you."

She could have walked out after slapping me and screaming that I had no right to say something like that to her. But I sensed she was the kind of woman who liked men to take chances with her.

She stubbed out her cigar and looked at me. I detected something in her deep brown eyes but I could not be sure what it was: Concern? Irritation? Desire? Perhaps she'd had a flash of intuition and clearly saw what was going to happen but believed she could do nothing to interfere with the workings of fate, and felt truly and profoundly sorry for my naive American belief that we have the ability to change the course of events.

"I hate this place," she said, gesturing toward Ocean Drive. "The mob scene. Let's get out of here. We can walk along the beach."

We dodged cars, tourists, models and Rollerbladers. Behind us I glimpsed the flash of cameras from the ghouls who kept gathering to have their pictures taken on the steps where Gianni Versace was murdered. People will do anything to touch celebrity.

When we reached the edge of the beach I wanted to keep walking out into the water so we could vanish into the darkness and re-emerge in some far corner of the world where we had no past and nobody knew us.

Instead we turned left, away from the lights and the crowds.

I imagined Magdalena beneath me, her eyes closed and legs spread apart, bloodred nails digging into the sheets.

I asked if she had seen or talked to Ernesto recently.

"No."

"He owes my company thirty thousand dollars."

No reaction.

"He seems to have fallen off the face of the earth," I said. "And now Frank has vanished too. It's all quite puzzling."

She stopped and turned toward me and looked up. She was nearly a foot shorter than I was but she had more knowledge than I did, so I was the one who felt intimidated.

"I want to give you some advice," she said. "As a friend. Because I like you." She paused and I knew the effect was for drama but I also found myself listening much more carefully than usual and I knew it was because I wanted this woman to keep talking to me. "Don't ask too many questions about Ernesto. He'll turn up when he wants to. And he'll pay your company. Most likely with interest."

"I'm happy to hear that," I said. "I really am. But I don't think that's gonna fly. I can't tell the bean counters in New York to get off my back just because some mystery woman assures me that everything will work out."

I bent down and picked a smooth stone out of the sand and tossed it up and down a few times, feeling its weight, before heaving it out into the ocean.

"Don't get me wrong," I said. "I like you too. And I appreciate the warning. But I have a job and I'd like to keep it."

I like you too. I couldn't believe I was uttering the same inanities I'd used at my first boy-girl dance in middle school.

I looked at her and despite the darkness I could see that her eyes were smiling at me, but I couldn't tell if it was mockery or genuine amusement.

"What happened to your husband?" I asked. "You must have a theory."

She shook her head. "Frank is secretive. At least he tries to be."

"Maybe he's trying to scare up some 'bidness.'"

"That could be it. But whatever happened, he wouldn't want me to go to the authorities. He hates cops. He thinks they're amateurs."

"Why is that?"

"They're always looking for simple explanations."

A party boat cruised by no more than a half mile offshore. It was lit with yellow and blue and green and purple but mostly with a throbbing strobe red and I could see it rocking back and forth, reacting to the energy of people dancing to deafening merengue. Magdalena watched too and I wondered what it would be like if we were on the boat together, both of us unattached and without a past and just getting to know each other.

"Why did you and your husband come to Florida?"

"I didn't want to come. But Frank insisted. He wanted to get in touch with Ernesto."

"How long had it been since they talked?"

"Almost ten years."

"Why did he want to see Ernesto again?"

"Frank had heard how successful he was. He wanted—what's the saying?—a piece of the action." She paused and looked out at the water again and I had the feeling that she, too, would have preferred to be on the party boat, where we each could have been . . . solicitous. "I told him that going back to your past is always a bad idea."

"Ernesto didn't want him involved."

"But Frank was determined. He felt that Ernesto owed him some favors."

"Favors for what?" I asked.

No response from Magdalena.

"For what happened in California?"

She started walking ahead of me, toward a low concrete structure that guarded a tangle of weeds and debris. I had a premonition that someone was waiting there, but I followed her anyway.

"Did Frank save Ernesto's life or something?" I asked.

We stopped beside the building. It was an abandoned bathhouse. Magdalena said she wondered if anything inside was still working and before I could answer she said she had to pee so badly she didn't care.

I waited, glancing around, never sitting, preparing for I-don't-know-who-or-what to swoop out of the night and engage me in a fight to the death. At one point I heard something snap behind me and I let out a little cry of terror and whirled around just in time to see a seagull trying to rip open a small bag of potato chips.

After waiting a few minutes I walked around the building, which was little more than a crumbling concrete block, before stopping outside the entrance and listening for any sounds within.

"Magdalena?" My voice was soft.

No reply.

"Magdalena?" A little louder.

Nothing.

I stepped closer and tried to see what was inside, but it was the color of ink.

"Magdalena?" Insistent. Almost a shout.

I went through the opening. Cobwebs brushed against my face. Dust filled my eyes and nostrils.

"Magdalena?" I was yelling now, and my voice was growing hoarse. "Are you there? Magdalena!"

I rammed my ankle against a cinderblock and let out a string of expletives that revealed the true extent of my vocabulary. Ahead I saw the outline of a doorway, and I limped toward it.

I was still calling Magdalena's name, not understanding why she had failed to respond, afraid of what I might find and of what might be waiting for me.

Through the doorway was a space even darker than the one I'd just left and I had the feeling of entering a void where there was no sensation except my own fear.

Something was behind me and I sensed its presence for only a moment before my ear was filled with an earsplitting scream that made me spin around, and suddenly I was bellowing in a voice that was not my own with my fists raised and my arms flailing forward at whatever it was that was tormenting me.

And then I heard the laugh. A deep, hearty cackle that was delighting in the consternation its possessor had caused.

Magdalena.

I sensed her only a few feet away.

"You bitch," I said. I wanted to be angry but I, too, was beginning to laugh, not only at the situation but in relief that she was here, and safe, and still with me. "You almost gave me a heart attack."

"Afraid of the dark, Garrett? Afraid of ghosts, or spiders? Are you a fraidycat?"

She laughed again and I joined in, the two of us now hysterical, forgetting what we had found so funny and laughing only for its own sake. I shortened my breath and regained my composure just enough to employ my best Goodfellas accent: "I ain't afraida nuttin', lady."

She burst out once more and between gulps of air said, "You could've fooled me."

With those words I found her. I could barely make out her features but I felt the silky texture of her long straight hair and the soft warmth of her skin and I could smell the traces of a perfume that reminded me of hyacinth. My mouth found hers and our tongues locked and I had suddenly forgotten about everything except her.

You would think I'd remember every detail, but in truth my desire was so overpowering that what happened next is a blur. I recall it only in pieces.

Pushing her against the wall. Pulling her panties down and hiking up her skirt. Magdalena undoing my belt. Unbuttoning my pants. Not seeing her but feeling her. Magdalena crying out as I entered her. Wrapping her legs around my waist.

Telling her I had never wanted a woman this much. That I had never felt so alive.

Magdalena murmuring in Spanish that I should go faster.

At the end, as I came, telling her I loved her.

SEVEN

With the care of an archaeologist excavating a site near the pyramids, Winston Copley examined the Krispy Kremes I had set out. "How many hits has your Website had?" I asked.

"Hundreds," Evan Copley replied.

Winston finally selected a lemon-filled thing and devoured it in three bites. A bit of goo dribbled from the corner of his mouth. I watched him with the slack-jawed astonishment I usually reserved for Nature Channel documentaries about predators on the Serengeti.

"Maybe a thousand since the start of the year," Evan continued.

I looked straight at him, then waved the business section of *The Herald* aloft like a talisman. "Do you know what the circulation of this paper is?" I asked.

"Four hundred thousand," the Copleys replied in unison.

"We need to make these pages," I said. "We need to get coverage. You've said that to me. Repeatedly."

The brothers nodded.

"I've got an idea that I think will do it."

The brothers nodded again and reached for more doughnuts. I asked if they wanted coffee and they declined. Evan said even decaf left him feeling nervous and jangly.

"So what's the goddamn problem?" I said.

"We don't think your idea is a bad one," Evan replied. Pieces of doughnut fell through his teeth and onto the floor. "We just don't think it's for us."

A knock at the door. The brothers looked at each other with alarm while I glanced at my watch. It was twenty after ten and my boss was interrupting right on schedule.

I told the Copleys I had no idea who it could be. When I opened the door, my boss asked if he was intruding.

"Well," I said, "as a matter of fact, you are. I've got the Copleys in here."

I opened the door all the way.

"Winston! Evan!" My boss stuck out his hand, which the brothers clasped with sugar-coated fingers. "I haven't seen you guys in a blue moon!" He paused before chortling to himself. "I was about to say I hadn't seen you in a coon's age, but we're all PC now."

This provoked peals of forced laughter.

My boss asked what was going on. Did he need to be brought up to speed?

I had talked to him earlier of course and he said the strip-malls-are-beautiful idea was the greatest thing since sliced bread and asked if there was anything he could do to help. I said we might have to double-team the Copleys.

My boss eased onto the couch in the corner, leaned back and interlaced his hands behind his head. I turned to the Copleys and asked if this was all right. They nodded but said nothing.

"Strip malls," I said.

"I'm all ears," my boss replied.

"A blight on the land. A parasitic reminder of mindless sprawl."

"I couldn't agree more."

"Cookie-cutter boxes sucking the energy out of America's down-towns."

"When you're right, you're right."

"The worst thing about life at the end of the century—after *The Jerry Springer Show*, of course."

"I wouldn't go that far. Jerry's funny sometimes."

I put my hand on my boss's shoulder, like a faith healer trying to drive out a demon. "You could not be more wrong, my friend," I said.

An image of Magdalena beneath me, eyes closed and mouth open, her breath short and quick as she scratched her nails down my back and softly said my name.

"Why am I wrong?" my boss asked.

He looked concerned, as if I had just forgotten the most important lines of a play.

I glanced at the floor and raised my eyes to his before beginning the spiel we had already practiced.

The average person may regard strip malls as an eyesore in the collective vision of America, I said in televangelist-like tones, but the average person has never invested with the Copley brothers. Their real estate investment trusts have consistently outperformed the S. & P. index, and canny investors have long realized that there is no better place to put their money. And why is this? Here's the answer, and it's an easy one to understand: Not only does the real estate appreciate in value, but the properties themselves are revenue-producing, thus providing a cushion against those inevitable, though short-lived, economic downturns. Yes, my friends, this is an opportunity that borders on the miraculous, if only you will believe.

"Say Hallelujah!" my boss shouted. "I believe in the Copley brothers!"

Winston and Evan exchanged doleful looks, as if they'd just heard there was a worldwide chocolate shortage.

"We appreciate the effort you're putting into this," Winston said. "We really do. But as we were telling Garrett, we're not sure this is the best approach for us."

"I like this idea," my boss said. "I like it a lot." He looked at the Copleys and stretched out his hands in a beseeching manner, as if he were a jury foreman trying to persuade the last holdout to go along. "Come on, guys. What have you got to lose?"

"More than you suspect," Evan said softly.

*　　*　　*

It was late afternoon and the sky had grown dark. Magdalena pulled the sheets around her and murmured in Spanish that it had been good. I walked to the window and parted the curtain.

Fat drops crashed against the glass. The clouds were so low they touched the buildings.

"Why are you looking at that?" she asked.

"It's interesting. The way it rains so hard."

"It happens every afternoon. You should be used to it by now."

I told her there were some things I'd never get used to.

I returned to her, slipping under the sheets and running my tongue over her shoulder, which tasted of salt. Magdalena asked how long we had.

Fifteen minutes.

She nodded and said in Spanish that she wanted me to hold her until she had to get dressed. She said she was tired and closed her eyes.

I stayed with her until the sound of water slamming against glass became so loud it seemed the window would break. Magdalena's breathing was deep and rhythmic and I walked across the room and opened the curtain.

The rain came down sideways, as if a giant hose had been turned against us. In the office building across the street, fluorescent lights bore down upon the cubicles. In one room a group of people sat at a table. In another some women huddled around a coffee urn and gestured extravagantly.

In the only room that was dark I saw three men in white shirts and ties; one of them had binoculars; he was pointing at our window.

I stepped back and wondered how much they had seen and whether the curtains had protected us from observation. The prospect of surveillance unsettled but thrilled me and I considered the other tools that could be used by anyone in the electronics age—video cameras, wiretaps, sensors that detect the heat of our bodies. None of us has a private life anymore.

An explosion of lightning blinded me. The thunder echoed so loudly it closed off my ears.

Seconds later, I heard shrieks in a tone filled with panic and edged with terror.

For a moment I could not move. I stood there, paralyzed, while Magdalena sat straight up in bed with terrible sounds coming from a dark place deep within her.

It took only three steps to reach her and I put my hands on her shoulders and told her it was all right, she should calm down, it was only thunder and it was outside and it could not harm us.

But she continued to scream.

My voice rose as I told her there was nothing to fear and her screams turned to sobs and I said there was nothing to be afraid of and finally I heard words coming from her as she buried her head against my shoulder.

"You weren't here," she said.

"It's all right."

"I woke up alone and you weren't here."

"It only took a second. I'm here now."

"I was so afraid."

We took our time getting dressed and paying the bill and walking to our respective cars. I was still intoxicated by my new love and wanted to bottle the feeling and keep it forever and wander through life in the hyped-up but dreamy state my emotions had created.

"Do you have to go back to the office?"

"I guess. I told them I'd be out most of the afternoon. With a client."

She giggled. She said I had provided excellent service.

I laughed and put my arm around her. We kissed and I could smell her hair, which had the scent of apples and made me think we were in a meadow instead of a parking garage and I had the sensation you always do at first, when you want to suck in your lover whole and never release her.

"Let's go somewhere," I said.

"What do you have in mind?"

"A cup of coffee. Perhaps with dessert."

She said she wanted to eat something fattening. She wanted to smoke too.

We drove around in Magdalena's Miata, but the best we could do was the Starbucks I usually frequented. We got our drinks and pastries and sat at a small round table high off the ground that looked as if it would topple over if we put all of our stuff on one side. But she couldn't smoke.

Magdalena asked what was wrong with my Rover and I described how the tires had been slashed. My dealer was having trouble finding new ones. In a certain way, Magdalena said, I was lucky. I could have been carjacked, or worse.

"There was something strange about it," I said. I told her about the note and as I did I felt I was entering a new realm of trust. I had told no one else about the message. Not even Helen.

Magdalena's eyebrows were knit together and she sighed and looked around the room and I could tell there was nothing she wanted more than the opportunity to puff one of those slim cigars she liked.

"What do you think?" I asked.

"*No sé.*"

"What's your theory? Was it Ernesto? Was he trying to make a point?"

Magdalena gave the classic look-around-the-room glance of someone who is afraid of being overheard before saying, "Ernesto has many secrets. I don't know all of them myself."

My wife held up the gigantic chef's hat she had given me for my birthday. I told her to go ahead and she placed it on my head, where it proceeded to droop into my eyes.

"I can't see a thing."

"You never can anyway."

I had the coals going and told Helen it was time for me to retreat to the kitchen to prepare my special sauce. Helen always asked me what ingredients I used and I always refused to tell her.

I lingered in the air-conditioning while Helen watched the fire. While I was mixing in the mustard she reached for my cell phone and then held it aloft as if it were a prize she'd just won.

I grabbed the chicken from the refrigerator and hurried out. About three steps out the door, I began to wilt in the humidity. I took the phone and slapped the chicken on the grill and began to brush the sauce over it. Helen's hand felt cold.

"This is Garry."

"It's me."

Magdalena.

My immediate thought was to talk about how good it had been during the afternoon and tell her I missed her and make plans for our next rendezvous. But then I remembered that my wife was standing five feet away from me.

"Thanks for getting back to me," I said. "That, uh, that thing we discussed. Do you have any ideas?"

She said she did have some ideas, and proceeded to describe some sexual acts she wanted to perform.

"That's, uh, that's an interesting proposal," I said as I flipped the chicken.

Magdalena laughed. She asked how close my wife was and I said I couldn't answer that.

"I wanted to tell you something," she said. "Seriously."

"What is it?"

"I talked to Ernesto today."

Solicitous, I thought. *Ernesto was solicitous.*

"That's interesting," I said. *"Dónde está?"*

"He wouldn't tell me. But he said you shouldn't worry. He'll be back soon and he wants to pick up where he left off. He thinks you're important to getting Tierra Grande off the ground."

"What about the money he owes?"

"He said he'll pay it in full. He needs a few days to pull everything together. Maybe even a week or two."

"I'll pass that along. Although I'm not sure how much good it will do."

"And, Garrett—one last thing."

"What is it?"

"Your wife suspects something."

I looked at Helen, who was looking around with the furrowed brow of a homeowner who likes the idea of a yard, but not the work or expense required to keep it up.

"Hey, honey," I said.

She turned when she heard my voice.

"Do you love me?"

"Sometimes," she replied.

Helen was propped against the headboard reading *Smart Money* while I stripped to my underwear. I heard the magazine smack onto her nightstand and waited for the sounds I had grown to expect after thirty-one months, two weeks and four days of marriage—the light snapping off, the rustle of sheets as she settled in, the soft sighs my wife let out as she let sleep come over her.

"Garry?"

"Yes, dear?"

"Can we talk?"

I put my shorts in the laundry bag before I turned to her. I thought I recognized Helen's look and asked if we were going to have the dog conversation.

"No," she said. "Actually, I was thinking about having the kid conversation."

I took off my shirt and balled it up in my hands and carefully shoved it on top of the shorts.

"We haven't had that one before," I said at last.

"Maybe we should. I'm not getting any younger."

"On your last birthday, you told me you were going to start counting backwards."

"Don't be glib, Garrett. This is serious."

"You want me to be serious? Here's what I think: Things are going pretty well now. Why upset the apple cart?"

"I like what we did tonight—staying home, being domestic. It seemed . . . " Helen paused, searching for the right word. She always prided herself on saying exactly what she meant. "Normal."

"You like it because we do it twice a week. How will you feel if we go out twice a year? If we stop having business dinners? If one of us has to stay home?"

"You don't have to be so negative."

"I'm not being negative. I'm trying to be realistic."

"If you don't want a child, just say so. I'm a grown woman. I can take the truth."

"Maybe we should start with a dog first and work our way up to it."

"Do you know what your problem is, Garrett?"

I closed my eyes and shook my head. Before you get married, nobody warns you that part of the deal is a lifetime of hearing about your faults and shortcomings.

Helen grabbed the magazine and angrily flipped through the pages. "You treat everything as a joke. Or something you can spin or manipulate. Well, this isn't a joke. This is as serious as you can get."

I went into the master bath and washed my face before flossing three times, all the while listening for the sound I wanted. Finally I heard the rustling of bedcovers as Helen settled in.

I waited a few minutes before stepping out and noiselessly sliding between the sheets. I felt sleep coming quickly but then Helen rolled over and put her hand on my chest. She kissed me full on the lips, her mouth open.

I responded, perhaps out of habit.

"Garry," she said as she bit the bottom of my ear. Long ago I had told her I enjoyed it.

"What?"

"Let's try."

EIGHT

The next two weeks were my happiest in Florida. I told my boss that I'd heard Ernesto would turn up soon, and would pay us what he owed. My boss looked as relieved as a man who had just passed a kidney stone. "Manna from heaven," he said as he e-mailed Collections in New York. "It's like manna from freaking heaven."

Josette and I kept looking for the perfect strip mall. We found a couple that were all right, but told ourselves there had to be a better one. I found that I didn't mind driving around Broward and Miami-Dade with a tattooed lesbian; in fact, I found that I enjoyed Josette's company.

What I recall most vividly, of course, was Magdalena. We were together almost every afternoon although I couldn't see her on the weekends, which stretched out interminably while I accompanied Helen to the beach or the movies, or to restaurants I'd once found interesting. On weekdays I enjoyed the anticipation of seeing my lover, and my breath would grow short and quick on my way to our assignations.

Magdalena always arrived first. I'd knock two times on the door, then three. The knocks matched the syllables in my name; we liked having a secret to share. She'd open the door and smile. She'd still be fully clothed because she knew I liked to watch her undress.

We'd kiss and she'd ask how my day had gone so far and I'd tell her, invariably, that it was about to get a lot better. She'd laugh and say I was incorrigible and I'd agree and we'd kiss again and laugh and wrap our arms around each other and after a few minutes she'd step away and unzip her dress and let it fall to the floor and then she'd kick off her shoes and walk toward me wearing only her lingerie. Usually it was black. I'd bend down and kiss her one more time, running my tongue over her teeth and ears and neck before biting her shoulder and then she'd sink down to her knees, and unbuckle my belt, and soon I'd be aware of nothing except the sensation of being lost in her.

We never discussed her husband, or Ernesto, or anything that could be considered "bidness." Instead we fantasized about what it might be like if we could get away for a few days together.

Some things went wrong, of course. Helen began to nag me about going sailing with a friend of hers from work named Diana. This woman went out on the water every weekend with her husband and children and Helen said she hadn't been sailing in years and she'd seen pictures of the kids and they looked adorable and Diana made it all sound like so much fun. I kept grunting and hoping Helen would forget about the topic.

But my biggest annoyance came from my dealer, who was unable to find tires to replace the ones that had been slashed. So I was forced to keep driving the Taurus, rather than my Rover, and whenever I was in the car I felt like a semiretired *schlemiel* on the lookout for an early bird special.

And then one day, as if prayers I hadn't made had nonetheless been answered, Helen came home from work with a dark look on her face. I asked what was wrong and she launched into a tirade about the idiots who ran her company but I didn't pay much attention because my experience in the private sector had taught me that idiots run just about every company. I was thinking of how much I'd rather be with Magdalena when I heard Helen say:

"So now they want me to go to New York."

"Why?" I asked.

"Three days of meetings. About that goddamn container port in the Amazon. We could handle everything in a two-hour conference call but they refuse to listen to me."

She sat heavily in a chair by the kitchen counter and poured herself a tall glass of chardonnay. I walked behind her and put my hands behind her neck and resisted the urge to break into the broadest grin I'd shown since I'd known her.

When I got to work Isabel was on the phone, gossiping in Spanglish with a girlfriend. I quietly asked if I had any messages. She looked annoyed and shook her head. As I walked toward my office she called out that the boss wanted to see me *ahora*. It was *muy importante*.

I put my briefcase under my desk and hung up my jacket. As I walked to my boss' office I snapped my suspenders against my Armani shirt before rapping on his door and pushing it open. He looked up at me with a startled expression. He was launching a screen saver but I could see he'd been playing backgammon.

"Garry? What's up?"

"You wanted to see me."

He looked around for a few seconds, as if he'd misplaced an important memo, before his eyes brightened.

"Right. Absolutely right. You've hit the nail on the head. As usual."

"What is it?"

I made a move to sit down but he waved me off. "This is minor. Totally unimportant. Won't take more than ten seconds." He paused and then shrugged, as if, unbelievably, he'd decided that the direct approach was best. "It's about Ernesto."

"What about him?"

"Collections is on my case again. They say it's been a couple of weeks and they want the thirty thousand. I tried to tell them that you can't lean on a man like Ernesto Rodriguez, but you know New York."

I told my boss that I'd see what I could find out.

He smiled and nodded and waved me off. I sensed that he wanted to return to his backgammon.

"You're a team player, Garry. That's what I keep telling them. A team player."

*   *   *

Magdalena asked me to zip her up and when I finished I ran my hands down her back and around her stomach. She leaned into my arms and brought up her hand and let it slide across my face. I licked her fingers as they passed by.

"Do you feel better now?" she asked.

"What makes you think I felt bad before?"

"I don't think you felt bad. You were—what's the term Americans use?—stressed out."

I told her that Collections was making noises about Ernesto. I felt Magdalena tighten slightly, as if she were an animal suddenly wary of surroundings she had assumed were familiar.

"Have you talked to him recently?" I asked.

She shook her head.

"Do you know where he is?"

"*No sé.*"

"Is he ever coming back?"

"He can't afford not to."

Magdalena whirled around and reached for my head and I responded, wrapping my arms around and kissing her passionately and of course I wanted her again but our time was running out.

It was only later, while I was driving to Hialeah, that I began to think she had simply wanted to stop talking about Ernesto.

Solicitous, I thought. *Ernesto was solicitous.*

I stopped at the storefront but I didn't even have to get out of the Taurus to see what had happened.

The office where Ernesto Rodriguez had once worked was shuttered. Iron gates stretched from the overhang to the pavement. There was no way to get within six feet of the windows or the door.

I got out of the car and walked up slowly to the gates. I expected to see a For Lease sign, but there was nothing but emptiness.

The sky was almost the color of night. The afternoon downpour was about to begin. I looked around but the street was deserted, although I had the creepy feeling that I was being watched.

I got back in the Taurus just before the rain started crashing. I turned on the wiper and my high beams and drove around to the Laundromat in back. I glanced into the alley that separated the buildings, but none of Ernesto's vans were there.

I ran into the Laundromat. In the two unprotected feet between the Taurus and the front door, I got drenched down to my underwear.

A teenage Latina was in back, stuffing several blankets into a heavy-duty washer. The girl had somehow slithered into a tight pair of capri pants and I made a note that if I ever had a daughter, I wouldn't allow her to wear something like that.

The old woman wasn't there. I tried to think of a line I could use.

"Señorita, por favor."

She glanced at me, then returned to the blankets and said, "What do you want?"

"Information, if you don't mind."

"I don't have any of that."

"I work for a company—we're Internet providers, and we're expanding. Always looking for new office space. I wondered if the building next door was available."

"I have no idea, señor."

"It looks vacant to me."

"It might be. I wouldn't know. I just started here."

"Have you ever seen anybody in there?"

She looked at me and before I could grin I heard a toilet flushing in back and a door creaking open. I knew what I was about to see and a voice inside told me to leave but I stayed rooted where I was. There was something forbidding about stepping outside, where the rain was cascading with tropical ferocity.

The old Cuban woman stepped out and nodded at me in recognition.

We were stuck in traffic and the radio was tuned to a station Helen liked. The air conditioner was erratic and Jewel was singing about her damn pancakes and I was tempted to start screaming, "He broke up with you! Get over it!"

Helen said she'd been thinking.

"I hate it when you do that."

I turned to my wife and was about to grin, but her glowering look froze the corners of my mouth.

"What have you been thinking about?"

"This New York trip."

"You keep telling me it's a waste of time."

"It is, for the company. But for me, it's been a catalyst. It's made me consider things long-term."

I shook my head and chuckled in my best befuddled-sitcom-dad manner. "As usual, honey, you're way ahead of me."

"I'm thinking of asking for a transfer back to New York."

If we'd been going faster, I would have slammed on the brakes. Instead I felt my mouth go dry and I was aware of my body temperature rising. I was sure that my cheeks were flushed.

"Are you, uh, are you sure about that?"

"I'm not sure. I said I was thinking about it."

"I thought you liked it here."

"It's all right. But when you get down to it, Miami's still a backwater."

"I don't think I could get a transfer. Ogilvie still pulls a lot of strings in New York."

"You could quit. This isn't like a couple of years ago, Garry. There are a lot more opportunities now. You could get a job with a dot-com or something."

An image of Magdalena climbing on top of me, snapping her head back and lolling her tongue out the side of her mouth while I cupped her breasts in my hands.

Suddenly something I regarded as salvation occurred to me. I turned to my wife and said, in my most solicitous voice, "But, darling, what if you're pregnant?"

Helen shook her head. "I don't think so, Garry. I feel crampy, funky—classic PMS. That's why I had that wine the other night."

She looked sharply at me and for a second I thought she knew all the thoughts in my mind.

"Besides, I know you don't want a kid. At least right now. We can move back to New York and see how we feel in a year or two. Maybe you'll be in a better mood, and we'll try again."

"But what about the house?"

"C'mon, Garry—half our stuff is still in boxes."

I parked the Taurus in a short-term lot and watched Helen assemble her suitcase and the thing it rolled on. She bit into her lower lip, which was a habit of hers whenever she was deep in contemplation.

"I think I'm gonna bring it up with them," she said at last.

I saw Helen to her plane. As I walked back to the short-term lot, I tried to come up with reasons for staying in Miami that would sound plausible to my wife.

When I spotted the Taurus, I stopped. Something was fluttering in the windshield wiper. I approached it slowly, as if it were some kind of explosive, but it only seemed to be a piece of plain white paper folded over, with dark lettering inside. I looked at it a second and considered tearing it up without even reading its contents. It didn't look like a ticket.

I opened it, of course. Read it, of course.

The note said, in writing I recognized from the time my tires had been slashed, "PLEASE STOP YOUR INQUIRIES. YOU WILL NOT BE WARNED AGAIN."

I backed away from the Taurus and looked around 360 degrees but saw only a few people straggling toward cars through humidity that was already crushing.

I slid in behind the wheel and turned on the air-conditioning and stuck the note in my briefcase where it joined the other one.

I almost jumped through the roof when my cell phone went off. I could not keep my voice from breaking as I answered.

"It's Josette. We found it."

"Found what?"

"The beautiful strip mall. It's on Route 84. In Davie. Horse country that's being turned into sprawl."

I told Josette to give me the exact location, which she did, and said she should meet me there as quickly as possible. I'd be there in forty-five minutes if the traffic gods were kind.

A tractor-trailer had jackknifed on the turnpike near the Miami-Dade/Broward line, clogging two lanes and sending pieces of gelatinous goo over the third.

I drummed my fingers on the dashboard and looked at my cell phone and listened to the radio. I hated all the music and eventually found my way to NPR. An earnest young woman was talking about a druglord in the federal penitentiary in Atlanta who was petitioning for an early release because he'd started a ministry. I rolled my eyes and popped in a Goo Goo Dolls tape and looked at my cell phone again. Every glance at it provoked an increasingly insistent voice.

Finally I picked up the phone and held it in my hand and debated with myself. I did not know how she'd respond if I called her. I wasn't sure I wanted to take the step, or if I could trust her. But finally I leaned back and reached over my shoulder into the pocket of my suit jacket, which I'd placed on a hanger. When I found my wallet I flipped through it until I discovered the business card I wanted.

The phone was answered by a clerk who sounded as if she'd need to rev it up several notches to reach ennui. I asked for Police Officer Pilar Hurtado, who was on the line within seconds.

"I don't know if you remember me."

"I'll know if you tell me who you are."

"My name is Garrett Doherty."

"Of course I remember you. And I'm sorry to tell you we've made no progress in the investigation. The people at the garage said they didn't see anything."

"Actually, um, that's, uh, not why I'm calling."

I've always disliked talking on the phone. My greatest ability is one-to-one communication—looking the other person in the eye, using my body language to convey sincerity and empathy and, above all, flashing my grin to show them I'm likable and easygoing and want to agree with them. On the phone I'm forced to rely solely on words, which some-times betray me.

"Then why are you calling, Mr. Doherty?"

"There was something I should have told you. About the incident. And something has just happened."

"You should have told me everything."

I sensed she was pulling out a notepad and pen. In the back of my head a dissenting voice told me to hang up now. Probably this conversa-tion was being taped and besides I was sending it out over the unscram-bled, unprotected air, where anybody with a scanner could pick it up.

I reached into the glove compartment and took out the notes that had now been left for me in the windshields of two vehicles. I wanted to read them to her exactly.

"That's interesting," she said when I was done. "Do you have any idea who could have done this?"

I felt like a cliff diver standing a hundred feet or more above boul-ders and swirling water.

"Can we go off the record, Officer?"

She paused a second before saying, "All right."

"Do you know Ernesto Rodriguez?"

I heard her gulping some air, and I realized that now she was the one who was afraid of the direction this conversation was taking.

"I've heard of him," she said slowly.

"I've done some business with Señor Rodriguez." I mentioned the thirty thousand dollars before describing the empty office, the house that wasn't his, the phone numbers that no longer worked.

I held back the encounter with the *puta* at the Orlando.

Police Officer Pilar Hurtado agreed that the events were strange. But, in and of themselves, they didn't necessarily mean anything.

Up ahead, vehicles slipped through the single open lane one by one.

"I suppose you could file a missing-person's report," she said. "You'd have to come down to headquarters and—"

"I'm not sure I want to do that."

"Then what do you want to do?"

I paused a second. I wasn't sure myself. "Well," I said, "these notes both popped up after I began asking questions about him. Perhaps I can give them to you." I laughed. "Just in case something happens to me."

There was a long pause before she said, "Okay."

I was almost past the site of the accident. On the shoulder were an ambulance and two state police cars, their flashing red lights barely visible under the tropical midday sun.

"Maybe you can come by my office," I said. "Tomorrow morning."

"Fair enough."

While I'd been stuck I had assumed that as soon as I got past the tractor-trailer I'd press the pedal to the floor and zoom away from the scene, leaving it behind me as quickly as I could. But off to the side, on the grassy shoulder, underneath a grove of tall and gentle southern pines, two state patrolmen were talking to a paramedic. All three seemed calm and unagitated, almost bored, as if they were discussing the weather or their families or the Hurricanes' chances of making it to the Orange Bowl.

Below them was a stretcher with a sheet pulled all the way over. It was stained a deep, angry red; from beneath it, a man's hairy arm dangled down, almost brushing the ground.

The sign said "Happy Land Mini Mall," but that was the only joyous thing I could see. Happy Land contained a 7-Eleven, a card shop, a place that claimed to sell real New York bagels, two vacant storefronts and, at the end, a business devoted to lamps. The strip mall was actually one long, low building made of concrete covered with pale pink plaster, lightly rippled to create a stucco effect. It could not have been more than five years old, but cracks were already visible.

On the other side of 84 were a Pep Boys, a Wendy's and a Dunkin' Donuts. Beyond them I caught glimpses of green occasionally broken by white rail fences—beautiful land that was now too expensive to resist development.

I saw Josette's Mustang, but not her. I had taken a few steps toward the stores—I figured she must be in one of them—when I heard my cell phone ring inside the Taurus. I never brought the cell to a meeting. I wanted people to think I was giving them my undivided attention, even when I wasn't.

I opened the car with the remote and waited for the blip before reaching inside, disabling the alarm, getting the phone.

"It's me." Josette's voice sounded edgy and bored at the same time.

"Where are you?"

"Inside the lamp store."

"I'll be there in a minute."

I put down the phone, re-engaged the alarm, locked the door again with the remote.

I remember all of these everyday details because of what happened next.

As I walked toward the lamp store I had the sensation that I was being watched by someone I could not see.

I looked around slowly. Parked on the other side of 84, in a dark green Oldsmobile sedan that had the unmistakable generic-car look of a rental, a man with binoculars was leaning through a rolled-down window.

He jerked his head inside the car. When he was in shadow he lowered the binoculars and raised the window and started the engine. The darkness obscured his features and he raised his arm to hide his face, like a celebrity fending off a swarm of paparazzi.

Still, in the few seconds I was able to see him, I could have sworn it was Ernesto Rodriguez.

I ran across the lot but the car pulled away. Traffic was swift and heavy on both sides of the road. I stopped on a grass strip that marked an uncertain boundary between the strip mall and 84 and leaned slightly into the street, trying to encourage the drivers to slow or brake for me.

A few honked. Many gave me angry glares.

The Oldsmobile was moving quickly, heading toward Lauderdale, its driver changing lanes erratically in an effort to make sure his tags couldn't be read. All I could make out were the first three markings—

J60—before the Oldsmobile swung directly in front of a gasoline truck, which let out a long blast.

As soon as I stepped inside I felt the sudden stale cold of air-conditioning. The store was stuffed with lamps of all kinds that seemed to be shoved wherever they could fit. Desk lamps were crammed in with antiques, which were packed on top of lamps with shades and lamps for end tables and stand-alones and halogens.

"Josette!"

"Over here!" Her voice came from the other side of a mountain of lampshades. "What happened? You get lost in the parking lot?"

Another voice called out asking if I was Mr. Doherty. I was happy she pronounced it correctly and replied that I was. It was a female voice whose owner's age I pegged at around forty-five and it said they had been waiting for me but in the meantime she had enjoyed the most interesting chat with Josette. As the woman spoke I recognized the broad flat tones of the Midwest.

"Sorry I'm late. I got stuck in traffic."

"That tie-up on the turnpike. It's all over the radio. Didn't you hear about it?"

"Not until I was in it."

I broke through a pile of boxes and saw Josette standing amid cartons marked "FRAGILE." She was wearing a tank top and for the first time I noticed that she didn't shave her armpits. Behind her was a tall, thin woman in a formless dress with blue trim. Her hair was going gray and she wore oversized glasses that were in constant danger of sliding off her nose.

Josette introduced us and I couldn't quite catch if the woman's name was Cary or Corey but I figured I was in enough trouble without asking her to repeat it. I shook her hand and was surprised at how strong her grip was. I said it was nice to meet her. She had quite a store here. I grinned.

"Josette's been telling me about your project," the woman said. "It sounds off-the-wall."

I admitted it was a little unusual.

"Don't be defensive," the woman said. "I love crazy stuff like that."

Josette turned to me and I could see that her face was slightly flushed and as soon as she spoke I noticed that her voice was tinged with the thrill of discovery.

"Isn't this the neatest place?"

I said it had a certain idiosyncratic charm.

"It's a mess," said the woman who was named Cary or Corey, and we all laughed.

She invited us to her office in back and asked if we'd like herbal tea. Josette accepted enthusiastically. I said I was trying to cut back on things that were good for me.

The office was immaculate, which was what I expected. People who display disorder in public always seek perfection in their private spaces. Cary/Corey filled a small electric pot with water and plugged it in while I told her that, technically, we didn't need the permission of any of the proprietors to launch our campaign, but of course it would be better if everyone was on board.

"You won't have any problems," she said as she poured some ginseng. "To be honest, we could use the publicity. We're a bit off the beaten track."

I looked at my watch and thought of the traffic-clogged drive back to Miami and told Josette I didn't have much time and we should talk to the other people who worked at the mall. I caught a flash of anger in her eyes—*You were late how dare you order me around*—and found myself grinning.

"I'll start now," I said. "You can join me after you finish your tea."

"That's fine."

I opened the door. It seemed impossible, but the store looked more cluttered than before, as if the lamps were reproducing themselves while no one was looking. I turned back to the owner and grinned again.

"Just one question," I said.

"What is it?"

"Why lamps?"

"They illuminate the world."

I smiled, mostly to myself. "Maybe that's what I have against them."

I stopped at the office before heading home. I was hoping to slide out before speaking to my boss but while I checked my e-mail I noticed that he was hovering outside my door, talking to Isabel, who doubtless was telling him I'd been out all day. My boss kept glancing at me in the manner of a person hoping to make eye contact.

I pulled out the notes I had found on the Rover and the Taurus and put them in an envelope, which I sealed. I wrote Officer Hurtado's name in big block letters and placed the envelope in my top drawer.

My boss walked in uninvited.

"Garry! You've been out of pocket all day."

As I locked my desk I told him about the strip mall. I said I was going to put in a call to the Copleys.

My boss clapped me on the back. "Great. Super." He paused and glanced down at the carpet. I knew he was going to ask a question that neither of us would like.

"Have you heard anything about Ernesto?"

I closed the door because I didn't want Isabel to overhear. I told my boss that Ernesto's office was shuttered and I had no way of reaching him, although my source assured me that he always honored his commitments and intended to come back and resume working on Tierra Grande.

I did not mention the man I thought was Ernesto staring at me from across the road at the Happy Land Mini Mall.

"But when will he come back?" my boss asked. "When, for the love of Jesus?"

"*No sé.*"

He looked at me as if my lapse into Spanish was unforgivable. Whenever two white guys get together in South Florida, there's a tacit bond that says you never slip into the increasingly dominant local language.

"I have to tell New York something." My boss sounded plaintive, like an eight-year-old trying to come up with an explanation for the broken cookie jar.

"Tell them I'm looking into it."

My boss looked at me sharply, as if he was wondering what kind of angle I was playing. But then he nodded and smiled. "Of course," he said. "That's good. Maybe the thing that'll save our butts. I'll just tell them, 'Doherty's handling that.'" He mispronounced my name, and I had to resist the urge to throttle him. "They know you in New York, and whenever I tell them you're handling a job, they just clam right up."

Because they're waiting for me to fail, I thought.

She pulled into my driveway shortly after nightfall. I opened the garage door so she could park the Miata unobserved by my neighbors. When she walked into the kitchen I grabbed her and she sank to her knees on the tiled floor and unbuckled my belt.

After a while I pulled her up and thought about leading her to the bedroom but this time I couldn't wait, I had to have her then and there so I unzipped her dress and pulled down her panties and dragged one of the chairs out from underneath the kitchen table. I sat down and let her slide on top of me and then I kissed her with the passion that seems so fierce when your love is forbidden and I wanted to hold her close like that forever.

When we were done, as our breathing slowed and we began to be capable of words and not just gasps and moans, Magdalena looked around and then gazed at me and smiled.

"*La buena casa*," she said.

I laughed and told her it was much better now that she was here. Magdalena asked where the bathroom was, so I led her by the hand to the master bedroom. As I pushed open the door I had the sense of seeing the place fresh; with a new person at my side, I had a new perspective.

I was struck by the room's softness and femininity; the Helen-ness of the space. Her dresser, much larger than mine. The sheets and bedspread with the floral pattern she had insisted on. Her vanity, smack by the window that caught the morning light.

Magdalena went into the bathroom while I sat on the edge of the bed. I had the sense that I was waiting, although I didn't know what for.

When my lover came out, she asked if it was all right if she smoked.

I wondered if I was being tested.

Finally I said I thought it was best if she went outside.

Magdalena nodded and said nothing but gave me a look that seemed almost contemptuous. She stayed a few feet ahead of me as she walked down the hall and through the living room and kitchen before sliding open the door to the patio and stepping outside. I saw the light of a flame and ash beginning to glow red.

I told myself I should go out there with her.

The phone rang and I considered letting the machine take it. It was seven-thirty and I figured it was a telemarketer trained to call at dinner time but then I thought it might be Helen and I was afraid that if I didn't answer, she might somehow realize what was going on.

Magdalena had said my wife suspected something. I hadn't asked my lover why she thought that. I was afraid that if I pressed too closely, Magdalena might retreat. But I was beginning to feel there were things about her that I had to know.

I picked up the phone and said hello in a warm, I-miss-you tone.

"Mr. Doherty."

The voice was deep and had a Latin tinge but also sounded angry. I felt I should recognize it even as it mispronounced my name.

"Yes," I said, my tone shifting to a neutral meter that indicated I wasn't sure where the conversation was going, or if I even wanted to be part of it.

"We just wanted to see if you were home."

This was followed by a click, and the hum of a broken connection.

I gazed at the phone as if it had turned into something that could harm me. Through the sliding door I could see a dark form that was raising and lowering a lighted ember. When I walked outside I was assaulted by humidity and a thousand microscopic bugs.

As I swatted at the insects, I asked Magdalena if she was hungry.

"You should smoke," she said. "It keeps them away."

I told her I'd consider taking it up because I needed more bad habits. In the meantime, I thought we should get something to eat.

She took another drag and seemed to shrug. "We could go somewhere, if that's what you want."

Conversations that begin this way lead almost inevitably to an analysis of various cuisines and restaurants, followed by speculation about whether the place is crowded and how long you have to wait if you don't have a reservation.

I imagined a big dark SUV speeding toward the house. Perhaps it had been stopped by a red light and the driver was hopping up and down in his seat, anxious to get going because the device next to him had a timer. It was easy to conjure the follow-up sights and sounds: blinding high-beams shining into the living room, screeching tires on the street outside, breaking glass and an explosion.

I said I felt a sudden urge to have Thai food. There was a place nearby we'd been meaning to check out.

Magdalena shrugged again and continued to puff on her slim cigar.

I asked if she liked Thai food.

She said it was all right. But as she'd said before, she didn't much care what we did.

"I thought I saw Ernesto today."

Magdalena looked at me as if I'd just announced I'd seen a vision of the Virgin.

I described the incident and asked what she thought.

She said she had no reason to doubt me.

"But why is Ernesto spying on me?"

"No sé. No soy Ernesto."

"But you've known him a long time."

She shook her head quickly and wagged her finger, as if I were a student who had failed to grasp an important part of the lesson. "I knew him a long time ago."

"Back then, did he do things like this? Disappear? Spy on people?"

I drank some tepid water that tasted as if it had been pumped through sediment. The restaurant was overlit and only one other couple was in it. Magdalena stared up at the ceiling and I had the feeling there was nothing she wanted more than to draw deeply on another slim cigar.

"He did disappear," she said. "But he always returned. We never worried about Ernesto. He's a survivor."

"What about spying?"

Magdalena shrugged. "He told you what he did."

"Fighting Communists. I'm still not sure I believe it."

"Ernesto had to do some bad things. I'm sure he wishes he didn't have to do them. But in his mind he justified all of it. Because of The Cause."

"What kind of bad things?"

"I don't want to talk about it."

"Drugs? Murder?" I grinned. "Cross-dressing?"

Her words came out, clipped and slow and on the verge of anger. "I really don't want to talk about it." She drew her fingers to her mouth, as if she did have that cigar she wanted. "Anyway, it's all in the past."

As I turned the corner I expected to see police cars and fire trucks, perhaps even an ambulance, gathered around the burnt-out husk of what had once been my home. I imagined neighbors I'd never met swarming about, momentarily gaining a sense of community because of a disaster that had not happened to them.

The street was dark and quiet. A few TVs glowed in living rooms.

I pulled into the driveway and opened the garage and let my headlights flood the space.

There was nothing out of the ordinary.

We entered the house through the kitchen. I turned on as many lights as I could and tried to walk softly and said nothing to Magdalena as I listened intently for unusual sounds.

"Are you all right?"

"I'm fine. Why?"

"You seem tense. *Qué tienes?*"

"*Nada.*"

She shook her head slightly and I knew she did not believe me and then a slight smile curled her lips and she said, "You're afraid you can't reload."

She walked toward the bedroom. Just before she entered it, she tossed back her head and laughed.

I almost followed her immediately but the blinking light on the answering machine caught my eye. I considered letting it wait before telling myself I had to hear it on the slight chance the message was important.

"Hi, it's me."

Helen's voice.

"I just wanted to see how you were. I'm sorry you're not there."

Was she checking in? Was this some form of surveillance?

The world was watching everything I did. My life belonged to everyone but me.

There was a pause, followed by the half laugh of a woman who doesn't believe the possibility she's suggesting: "God, I hope you're still not at work."

I erased the message and took a few steps toward the room where my lover was waiting. All I could think of was how badly I wanted her.

But then I stopped. For the first time since I'd met Magdalena, I tried to let my rational side analyze her actions.

Her husband had disappeared.

She did not know where he was.

She did not seem concerned about him.

She had begun an affair.

Despite the air-conditioning, I felt myself starting to sweat as I resumed walking toward the bedroom. I could picture a goon waiting just behind the door, ready to attack as soon as I stepped inside. Perhaps it would be the burly young Latino who had taken me and Josette into Ernesto's office. I could also see somebody lingering in either the bathroom or the closet, an ally of Magdalena's in whatever game she was involved in, waiting until I had climbed into bed with her to wreak whatever havoc they thought I deserved.

When I stepped into the bedroom, Magdalena's back was to me. She was perched on the edge of the bed as she took off her earrings and put them on the dresser.

Helen's dresser.

I should have been filled with guilt or self-loathing but the sight of Magdalena casually removing her things seemed everyday, as if she belonged in my life.

I walked around the bed and stopped directly in front of her. She reached forward and I expected the expert unbuckling of a belt and lowering of a zipper, followed by her head leaning forward as her hands stroked and massaged me.

But what she did was this: She put her arms around my waist, and let her cheek rest against my stomach.

And I ran my hands through her hair, and began to murmur in my imperfect Spanish how much I wanted and loved her.

She turned her head again to look up at me, and I lowered myself on top of her as she fell back on the bed.

An image of Magdalena, later that night, her legs spread apart and her upper lip biting into her lower one, urging me in Spanish to go harder, faster, deeper.

NINE

As she sat outside my door, tapping her shoe on the carpet, Police Officer Pilar Hurtado looked repeatedly at her watch. I could tell Isabel was about to say something—most likely about the time—so I brushed past her and walked up to Hurtado and extended my hand.

"Thank you for coming. Sorry I'm late. Traffic was a nightmare."

An image of Magdalena, wiping the sleep from her eyes and smiling at me as I rolled on top of her.

Hurtado took my hand and said she understood. I asked if she wanted anything and she said no and I made the offer again, this time specifying that I'd be happy to get her coffee or tea or juice or water. Anything she wanted, even a doughnut. All she had to do was ask.

"Make them feel at ease," Lisa Shapiro once told me. "Get them comfortable. Then spring your trap."

Police Officer Pilar Hurtado shook her head. She appreciated my generosity but she couldn't stay long. "Besides," she said, "I don't eat doughnuts."

She said this proudly, as if she'd quit a two-pack-a-day habit cold turkey.

"Why not?"

"You know—the stereotype."

I thought of the cops in the neighborhood I'd grown up in, congregating all day at the doughnut shop on Route 3. As long as you didn't rob that store, the standing joke went, you could get away with anything.

I chuckled at the memory as I unlocked my desk drawer and pulled it open and got ready to take out the notes I'd left in the envelope marked with her name. I imagined handing it to her and telling her to read the contents in private whenever she had a chance. I already knew what they said.

The envelope was gone. I had left it on top so it would be easy to find but now it had disappeared and I pushed all the papers aside in a search that was frantic and futile.

"I don't understand it."

"Don't understand what?"

"The notes. They're not here. I put them here last night. I know I did."

I expected Hurtado to say "Sure you did" in the cajoling tones of sympathy you use for people who are flaking out and I could see myself insisting, with greater and greater fervor, that I had *in fact* left the notes in my desk, they were *right there,* I knew *right where I left them*—going on and on until I sounded like the only character in a *Twilight Zone* episode who can see the creatures that are about to invade Earth.

I looked through the other drawers and got down on my hands and knees to search on the floor on the chance that the envelope had somehow fallen out. All the while I kept saying that I didn't understand.

"It's okay."

The voice came from almost directly above me and I was so startled I raised my head and smacked it against the bottom of my desk.

"Are you all right?"

I stood up. I felt woozy.

Hurtado said she believed my story.

"You do?"

"You seem like a responsible man."

"I try to be."

"You say you put the notes in an envelope."

"That's correct."

"And you put the envelope in your desk drawer?"

"Right."

"And you locked the drawer?"

"Yes."

"Does anybody else have a key?"

"Not to my knowledge."

"Was anything else taken?"

"No."

She stood with her arms folded and her head down, as if she were thinking deeply about something. "I'd advise you to change the lock on your desk," she said at last. "And make sure no one else has the key."

"Okay."

"The note," she said. "The one you found on your Range Rover. You had it in your possession the first time we spoke, didn't you?"

I nodded. I knew where she was going but I was still reluctant to volunteer anything.

"Why didn't you give it to me then?"

"I don't know. I should have. I realize that now."

"In the future," she said, "if this matter continues, don't hold anything back from me."

She turned and headed for the door, doubtless thinking that we had said everything we needed to.

"There is one thing, Officer."

She looked back at me. Her face had a what-is-it-now? expression.

I told her what had happened at the Happy Land Mini Mall. By the end of my description, she was taking notes.

"That's good," she said. "That means Ernesto Rodriguez is no longer missing."

"But why is he spying on me?"

"I don't know, Mr. Doherty." She pronounced my last name correctly, and for a moment I was grateful. "Do you have any enemies?"

I told her I was an upper middle-class American male with a wife and a job and an SUV and a home in the suburbs that was gradually filling up with too many gadgets. There might be people who hated what I represented, but I could think of no one who wished me ill.

I was lying of course. Police Officer Pilar Hurtado had asked me to be candid but I had reverted to my habits of dodging and spinning. I could have mentioned the call I'd received at my house the night before or what I'd learned from the *puta* at the Orlando. But a conversation like that would get me talking about Frank Hedges, and from there I'd go inevitably to Magdalena.

There is a man, I could have said. *I'm making love to his wife. If he's still alive, I'm sure he's not happy about it. But Ernesto may have killed him— which would be lucky for me, wouldn't it?*

Hurtado put her notebook away. In the absence of a formal request, she said, there was nothing the department could do.

"Maybe there is. Informally."

"What do you mean?"

"Tell everyone you received an anonymous tip." I grinned. "Ernesto Rodriguez has disappeared. Check out his office in Hialeah. It's vacant and shuttered. And then just keep your ears open. Maybe somebody will hear something. Or see something."

She was silent, and in her silence I could almost hear her thinking. There's something about a mystery that people can't resist.

"His car was a rental," I said.

"How can you be sure?"

"I can't. But his tags started with J60."

She nodded slowly. Those were rental tags.

"Where did he get it?" I asked. "Why is he driving around in a rental? Who or what is he afraid of?"

There were three messages on my voicemail when I returned from lunch. The first was from Winston Copley, who said he and Evan had discussed the matter between them and felt the Happy Land Mini Mall was as good a place as any to launch the campaign, even though they remained dubious about it. The second was from my dealer, who said— in portentous tones that lacked only a drumroll in the background—my Rover was ready and if I didn't pick it up by nightfall they'd have to park it on the street because space on the lot was limited.

The third call was from Helen. She said she was on a break between meetings and had some news to tell me, but she supposed it would be better if she did it in person. She giggled and said she hoped the suspense was killing me.

Just before she hung up, she also said, "I love you."

I wondered what the news was. My wife was not the type of woman given to giggling or to breathlessly announcing that she had a secret, like a schoolgirl swept up in the swirl of her first crush. I suspected the worst: She'd asked for the transfer back to New York and her supervisors had agreed and told her they wanted it done as quickly as possible.

I should have called. I had the number for her pager. I imagined Helen in the middle of a meeting, trying hard to mask the boredom she felt while people who knew less than she did debated the merits of the Brazilian project. The beeper would go off and she'd say "excuse me" softly to the people around her and check whom the call was from and when she recognized my number she'd smile and, if the discussion had gone in circles once too often, push herself away from the table and say she had to return the call, it was from Miami and it might be important.

But I knew what I wanted, even without acknowledging it to myself: I wanted the Rover back and I wanted to drive it on a trip that might last overnight and I wanted to go with the woman whose company I most enjoyed.

Magdalena met me downtown and brought a change of clothes. I helped her into the Rover and she said she liked sitting so high, she could see everything and felt protected. When I started the vehicle she asked where we were going.

"Guess."

"The Everglades."

"How'd you know?"

"I can read your mind."

"If you could read my mind, you'd be undressing."

"We'll have time for that later."

It took about an hour to drive to the visitors' center and while we were on the road Magdalena said she wanted to know about my life, so

I described growing up in New Jersey and playing Little League and going to Catholic school.

"Catholic school?" She seemed surprised. Her eyebrows almost reached her hairline. "Obviously, it didn't take."

"Thank God for that."

She asked why I went into public relations and I said I'd started out in journalism but soon realized that the real power lay with people who could manipulate or orchestrate events, not with those who merely recorded them.

Magdalena nodded. She said I made sense.

Of course I'd told her only a part of the reason. I had used the same line on Magdalena that I'd used on Lisa Shapiro the day I walked into her office, at a time when I was desperate to escape the New England cowtown to which I'd been exiled and desperate to get to New York to become part of something that seemed much bigger than I was and desperate most of all to escape a career that was already failing.

I gave Lisa my line and a grin I'd been practicing in the mirror. I kept my eyes steady with hers and she nodded at me and stood abruptly and said we should get some lunch. We went to a trendy bistro with a wrought-iron facade and the headwaiter seated us immediately and said he was delighted to see Ms. Shapiro again. His accent sounded vaguely European and I wondered if it was authentic.

I looked around at the neatly arranged tables, with silk napkins and gleaming silverware and sharply dressed people talking in low tones about matters I assumed were important, and told myself this was the kind of life I wanted and deserved.

"I'm not an idiot," Lisa said.

I told myself I couldn't have heard her correctly so I pushed my menu aside and folded my hands together on the table and said, in my best schoolboy manner, "Excuse me?"

"You heard." She glanced down at the menu and curled her lips tightly. Lisa was a big woman and it seemed as if she was engaged in internal combat, with her mind suggesting eggplant while her stomach demanded steak, medium rare, with *pommes frites*.

I wondered if I was being tested and decided I was. This woman was using crude intimidation, trying to see how easy it was to rattle or break me.

I told myself to stay calm and look right at her and talk in a calm, unhurried way. Most of all, I told myself to think about everything I was saying.

"I don't understand what you're getting at," I said.

"That's better." Lisa folded her menu and tossed it down. Within seconds a waiter appeared and she ordered the steak, medium rare, with *pommes frites*. I got the same.

Lisa stared at the bread that had been placed between us and finally, with a bit of a sigh, took a slice and spread butter on both sides. I did the same.

"That line you gave me," she said between bites. "Back in my office. It's good. Clever, glib, sounds like the kind of thing we want to hear. Some of the people I work with . . ." She shook her head. A few crumbs trickled from the corner of her mouth. "There's one guy we have. His name's Ogilvie. My fellow VP. If he'd heard that line he would have hired you on the spot. Probably put you on the fast track, too. Because he's smooth. He's slick. And he wants everyone who works for him to be smooth and slick as well." She took another bite of bread and I fought the urge to look around the room. I could hear nothing else and by now I was sure everyone in the restaurant was listening to us. "And Ogilvie thinks that's all PR is," Lisa said. "And that's what the people who work for him think. And it is part of the job; I'll grant them that. But do you know what PR is most of all?"

I shook my head. I had no idea what she was getting at and I felt thoroughly uncomfortable and at that moment I was silently cursing the college classmate who had steered me toward this interview.

"It's about making people pay attention."

I was still locked into her eyes, which were clear and green and didn't seem to go with anything else about her. I nodded and smiled and told her I got the point.

"What are you doing?"

Magdalena's voice crashed into my consciousness. Her words were soft but sharp and full of incredulity.

I was surrounded by pine and cypress. I tried to remember where I was.

"You missed the visitors' center."

"Oh, Christ, I'm sorry. My mind is drifting."

"Drifting to what? Getting us killed?"

"To somebody I used to know."

"Back when you were a Catholic?"

"After that."

We pulled into the parking lot and got out of the Rover and it felt good to stretch my legs even though we were at ground zero of all the humidity in the world. I took Magdalena's hand and we trudged along a wooden walkway that was raised ten feet above stagnant water. Signs pointed out various types of flora, or noted the kinds of birds that liked to nest in the area.

"I don't see any alligators," Magdalena said.

"You sound disappointed."

"I've only seen them in zoos. I thought I had a chance."

Beneath us something stirred and I saw an object the color of the water swinging from side to side before I realized it was the tail of a nine-foot-long alligator that was moving sluggishly through the slough. I put my arm around Magdalena and pointed down and heard her gasp a bit as the gator swam directly under the walkway.

"I hope he doesn't attack us," my lover said.

"They don't attack humans," I replied with more confidence than I felt. "Except in self-defense. Or else if they're very hungry."

With that I let my arm fall down to the back of her thigh, which I grabbed while making a ferocious chomping sound right in her ear. She jumped several inches off the ground and turned to me with a mixture of fury and laughter. *Bastardo,* " she said.

"What's the matter?" I said. "Afraid of a little alligator?"

"I ain't afraid of nothin'," she said in a not entirely convincing attempt at an American accent.

Both of us laughed. We strolled along the walkway, drunk on each other.

As we regained control of ourselves we began to look around. Lying on top of the water and the banks of the slough—always blending in with the water and the grass and the mud—were dozens of alligators. They had been there all along. We just didn't know how to look.

"They're not doing anything," Magdalena said.

"I've studied animals."

"Now you're a zoologist."

Giggling from my lover. I felt another wave of senseless guffaws about to come over us.

"I'm eminently qualified. I've seen lots of documentaries on the Nature Channel." I felt Magdalena shaking in my arms. "And this is what animals do—they eat, and they sleep, and they make little animals."

Magdalena fell against me and laughed for minutes and rubbed her head against my chest and said she liked this, she liked being away from everyone and everything and only caring about enjoying the moment.

We looked over the railing. An alligator was at the edge of the water, lying on its side, as if it were about to roll over and plop into the slough.

But it didn't do what I expected. It remained where it was and flicked its tail and used one of its legs to dig into the muddy bank, and suddenly dozens of small fish and frogs were leaping in the air and the alligator was snapping, opening its huge jaws as wide as they would go before biting down. Blood seeped between its teeth as the gator, now seemingly content, finally rolled onto its stomach and floated down the stream.

When we returned to her office, Lisa Shapiro waved me to a seat and opened her top desk drawer and took out a box of cigars. She extended them toward me but I shook my head. She removed a stogie and ran it under her nose before clipping off the tip and lighting it. She said she got these things from Cuba. She said she knew someone.

"I know why you want to get out of journalism," she said. "I used to be in it myself. The pay sucks, you work nights and weekends, and you can't get the holidays off. It seems glamorous, but anybody with any sanity gets out as quickly as they can."

I told her she was wrong. Those were not the reasons I wanted to change careers. I was amazed the words were escaping my mouth but I suspected this woman would accept nothing less than absolute honesty, even if it meant disagreeing with something she had said hundreds of times.

She puffed her cigar before leaning back in her chair and putting her feet on the desk.

"They why do you want to leave?" she asked.

I told her about the city councilman and his son the quarterback and how I'd found myself exiled to a place that was virtually Labrador. Lisa walked to the window and looked out at the late afternoon shadows. The last rays of sun were easing through and they magnified the smoke that surrounded her.

"I'm glad you told me that," she said. "You've learned an important lesson—you have to know who you can fuck with, and who gets a pass. It's a good thing you learned it at a young age, when the stakes are low."

She stuck the cigar between her teeth as she strode back to her desk.

"Actually, I'm amazed they didn't fire you."

"Garrett? Are you with me?"

Magdalena's voice, a few feet away and soft in my ear.

I was supposed to be looking at the road but I turned to her and grinned and told her I loved her.

She put her hand on my stomach and let it slide down and for a moment I imagined her undoing my belt and zipper and leaning over to take me in her mouth.

"Sometimes it seems like your mind drifts," she said. "Like you're a thousand miles away from me."

We ended up on the other side of the Everglades, in a small tourist town with parking lots, a convenience store, a couple of docks and a motel with a restaurant. I thought about checking if any rooms were available but before I could say anything Magdalena asked, in the tones of a teenager who's been dragged along on a family vacation, "What are we going to do *here?*"

"We can take a boat," I said. "We can watch the sunset out in the bay."

We started walking toward one of the docks. Going in any other direction seemed pointless.

"I didn't know you were the type," Magdalena said.

"Type for what?"

"Looking at sunsets."

"I am when I'm with the right person."

Magdalena shook her head and slipped her hand into mine and kissed me lightly. "You're good," she said. "You're very good."

We sat at the edge of the dock and let our legs dangle as we pressed our mouths together.

An image of Magdalena on all fours on a king-size bed, looking over her shoulder and biting her lower lip as she waited to accept me.

And then came the sound; one I knew well; the click and whir of a camera only a professional would use.

Magdalena jumped. I turned and saw a ponytailed man, gray-haired and heavyset. He was putting what looked like a 35-millimeter camera back in its case.

"What are you doing?" I asked.

"Taking your picture." He wore fatigues and an army jacket and I figured he was one of those journalistic combat junkies whose mind had never left Vietnam. He took out a pen and a small notepad. "Should come out nice, too. Now I just wanna nail a couple of things down, like your names and—"

"You have no right!"

Magdalena was shrieking in a voice filled with panic and fury.

I wondered what was inside her. What was forcing these things to come out.

"An ambush! That's what it was!"

"You were in a public place."

"You're a stalker!"

"I can do whatever—"

"I demand—"

"You're acting like—"

She lunged for his case but he clamped her wrist with a hairy hand and she cursed at him in Spanish and he told her not to talk to him that way.

I got between them and asked her to calm down and give me a chance to work everything out.

To trust me.

I draped my arm around the photographer's shoulder and led him a few steps away. Magdalena marched down the dock and reached into her bag and took out one of her slim cigars.

I turned to the photographer and grinned.

"It doesn't matter if you don't give me your names," he said. "My editors will figure out a way to run the picture."

"Who do you work for?"

"*The Herald.*"

"I know some people there. Victor DeLuca?"

The photographer shook his head. He said he hardly ever worked for the business section. Mostly he did sports but he'd taken the day off to go fishing and he always brought along his equipment because you never know what might happen and when he'd seen us he'd just started to follow at a discreet distance because he thought something interesting might happen—he'd been shooting pictures for thirty years, he had a sense for these things—and when we sat down and started kissing there was something about the play of our bodies and the water and the late-afternoon sun that seemed striking.

I kept nodding. I was afraid he was going to tell me what f-stop he used and how fast the film was.

He said his bosses had told him he needed to shoot more feature pics so he was always on the lookout and he thought he had a winner here.

I motioned toward Magdalena, whose hand was shaking as she tried to light her cigar. "The lady and I."

"Yeah?"

"We're not married."

"So?"

"To each other."

I pointed to the gold band on my ring finger and the photographer looked puzzled, as if I were explaining an arcane facet of metallurgy, before his eyes went wide and he began to chuckle.

"Oh," he said. Chuckling louder. "I see." His chuckles turned to outright laughter. "I get it." He began laughing so hard I thought he might rupture a couple of organs.

"I knew you would."

"I'm not looking to cause you any trouble or anything. So I'll just . . ."

He motioned toward his camera case, as if he were ready to leave the scene and now regretted ever spotting us.

I kept my hand on his shoulder. I was surprised how strong my grip was.

"The film," I said.

"What about it?"

I grinned again. "I can tell you're a reasonable man. But you can never tell."

Genuine puzzlement filled his eyes.

"Your editors. What if they see the picture? Inadvertently, of course. What if they decide to run it?"

"You don't have to worry."

He stretched toward his camera case. I kept my grip on his shoulder. "I do worry," I said.

Magdalena was a few feet away. She was puffing furiously, and her eyes were dark and suffused with hatred.

"I can't give you my film," the photographer said.

Magdalena stepped toward us. I was afraid of what she might do.

"Why not?" I asked. I tried to keep my voice reasonable even as I gripped his shoulder more forcefully. "Do you have a good shot in there somewhere?"

"No," he said. Sweat streamed down his neck and his shirt was damp, with stains beginning to show. He said his company was tight with a buck, but what company wasn't these days? If he went back to the office missing a roll of film, the bean counters were likely to dock it from his pay.

I told him I understood. As I reached for my wallet, Magdalena glared at me. I told the photographer I didn't want to do him any harm, financial or otherwise. If he was going to give up something, he should be compensated.

I slipped a hundred-dollar bill from my wallet.

The photographer said he thought this would cover his expenses. He laughed and said he might even be able to buy a nice dinner. He rewound the film and I put out my left hand and he smacked the canister into it before sliding the bill all the way out. I told him to enjoy his evening and walked over to Magdalena, flipping the film in my hand as if it were a baseball autographed by El Duque himself.

"You shouldn't have done that," she said.

"Done what?"

"Paid him. Especially that amount. Disgraceful."

"It was a business transaction."

I tossed the canister to her and she flung it into the water before walking away from me.

"You should have taken it from him," she said. "He had no right to do what he did."

"He's just trying to do his job."

"How do you know? How do you know he's legitimate? He says he works for a newspaper. Who would employ a man who looks like that?"

"Have you ever worked with photographers? Most of them are feral."

"Go ahead. Make a joke of it. That's how you resolve every situation."

"I don't think you appreciate what happened," I said. My anger was rising. It was a side of my makeup that I always tried to suppress. "I just got us out of a tight spot, and all you can do is criticize me."

She stopped and looked down at her shoes. Her breath grew quick and short.

"Do you know how I felt when he took that picture?" she asked. "Do you know how I still feel?"

I shook my head.

"Violated."

We paid ten dollars apiece and boarded a flat-bottomed boat that took us into the bay. A guide talked in a monotone about the birds nesting on the small islands scattered around. They used to live on the mainland but lost their food supply as the ecosystem changed.

A few tourists snapped pictures.

The guide said that sometimes you could see dolphins.

I sat with my arms folded across my chest. I did not want to touch Magdalena. I stared ahead at the sinking sun.

The guide said the fish population in the bay had declined markedly over the years. Efforts were being made to stabilize it.

From behind us I heard a shriek of joy. A little girl in a T-shirt and baggy shorts was pointing to the side and screaming, "I saw one! I did! I swear I did!"

I got up and walked over and wondered how long I could remain angry.

The girl kept saying she had really seen one and the guide said that sometimes dolphins stayed underwater for ten minutes or more. The dolphin population had fallen drastically too, of course. Although it was no longer legal to hunt dolphins, they often became entangled in fishing nets.

I was about to head back to my seat when the girl cried out, "There he is!"

Behind the boat, a sleek gray form leaped out of the water. The dolphin's skin glistened as it caught the last bit of daylight.

I was imagining a silent drive back to Miami with nothing surrounding us but darkness. And then it happened: a feeling I had not experienced until recently, but one I was beginning to recognize—the creepy sensation that someone was watching me.

I looked across the parking lot and saw a solitary car on the far end. The brief tropical twilight was almost over and I could not make out every detail but I was relatively certain of what I saw: A dark Oldsmobile, an obvious rental, with its passenger window down and someone whose face was obscured peering out, binoculars in his hands.

I did not think it was Ernesto. His frame seemed bulkier and somehow younger. But, even though I couldn't see the tags, I felt it was the same car I'd observed near the Happy Land Mini Mall.

I ran toward the Olds. It was difficult to tell through the darkening night, but I convinced myself that the eyes of whoever was behind the wheel went wide as he threw down his binoculars and jerked his head inside the car.

Windows up. Engine on. He lit the Oldsmobile's high beams and sped away, the rear wheels squealing as they kicked up dirt and gravel. The car faded into the night before I was halfway across the lot but, as it slipped away, I saw the first markings on its tag: J60.

Follow him.

The thought entered my mind immediately, an unbidden idea that made sense at the moment.

I searched for Magdalena, feeling an instant of panic because I did not see her at first.

My lover stood at the foot of the dock. She had her hands on her hips and was shaking her head slightly, as if she disapproved of everything I had been doing for hours.

I ran toward her and grabbed her by the wrist and tried to take her with me as I made my way to the Rover.

Why didn't they trash it?

Magdalena stumbled behind me, but I did not loosen my grip.

"What are you doing?"

I did not reply.

"Loco. Estás loco."

About ten yards from the Rover another thought struck me and at first I thought it was fanciful but then I persuaded myself it was the only explanation for why my tormentors had left my vehicle intact.

I stopped abruptly and told Magdalena to stand behind me. I backed up a few feet, pointed my remote at the Rover and cringed, bracing my body for an explosion.

All I heard was a click as the doors unlocked.

I told Magdalena to wait. In fact it would be best if she hid behind something until I got the engine going. She asked what I was talking about but before I could answer I had gone the final few feet and jumped into the Rover and slid in the key and turned the ignition.

I waited a few seconds and prepared myself for anything other than what I heard, which was the sound of an engine running smoothly.

I pushed open the passenger door. Magdalena stood only a few feet away. She had not sought shelter.

"Get in."

"*Qué?*"

"Get in!"

Magdalena walked slowly toward the Rover. She was still looking at me as if I had lost all sense and reason.

"Magdalena! *Ahora!*"

She climbed up and in and closed the door half-heartedly. I took off, heading back into the heart of the Everglades.

Magdalena said she was hungry.

I tried to calculate how much of a head start the Oldsmobile had. Perhaps two minutes. Certainly no more than three.

Magdalena said she wanted to stay for dinner.

There was no illumination and the road twisted, but it was smooth and flat and I told myself I could do seventy-five with no problem.

Magdalena asked what I thought I was doing.

I pressed the accelerator to the floor. The Rover gained speed and soon the trees were whizzing by and only a narrow shaft ahead of me was lit and I felt as if I were playing a video game, except the stakes were real.

Magdalena asked if I minded telling her what this was about.

I hit seventy-five but still felt I was going too slowly so I nudged the Rover up to eighty. Some of the scrawny scrub pines had taken root close to the road. I'd been told they had sprouted in the past few years, after Hurricane Andrew cleared out much of the old growth.

Magdalena asked if it was absolutely necessary to go this fast.

I said it was.

Magdalena said I was making her nervous.

I said I didn't care.

Magdalena said that if she didn't know better, she'd swear I was trying to get both of us killed.

Up ahead I glimpsed a car that disappeared when it followed a bend in the road.

I nudged the accelerator. The Rover was doing eighty-five. We careered around a turn and I heard the tires squeal and felt the body of the SUV shift to the left.

Magdalena said she wished I would slow down.

It was there. Clearly ahead on a straightaway although I wasn't close enough to see its tags.

I wondered what I would do when I caught up to him.

I wondered if he had a gun.

I asked Magdalena if she could make out the tags on the car ahead of us.

She said she was too terrified to look.

I told her nothing was going to happen to us.

She asked in an emphatic tone—raising her voice in a way that demanded I finally supply a truthful answer—exactly what I was trying to do.

I said I wanted to catch up to the car ahead of us.

"*Por qué?*"

I said it was the same car I'd seen the day before across the road from Happy Land. It was the car from which Ernesto Rodriguez had been spying on me.

Magdalena said she was sure of it now. I was *loco*.

I was gaining on the Oldsmobile and I think he became aware of me because he began to pick up his speed but I knew I'd overtake him soon. I told myself it was important to have a plan, to know exactly what I was going to do when I reached him, and I envisioned passing him on the right and then nudging him over so he'd pull onto the shoulder and as he slowed I would—

"Watch out!"

It was Magdalena's voice, registering a note of panic I had never heard before, and I turned involuntarily to look at my lover and her eyes were fixed on a point not far in front of the Rover and when I swung my head back I saw a blur of something in front of us and I heard myself yelling, although I'd swear the sound originated from somewhere outside of me, and suddenly we were spinning and there seemed to be nothing I could do to make it stop and I felt the vehicle start to tip and for a moment I was sure it was going to roll over and I offered a prayer to a deity I barely believed in and then, somehow, my vehicle righted itself, and stopped.

I tried to get my bearings. We had spun off the road and the Rover had come to a halt only a few feet from a grove of pines. I wasn't even sure if we were pointing in the right direction.

I eased the Rover back onto the road.

Magdalena asked if I'd be careful.

I promised her I would.

I started the Rover at a slow pace toward what I thought was the east. Just as we resumed our drive I saw something move off to the right and I slowed, wondering if this was the blur that had almost caused me to crash.

Standing on the side of the road, just outside a thicket of bushes, a tall but gaunt panther with cobalt eyes stared as we cruised by its lair.

We stopped at a Friday's in the first strip mall we saw and I made a lame joke about being back in civilization. Magdalena rolled her eyes and shook her head. We took a booth and each ordered a burger and a beer and then sat uncomfortably, glancing past each other as we pretended to be mesmerized by faux ferns and fake wood paneling.

Finally I looked directly at Magdalena, and grinned. She shook her head, as if saying, "It's not going to work." So I started to do something I occasionally engage in when I feel awkward or stressed: I chattered. I talked about how happy I was to get the Rover back and how interesting I thought the Everglades were and how much I had enjoyed seeing a dolphin. I said that if I had to do it over again, I would have insisted that the strip mall for the Copleys' campaign contain a bar or at least a liquor store. I wondered what kind of profit a typical Friday's returned and whether the humidity would break before Christmas.

"You may have been right," Magdalena said.

"Huh? What?" I found it hard to believe she'd been listening to me.

"Before," she said. "The more I think about it."

"About what?"

"That car you were chasing. Maybe it did have a connection to Ernesto."

All my distractions disappeared as I focused on her face, which had the faraway look of a woman trying to recall her first boyfriend.

"What makes you say that?"

"He's told me he likes that part of the Everglades. He likes to go fishing there. He says it's very peaceful, but it's also easy to get to."

"When did he tell you this?"

"A while ago."

"Why didn't you tell me?"

"I only thought of it. *Ahora.*"

I wasn't sure I believed her and it was that uncertainty, more than anything else, that made my anger start to rise. We were in a public place and it was important to maintain a calm facade but I found myself slapping my palm against the table harder than I intended.

"You only thought of it now?"

"*Sí.*"

"I would have liked to have known about this before."

"*Por qué?*"

"I would have had my guard up. I would have been careful. I would have asked people if they'd seen him."

"And what would you have done if you'd found him?"

"Told him to pay my company the thirty thousand. If I got ambitious, I would have asked him if he killed your husband."

I stopped. The bar was noisy with people who had lingered long after happy hour, and the sound system was blaring the latest shrieks by Mariah Carey. I doubted that anyone had heard me.

"Ernesto didn't kill my husband," Magdalena said softly.

"What makes you say that?" I could not keep the contempt from my voice. "Women's intuition?"

"I'd know if Frank was dead. Arrangements have been made."

She sat at the foot of the bed, hunched over as if something hurt inside, and asked if I was angry with her.

"What makes you say that?"

"The way you made love to me."

I'd been furious all the way home and as soon as we entered the bedroom I whipped off my belt and threw it to the floor while she took off her earrings with great deliberation. I flung my shoes into the closet, where they crashed into the wall and made a sound like a body falling.

Magdalena had looked at me as if I were a three-year-old on the verge of a temper tantrum. For a moment I thought I might get a time-out.

I ripped off my shirt. If I'd been thinking clearly I would have been afraid of tearing some buttons.

Magdalena turned her back to me and pulled off her top. Then she faced me. She was smiling.

I stepped toward her and yanked down her pants and pushed her onto the bed. As I got on top she asked what I was doing.

I said nothing all the way through.

An image of Magdalena when it was over, a small tear trickling down the left side of her nose.

TEN

As soon as the Miata turned the corner I stripped the bed and put on the pale blue cotton sheets that I knew Helen liked.

At the office I began writing an over-the-top cover letter about the strip-mall campaign. My phone rang within five minutes. I looked through the glass wall and saw Isabel filing her nails and decided it was time to act like the abusive manager I'd always sworn I'd never become.

I yanked open the door and called out, more loudly than was necessary, so everyone near us could hear, "Could you do your job, Isabel, and answer the phone?"

She let the phone ring one more time before she picked up the receiver and mispronounced my name.

I returned to the cover letter. A few minutes later the door to my office opened. "Officer Hurtado called," Isabel said, the level of her voice matching my own. "She wants you to call her as soon as possible. She says you know her number."

I nodded, as if I was expecting the message. *"Gracias."*

"De nada."

"That matter we discussed," Pilar Hurtado said.

"Yes?" I uncapped my pen. It was an expensive gift from my in-laws that I at first dismissed as an unnecessary adornment, but had grown to like.

"I made some inquiries. Unofficially. This has to remain unofficial."

"I understand."

"The car was most likely rented from the Rock Bottom lot near Fort Lauderdale Airport."

"What do you mean, 'most likely'?"

"They have a lot of cars like that. Oldsmobiles with J60 tags. No one else was a candidate."

As I crawled up 95, I called Victor DeLuca. After identification and pleasantries, I asked how his son's soccer team was doing.

"He scored the winning goal the other night." Victor's voice had more than a normal tone of pride, as if he had taught the boy how to perform under pressure. "It was beautiful. He slipped through three defenders. I have it on tape and I still don't know how he did it. He shot the ball high into the corner, from an impossible angle. Unbelievable. Did I mention that I have it on tape?"

"If he gets any better, he'll need his own PR man. Tell him I'm available."

"We don't need anything like that. Yet."

"Too bad. I'm always looking for business."

Laughter on both ends.

"I sent you a fax earlier. I wanted to make sure you got it."

Victor said he had. He also said that in a city where strange things came across his desk all the time, this was one of the strangest.

"Good!" I said, forcing my voice into a zone of conviviality I was not actually feeling. "We're trying to break through the clutter. Make our idea truly stand out."

"It does stand out," Victor said. "It makes me think you've lost your mind."

"You've heard of the Copleys?"

"Yeah."

"But you've never covered them."

"A lot of people do REITs."

"We're doing them differently."

I described how we'd kick off the campaign. Besides the Fourth-of-July style oratory, some of Josette's artists would be at the strip mall, painting murals and installing sculpture as a visual testament to the Copley brothers' financial plan. South Florida would witness the true unification of art and commerce.

"What happens when the environmentalists find out?" Victor asked.

"Can we go off the record?" These words are catnip to reporters and editors, who believe "off the record" is always a prelude to important information.

"I don't see why not."

"We're telling them. We want them to protest. We'll be all over the eleven o'clock news, especially if it's a slow day."

I could hear him chuckling. He said he didn't know if he should send a reporter from his department or just hand the damn thing over to Lifestyles.

"Compromise," I said. "Send two reporters. One from each section."

Suddenly, out of nowhere, as if this man with whom I had a telephone relationship could read my mind, Victor DeLuca asked me this: "How's Ernesto doing?"

I did not answer right away. I wondered if Victor knew something or if he was trying to get information or if he was just genuinely curious.

I found myself grinning, purely out of reflex. "Fine. Ernesto's fine."

"Can you tell him to give our reporter a call? We really want to do that story about Tierra Grande."

"I'm trying," I said. "Ernesto's extremely busy. He's been hard to reach, even for me."

"I don't understand it," Victor DeLuca said. "Ernesto says he wants publicity, and then when we're ready to give it to him, he plays hard to get." Victor said the same thing had happened about ten years ago, when Ernesto began his climb up the real-estate ladder. *The Herald* assigned a reporter named Miriam Goldberg to do an in-depth feature, which she pursued in gung-ho fashion for a few weeks. But then something happened. Victor was never able to figure out what it was. But she suddenly said she wanted to drop the story and three weeks later she'd quit *The Herald* and moved to Kansas City.

"What the hell did she do that for?" I asked.

"She said she wanted to live in America."

Rock Bottom Car Rental was up U.S. 1 about a half mile from Fort Lauderdale Airport, in a small lot on a stretch of road where the rental companies that serve tourists and business travelers began giving way to used-car dealers and junkyards.

As I walked through the wet blanket of humidity, I looked around but tried not to appear too curious. Several dark green Oldsmobile sedans were clumped in a dull mass. A few Cadillacs were close to the office.

I entered refrigeration, shaking a bit as I got used to the cold. Behind the counter was an overweight, bored-looking black girl with hair extensions. She chewed gum slowly and made no effort to acknowledge my presence, even though we were the only two people in the room.

I walked up to her and grinned.

"You have a reservation?"

"It's a little more complicated than that."

She rolled her eyes.

I put my elbows on the counter and leaned toward her. Grinned again. She snapped her gum.

"I'm the financial officer at a public relations company."

"Congratulations."

"We have a policy—when we send our people out, we tell them to use the best. They're supposed to rent Cadillacs."

More gum chewing. She barely looked at me.

"I suspect one of our guys isn't doing that. I think he's renting Oldsmobiles and pocketing the change."

"What's the difference? You're spending the money anyway."

"We want our people to make a good impression. As I said, we're in public relations."

I took out a picture of Ernesto that I'd cut from a brochure we'd done about Tierra Grande. I handed it to the girl and asked if she recognized this man. She gave it right back and said she never remembered anyone who came in. I glanced around the room, which had the aura of a place that hadn't seen another person step inside it for hours, if not days.

"Because you have so many customers, right?"

She looked at me sharply. I felt as if I finally had her attention and slid the picture back to her.

"He might still have the car out," I said. "Take your time. Tell me if you recognize him."

She picked it up. Her gum chewing slowed.

"I did see him," she said. "He returned the car this morning."

I thanked her and said I appreciated the information.

"He paid cash," she said. "That's why I remember."

I slapped my palm on the counter in a gesture that was half theatrical and half genuine frustration. If Ernesto was paying cash for everything, there'd be no paper trail.

"We do keep records of our cash transactions," the girl said. She was suddenly more than cooperative, like an overeager schoolkid volunteering to do extra homework. "They're in a separate file in the computer."

I leaned closer to her and grinned again. Gum-chewing smacks echoed in my ear.

"You're doing great," I said. "You're helping me a lot."

She nodded happily. Her eyes seemed to light up. I wondered if anyone had ever paid her a compliment.

"Could you do me a favor?" I asked.

"Sure."

"Could you print out a copy of the receipt you gave him?"

She said it would take a minute. While we waited for it to print I asked her where she lived and if she went to school and what her plans for the future were. I have to confess that I don't recall her answers, although they may have involved opening a hair salon.

With the self-satisfied pride of a person who has solved a difficult puzzle, the girl tore off the receipt and handed it to me. Ernesto had rented the car for five days, at a total cost of $181.92. I imagined him driving around the Generica west of Fort Lauderdale, checking into a different cheap motel every night, always paying cash and leaving early in the morning, on the run from . . .

From what?

I wondered if he was still in Florida. It would be simple to drop off the car and board a bus to the airport. From there he could go anywhere.

When I saw the name he had used, I smiled. According to the Rock Bottom Car Rental Agency, the dark green Oldsmobile sedan, tag number J60 XFT, had been rented to Francisco Seto. I imagined telling Magdalena and both of us laughing. That would cause us to try out aliases, coming up with increasingly improbable names for ourselves that would soon resemble the ones used by professional wrestlers. We'd be convulsing as we lay together in bed, and finally I'd roll on top and kiss her while we both still laughed and then I'd work my way down her body and listen with prurient contentment as her laughs turned to sighs and then moans.

"Sir? *Sir?*"

The black girl's voice invaded my consciousness and when I looked at her she was like a background figure suddenly being rack-focused into the forefront.

"Sorry," I said, and grinned, hoping that would work. "I didn't hear you. What was that again?"

"Is there anything else I can help you with?"

I told her I didn't think so and stepped away. But then a thought crashed into my head.

She had resumed her previous stance—back hunched, shoulders slumped, a look somewhere between a scowl and indifference plastered on her face.

"There is one more thing," I said.

No response. I wondered if I had used up her daily quotient of civility.

"I haven't seen Mr. Seto today. When he left, did you happen to notice if he went to the airport, or took a taxi, or . . ."

"There was somebody waiting for him," she said quickly, as if she'd been waiting for me to ask the question.

"Really? What did he look like?"

"It was a lady."

"Then what did she look like?"

"Very pretty, but kind of short. Long dark hair parted in the middle."

I felt my breath begin to leave me.

"Bright red nail polish—I wish I knew the shade; I'd get some myself."

If I lived in another climate, I would have stepped outside to get some air.

"Dark eyes, beautiful skin—and her dress was definitely not off the rack, you know what I mean?"

I'd read stories about deep-sea divers who came up too quickly after plunging to the ocean floor and I told myself this was the same sensation; the world itself was disorienting, the very act of breathing painful.

"Do you know her?" the girl asked.

I used all my self-control as I asked the following question in quiet and even tones: "A red Miata?"

"That's right."

"I know her."

I gave the girl a twenty. She told me to have a nice day, and I somehow managed not to laugh.

My Rover wound up in front of Red White & Blew, almost as if my vehicle were telling me that this was a place where I could find refuge or, at the least, a degree of solace.

The gallery was empty. I looked at the celebration of the tacky and banal, the almost unironic appreciation of kitsch, and tried to persuade myself that some things in life are what they seem to be, with no subtexts or secret meanings or hidden agendas.

Five minutes passed before I called out Josette's name—softly at first, gradually raising my voice to its normal volume.

I stepped behind the counter where Josette and Teresa transacted what little business they did. There was still no sign of anyone. I peered down the hallway that led to the offices and storerooms in back. I listened for sounds of movement or muffled conversation.

Nothing.

"Josette?"

No response.

I pictured her bound and gagged, her almost naked body lifeless or close to it, blood spattered across the paintings she kept in back. I imagined a piece of paper next to her, folded neatly, with my name on it in handwriting I recognized.

Halfway down the hall I heard a sound that was surprisingly high-pitched. I stopped and cocked my ear and tried to catch whatever noise was traveling from a far back room.

It sounded like giggling.

I walked as softly as I could toward the source of the sound, which changed from giggles to deep sighs and finally a shout.

I stopped outside the room where the noises were coming from. The door was open a crack and I almost pushed it open all the way, but the sight I observed made me draw back.

Josette was on a couch and she was, in fact, naked. I'd never realized how many tattoos she had. Her legs were spread wide and her eyes were closed and her face was twisted with the pleasant contortions of a woman on the verge of sexual ecstasy.

From where I stood, it seemed as if a mass of gray hair was attached to her genitalia. Even from behind, I knew who it was. The lady from the lamp store. Cary or Corey. I wished I'd gotten her name straight.

Back at the office I listened to a voicemail from Sebastian Overstreet, who wanted to know if I had talked to Ernesto recently. Echoing Victor DeLuca almost word for word, the reporter said his editors were really anxious for that story about Tierra Grande.

As I hit his number I prayed that he wouldn't be at his desk, but my years-long absence from church must have been noted because he answered on the first ring.

"Ernesto's a busy man," I said. "I told that to Victor."

"I understand."

"It's been tough to pin him down. But I'll try him again. How are you doing?"

"I'm fine. When did you talk to Mr. Rodriguez?"

"A few days ago. We keep missing each other."

"I tried to reach him myself."

I found myself grinning tightly. "You should really go through me, Sebastian."

"Did you know that his number's been disconnected? And there isn't a new one?"

"It's a snafu. He changed providers."

"Could you give me his new number?"

"Uh, well, to be honest, I'm not sure he'd want me to do that."

"Why not?"

"He's cautious about giving people access."

"I've thought about swinging by his office."

"Don't do that." I immediately regretted my vehemence, and grinned again. I wondered why I did that when no one could see me. "If you show up unannounced, he might kick you out. Permanently."

I wondered if Ernesto and Magdalena were lovers.

The thought crashed through unbidden, like a drunken relative staggering in during your favorite daughter's wedding.

Solicitous, I kept thinking. *Ernesto was solicitous.*

Magdalena had misled me and my initial suspicions were correct: Ernesto had killed Frank Hedges. She had been waiting for me and not her husband that night at the Orlando because she wanted to keep me close so they could know if I was on the verge of discovering something that might ruin their plans.

Ernesto and Magdalena were going to disappear together. Perhaps they were already gone. I pictured them driving to the airport in her Miata and boarding a plane for South America. In years to come, on the rare occasions they mentioned my name, they would laugh uproariously at the light-skinned man they had manipulated so easily.

I picked up my phone and punched in the number I knew by heart.

I did not expect an answer.

I told myself she was gone.

"Hola."

Her voice. Even in perfunctory greeting, it thrilled me.

"It's me."

"Cómo estás?"

My tongue felt bloated. Everything I said sounded thick and stupid.

"Bueno," I said. *"Cómo estás?"*

"Bien. Are you sure you're all right?"

I almost told her the truth: I wasn't all right and hadn't been since my visit to the car rental. And I wasn't going to be all right until I found out what she was doing with Ernesto and what the man I was beginning to regard as my former client was trying to do.

"I'm okay," I said. "I wanted to see you. That's all."

"Cuándo?"

"Ahora."

"I thought your wife was landing soon. I thought you were still mad from last night."

"I want to ask you something."

"Ask me now."

"I can't do it over the phone. I have to see you."

I sat by myself at a rickety table in a lounge at an airport hotel and told the bartender I was expecting a lady to join me but in the meantime I'd like a beer. As I sipped it I kept looking around for something to shove under the table to steady it.

I told myself that after I asked Magdalena my question, I'd pick up Helen. I'd drive my wife home and make love to her and the two of us would move back to New York and get on with our lives and I would never again be unfaithful to anyone.

Magdalena walked in, wearing a short dress with a checked print and three bracelets on each wrist. Her hair fell past her bare shoulders. Every man in the room stared at her and then at me as she stopped at the table and smiled and sat down.

The bartender appeared right away. Magdalena ordered a frozen daiquiri. I kept wishing the damn table would remain steady.

"So," she said.

"So."

"You wanted to ask me a question."

As I nodded, I felt my resolve melting away. I asked how her day had been.

"Is that your question? You couldn't ask me that over the phone?"

"I'm leading up to it."

"My day has been . . . uneventful."

Her drink appeared. I smiled at her.

"I wound up in Fort Lauderdale. On business. I stumbled upon two women engaged in a sex act."

Magdalena took the first sip of her drink. "Then you had a more interesting day than I did."

"I don't think so."

She put her drink down hard. The table wobbled. "What do you mean by that?"

"I told you I had a question." It was important to keep my voice low. I felt I was skirting the edge of danger and I did not want anyone around us to overhear. You never know who might be eavesdropping.

"My question is this: Where's Ernesto?"

"I've told you. *No sé.*"

"Are you having an affair with him?"

She looked at me with the kind of astonishment that villagers in Nazareth must have expressed when Joseph the carpenter started telling them about his wife's virgin birth. And then she burst out laughing, slowly lifting her hand to her mouth in a halfhearted attempt to conceal her amusement.

"You are too much," she said. "Too, too much."

"I'm glad you find me so amusing."

"I do. I really do."

"Then maybe you can tell me where you took Ernesto after he dropped off the rental car this morning. Since I amuse you so much."

She stopped laughing. Her hand dropped to the side. She reached for her drink and almost tipped it over and glanced at me before looking away.

"Have you been spying on me?"

"No. But I have been trying to find Ernesto. You know that. And apparently you know where he's been all along and you haven't told me."

"*No es verdad,*" she said. Her words were swift and I could not tell if she was being truthful or if a plausible story had just occurred to her. She said Ernesto had called in the morning, shortly after she left me. She was surprised to hear from him of course and she asked where he was but he wouldn't tell her. He said he needed a favor. She asked what it was and he said he shouldn't have to explain and she thought about if for a few moments before deciding that he was right; she owed something to this man who had always been kind to her. So she said yes before knowing exactly what he wanted. And what he wanted was simple—she didn't know why he demanded a loyalty test.

"He told me he was returning a car. And he needed someone to pick him up."

"Where did you take him?"

"To the airport."

"Where did he go?"

"He didn't tell me."

"What airline?"

"American."

"Foreign or domestic?"

"Foreign."

"Why call you? Why not just take a shuttle bus or taxi to the airport?"

"Ernesto doesn't trust strangers."

"Strangers you can trust," I said. "It's friends you have to watch out for."

Magdalena reached into her bag and took out one of the slim cigars she favored. She started to light it before I tapped her on the wrist and pointed to the sign over us that said, "*NO FUMAR.*" She shook her head and put the cigar back and said she couldn't believe that a country that spent so much time talking about freedom would forbid people from smoking if they wanted to. No matter how much time she spent in the United States, she'd never understand it.

"What did you and Ernesto talk about?"

"When did you turn into a cop?"

"I'm curious. Humor me."

"We talked about you."

I always try to appear unsurprised, to make it seem as if the words I've just heard were exactly the ones I was expecting. But in this instance my facade must have cracked; I was amazed, and my jaw swung down until it almost hit my chest.

"He knows you've been trying to find him. He recommends that you stop."

"If he's out of the country, I won't have a choice."

Magdalena leaned back and tilted her head toward the ceiling. She seemed to be trying to pick the right words out of the air.

"He knows about us," she said.

I imagined Ernesto or his people keeping me under surveillance—dull duty until Magdalena showed up—and wondered if I had exposed myself to some form of extortion.

"He doesn't disapprove," Magdalena said. "But he thinks we should be more discreet. I told him it wouldn't be necessary. Because I thought it was over. By your choice."

"Did you say anything else to him?"

"No. That was when I dropped him off."

"What about his family? How will they manage without him?"

"I wouldn't worry about Luisa and the children. He never does."

Solicitous, I thought. *Ernesto has always been solicitous.*

I drank the last of my beer and told myself I didn't need another because I was about to leave. I put my elbows on the table and leaned close to her and spoke softly.

"I'm not an idiot," I said.

Magdalena looked at me sharply. "Excuse me?"

"You heard." I was within inches of her and I could smell the perfume that reminded me of hyacinth and for a moment I was intoxicated—I wanted to let her surround and capture me—but then I looked into her eyes and they seemed tired, almost dead, and I told myself that she was concealing something.

"Ernesto killed your husband," I said in a voice so low I could barely make it out myself. "And now you're waiting for him. He'll get himself set up somewhere in Latin America and then you'll be on the next flight out of here."

Magdalena slammed her drink on the table with so much force I was afraid the glass would break.

"Go to hell," she said before pushing back her chair and rising to her feet. I sensed that she was debating with herself about whether to spit at me before she turned and left.

I should have let her go. I had told myself I was ready to let it happen, but now that she was literally walking out of my life, a craving came over me that must be what junkies experience when they go into withdrawal.

I slapped a twenty on the table and ran out of the room.

She was in the lobby. Almost out the door. A porter smiled at her as she passed.

I ran faster. If she got away, she'd be lost to me forever.

"Magdalena!"

I wasn't shouting.

"Magdalena!"

That word did not come from me.

She stopped. Her back tensed, as if she was both frightened and attracted by the voice she was hearing.

I caught up with her and breathlessly puffed out the first words I could think of: "I'm sorry. I'm so, so sorry."

"Don't be—"

"I had no right—"

"If you only knew—"

"I promise I won't—"

"Don't say anything—"

And then my arms were around her and she had embraced me and we were kissing and I was telling myself it was better now, even better than before, because we had somehow crossed the threshold from lust to love and from desire to need.

I pulled back a few inches and looked at her directly. I was amazed at what I was about to say, but the words came out anyway: "You don't love Frank."

She shook her head. "No. Not for a long time."

What happened next is a kaleidoscope of moments that barely seem connected to one another:

Stumbling toward the front desk and asking if a room was available; laughing when the clerk wanted to know how much luggage we had; groping each other as the elevator rose and feeling her thighs her hips her waist and breasts; throwing off our clothes when we entered the room; hearing her moan as I tasted her; seeing my lover roll her eyes as she urged me in Spanish to go faster.

We lay together awhile. She told me that Frank still had an arrangement with someone in the government: he checked in every forty-eight hours, no matter where he was, and if this person didn't hear from her husband, Magdalena would get a call. So far, she had heard *nada*.

"He vanished right after their argument," I said. "Did Ernesto scare him into disappearing?"

Magdalena took out one of her slim cigars and let a long plume of smoke float up toward the air-conditioning vent. "Could be. This is not a good time to be on Ernesto's bad side."

"What do you mean?"

"Tierra Grande. What's the phrase—'biting off more than you can swallow'?"

"Close enough. I get the point."

"Ernesto will raise the money. But it's best not to bother him for a while. At this point, he really resents . . . distractions."

"How will he get the money?"

"He didn't tell me."

"But you think you know?"

She nodded.

"And you think it's best if I don't know?"

She nodded again, and smiled, and let her cigar rest in an ashtray on the nightstand. She put her arms around me and her eyes seemed to have sprung to life and I had to have her again. She gasped when I entered her and then told me how much she liked it and finally she said, so quietly I wasn't sure I was supposed to hear it, *"Te quiero,"* and, for that moment at least, I was happy.

When I got home it looked as if all the lights were off. I turned on the overhead in the kitchen and drank three cups of water from the large cooler that Helen insisted we keep beside the refrigerator. In the guest bathroom I washed my face with the antibacterial liquid soap that my wife liked to use and found the spare toothbrush she had stashed in the back of the medicine cabinet. I examined the floss that she'd bought but it wasn't the kind I preferred so I decided to skip it. Missing one night wouldn't make my teeth fall out.

I walked back across the house and stopped outside our bedroom and put my hand on the knob. But then I paused. I had a premonition that I was about to discover something that meant my life was going to change.

I am an American, born and raised in the latter part of the twentieth century, and years of media conditioning fed a tabloid-drenched vision of my wife's body sprawled across the mattress, the wounds too horrible to glance at, a message on the walls written in blood that was still dripping even as I ran out and found the phone and called the police.

The questions would come of course: Where were you, who were you with, why were you there, do you have any enemies, can anyone back up your story?

A vision of Magdalena trying to enter police headquarters, a kerchief wrapped around her head while a hand shielded her face from a battalion of photographers.

I opened the door slowly in a futile attempt to stop it from creaking.

Everything seemed in order. The drawers to our bureaus were shut and the closet doors were closed and Helen's lipstick and makeup were arranged neatly on her vanity.

I saw all these things clearly because the light on Helen's nightstand was on. My wife was propped up in bed with a pillow supporting her back. She was reading a copy of *Forbes*.

"Hello, Garrett."

"Hi."

"You weren't at the airport."

"I had to entertain one of our clients. I should have left a message for you."

"I waited a half hour. Then I called a car service."

I told her I was sorry and apologized for getting home so late. I should have called. I had no idea what got into me.

"I had the whole thing planned out. I wanted to have dinner together. There's something I have to tell you."

I apologized again to my wife and suggested we go out for dinner the next night.

"I wanted it to be tonight." She was trying to control her voice, but it was rising. "I had something to say to you. Something important." She flipped through the pages forcefully.

"Tell me now."

"It doesn't work that way, Garrett. You can't come waltzing in here whenever you feel like and pretend everything is okay. Because it isn't."

I said she didn't have to say anything if that's how she felt. In fact I'd prefer it that way. I was tired. It was late. I wanted to sleep.

"I thought you'd be happy. I thought you'd want to know. But now I realize you just don't give a shit."

I lifted the covers and slipped in and pulled a blanket up to my chin to ward off the dry cool of the air-conditioning.

"You got the transfer back to New York," I said. "Great. Just great. When do you start?"

She threw the magazine down on her nightstand, where it landed with a wet-sounding *thwap*.

"That's not it," she said. "That's not it at all. I didn't ask for a transfer, Garrett. Do you know why?"

I rolled over and opened my eyes. The backlight from the lamp on Helen's nightstand created a glow behind her that reminded me of a halo, and for a second I thought I'd never seen her look more beautiful. Her nightgown strap fell from her shoulder and I could see the water in her eyes but she blinked rapidly; she held it in; she would not let me know how much I'd hurt her.

"I'm going to have a baby."

ELEVEN

My boss stared wide-eyed at his computer screen, as if he'd discovered an uncommonly graphic pornographic Website.

"I got an e-mail this morning," he said. "Highest priority. Very important. From New York."

"About Ernesto?"

"Bingo."

I shrugged and decided there was nothing to lose by telling him the truth about the client he had wanted to land so desperately: One day before, Ernesto Rodriguez had dropped off a rental car near Fort Lauderdale Airport before being driven to the American Airlines foreign flights counter.

My boss slammed his palm against the side of his computer, as if that might kick the offending message out of his system.

"You mean he's flown the coop? Say it ain't so."

He put his head in his hands and shook it from side to side. I had last seen grieving like that in the neighborhood where I grew up, when old Mrs. Martinelli lost her husband. She wailed for days, and the only thing she'd ever done with the man was argue.

"What can we tell them?" my boss kept asking. "What on earth can we tell them?"

"The truth," I said.

My boss looked at me as if I had suggested he sprout wings and fly.

"We don't know where he is," I said. "We believe he's out of the country. If he comes back, we'll get the money."

"You don't understand." My boss sounded as if he were lamenting the dead. "You just don't understand."

"Technically, we could get a civil judgment against him. We could put a lien on his assets, assuming he has any. But that would just piss off every Cuban in Miami."

"They want my ass on a platter." My boss slammed his palm on his desk. "Those bastards in New York have it in for me. They've wanted to get rid me of me for months. And now they've got something to hang around my neck. I'm so tied up in knots I haven't been getting my eight hours of shut-eye."

He looked at me out of the corner of his eyes and I knew what he was thinking: I was an agent of his destruction, sent down from New York in a cleverly concealed plan that would result in my takeover of the Miami office.

"Underperforming," he muttered. "That's what they told me a few months ago. The office was underperforming."

Magdalena had said she didn't know where Ernesto went, and I had chosen to believe her. My only unexamined lead had come inadvertently from Victor DeLuca, so I called *The Kansas City Star* and asked for Miriam Goldberg. I believed I would find her easily. In the heartland, I told myself, her name must be exotic.

An operator told me that nobody with that name worked at the newspaper.

"Hmmmm. Maybe she doesn't work there anymore. I believe she is, or was, a reporter in the business section. Could you put me through?"

"Certainly, sir."

A clerk answered and I said I was trying to locate a woman named Miriam Goldberg. I believed she had once been a reporter on the staff.

"What?" asked the clerk, sounding like a kid who was too tired from going to school and holding down three jobs.

I explained my problem, more slowly this time. The clerk said he'd never heard of the woman. I could tell I was seconds away from being hung up on.

"Maybe you could ask around," I said. "Somebody might know where she is. I'm calling from Miami and it's really important." I found myself grinning.

I heard muffled voices and questions directed into the air followed by shouted replies I could not decipher. Finally a woman's voice came on the line. She sounded as if she were speaking from the bottom of a well. "Are you talking about Mims?"

I had no idea, but said I was.

"She got married. To a man named Schiffer."

"I see. I hadn't heard. Maybe that's why I'm having so much trouble finding her."

"It's not only that. She doesn't work in this department anymore."

"Oh."

"She's the food editor now."

I tried to imagine the leap from covering markets and start-ups to editing stories about leftovers, but my mind refused to comprehend it. Instead I asked to be put through to Miriam Schiffer née Goldberg.

The line went dead. I rolled my eyes and cursed silently in Spanglish before hitting redial. After a few minutes, I finally connected with a live person in the food department.

I asked for Miriam Schiffer.

The voice on the other end belonged to a middle-aged woman and I could picture her after the first syllable she uttered—a woman barely able to fit her body in a chair, her roots showing and a dress from Sears draped over her like a dropcloth.

She asked who was calling.

I identified myself. I said Mrs. Schiffer didn't know me.

The woman asked what I was calling about. I heard cellophane being unwrapped, followed by chewing sounds.

I said I was calling from Miami. I had a couple of questions I wanted to ask her.

"Some man from Miami," I heard in muffled tones, as if a hand had been placed inexpertly over the phone. "He said he wanted to ask you some questions. His name sounded Irish. Maybe he's with the police."

"Yes?"

Miriam Schiffer née Goldberg's voice had the clear, no-nonsense tones of a professional woman who had grown accustomed to juggling three or four roles. But in that single word I also heard a wariness that went beyond the skepticism that journalists maintain by both habit and training; there was a shakiness that bordered on fear.

I identified myself and told her I was in public relations. I said I knew Victor DeLuca.

She asked how he was.

I said he was fine. His son was a high school soccer star.

She said she remembered when the boy was just starting kindergarten. Time moves on, whether you want it to or not.

She asked why I was calling. She said it had been a long time since she had talked to someone from Miami.

I said it was about a client. Victor had told me she once tried to do a story about him, but it didn't pan out.

Miriam Schiffer née Goldberg laughed. She said she had spent most of her life working on things that didn't pan out.

"It's about Ernesto Rodriguez," I said.

Although I couldn't see her, I sensed her face muscles tightening.

"I don't want to say anything about him."

"Why not?"

"It's in my past. I want to leave it that way."

I started speaking quickly, which is my usual habit when I'm not telling the entire truth. I told Miriam Schiffer née Goldberg that I was working on a real-estate project with Ernesto and a *Herald* reporter was asking about the financing and I'd been unable to come up with satisfactory answers.

"Why don't you ask Ernesto?"

"He's out of town. Victor said you tried to do something similar on another project Ernesto did. I was just wondering if you could give me some guidance."

"The best guidance I can give you is this: Drop it. And get as far away from Ernesto as possible."

"I can't do that. He's already hired me. And the reporter is quite persistent. He's young. Gung ho. You know how it goes."

"Tell him to do stories about lifestyles. Or celebrities. Those are the only things people care about anymore."

"I can't believe this," I said. "I'm trying to help out the media, but the media isn't helping me."

Miriam Schiffer née Goldberg sighed, as if she couldn't believe she was falling into a guilt trap that had been set by somebody who lied for a living. Finally she said this, although she sounded as reluctant as a witness who's been compelled to testify against her best friend: "Victor's memory is a little faulty. I did do one story. Back when Ernesto bought that hotel. The Orlando. It was in '86 or '87. Check it out."

"Why?"

"You sound like a bright guy, Mr. Doherty."

She pronounced my name correctly, and I was grateful. "If you read between the lines, you'll be able to figure it out."

During my short career in journalism, one of the things that amazed me was the amount of information available to the public. Anybody can walk into a place where records are stored and ask to see one of the myriad documents that are filed with the recordkeepers of democracy: deeds and titles, minutes of city council hearings, certificates of births and deaths. Of course the few members of the citizenry who actually look at these things are dismissed as cranks and eccentrics.

I walked into the Miami Beach City Hall and found the records bureau at the end of a long corridor in the basement. The door creaked when I pushed it, as if it were unused to being opened. A few feet inside was a counter with no one behind it and I wondered if I would stand there for hours or perhaps days, shriveling away while waiting for assistance.

I heard a voice coming from behind a stack of files. The voice surprised me—I'd been expecting a sixtysomething woman with blue hair who knew where everything was and could talk about the city's history in the kind of detail possessed only by someone who spent a lot of time in the presence of the past. But the voice sounded young and I thought I glimpsed the top of the head it belonged to—hair that was spiked and dyed flaming orange, and a body that was no doubt comfortable only in leather.

"It's so unfair," the voice was saying. "Melt is a great club. Who's going to run it if he's in jail? The whole thing happened five years ago and you'd think they'd get over it. So what if he killed somebody?"

I coughed, perhaps more loudly than necessary, and saw the head swing out from behind the stack. She was about twenty-five, perhaps pretty under the makeup, with studs on both her ears and in both her nostrils.

"Oh my God, somebody's here."

I heard a phone being put down. She walked up to me and looked astonished that she actually had a customer.

I grinned and said I wanted to check all records regarding any sales of the Hotel Orlando dating back to—and here I leaned back and gazed at the ceiling, as if I were literally picking a figure out of the air—oh, let's say 1980.

She nodded and said okay and asked if I could wait a few minutes while she found it.

I grinned again. "No problem."

She disappeared but a moment later I heard her voice: "The Orlando. That's one of the small ones, isn't it?"

"I hadn't thought of it that way. But I guess it is."

She returned with a few pieces of paper that looked as if they'd just come out of a printer that hadn't been replaced since Catfish Hunter last pitched for the Yankees. I took them and started to look through. The current owner had a name I recognized—a club impresario with several stints at the Betty Ford Center and a couple of no-contest pleas for tax evasion. He was the latest in a long line of proprietors; if I was reading the records correctly, during the nineties nobody had owned the hotel for more than ten months, and each time it sold, the price had been marked up significantly.

I flipped the page and looked at the records for the eighties, which were much less extensive. In 1989, the Orlando had been sold to Takashiro Matsuda, whose primary residence was listed as Kyoto. The seller was Ernesto Rodriguez, who had taken advantage during the days when the Japanese had money and were willing to overpay. Mr. Matsuda had purchased the hotel for a million and a half dollars.

The previous sale had occurred on February 5, 1987, when Ernesto Rodriguez had purchased the Hotel Orlando from a man named Solomon Weinstein for one hundred thousand dollars. Even with my limited math skills, I was impressed by the profit Ernesto had made.

An image of Magdalena curled in my arms, her breathing quick and shallow as she enjoyed the afterglow of her orgasm. In a low tone I said I had a question for her and she asked what it was and I said it was about Ernesto and it concerned what had happened a long time ago. I said I wanted to know everything and my lover said she understood; she was ready to answer all the questions I had.

I cleared my throat. The orange-topped head popped over a stack.

"I'm not sure I made myself clear. I asked for the records going back to 1980."

"That's what I gave you." A note of peevishness crept into her voice. If I didn't let her nap, she'd fall asleep during tonight's rave.

"But the first sale that's recorded was in 1987."

"Maybe the guy who sold it had owned the place for a long time."

That possibility hadn't occurred to me. I was used to a frenzied pace of acquisition and unloading. The idea of purchasing a piece of real estate, and holding on to it, struck me as just slightly less odd than taking vows of poverty, chastity and obedience.

"When did Solomon Weinstein buy the Orlando?"

Heavy sighs. I was demanding more work than she had been anticipating, probably more work than she had done in a week. I heard a computer being booted and the repeated clicking of a mouse and, after a few minutes, a slow printer spewing out some information.

Stud Girl appeared, slapped the paper on the counter and said "Here!" before withdrawing to whatever place she preferred to occupy.

According to the statement in front of me, Solomon Weinstein had purchased the Hotel Orlando on November 2, 1949, for fifteen thousand dollars.

It was a lot of money back then.

An image of Magdalena from minutes before; my face between her legs and my lover grabbing my hair and saying in Spanish that she wanted this to continue until her death and beyond.

"Can't you talk about something other than Ernesto?"

"He's someone we have in common."

"Whenever I'm with you, I feel like you're interrogating me."

"I had a question. I thought you might have an answer."

"*No sé.* What's so hard about that to understand?"

I had asked Magdalena in what I imagined was a tone of hazy post-coital wondering if she had any idea how Ernesto had raised one hundred thousand dollars to buy the Orlando in 1987. She had seen right through me of course. To Magdalena, I was always transparent.

My lover stubbed out her cigar in an ashtray and wrapped her arms around my back. As she rested her head against my chest, she said there was a story she wanted to tell that she had heard from her grandmother many years ago . . .

There was a man who loved a beautiful woman with all of his heart but whenever he got near her he became tongue-tied so his worship was from afar. The woman had many admirers and of course she married one of them but he turned out to be cruel. He beat and insulted her and made her life a misery. Anyway the man who worshipped her was struck by a passing car one day as he tried to cross the street and as he lay there in agony, his life ebbing away, his one last wish was that he could be close to the woman he loved before he left the earth. Perhaps there are such things as angels because the man's soul found its way into the body

of a dog that roamed the street in front of the woman's house. He trot-
ted back and forth for hours every day, sometimes catching a glimpse of
her through the gate, but his joy at seeing her was tempered by the obvious signs of her growing unhappiness: she stopped wearing makeup, she
let her hair become unkempt, she wore clothes that drooped loose and
wrinkled around her. One night he heard her screaming from within;
the sound of leather striking flesh filled his ears and he sensed the creep-
ing approach of a slow and bloody death. Somehow he found the
strength and energy to bound over the concrete wall that separated the
house from the rest of the world and he leaped through a window and
did not mind the pain inflicted by the shattering glass; he rushed up the
stairs and found them in their bedroom, the woman he loved holding
up her arms in an increasingly futile effort to ward off the blows from
her husband, who in a drunken rage had hauled out a horsewhip and
was intent on using it until there was no resistance. So the creature who
worshipped the woman jumped on her husband and knocked him to the
floor and they bit and growled and fought until finally all the life had
flowed out of the cruel man and there was no danger anymore to anyone. In gratitude the woman bathed the dog and dressed his wounds
and of course she kept him; and every night for as long as he lived he
slept at the foot of her bed.

The library was long and low and next to a Blockbuster that was so
crowded the customers' cars and minivans and SUVs spilled into the
road. The library's lot was almost empty, so I parked near the door.
When I told the woman at the front desk that I was looking for copies
of *The Herald* from February 1987, she looked at me as if I had asked
her to disrobe.

She looked around in what seemed like desperation. Directly behind
her was a girl playing a game of computer solitaire. She asked the girl in
Spanish what the hell I was looking for and the girl turned around and
shrugged and went back to her game. Black ten on the red jack.

I leaned forward and put my hands on the desk. The woman drew
back from me.

"*Por favor,*" I said. "This is a library, isn't it?"

"There's no need to be insulting, señor."

"If you tell me where you keep your back copies of *The Herald,* I can find what I need by myself."

She pointed in a direction that was vaguely to my right. I nodded and stepped away and wandered between rows of reference materials that were encrusted with a deep layer of dust. After what seemed like an hour of searching, I finally saw, on a top shelf I could barely reach, bound copies of *The Miami Herald* with dates so faded I could barely make them out.

I was amazed this stuff wasn't on a computer or at least microfilm, but as I looked around at the dirt that covered everything and the way the nearly deserted building seemed to sag, I realized it was amazing that this place had enough of a budget to stay open at all. There's an awful lot of money in this country, and we've decided to keep it all for ourselves.

I removed the book and sat at a table that was stained by years of spilled drinks and opened the heavy cover and felt it stick to whatever was now beneath it. I flipped through the pages and found the yellowing edition of February 6, 1987. The front page was dominated by stories about Iran-contra and a proposal to allow one more flight a week between Miami and Havana. Leaders of the Cuban-American community were opposed to anything that might look like a softening of the embargo.

I went through the front section before turning to Business. There was nothing on the first page by Miriam Goldberg and I kept going past ads for stores that had long since gone out of business until finally, on the next-to-last page of the section, I found what I wanted.

Under a headline that said "Onetime Janitor Buys Beach Landmark," Miriam Goldberg recounted the purchase of the Hotel Orlando in standard journalistic boilerplate. I went through the story slowly. I wondered exactly what I was supposed to figure out by reading between the lines.

The information toward which Miriam Schiffer née Goldberg had tried to steer me was, of course, in the last two paragraphs. I read them three times to make sure I understood. According to her reporting, Ernesto Rodriguez refused to reveal who his backers were, although he also said he'd been quite thrifty and had saved most of his janitor's salary in the hope that an opportunity like this would arise. I could almost see a collective arching of the newspaper's eyebrows. The article also noted that nobody involved in the dealings would reveal what the price had been. Miriam Goldberg must have written the story before the deed was filed, and no one else had ever bothered to check.

At the end of the article, the reporter noted that Solomon Weinstein had once vowed never to sell the hotel, which was the first property he had purchased on Miami Beach. A small picture accompanied the words. It showed Ernesto, smiling slightly, shaking hands with Weinstein, who was propped up in bed in an assisted-living facility in Bal Harbor. Weinstein looked cadaverous, while Ernesto more than slightly resembled a vulture.

When I got home I went through the mail. None of it was interesting. I got a beer from the refrigerator and turned on *SportsCenter* and considered my next move. As I watched the highlights of an afternoon game from Wrigley Field, I had one of those bursts of inspiration that creative people are supposed to have all the time, but that actually occur once every other year.

I could call Victor DeLuca and ask about Solomon Weinstein. I'd tell Victor that my company was getting involved in a promotion of the Art Deco Historic District and was trying to find information on Miami Beach's pioneers.

Helen burst through the front door. Her arms were filled with bags. I smelled Chinese food coming from one of them. Helen said she'd gotten takeout on her way home. She hoped I didn't mind.

I asked what was in the other bags.

"Books," she said.

"Books?"

"Pregnancy and childbirth. You wouldn't believe how much stuff is out there." She started singing "Too Much Information" as she removed a half-dozen paperbacks, all of them with basically the same title. "You know how I felt crampy before I went to New York? Turns out that the signs of early pregnancy are almost identical to premenstrual. Why doesn't anybody tell you that before you go through it?"

I asked if I had time to make a phone call.

She said I did if I kept it short. She'd have the food on plates in a couple of minutes.

I muted *SportsCenter* and called *The Herald*. The clerk answered in a barely audible voice and did not even ask who I was when I requested the business editor.

"We're going sailing on Saturday," Helen announced as she scooped rice into a bowl.

"We are?"

"Diana asked me today and I said yes. Because I felt like it."

"That's fine, dear."

Victor picked up the phone and his voice sounded flat, as if all the air had been sucked out of him. I said I knew he was probably right on deadline, but there was something I wanted to ask. I spun out my imaginary tale about Miami Beach and said there was a name that kept cropping up: Solomon Weinstein. I asked Victor if he knew anything about the guy.

He said that if he remembered correctly, Weinstein had owned many of the apartments and hotels on the beach for a long, long time. He'd started buying them shortly after World War II and hadn't gotten rid of the last one until the eighties, when his health began to fail. To be honest about it, the guy was little better than a slumlord. The area didn't turn around until he was out of the picture.

I said I was interested in talking to people who had known him. I asked if he knew when Weinstein's obituary ran.

"I think he's still alive."

"You're kidding."

"He's probably in his nineties—wherever he is—but we definitely haven't run his obit. We've got one ready."

"But you don't know where he is?"

"Haven't a clue."

Victor's voice sounded dispirited, as if he'd suddenly realized that nothing in the world had any meaning whatsoever.

Helen said the food was ready.

I asked Victor if something was wrong.

"What? Oh, I think it's—I'm sorry, Garry. I guess you haven't heard."

"Heard what?"

Something invisible began to press around my neck.

"Christ, Garry—there's no good way to say this."

I wondered why it was so hard to breathe.

"It's Sebastian Overstreet. He was in a crash late this afternoon. Only a couple of hours ago. On the turnpike."

"That's too bad. I didn't know. How—"

"He's dead."

My breath came in spurts but I also had to admit that, on a level deep within me, in a part of my character of which I am profoundly ashamed, I felt a sense of relief.

"He was in Hialeah," Victor DeLuca was saying. "He wanted to check out Ernesto's place for himself."

I said nothing.

"He called me from there but I was in a meeting. He told my secretary he'd found something interesting."

"Is that right?"

"He said he was coming straight back to the office. I still can't figure out why he was on the turnpike."

"Maybe 95 was backed up."

"Yeah. That must be it." Victor paused. There seemed to be something he needed to let out so I stayed on the line even though I could hear Helen saying that she'd appreciate it if I got off the phone before the food got cold.

"Twenty-three years old," Victor DeLuca said. "It's so goddamn unfair."

TWELVE

oconut Grove was deserted except for a few trendoids in purple hair trying to find a place where they could get waffles and a double espresso. I parked the Rover and took out a cooler that seemed to contain at least half our belongings.

Helen saw them first and waved vigorously from the foot of the pier while jumping up and down like a preteen who has just spotted her favorite rock star. She walked quickly onto the pier while I lumbered behind.

"Who are these people again?" I asked.

"I've told you, Garrett. A thousand times."

"You're always telling me how oblivious I am. Have some compassion."

The people were Helen's friend Diana, her husband Richard ("Not Rich or Rick or Dick; he hates nicknames") and their two children, Melissa and Eric. Their boat was a thirty-foot ketch called *Rudder Chaos* and they went sailing every Saturday and Sunday from early morning until nightfall.

Helen and Diana greeted each other with hugs and kisses. I then saw Helen being introduced to Richard, a man with the air of a high school athlete who has begun to let his stomach settle and expand. Two little creatures wrapped in bright orange life vests darted around the deck.

"You shouldn't have," Diana said when she saw me with the cooler.

I handed it to Richard, who took it as easily as if he were removing a plate from a cabinet. I jumped aboard, shook hands with our hosts and smiled at the children, who seemed uninterested.

"Can you untie us from the dock, Garry?"

"Sure thing, Dic—Richard."

I didn't tell him I'd never been on a boat before.

After a couple of attempts, I disengaged the rope that tied the boat's stern to the dock. Diana coiled and stowed the line with the ease of a woman who wasn't thinking about what she was doing. As the boat began to swing away, I clambered toward the bow and lunged toward the rope and somehow managed to throw it behind me before I began to slip and for a second I saw myself pitching into the water or knocking my head against the hard wooden piles but right at the edge my feet firmly gripped the deck. I righted myself and stumbled toward the stern.

"You all right?" Richard asked.

"No problem."

"He almost fell into the water, Daddy."

"It would have been cool."

Richard engaged the motor and steered us into the bay while Diana and Helen talked about people at their office. I turned to Richard and asked if he thought the Dolphins had a chance of making the playoffs. This produced a lengthy response that dwelt on the inadequacies of the tight ends, secondary and coaching staff. I half listened as I took in the green shore of Key Biscayne and the teal-colored water and the still-rising sun glinting off the glass towers downtown. I felt drowsy and peaceful and told myself that perhaps this wasn't such a bad idea after all.

"What do you think, Garry?"

"I agree with you, Dic—Richard. They've got problems."

"But they've still got some good players."

"True enough. Marino." I couldn't name anybody else on the team.

"Of course, we don't root for the Dolphins. We're not from around here."

"Nobody is."

"Are you talking about football again?" Diana asked.

Her hair was wrapped in a kerchief and her eyes were hidden behind Ray-Bans. I couldn't tell if she was pretty.

"It's my fault," I said. "I brought it up."

Eric said he liked sports. Especially soccer. Melissa mentioned that she was taking ballet lessons.

I turned to Richard and asked what brought him to Miami.

"Work."

"What do you do?"

"FBI."

"Oh." I had assumed he was in banking or finance, trying like so many other people to cash in on the El Dorado of the Western Hemisphere's increasingly unregulated boom. But when I looked at him more closely I noticed the cropped hair, ramrod posture and don't-fuck-with-me attitude so prevalent in law enforcement. "That must be interesting work."

"It is. Down here."

Eric announced that his dad put people in jail. Melissa said she was going to be in the school play.

Out in the bay, the slightest of breezes was coming in from the ocean. Diana took the tiller while Richard climbed over the cabin and stood below the mast and hoisted the sail, which fluffed out when Diana aimed the boat away from the wind. Melissa and Eric said they were hungry. Richard took the tiller while Diana told the kids to wait a minute. Helen asked if there was anything she could do.

"Do we have a destination, Richard?"

"There's a beach on Virginia Key. Hardly anybody uses it anymore. It's good for the kids. They can run around all they want."

"Why doesn't anybody use it anymore?" I envisioned toxic chemicals and abandoned syringes.

"It was a segregated beach. It's hard to reach. Used to be for niggers only."

I've spent my career in and around the media, where white people have to at least pretend to be broad-minded. Dealing with authentic middle-class Caucasians is always eye-opening.

Melissa was performing an intricate hopscotch pattern in the sand while Eric ran into the water and back out again in what seemed like continuous motion. Helen and Diana were sitting on a blanket and talking. Despite my sunblock, I felt as if my skin were being seared and blistered. Beside me, Richard reclined in a beach chair and popped open his second can of Bud.

He asked if I was sure I didn't want one.

I told him I hardly ever drank during the day.

He said drinking during the day was the whole point of sailing, then tilted his head back and chugged about half the can. He motioned toward our wives and asked what they were talking about.

I cupped my ear. Diana was saying she was so glad they had decided to do this. Richard had really wanted to meet us.

I turned to Richard and said it wasn't important and he said it was fucking amazing how women could spend hours talking about shit. He asked what my favorite sport was.

"Baseball."

"Too slow."

"I like basketball too."

He grimaced as if his beer had just gone flat. "Fucking African ballet," he said as he finished his Bud and crumpled the can in his right hand. He reached into the cooler and took out another beer. "I shouldn't have said that," he said as he popped it open. "Not PC."

"That's all right. I'm not a reporter." I grinned. "Although I used to be."

"Thank God you got over it." He took a few swigs and put his beer in the sand. "You haven't told me much about yourself."

"My life's not very interesting."

"You don't think working with Ernesto Rodriguez is interesting?"

I could have responded to this with shock or surprise or denial, but I remembered something Lisa once told me as she sat in her office in the early evening. We were drinking neat whiskey. Smoke curled up from one of her stogies.

"Never get defensive," she said. "Only losers play defense."

I picked up a stick and made a smiley face in the sand. "You know Ernesto?" I said in what I hoped was a nonchalant tone.

He laughed. It was the laugh of a man whose idea of a good joke is poking out the eyes of his neighbor's cat. "Oh, yeah. I know Ernesto."

"How?"

"I shouldn't be telling you this." He tilted his head back, drank some more beer, then said, "Ah, fuck it," as he reached into the cooler again. He asked if I was sure I didn't want one. "Ernesto has contacts. You know what I mean?"

"He knows a lot of people."

"He knows the right people. You know what I mean?"

I looked at him directly and felt as if I was raising the ante on a guy whose hand wasn't quite as good as he thought. "No, Richard, I don't know what you mean."

"Ah, fuck it," he said again as he chugged away. "Ernesto's made and lost a lot of money over the years. And so he's done business with people who aren't quite on the legitimate side of importing and export-ing. You know what I mean?"

"Drugs," I said.

Richard knocked back the rest of his Bud and threw the can toward the water. I later saw pictures of the beach at Virginia Key from the for-ties, when it was packed with people under large signs that said, "COLORED ONLY." The sand was smooth and gleaming.

"Ernesto's helped us out for a long time," Richard said. "He'll drop the word on somebody, and usually his information turns out solid."

I wondered why he was telling me this.

"So we look out for him. One hand washes the other. You know what I mean?"

"I think I do."

"There have been rumors about Ernesto over the years. You've heard about them, haven't you?"

I had, but I shook my head.

"We've never pinned anything on him. If he is involved in anything, he's far too smart to get caught. And even if something came up . . ." Richard's voice trailed off as he reached for another beer. He opened it and chugged some more. "Washington would like to keep Ernesto around."

"Why?"

"Castro's not gonna live forever. Five years after he's gone, we'll be all over the fucking island. It'll be just like the fifties, except Disney will run the casinos. And it'll be a lot easier for us if people like Ernesto are in charge of things. People we can rely on."

"That might not happen for a long time," I said. "Castro's parents lived into their nineties." I had gleaned this fact from a magazine article and it had been clinging to my brain like a barnacle. I was overjoyed it had finally proved useful.

Richard looked at me as if I'd just said I understood superstring theory. "Is that right?" he asked.

I nodded.

"Fuck," he said as he drank more Bud. "I wonder if anyone in Washington knows that."

Eric kept trying to create a mound of wet sand at the water's edge, but after a few seconds of adding to it he'd become frustrated and fling some of the gunk into the water. Melissa seemed to have grown tired and was resting her head on the lap of her mother, who continued talking with Helen.

"You're good, Garry," Richard said.

"Excuse me?"

"You don't give anything away, do you? When I mentioned Ernesto's name, ninety-nine guys out of a hundred would have asked, 'How do you know I do business with him?' They would have been a little nervous, too. Not you. Cool as a cucumber."

I erased the smiley face and started to draw geometric patterns—squares, circles, triangles and trapezoids. I reminded myself that I was sober and Richard wasn't. After a few seconds I turned to him and grinned.

"I haven't talked to Ernesto in a while. Have you?"

Richard shook his head. He said he'd gotten word that I was looking for him.

"He owes my company some money," I said. "That's the only thing I'm interested in."

An image of Magdalena, standing in a doorway, smiling slightly, letting the last of her clothes fall to the floor before extending her arm toward me.

*   *   *

As Helen climbed into bed with me, I thought I could detect the faintest trace of swelling underneath her nightgown. She turned on her night light and propped herself against the headboard and began reading a maternity magazine that was bigger than the Yellow Pages.

I drew the covers over my shoulders and around my chin to ward off the air-conditioned chill. I looked forward to the dry season, when I could breathe air that didn't come from a machine.

"Did you have fun today?" Helen asked.

"I guess."

"I liked it. That's the kind of life I want. Is that too much to ask?"

"You want me to be an FBI agent?"

"One of the reasons I married you, Garrett, is your sense of humor. But it's like my mother always said: 'Be careful what you wish for.'"

"I'll try to be less humorous in the future."

"I think we should have two kids. Maybe three. And we have to think about where we should live. The schools down here stink. So after my maternity leave, I'm gonna ask for that transfer. We could live in Long Island or Westchester and then we can . . ."

We'd live in a colonial and I'd commute every workday to a job I loathed in a railcar packed with people who despised their own jobs and on the weekends I'd use my Rover to drive my still-theoretical children to soccer practice where I'd talk on the sidelines with the other parents about the Dow and the Knicks and how much different school was when we were kids. I might even go back to church.

THIRTEEN

All I had was information from a photo caption that was more than ten years old but I didn't have any other ideas so I called the Palm Grove Healthcare Center in Bal Harbor and said I was looking for someone. I was calling on behalf of some distant family members in New York. They were planning a gathering of all their relatives and they were trying to track down everybody and the last information they had on this man was from years ago but this seemed like a place to start.

The voice on the other had said nothing since answering the phone.

I said I was looking for Solomon Weinstein. I wondered if he was still a resident or if the facility had any record of what might have happened to him.

No response. I doubted anyone had been listening to me.

I waited a few minutes. Said "hello" several times into the mouthpiece. And then a voice came on, a voice that sounded bored and blasé and most of all offended that I had asked it to do some work.

"Mr. Weinstein is no longer with us. He transferred to the Palmetto Seniors Center on August 24, 1995."

"Why did he—"

I heard a click and a hum.

Magdalena collapsed on top of me and I wrapped my arms around her. I liked the way we were entwined from our heads to our feet, as if we were joined and, for a few moments at least, there was no way to separate us.

My lover brushed her lips against my ear. *"Maravilloso."*

I had thought of telling her that Helen was pregnant.

Magdalena's face was only a few inches from mine and when she opened her eyes she seemed to see something inside me because she asked, "What's wrong?"

"Nothing."

"Don't lie to me, Garrett."

I was still inside her. I liked how it felt.

"What would you do if Frank came back?"

She turned her head and rested it against my shoulder. "I try not to think about it. When I'm with you, I try not to think about anything. Except the moment."

I ran my hands through her long straight hair and felt her chest swelling and receding against mine.

"There are so many things," I said.

It sounded like the kind of idle but breathless statement that lovers make, words that do not demand a response. But I was leading up to something.

"There are so many things I want to know about you."

She opened her eyes and looked directly into mine. Our faces were only inches apart and she shook her head slightly.

"You don't," she said.

The Palmetto Seniors Center was made of crumbling white brick overbaked by the sun. I parked in the lot and walked up litter-strewn steps and as soon as I stepped inside I was almost overpowered by the stench of human waste. The air-conditioning wasn't working and I took my breath in short quick bursts and told myself this whole thing would take only minutes.

I strode to the main desk, which was covered with old magazines and fast-food containers and coffee stains. A lone woman sat there. I guessed she was Haitian and in the country illegally.

I smashed my hand down so hard on the counter that I sent some detritus flying and in a VERY LOUD VOICE I said I was Solomon Weinstein's grandson and had just found out he was in this horrible place and I demanded to see him immediately because I wanted to make sure he was all right and if I didn't get in I was going to complain to the authorities and make damn certain this entire operation was shut down.

The woman behind the counter shook her head. In an uncertain but lilting voice she said, "What you saying, sir? What you saying?"

I leaned over the counter and spoke slowly. "My grandfather. Solomon Weinstein. I have to see him. Right now."

"I do not know," she said. "I do not know of such a man."

"Oh my God. Is he dead? Why didn't anyone tell me?"

"I do not know. I do not know anything."

"Can I see if he's here? Is there a way of checking?"

The woman reached down and lifted up a big blue book covered with dust. She put it on the counter and said: "Here. Check here. In here."

I opened pages that creaked and crackled with each turn. There was no particular order to the names—they were not listed alphabetically nor were they arranged by date of entry. Instead they'd been scrawled into any space available.

I found his name on the seventh page. He was in a room on the second floor. The entry listed his birthdate and Social Security number and how much a month he was paying. Almost all the money came from Medicare. The listing noted the day he'd been admitted.

I passed by open rooms that contained dazed-looking survivors staring at televisions turned on full blast. A few solitary people with walkers clogged the hall. "Can you help me?" one of them asked. "Sir? Can you help me?"

I opened the door to the stairwell and the smell of piss and shit was almost unbearable and I tried not to breathe and tried not to puke as I raced up the steps. In a corner I saw a shriveled form and wondered if it was alive or dead.

Only a few of the second-floor rooms had numbers. But I thought I had the sequence figured out and finally stopped in the doorway of what I believed was the right one. The television was on to *Judge Judy*, and she was berating a guy for not repaying a five-hundred-dollar debt.

I looked at the shrunken figure on the bed. The only sign of life came from the labored breaths that caused his chest to rise and fall every few seconds.

"Mr. Weinstein!"

I was shouting over the TV.

"Mr. Weinstein!"

I wondered if he could hear me or if he could hear anything or was even capable of being aware anymore.

"Can you hear me? Mr. Weinstein!"

His eyes flickered. I imagined they'd once burned with intelligence.

I pointed at the TV and asked if it was all right to turn down the sound.

No movement from him at all. I lowered the volume until it was a loud hum.

I did not close the door. I stepped close to the bed so no one could see me from the hall.

I said I was sorry to bother him but there were some questions I wanted to ask. I identified myself and said I was working with Ernesto Rodriguez.

He tried to raise his hand, as if he needed to shoo away a fly.

"Go away."

I don't believe in ghosts or mediums and there are times when I question the existence of an afterlife, but if I ever heard anything coming from the other side, it was the voice of Solomon Weinstein.

I said I wanted to ask him about Ernesto.

Weinstein shook his head. The effort seemed to require all his energy.

I asked him why he had sold the Orlando after vowing to hold on to it, no matter what.

Solomon Weinstein opened his mouth slightly and gasped for air. I wondered what deep-seated force kept him alive and decided it was the fear of what might be waiting for him.

"I'm not going to leave, Mr. Weinstein. I'm not going to leave until you tell me what I want to know."

He closed his eyes.

"What did he offer you? Why did you sell it to him?"

"Cash."

At first I wasn't sure if Weinstein had said anything or if the word I thought I had heard was merely part of his wheezing. I brought my head even closer to his and decided it would be best if I lowered my voice as much as possible.

"Ernesto paid cash for the hotel?"

Weinstein nodded, almost imperceptibly.

"It was one hundred thousand dollars. How did he get that kind of cash?"

"How do you think?"

"Drugs?"

Weinstein said nothing.

"Why did you take it?" I asked. "Why did you take drug money?"

"I needed it. Cash."

I did not have to ask where the money had gone: Solomon Weinstein needed round-the-clock care and a pharmacy full of medicines and he could stay at a top-flight institution for a long time if he paid it under the table.

He had not figured on living this long. He had not anticipated ending his life in a place like this.

"Thank you, Mr. Weinstein. I know this was hard for you."

I drew my head away from his and was about to return the TV to its top-volume setting when I felt a grip of bony fingers on my wrist and almost jumped in fright. Solomon Weinstein lifted his head an inch from the pillow and his eyes flashed and for a moment I saw the fierceness and steel that must have made him formidable.

"Take me with you."

I almost shouted "No!" but instead I shook my wrist as vigorously as

I could. His hand broke away and his head fell back. As I passed the TV I put the sound back to full. Judge Judy told a guy whose shirttail was hanging out that he had to get his life together.

When I stepped out of the room I almost walked right into a heavyset Latino in a white smock. Aside from the woman at the desk, this was the first indication that the Palmetto Seniors Center had any staff members.

"*Quién?*" he asked.

I understood the question. On a deeper level, I understood the menacing tone in which it was asked.

"I'm his grandson," I said.

He pointed toward Weinstein's room.

"*No familia.*"

I stood straighter and looked the man directly in the eyes and raised my voice and said, "I am his family. I just found out he's here and I can't believe how filthy and slipshod everything is." I pointed my index finger at him and said, "I'm coming back in a few days and I expect everything to be cleaned up or I'm reporting this shithole to the authorities. Don't pretend you don't understand."

I started to walk out but expected him to stop me. I listened for heavy footsteps and wondered if I'd be able to run in my four-hundred-dollar Kenneth Cole shoes and feared slipping on a pool of urine or a mound of excrement. I entered the stairwell and held my breath and walked down to the ground floor and past the desk and out into damp heavy air that was laced with auto exhaust.

Winston Copley grunted as I told him that Josette had an actor friend who'd agreed to serve as our spokesman during the strip-mall rally and any subsequent media appearances.

"Just wait until the kickoff," I said. "It'll all be worth it."

"That's something we wanted to discuss."

I did not like what I heard in his voice. It sounded like the type of pent-up anger you acquire when you haven't talked for a long time to someone who's harming you.

"We're not sure we want to attend."

"You have to attend."

"We're not sure we want to."

Wanting has nothing to do with it. This is your company and I'm doing my best to make it a success even if you don't give a shit and Josette and I have worked our asses off, so you two fat fucks are gonna show up.

"You and Evan own the company," I said in what I hoped was a tone of mild reproach. "You have to be there. You don't have to say anything."

"Then why bother? You and Josette have everything well in hand."

I remembered Lisa sucking on a cigar stub and knocking down another whiskey. She leaned forward and pointed the stogie at my face. "Sometimes," she said, "you might have to tell them the truth."

So I said this to Winston Copley: "It'll look awfully strange if you're absent."

"It'll be awfully strange anyway."

"That's not the point." My tone was becoming sharper and part of me said I should control it but another part said my outburst was justified. "The point is that you and Evan own the company. The point is that we'll have lots of media there. The point is that they'll want to know who the bosses are. You can refer all the questions to me or Josette or the actor. But you have to be there. Both of you. That's not negotiable."

Winston Copley could have hung up on me, or threatened to take his business elsewhere, or reminded me that he was the client and I was merely a hired gun. But I have discovered one overriding rule of life; it was unpleasant to learn and it's uncomfortable to impart, but I speak with the conviction of a longtime disbeliever who has reluctantly embraced faith.

When you yell at people, they do what you tell them.

Salazar smiled and stood as we approached. He clasped both of Helen's hands and raised her right one to his lips. My wife blushed.

"Please, Jorge, you don't have to."

"I insist. An old-fashioned custom, but one I enjoy."

He turned to me and we engaged in macho bone-crunching before settling in the booth, which was semicircular. Helen sat in the middle. The place was an Argentinian steakhouse furnished in a deep, smoky wood that already seemed fifty years old. The decor made me think of juntas and fugitive Nazis and Madonna singing badly. Salazar said the wine list was excellent. Helen said she wouldn't be drinking.

"Is there anything you would like?" Salazar asked me.

"Whatever you prefer."

In that case, he said, the restaurant had a Chilean merlot he especially enjoyed. He had recommended the wine to the steward himself.

"It's so neat you know that," Helen said. I looked at her more sharply than I intended. "Neat" was not a word my wife usually employed. It made her sound like a cheerleader. "I'm an idiot about wine. I feel I should know more."

"You're an intelligent woman," Salazar said. "I'm sure I could teach you a few things in very little time. It's not—what is the term you Americans use?—rocket science."

He smiled again. Helen returned it. I drummed my fingers on the table.

Salazar went on: "But you said you didn't want any. Are you sure?"

He stared directly into her eyes. Finally Helen looked away.

"I shouldn't. I mean, I don't want to. But thank you for asking. It's nice to be asked."

They talked about Brazil. The *real* had just been devalued and the political situation seemed to be stabilizing but there was still a great deal of uncertainty that was nonetheless mingled with opportunity.

"That's why I called you today," Salazar said to my wife. "I thought if you and I could meet privately, we could resolve some issues. I don't know what you discussed in New York, but the government's decision— it changes everything."

"Only some things, Jorge."

"The container port. Surely you'll agree it's more viable now."

"Marginally. I'll be honest with you: New York isn't crazy about it. Although nobody has made a final decision."

"Our goods will be much cheaper to produce. We have plans—you've seen them." Salazar leaned into the table and looked at me for the first time since we sat down, literally going around Helen, trying to appeal to me *mano-a-mano* and, without really saying it, conveying the message of *Can't you talk some sense to your wife?* "You should see the plans, Mr. Doherty. Beautiful things. Works of art. The largest container port in South America. Its location provides access to the interior. Surrounding the port itself are dozens of factories. Transportation costs will be negligible. Thousands of people will be employed while billions of dollars come into our country. We will make quality goods, inexpensively, that the rest of the world is waiting to buy."

Before I could respond, Helen said, "I've told you before, Jorge—the problem with emerging markets is that sometimes they never emerge."

I grinned and looked straight at Salazar while I took the first sip of the wine. It was excellent and tasted familiar. I decided to say nothing about it.

"I'm just a public-relations man. You guys are out of my league."

I felt Helen's hand slip under the table and squeeze mine.

"No, Mr. Doherty, you do the hardest thing of all." Salazar paused while he sipped the merlot. "You try to capture the public's attention."

I mumbled a few words about it not being so difficult once you figured out a few things.

"Do you like the wine?" he asked.

"It's not bad."

I suddenly realized it was the same merlot Ernesto Rodriguez had ordered the night I met Magdalena.

We settled into neutral areas of conversation, such as films and music and Americans' inability to enjoy soccer. ("Too much violence in the stands," I said, "and not enough in the game.")

After the waitstaff removed our appetizers, Salazar asked—in an idle, how-do-you-like-the-weather tone—if I'd heard from Ernesto lately.

Is he interrogating me? Or is he just making conversation?

"I haven't," I said before flashing my grin. "Have you?"

"He owes you money," Salazar said.

I told him the bean counters in New York were adamant about getting what Ernesto owed us.

"Don't you think it's strange?" Salazar said. "A man as important as Ernesto Rodriguez disappears, and nobody seems to care."

I began to wonder if it was me, and not Helen, that Salazar really wanted to talk to. Then I wondered why he hadn't just called me directly until I realized that an innocuous business dinner with Helen—her husband tagging along, strictly for decoration—was the perfect cover.

"The last I heard about Ernesto, he was heading to a foreign airlines counter at Fort Lauderdale Airport."

"I talked to him today," Salazar said.

I almost let my wineglass slip through my fingers.

"How is he?" I asked.

"He's in excellent health," Salazar said. "He sends his best wishes—to both of you."

Solicitous, I thought. *Ernesto was solicitous.*

"Where is he?" I asked.

"I did not ask. I would guess he's in South America, by the sound of the connection."

"What's he doing there?"

"Raising money. I think Tierra Grande has turned out to be a bit more complicated than he envisioned. He's still optimistic, though. He looks forward to doing great work with you."

Salazar lifted his glass toward me.

"Will Ernesto raise the money?" I asked.

Salazar shrugged.

"How is he raising it?"

Salazar shrugged again.

I swirled the wine around in my glass and decided to throw out a line. I hoped it sounded like chitchat. There were things I had to know that no one wanted to tell me.

"You did business with Ernesto." It was a half-statement, half question, as if I were trying to recall the name of a band that had recorded a
couple of hits twenty years ago.

"A little," Salazar said. "We were competitors too."

"Was this in California?"

Salazar raised his eyebrows, as if I'd just nailed the answer to a seemingly impossible trivia question. "If he talked about California, Ernesto
must have taken you into his confidence."

"He didn't say much. But word gets around. No matter what you
intend."

*An image of Magdalena beside me, our bellies touching as I ran my hand
over her hips and down her thigh. My lover saying she wished it could always
be like this.*

"I asked Ernesto what he did in California." The wine was making
me bolder. "And he told me he fought Communists."

The waitstaff slid our plates in front of us.

"You sound skeptical," Salazar said.

"Perhaps I am."

"You must remember that Ernesto has been fighting Communists
for a long, long time. Since before you were born."

"I'm not sure how you fight Communists from California."

"You use it as a base, Mr. Doherty." He mispronounced my name
and I thought it was deliberate.

"And where do you go? From your base?"

"Wherever you have to."

I started to eat my steak. I'd ordered it medium rare and the kitchen
had undercooked it a bit, so the bloodred juice spread over the plate as I
cut.

"You said you were competitors. So what did you do, Jorge—help
the Communists?" I grinned, but didn't mean it.

"Even in noble work, Mr. Doherty, there's only so much business to
go around." Salazar smiled, as if he were remembering a particularly
trying time that he was glad to have survived. "I used to see Ernesto in
the strangest places: Panama, Guatemala, El Salvador. He always

seemed to have one more contact than I did. Once I was in the Caribbean. On a vacation, of all things. My first one in years. And guess who was staying at the resort as well?"

I smiled mirthlessly and sipped my wine and said nothing.

"He was with a woman. Not Luisa. She was young and very beautiful."

The wine began to taste sour in my mouth.

"She had dark skin and long straight hair."

I realized that Ernesto had told him to say these things to me and I wanted to scream *stopit stopit stopit*.

"Luminous eyes."

I felt my heart rising into my throat and I knew, just knew, that my dinner companions were aware of what I was thinking and what I had done and were ready to pass judgment on me.

"In fact, Mr. Doherty, she was as beautiful as your wife."

I turned my head and looked directly past Helen and into Salazar's eyes, which I was convinced were mocking me. Somehow I managed to grin.

"Nobody is as beautiful as my wife, Jorge."

An image of Magdalena, a smile dancing across her lips as she rested her head on the pillow and spread her legs wide.

I lay in bed hoping sleep would overtake me before Helen finished her ablutions. But my brain was racing. I told myself I should stop wanting a woman who delighted in keeping secrets from me. I was a married man with a pregnant wife and I should concentrate on my commitments—even embrace them—and let everything else fade away.

I imagined myself on a psychiatrist's couch. The shrink was one of the few Freudians left. He would not allow eye contact as he lectured me in the heavy Teutonic accent of *Mitteleuropa*. He would review my situation: I was a white, college-educated, upper middle-class male professional in his early thirties with a three-bedroom house and an SUV and enough credit cards to finance a small war. I was married to a woman of similar station. She was smart and funny and attractive and I had no doubt that she loved me. This woman was carrying my child and, if I had any decency at all, I should have felt overwhelming gratitude.

Despite all my advantages, I was engaged in conduct that was foolhardy. Perhaps even reckless. The doctor would ponder this for a moment: Did I have a poor self-image? Perhaps I secretly wanted to be caught. Part of me lusted after the forbidden fruit but an even bigger portion craved punishment for my sins, both real and theoretical. It was all related to my Catholic upbringing and those twelve years with the Presentation Sisters and Christian Brothers. My sense of guilt, the psychiatrist would tell me, was overwhelming.

Perhaps I would dispute this. Guilt was a Jewish phenomenon. Catholic school survivors usually had overpowering sensations of dread.

More than likely I'd just grin, even though he couldn't see me.

Ya got me, Doc.

He would call attention to my lover, the mystery woman with the shady past. She was married to a man who seemed capable of violence. She had longtime links to another man, a client of mine, who had been and perhaps still was involved in illicit activities.

Solicitous, I would think. *Ernesto was solicitous.*

The psychiatrist would say he was going to ask me a question. It seemed simple, but he wanted me to think carefully before answering. He would ask if I was capable of careful thought.

I believe so.

"Why are you doing this?" he would say. "Why are you doing this to yourself and your wife?"

I would wait a few seconds before replying. Finally I'd grin again.

I'll be honest with ya, Doc—I don't know why I do a goddamn thing.

Of course this would be dishonest. People who demand the truth are the least likely to get it. There is a phrase I have heard over the years; I believe it originated with the French. They are a group of people for whom I have little use, but the words have lingered in my mind:

The heart has its reasons, which reason knows nothing of.

As I lay in bed, I tried to summon the feelings I had whenever Magdalena ran her hands down my back. I thought of the way my lover's eyes burned when she was angry and how her hair always smelled faintly of apples and of how much I wanted to be with her. All my life I have grown tired of the people I know—friends and colleagues, teachers and parents. But I never grew tired of her.

The door to the bathroom opened. Helen walked toward me as she rubbed lotion over her hands.

"Are you asleep, Garry?"

"Not yet."

"I've been thinking. It's never too early to start talking about names."

FOURTEEN

Solomon Weinstein's obituary was stripped across the top of *The Herald*'s metro section.

It said he had died of natural causes at the age of ninety-four at the Palmetto Seniors Center. There were no survivors.

Magdalena wrapped her arms around my back as we finished. After a minute or two of nothing but breathing, she asked what I was thinking.

"That I'd like to go away."

Magdalena said a long weekend in the Bahamas or Key West would be nice. We could get away from everything and just be together and for a few days at least nothing would matter.

"I was thinking I'd like to go away permanently. With you."

My winning-the-lottery fantasy had evolved this way: I'd buy a boat, at least a sixty-footer, and drive Magdalena down to the dock without telling her where we were going or why. I'd take her hand and walk her out to the boat, gleaming white and named *Te Quiero*. She'd ask me what I was doing and I'd tell her to get on board. The boat was mine. I meant ours. I'd stretch my arm and she'd grab it and jump on board and I'd cut the line to the dock and we'd go out into the ocean and leave everything behind forever.

Magdalena propped herself up and lit one of her slim cigars. "You say that now. How will you feel later?"

"I don't know. I suppose it depends on—" I stopped myself. I was about to say *how much I trust you.*

"Depends on what?"

She blew some smoke and watched it rise toward the air-conditioning vent. I said nothing for a few moments, then asked if she knew a man named Jorge Salazar. She leaned her head back and seemed to be trying to recall a fact she'd once had to learn, but regarded as unimportant.

"I think so," she said. "He's from Brazil."

"I had dinner with him. He mentioned a time when he was in the Caribbean. Years ago. He crossed paths with Ernesto. Who was with a woman. Much younger. Not his wife."

Magdalena stubbed out her cigar and got out of bed and walked toward the bathroom. She began to run the water and I had the feeling that she was trying to wash away all the men she had ever known.

"I remember him now," she said. "He reminded me of a ferret. And the way he ogled me." She walked back toward the bed. She was wiping her hands furiously with a small towel. "I remember that vacation. If you want to call it that. I was with Frank. He spent most of it in our hotel room. Sick to his stomach. It was something in the water." She threw the towel in my face and I was surprised by how much force she put into it; the towel was wet and heavy and it stung when it struck me. "Everybody thinks Ernesto and I were lovers. Even you."

Solicitous, I thought. *Ernesto was solicitous.*

Magdalena put on her slip and began attaching her earrings.

"There are things in the past, Garrett. Things in the past that are best left there."

"What did you do back then? With Frank and Ernesto?"

"I was young. Let's leave it at that."

"I was young once, too. I'm not running away from anything."

"Did you ever do anything you regret?"

"No."

"You're lying."

*   *   *

I sat in the Rover after work. I didn't feel like driving home so I just stayed there and thought about what Magdalena had said. I didn't even turn on the radio and I remembered the day Lisa told me to see her after I'd wrapped up everything. The invitation was unusual. I often stopped by informally on my way out to hear the latest gossip or just listen to the way she talked. Sometimes I'd stay for an hour or more. I always loved to hear Lisa talk.

I was up for a promotion and Lisa had told me I was a shoo-in and I guessed she was going to tell me that the job was mine and offer me one of her Cuban cigars and perhaps even open a bottle of champagne.

The door to her office was open but I rapped on it anyway. She told me to come in. She wore dark trousers, as she always did, and her feet were propped on her desk. The early evening sun was shining directly through her window and a stogie dangled between her fingers and a tumbler of neat whiskey was perched on the desk within easy reach.

"You wanted to see me?"

Lisa told me to have a seat and asked if I wanted a drink. I said it sounded like a good idea. She swung her feet down and reached into her bottom drawer and took out a bottle of Seagram's and a big glass that she filled almost all the way.

"What the hell is this?" I asked as she pushed it toward me.

She told me to drink up. I thought this might be a management initiation rite so I knocked back my head and took a big gulp. The whiskey smelled warm in my nostrils and burned all the way down to my stomach. It did not taste good but I liked the way my head started to buzz.

"I've got something to tell you," Lisa said.

"Go ahead."

I snapped my head back and took another gulp. I was enjoying what the alcohol was doing.

"You didn't get the job."

"What?"

The word echoed around the room.

"You didn't get it. Cooperman's gonna tell you tomorrow but I thought it was better if you heard it from me. Now. This way you won't make an ass of yourself when you get the bad news." She paused before adding, "I'm sorry, Garry."

"You said it was mine."

"I was wrong."

"Fuck." I slammed the drink down and started to stalk around the room. The job came with its own office and paid twenty thousand a year more. I'd mentally spent the money on new electronics and a Hawaiian vacation.

"You're taking this like a man," Lisa said. "Badly."

"Who got the job?"

"That's not important."

"It is to me."

"Joe Winthrop."

"Christ, I'm better than he is."

I was bellowing like a mortally wounded animal.

"I agree. But my opinion didn't carry the day. At the last minute, Ogilvie pushed hard for Winthrop. I wasn't expecting that. Shit, I hate being outmaneuvered by that sonuvabitch."

"Winthrop got it because he's black."

"That's not the reason, Garry."

"If they wanted to make a goddamn affirmative-action hire, they should have just said so."

"That's not the reason."

"I wouldn't have applied for the job and I wouldn't have wasted my time and—"

"Goddamnit, Garry, will you shut up and listen to me?"

With the exception of taking the Lord's name in vain, those were exactly the words and tone the nuns used to employ when I failed to grasp an obvious precept of proper conduct.

"What do you know about Joe?" Lisa asked.

"Nice guy. Went to Rutgers. Does a decent job—don't get me wrong, I like Joe."

"So do I. Keep going."

"I don't know what else to say. It's not like we hang out together."

"Why don't you hang out together?"

"He always has a train to catch. Back to Westchester or Long Island or wherever the fuck he lives."

"It's New Jersey. In a house. With a mortgage. And a wife and kids. Although the mortgage is what's most important."

"What are you getting at?"

"Christ, Garrett, you're usually not this stupid."

I did not respond.

"He's a family man. Tied down. Joe Winthrop isn't going anywhere. He's got a three-bedroom colonial in Montclair and two kids to put through college. You're Mr. East Village Man About Town with a different girlfriend every week. You might be gone in a year."

"I'm not planning to go anywhere."

"I'm sure you mean that. But things happen."

"Maybe I should look around. This company obviously doesn't value my work."

"Get off it, will you? The same thing's gonna happen wherever you go. Corporate America likes its men married and its women gay."

I looked at my glass. I must have kept knocking the stuff back because the whiskey was almost gone, although I was so worked up I felt no effect anymore except for a flush in my cheeks.

"So what should I do? Get married?"

"If you're serious about working here—or anywhere else in this business—the answer is yes."

"Great. Fucking great."

"The world's not fair, Garry. Better you find it out while you're still a young man. Want a refill?"

The next day, with my head feeling as if it had been worked over by a couple of loan sharks, Scott Cooperman called me into his office and told me the news I was now expecting. I said that while I was disappointed in being passed over, I thought Joe Winthrop was an excellent choice and I'd do everything I could to make him a success in his new position. That weekend, I proposed to Helen. She was surprised. Almost taken aback. She said she had no idea I felt this way and she was flattered and didn't know how to reply. I said the whole thing had come to me suddenly; in a flash of insight almost biblical in its nature, I realized I wanted to marry her.

And then I grinned.

My boss asked if I wanted some coffee and looked surprised when I declined. He said he was already on his third cup.

"What's up?" I asked.

"The stock market," he said. He started to laugh and I did too. He put his feet on his desk and looked at the ceiling and laced his fingers behind his neck. "That's what I should've done."

"Excuse me?"

"The market. I should've hooked up with Merrill Lynch. Dean Witter. One of those guys."

"Goldman Sachs."

"Too many Jews."

I didn't know what to say. Blunt expressions of prejudice always surprise me. I keep thinking that we—the allegedly educated people who work in offices and wear expensive clothes and live in nice houses in upscale neighborhoods—are beyond all that. But we're not. Not when we're behind closed doors and among ourselves.

"I'd be on Easy Street," my boss was saying. "Living the life of Riley. Bonuses and stock options out the ying-yang. Instead I did this. Shit."

I asked him what was wrong.

He put his feet back on the floor and pushed a piece of paper toward me. "I got this e-mail at home last night. At home. The bastards can't leave me alone."

I looked over the message. It was from the chief financial officer and it demanded an immediate accounting of the thirty thousand dollars that Ernesto Rodriguez owed our company. The time to settle this matter had long since passed.

"They're busting my balls. Just busting my balls. If they want to fire me, they should lower the boom already. Just stop busting my balls."

"We could try to smoke him out."

My boss looked at me strangely, as if he was startled I was still in the room.

"We could file a missing-person report," I said. "Then leak word to *The Herald*. If this becomes public, it might force Ernesto to come back. If only to declare that he's still around and it was all a misunderstanding and nothing's wrong."

My boss nodded, as if he liked what I was saying. But then he started shaking his head.

"There's a problem, Garry."

"Okay."

"A big problem. Very big. Fucking huge."

"All right."

"If word gets around that Ernesto hired us, but then we turned on him when something came up . . . something he wanted to keep confidential . . ."

"I'll give it to them off the record."

"Ernesto has ways. He'll find out."

"Can't we just eat the money?"

"New York won't allow it."

I told my boss I'd redouble my efforts to find Ernesto Rodriguez.

An image of Magdalena, gently guiding me into her. Then telling me to go faster. Saying she wanted it to be like this always and would go with me wherever I wanted.

"I just had a brainstorm," my boss said.

"I'm all ears." I wondered if using cliches was contagious.

"How's that thing you're doing with the Copleys? 'Strip Malls Are Wonderful,' or whatever the fuck it is?"

"It's going all right."

"When will you be ready?"

"About a week." It was a guess.

"The sooner the better. We need a success. Something to divert New York's attention."

I was surfing the Net and looking for something—anything—about Ernesto Rodriguez, a nugget of information that might tell me where he was, when my office door crashed open. I reacted with a start, the way you do when a dream is interrupted.

Isabel stood in the frame.

"I told you I didn't want to be disturbed."

"There's a lady on the phone for you."

"Who?"

"She wouldn't give her name. She says it's *muy importante.*"

My secretary walked away. Under her breath, I heard her cursing in Spanish because she had chipped a nail.

I picked up the phone and identified myself as warmly as I could. I was about to say that I wished she was with me this moment so she could sit on my lap while I lowered my pants and let my hands run under her dress so I could feel her warm soft skin.

"Mr. Doherty?" The words had a professional tone.

"Yes?"

"This is Officer Hurtado."

"Of course. How are you?"

"About that man we've been discussing. Are you still interested?"

"Very much so."

"There are some things I'd like to tell you. Could we meet somewhere?"

Police Officer Pilar Hurtado sat by herself in the Starbucks a block from my office. She had removed her hat, which took up almost the entire area of the small table she had chosen. The crowd of goateed *artistes* and double-breasted businessmen walked more widely around her than was necessary.

I sat opposite her and grinned and said I was glad to see her again.

"That man we've discussed. I've asked some questions about him."

Her voice was so low I could barely hear her over the Spanglish in the background and the Mozart on the sound system. She kept looking around, as if she expected to see somebody she was trying to avoid.

"I believe that man is not what he purports to be."

She lowered her head. Our lips were almost touching and someone observing us might have thought I had this kinky thing about female cops in uniform.

"I believe he is running drugs into this country."

I tried to pretend I was surprised, and said, "I don't think Ernesto would get mixed up in something that could send him to jail."

Tell me what you know, I thought. *Or at least what you suspect.*

Police Officer Pilar Hurtado shook her head vigorously, as if I was obstinately refusing to acknowledge an obvious truth.

"He is protected," she said. "At the highest levels. I believe it has gone on for a long time."

I realized it was likely that Ernesto had been laundering drug money through his real estate company, which would explain why he was so adamant about not discussing the financing of Tierra Grande. The project needed more funds than he'd anticipated, and now he was trying to raise them the best way he knew.

I asked if she had any idea of Ernesto's whereabouts. Pilar Hurtado shook her head. She said it seemed as if he had been swallowed up by the earth and I had an epiphany:

He's in the Everglades. He has a place where he hides and he's not coming out until he wants to, or until events force him.

I asked if she had any theories about why he had vanished. She said the more she looked into his life, the more she had the sense that his past was catching up with him.

I needed to talk to him. But my questions would not be concerned about his actions or motivation. I wanted to ask him about Magdalena and what she had been like and what they had done together and whether there was a chance that she really loved me.

Solicitous, I kept thinking. *Ernesto was solicitous.*

I tried to pick up my drink. My head felt jangly with the dull throb of too much caffeine and my hand shook as I wrapped it around the cup and I told myself not to have any more; I was tense and wired and it wasn't even noon.

"There's a man I think you should talk to," Pilar Hurtado said.

"Who?"

"His name is Duncan McNabb. He's in the federal prison in Atlanta. Maximum security."

"Why should I talk to him?"

"Do a Nexis search. He was in the papers about ten years ago."

"What will he tell me?"

"I'm not sure exactly. I haven't spoken to him. It would create suspicion. People are already wondering why I'm asking about the individual in question."

"How do I get in to see this McNabb guy?"

"Make something up. You're good at that."

Rain crashed against the window as Magdalena wrapped her mouth around me. I closed my eyes and told her to take it slowly.

I liked listening to the storm outside. I liked hearing the violence while knowing I was safe. I liked what she was doing and wanted to make it last.

When we were done she laid her head against my chest.

"I've thought about what you said. The last time." Her words were so soft I could barely hear them. "About going away."

I nodded and let her hair slide between my fingers.

"We could do it."

Thunder crashed just outside the room and I felt her jump a bit so I put my hand on her shoulder. Her skin felt warm and goose-bumpy, as if she was somehow comfortable and frightened at the same time.

"We'd need new identities but I know how to arrange them. We could go to Costa Rica. It's beautiful."

I kissed her lightly and ran my hand along the curve of her hip.

"You don't want to go back to Mexico, huh?"

She shook her head.

"You must have been poor."

"My father was a businessman. I was bored."

"Frank and then Ernesto—they took you away from all that?"

"*Sí*. At the time, it's what I thought I wanted."

"And what do you want now?"

"To start over."

She rolled her head so she was looking directly in my eyes and I sensed that she knew the power she possessed.

"We have a chance," she said. "But it won't last long. Do you want to do it? Do you want to go with me?"

My heart tried to burst through my chest and I tried to say something, but nothing would come out of my throat. It's one thing to idly consider a possibility, and entirely another when it suddenly threatens to become reality.

All I could do was nod.

When I got back to the office I did a Nexis search and came up with 512 matches for Duncan McNabb. Most of the items were from the late eighties and early nineties and came out of Southern California. McNabb was known as Drive-by Duncan and he had ended up being sentenced to a gazillion years in prison on an assortment of federal drug charges. According to the federal government, Drive-by Duncan McNabb had been one of the first and largest crack dealers in the United States. He had used his connections with West Coast gangs to distribute the drug along the Pacific before spreading it throughout much of the country. Several officials with the Justice Department said that Duncan McNabb had caused more destruction than any criminal they'd ever encountered.

McNabb did not deny the charges. At his trial he claimed the government approved of what he'd been doing because of his chief business partner, a Cuban who used his profits for anti-Communist activities.

The judge cut off Drive-by Duncan and ruled him out of order. The defendant McNabb had presented no evidence to back up these assertions. Besides, they were irrelevant to the charges.

Drive-by Duncan said he wasn't good with the fancy words the judge was using. He was just speaking the truth.

After his conviction, McNabb's case became mired in the appeals process. His motions—for a new trial, for his immediate release, for a reduction in his sentence—were routinely denied. After a few years he wound up working in the prison library in Lompoc, and the stories about him became perfunctory.

In the mid-nineties a left-wing magazine named *Barricades* ran a lengthy story that it called "The Curious Case of Duncan McNabb." In the overwrought, first-person style so common among polemical rags, the reporter took up McNabb's cause (while noting that he had been, when you got down to it, nothing but an entrepreneur) and embraced everything the convicted crack dealer had said—without, as far as I could tell, offering much in the way of corroboration.

Far down in the story, the reporter worked her prose into a state of indignation. "The question the authorities never seemed to bother to ask was this: Where did Duncan McNabb—an admitted drug dealer, but one who was strictly small-time—get the funding to finance the largest drug-selling network in the history of the United States? It seems ludicrous to believe he came up with all of it himself—or sprouted fully formed from the head of Zeus, ready to spread crack throughout the western half of the continent—but that is what the government asserts."

I found myself nodding. The reporter, whose name was Gretchen Montgomery, had asked a question that seemed beyond the grasp of the media types who had covered McNabb's trial—a question, in fact, that had not been raised by the man's attorneys.

In the last paragraph, Gretchen Montgomery roused herself into a final bit of righteousness: "Perhaps now the time has come for people concerned about justice to take seriously the claims made by Duncan McNabb. Perhaps someone will look for the man he worked with—a middle-aged Cuban from Miami, an allegedly distinguished gentleman with a dark mustache and a thick head of hair turning to gray."

I had to go on. It was like reading a diary that revealed the most depraved thoughts of someone you respected.

"Perhaps they will search for this man's accomplice, a younger Anglo—a thin man with a hawklike nose who spoke infrequently, but with the unmistakable twang of Texas."

I wanted the story to stop. But it continued.

"Perhaps they will look for the beautiful young Latina who accompanied them. If nothing else, *that* ought to interest the men who are supposed to investigate crimes in this country."

It was well after six and I knew I should leave but I stayed rooted to where I was. A subsequent article in *Barricades*, also by Gretchen Montgomery, noted in ever more purple prose that shortly after her first story appeared, Duncan McNabb was transferred from Lompoc to the maximum security federal prison in Atlanta, where he was kept in solitary confinement twenty-three hours a day.

The authorities alleged he'd been planning to escape. They said he was still a very dangerous man.

Gretchen Montgomery said this was bullshit. He'd been sent across the country as punishment for speaking out. From the day he entered the system, Duncan McNabb had been a model inmate. He'd even founded a prison ministry.

I should have gone home to my wife. My pregnant wife. But I was entrapped by the awful thrill of discovery.

I figured it would be easy to find Gretchen Montgomery. A few clicks of the mouse and I'd learn where she was working and then reach for the phone. I started running through stories she had written, almost all for left-leaning publications in Seattle and the Bay Area. She seemed intent on exposing corporate greed and the government's complicity in it and I remembered why I had gone into journalism: I once thought that people wanted to make the world a better place and would be roused into action if only the truth were revealed.

In a way, I admired Gretchen Montgomery, although I wondered how she would handle her inevitable disillusionment.

She never reached that point.

On April 23, 1997, a story in *The San Francisco Examiner* said that a freelance journalist who had written a number of controversial articles had been found dead in her apartment in the Tenderloin District. The police said it was an apparent robbery. The place had been ransacked and there was no telling how much had been taken, although her friends said she didn't have much worth stealing. She'd been bound and gagged to a chair in her living room and her throat was slashed and there were burns over much of her body that looked as if they'd been caused by heavy, hand-rolled cigarettes.

I got up and walked to the watercooler and gulped down several small cups. Then I resumed surfing for information about Drive-by Duncan. His attorneys had continued filing appeals but they became more desultory, his bids for freedom now filled more with rote than passion. The last motion was languishing in a low-level federal court. It asked for Duncan McNabb's immediate release from incarceration. He was a stellar inmate with no blemishes on his record and he was a leader in the prison's Bible study program now that he was no longer confined to his cell twenty-three hours a day.

Duncan McNabb's attorney was listed as Kendall Poltrane, of Poltrane Wilkes and Johnson, a firm in Atlanta.

I got the number from Atlanta Information. I wasn't surprised when I called the office and got a recording. I told myself I'd have to try again in the morning. But the last menu option was "pound zero" to talk to a live person, and I hit it in the thought that someone might still be there.

Somebody was. From the tired sound of her voice, I guessed it was a girl who was balancing two part-time jobs and a full course load at a local college. I said I was looking for Kendall Poltrane and wondered if he might be around. She told me to hang on for a minute.

"This is Kendall Poltrane."

It was a sonorous voice, basso profundo, and I imagined it belonged to a tall and distinguished-looking middle-aged black man, a church-going pillar of his community who sat in front at services every Sunday and sang loudly in praise of the Lord. I also wondered how he justified having clients like the largest crack dealer in American history, but our contradictions are what make us interesting.

I identified myself and said I was interested in one of his clients: Duncan McNabb.

"We're expecting a decision from the appellate court," Kendall Poltrane said. "Why don't you call back in a few days?"

Because I don't have a few days.

"How do you think it'll go?" I asked in the breezy manner of a casual fan assessing the Braves' chances of making it back to the World Series.

"One never knows," Kendall Poltrane said. "That's why you have appeals."

"Your client has been appealing ever since he was sentenced," I said. "That's ten years now. He hasn't done too well."

There was a long pause and at first I thought Kendall Poltrane had hung up the phone, dismissing this call from some smart-alecky white man as nothing more than a prank.

"Why are you interested in Mr. McNabb?" the lawyer asked at last.

I'd been expecting this question. I'd even jotted down some notes to help me explain why I was doing this. I told Kendall Poltrane in guarded tones that I represented some people who were interested in publicizing the most egregious cases of injustice being perpetrated in the United States.

I almost heard Kendall Poltrane nodding. I pictured him as a man with a massive head that he moved only when it was absolutely necessary.

"Yes," he said. "The war on drugs has produced a lot of collateral damage."

I told him that the people I worked for had come across Duncan McNabb's name while they were doing research on this project and they thought he was a candidate for their cause. That was where I came in. They wanted me to talk to him to see if he'd be an appropriate symbol. We were, after all, talking about a public relations campaign.

Helen's minivan was in the driveway but the house was dark except for the purplish glow in the living room that indicated the television was on. I stepped inside our home and felt a chill that I told myself was just too much air-conditioning.

I walked into the living room. Helen was on the couch. Her arms were folded in front of her.

"This program is interesting," she said. "*When Good Pets Go Bad.* These poor people. They take animals into their homes and make them a part of their lives. Feed them, walk them, bathe them. They think the animals love them. But then—"

And here my wife snapped her fingers.

"—they turn vicious. Attack the owners and their families. Turn everybody's life into a living hell."

Helen turned around. Her eyes were rimmed with red and I could tell she had wanted to cry but had willed herself not to.

"How is she?"

"Who?"

"Oh, come on, Garrett. Do you think I'm stupid?"

A voice inside me told me that the best thing to do was to turn around and walk out of the house, but my legs would not move. Helen approached me and it seemed as if she was trying to stand as straight as she could. My wife was only two inches shorter than me and she was trying to walk with the kind of swagger she must have associated with men.

"Do you think I don't know?" she said. "Do you think you're so clever I can't tell what you're doing?"

Her voice was rising. The harsh tone of accusation filled the stale air.

"Do you think I don't know when you've been with her? Do you think I can't tell from the way you act? Do you think I can't smell her on you? Tell me, Garrett. Tell me!"

Lying seemed pointless; confession premature and insincere. I had enjoyed every moment with Magdalena. Those stolen hours were filled with zest and passion. When I looked at the future Helen wanted for me, I did not see life. Only existence.

My wife raised her fists and began pounding them against my shoulders.

"Say something, Garrett! Say something to me! I had a sonogram today and you weren't even there. You didn't even call. You sonuvabitch!"

I tried to put my arms around her. Helen pushed herself away.

"Don't touch me! How can you touch me after you've been with her?"

She ran down the hall, her feet striking the carpet with a curiously soft sound. But there was no mistaking the hard intention of the bedroom door slamming shut.

As I walked after her, I told myself I was being calm and deliberate.

"Helen."

It was the first word I'd said since entering the house.

"Helen."

I put my hand on the doorknob, which was locked of course.

"C'mon, Helen, open the door. We need to talk."

"Get out of here!" The door muffled her voice, but there was no mistaking its fury. "Go back to her! Go back to your whore!"

Something icy entered my blood.

"Helen."

My voice was shorter and quicker, almost breathless.

"Go back to your whore if that's what you want!"

"Stop it, Helen."

"How do you think I feel when I answer your cell phone and hear her voice?"

"Cut it out, Helen."

"Why should I? I'm not the one who told you to fuck that whore every day!"

There is a problem with having a calm facade, with always grinning at others and agreeing with them, with consciously and constantly striving to be pleasant. When the facade cracks, all the bile that has stored up comes pouring through and there is no way to contain or control it.

"Don't call her that!"

It was my voice screaming, although it seemed to come from somewhere outside me.

"Go back to your whore!"

"Don't you dare call her that!"

What happened next is a jumble of sounds I can barely recall. I slammed my body against the door and it cracked open—plywood that the developer had insisted was mahogany; hinges, supposedly brass, flying upward and revealing themselves to be made of scrap—and Helen was shrieking and backing away from me, her arms extended full length as if she were a wounded lioness trying to protect her cubs. And I was yelling; full throat; top of my lungs—

"You sanctimonious bitch! Who the fuck made you so perfect?"

Helen threw a hairbrush at me but I swatted it away. She yelled for me to go back to my whore and I screamed back that she should shut up and she grabbed some cosmetic cases from the top of her vanity and hurled them at me and I kept coming toward her, relentlessly, like a destructive machine set on autopilot.

My wife backed into the bathroom and closed the door. I heard her lock it.

"Get away from me, Garrett. Just leave me alone."

She was sobbing now. I had broken her down. In retrospect I'm repulsed, but at that moment I felt satisfied.

But I was not finished.

I crashed my shoulder against the bathroom door, which was sturdier than the one to the bedroom but it started to give way and with two more shoves it, too, flew off its hinges.

Helen cowered in the tub with the shower curtain wrapped around her, as if this thin plastic sheet would somehow protect her.

I tore the curtain away and flung it against the wall and reached down and picked her up and felt her body shaking in my hands.

I thought about hitting her. I considering shoving her against the wall or slamming her head on the tiles or finding some kind of a heavy object and striking her with it. There are so many ways to injure people. So many ways to destroy them.

But I did none of those things. Instead I grasped her shoulders and yelled directly into her face, "Don't you ever use that word about her! Don't you dare!"

Helen said something but I couldn't hear it properly at first because by now she was bent over and sobbing, almost as if she'd been snapped in two.

But then, after a while, I was able to make out her words while she repeated them. It almost sounded as if she were reciting a lament for the dead as she said, over and over, her voice rising and falling like ocean waves, "Why are you doing this to me?"

FIFTEEN

I spent the night on the futon in the guest room. When I woke up the next morning, Helen was gone. She had packed as many of her clothes as she could into the two suitcases she normally kept in the garage. She did not leave a note.

When I got to work I called Josette and asked how soon she could be ready for the rally if she really pushed it.

"Two days," she said. "But do you think—"

"Let's do it."

I phoned all my media contacts, most of whom said they'd send a reporter if it was a slow news day. This was not exactly the response I wanted, so I drew up a letterhead for a group I named Greenspace and spelled out in detail the terrible threat to South Florida's delicate ecosystem that was being posed by the Copley brothers and their strip-mall campaign. I faxed the letter to every public interest group and media outlet I could find in the phone book.

When I met Magdalena in the early afternoon she said I was tense and needed to relax. I did not disagree. She asked what was going on in my life and I told her I was starting to feel overwhelmed. My lover asked again if I'd thought any more about going away with her. We could disappear into the rain forest and never emerge, the two of us making love on languid afternoons and worrying only about pleasing each other.

I still could not find the words to agree. There were things I needed to find out that I knew I would not get from her. So I just nodded and grunted and hoped she would interpret these as masculine signs of assent.

Late in the day Victor DeLuca phoned to say he'd been swamped by calls from environmental organizations protesting the Copley brothers campaign. He asked if I was behind this and I said I could neither confirm nor deny and he told me I was a slick bastard.

As I locked my desk for the night and prepared to return to a house I now had to myself, the phone rang. I thought of letting my voicemail take it but then I thought it might be Magdalena, saying in a breathless tone that our new identities were ready and she was prepared to leave tonight.

I wondered what I would do if I had to decide.

I picked up the phone and identified myself and heard the sonorous tones of Kendall Poltrane. He told me that he had pulled some strings. In fact, he had pulled many strings. He said I could see his client the next day, and the opportunity might not arise again for a month or more.

Kendall Poltrane drove through the Generica outside Atlanta, a stop-and-go journey past subdivisions and strip malls on four-lane roads lined with Taco Bells. When we got to the prison we cleared security at the front gate and then went through more security once we were inside. We had to pass through another checkpoint outside the room where we could meet the prisoner.

An image of Magdalena stepping into the shower, turning on the water and letting it run until her hair was matted and her skin glistening, then turning to me and smiling and beckoning with her finger that I should join her.

The guard stood aside as the heavy metal door swung open. Poltrane and I stepped into a high but narrow room that was illuminated by a single bulb screwed into a socket in the ceiling. Sitting at a rickety card table, with his manacled hands folded in front of him, was a wiry African-American who had the hard face and eyes of a thirty-year-old who has seen enough for eternity. He looked at me and did not blink and I noticed how the light glinted off the crucifix that hung around his neck. He wore baggy prison grays and I wondered how he'd managed to convince the guards to let him wear the cross.

"This is the man I talked to you about," Kendall Poltrane said to him.

"Peace," Drive-by Duncan McNabb said to me.

I turned to Poltrane and adopted a hesitating voice, as if I'd just thought of something and hated what I was about to say, but felt compelled to raise the point anyway: "I was wondering, sir, if you please . . ."

The lawyer leaned closer to me. The catch in my voice must have convinced him of my sincerity.

"Would it be all right if I talked to Mr. McNabb alone? The people I represent would prefer it that way. It's up to you, of course. I'll understand if you feel you need to be here, but I'll have to note it in my report."

A curious look came over Kendall Poltrane, as if he was wondering why I hadn't raised this point earlier. He turned to Drive-by Duncan McNabb, who clasped his hands and closed his eyes and lowered his head. I saw his lips moving and then he raised his head and looked at the ceiling and nodded.

"It's all right," Duncan McNabb said in a voice of otherworldly calm. "The Lord wants him to be here."

Kendall Poltrane slipped out of the room. I walked toward Drive-by Duncan and kept wishing he would avert his eyes or at least blink a few times. But all he did was stare at me, as if he felt he could learn everything about my life if he looked at me long enough.

I put my briefcase on the table and snapped it open and started to go through it as if I were searching for something, although I knew exactly what I wanted and where it was.

"You seem troubled," Duncan McNabb said.

I took out the pictures I had brought but kept them in front of me. I did not want to show them yet.

"You must let the Lord into your life," McNabb said. "He will show you the true path. The right path. It all flows through Him."

"I represent some people who believe you have suffered an injustice."

"Injustice. Like Christ. He died for our sins even though He Himself was blameless."

I looked directly at Duncan McNabb. I thought he might be yanking my chain but his eyes had an ethereal glow.

"I want you to tell me about how you were arrested."

Duncan McNabb's eyes clouded over and I believed he was remembering his younger, angrier self. "It was a setup," he said. Then his calm returned. "Like Gethsemane."

"You alleged that you did business with some men who claimed to work for the government."

"They did Caesar's bidding. And I obeyed them. That was my downfall."

"How did you meet them?"

Duncan McNabb sighed. He said he was not proud of who he was or what he had done.

I told him that if there was any chance of changing the present, it was vital I learn about the past.

Magdalena, I almost said. *What can you tell me about Magdalena?* But I had to wait. It was not yet time to ask.

Duncan McNabb said he was a member of the Bloods in South-Central L.A. One day he was playing ball with some of his friends when he saw two men standing off to the side, watching the game as if they were scouts for the Lakers. In particular they kept looking at him and eventually they ticked him off so much that he stopped playing.

Who are you looking at?

We're looking at you.

One of the guys was Latin and the other was white. The Latin guy in particular surprised him. He didn't sound like a Mexican and he was darker than a Mexican too.

What are you looking at me for?

Duncan's homeboys had surrounded the guys but the two of them stayed cool, with their arms folded across their chests and their backs leaning against the chain-link fence.

You're Duncan McNabb.

You got that right.

We have a business proposition.

Go ahead.

We want to talk about it privately.

Duncan raised himself to his full height and decided to show his homies whose side he was on and he told these guys that if they had anything to say, they could say it in front of everyone.

This produced nods from the group and cries of "You got that right."

In that case, the Latin said, they had nothing to discuss. They were sorry for interrupting the game and hoped everyone had a nice day. Duncan McNabb was about to chalk this up as just another piece of weirdness in a life that was full of it when he noticed the car they were walking toward.

The late model BMW was gleaming in the sun. Its windows were tinted and it was the kind of car Duncan McNabb had always wanted to own.

The men took their time getting into it, as if they wanted Duncan to get a good look at what he was passing up.

"Better see what the men have to say," one of his friends said.

Duncan McNabb ran across the playground and slipped through a hole in the fence and walked up to the BMW while the white guy turned the ignition. Duncan smiled and made a motion that indicated the driver should lower his window. Which he did.

What's up?

The Latin leaned forward in the passenger seat and turned his head and asked Duncan if he'd like to talk now.

Got that right.

The Latin told him to get in the car.

Duncan McNabb did. It was as nice as he had imagined, with soft leather seats and air-conditioning and a great sound system. Duncan McNabb found himself running his hands over all the objects in the car to assure himself they were real.

The men drove slowly around the neighborhood, as if the guys in front were familiar with the streets. It occurred to Duncan McNabb that these men had been watching him for quite some time.

"You know people around here, don't you?" the Latin asked.

It seemed that he would do the talking. Although the other one was kind of skinny, he had an aura of menace that Duncan McNabb respected.

I know lots of people.

And you do business with them?

That's correct.

Would you like to do more business?

I'm always looking to expand.

They continued to drive slowly along the streets where Duncan McNabb had lived his life. He recognized the stores and the schools and the kids playing in their yards, and he thought it wasn't such a bad place despite what the white people said.

The Latin and his partner were importers. They had access to stuff. Lots of stuff. They needed a distributor. Duncan McNabb asked them what kind of stuff in particular they were talking about and the Latin pulled out a small manila packet and handed it over. Duncan McNabb looked inside and saw what appeared to be a small, dirty rock.

What's this?

Cocaine.

Doesn't look like anything I recognize. Besides, I don't work with that shit. Too expensive.

This is affordable. You smoke it. Five dollars a pop.

They told him to try it. So he did. He never sold anything he hadn't tested himself.

The stuff was unbelievable, the best he'd ever used. Of course he craved more as soon as the high wore off, but he told himself that was good. It would make people buy more.

He started meeting regularly with his suppliers, who showed him how to turn the raw cocaine into rocks he could sell. Drive-by Duncan set up a small plant in his mother's garage. The demand was immediate. He couldn't keep pace with how much the people wanted. Soon he was selling it for ten dollars a pop, sometimes twenty, and he needed to produce more, so he moved his operation into the ground floor of an old warehouse and his suppliers provided more and still he couldn't keep up.

Stories started spreading about how good this stuff was and soon Duncan McNabb began going to other cities to set up operations for supply, distribution and manufacture, and still he needed more and he worried about getting it but his suppliers almost always had enough. Drive-by Duncan bought a big house in Baldwin Hills and put his mother there and felt good that he'd been able to take care of her. He acquired a BMW and a Cadillac and a Rolls and a Jaguar, and when he felt he had enough cars he purchased a boat. He told himself he had everything he'd ever wanted. He told himself he was happy.

But Duncan McNabb read the newspapers and watched CNN and he knew what was going on. People wanted this stuff too badly. They were robbing and killing, neglecting their kids, abandoning everything in their lives except the desire to get high. He told himself that none of this was his problem but then he saw his name in the *Los Angeles Times* with the sheriff's department saying he was the biggest dealer in all of California.

Duncan McNabb was not a stupid man. He knew he should be concerned. People don't go mentioning your name to the newspapers that way unless they have something bad in mind.

His suppliers assured him that nothing would happen. They knew people. Everything was protected.

One day Duncan McNabb got a call at home. He was in a haze because he'd been smoking some stuff but a guy at the warehouse was on the line saying they'd just gotten a really bad batch and he'd better come down to look for himself. So Duncan got one of his assistants to drive him and he sat in the backseat swearing at his suppliers for sending stuff that was barely better than baking powder and vowing up and down that he was going to nail them, seek vengeance, make them fear the power of Drive-by Duncan McNabb. By the time they arrived he'd straightened out a bit and his top man at the plant was surprised to see him and asked why he was there and Duncan said he'd just got word that they'd received some really bad stuff and the guy shook his head and said somebody was pulling his leg; they'd just gotten their latest shipment, right on schedule, and it was very fine indeed.

The warehouse walls started shaking and at first they all thought it was an earthquake and then this big battering ram came through the door; the thing looked like a tank and it was followed by what seemed like hundreds of cops with rifles and machine guns and they were ordering everyone to put their hands up and then lie on the floor or else they were going to get their heads blown off.

Duncan McNabb knew he'd been set up and in a way he wasn't surprised it had ended this way, but what he hadn't expected was this: On his way to central booking, as he rode in the back of a van packed with the people who had worked for him, with his hands and legs shackled, he looked out the slits at the neighborhood he had left behind. And what he saw was this: storefronts burned out and boarded up; houses with metal bars over their windows; schools surrounded by barbed-wire fences; no children playing outside; no signs of life at all.

Once he was in custody, he thought he knew what was going to happen. The cops and the feds and the DA's office would want to know who was supplying him and, after suitable negotiations, Drive-by Duncan would tell them all about his suppliers. He was ready to do it. All they had to do was ask.

But nobody did.

Duncan McNabb was kept in solitary and his assets were seized and his mother was thrown out of the house in Baldwin Hills. When he finally got a bail hearing, his attorney approached the bench and in a private conference told the government's lawyers that his client was ready to cooperate.

The government said it wasn't interested.

Don't you want to know who supplied him?

Not really. He's the one we're after.

But he wasn't the supplier. He didn't bring the drugs into the country.

Doesn't matter.

I was looking directly into Duncan McNabb's eyes and I was trying to decide how much of this I should believe. He had the unblinking stare that marked him as either a true believer or a fanatic. Of course the line between the two is awfully thin.

I arranged the pictures I had brought with me. Before I could say anything, Duncan McNabb's eyes flashed and he raised both his fists and slammed them down on one of the photos.

"This is the man," he said.

I slid the picture away from him and turned it around so I could see. It was Ernesto.

"The man he was with," I said. "Describe him."

He said the guy was tall and thin and had a beaklike nose and spoke like some kind of hick. He was clean-shaven and had deepset brown eyes and looked to be younger than the other guy—around thirty or so. He was quiet unless he had a few drinks. Then he got loud and insulted everybody.

I cleared my throat. I wanted my next question to sound as innocuous as possible although I felt my stomach rising and my heart racing and beads of sweat beginning to break out on my forehead.

"Was there anybody else with them?"

Duncan McNabb nodded. "A woman."

"Who was she with?"

"The white guy. But the Latin guy liked her. You can tell."

Solicitous, I thought. *Ernesto was solicitous.*

"Tell me about her."

The woman was fine. More than fine. She was the kind of woman every man in the room wanted to go home with. She wasn't tall but her body was outstanding, like something out of a painting. She was Latin too and she had dark brown hair and smoldering eyes and all in all, back in those days, back when he was wild and before his life had been saved by the Lord, Duncan McNabb thought she was the most delectable piece of arm candy he'd ever seen.

So far none of this surprised me. I told myself that perhaps it would be okay.

Duncan McNabb said the woman was about eighteen years old.

I told myself it was the right age for her back then.

Duncan McNabb said one night in particular stood out. He was having a meeting with his suppliers about a late shipment. Usually they delivered like clockwork and his organization had grown to depend on their precision but now everything was messed up and he was in a foul mood as he walked into the motel room they'd rented near the airport. Drive-by Duncan McNabb began hollering at his suppliers: they were the worst people he'd ever dealt with in his life, he had half a mind to kill them right now.

They apologized and said it wouldn't happen again. They wanted to continue their business relationship. It was important to them.

Drive-by Duncan had been smoking a little before the meeting. He was not thinking with his usual lucidity.

He reached into his knapsack and brought out a gun. It was a heavy-duty automatic and he started waving it around saying he was gonna blow their heads off. His homies encouraged him:

You tell 'em, Duncan.

Don't back down.

Don't take any more shit from these fuckers.

He stopped himself and shook his head and told me he was sorry. He was trying not to use language like that anymore. I told him I'd heard worse things in boardrooms.

Duncan McNabb said he felt something else going on in the room, something he should check out even while he continued berating his suppliers. So he turned and looked over his left shoulder, toward the bathroom.

Standing in the frame was the woman, who had always been silent in all the meetings they'd ever had.

She was pointing a gun right at his head. Her hand was steady and from the expression on her face, he could tell that she was willing to shoot.

Drive-by Duncan and his homies grew quiet. The situation suddenly seemed more serious than he'd anticipated.

"Put the gun away," the woman said in an accent so thick Drive-by Duncan had a hard time understanding.

He realized that a lot of lives were riding on what he did next.

So he laughed. He laughed loud and long and said he'd gotten a little agitated but he was just upset because things weren't going according to plan. He said he agreed with his suppliers. A little misunderstanding was no reason to destroy a good business.

For a few seconds he heard nothing but silence. This was the tensest moment Drive-by Duncan had ever experienced. He didn't know what his homies would do and he was praying—yes, praying, to the Lord above, something he never did in those days, perhaps it was a sign of the direction his life was meant to take—that nobody did anything stupid.

And then his homies started to laugh and his suppliers chuckled a bit and Drive-by Duncan put his gun back in his knapsack, which he tied tightly to show his good faith.

The woman started moving toward the door. She lowered her gun but did not put it away and started talking in Spanish to the two guys, who nodded their heads rapidly, as if they agreed with everything she was saying. As if they were used to agreeing with her. The man with the mustache, the man who did almost all the talking, the man I assumed was Ernesto Rodriguez, turned to Drive-by Duncan and said the next shipment would be delivered in two days to the usual location and there would be a ten percent discount because of the inconvenience.

Drive-by Duncan high-fived his crew. They'd done the right thing.

The two men reached for the door. The woman said something else to them, and the man with the mustache turned to Duncan McNabb and said, quietly and evenly, in a tone that made it clear he was not screwing around: "Señor McNabb. Don't ever threaten us again. You have no idea of the stakes involved in this operation."

They left the room. It was the last time Drive-by Duncan ever saw the woman. But he had the sense, from that encounter, that she was much more than a decoration.

I pulled a handkerchief from my jacket and mopped off the sweat that had been running down from my hairline.

The handkerchief was part of a set that was monogrammed with my initials. Helen had given it to me for my last birthday.

"It's hot in here," I said. I smiled weakly. "It's terrible what you guys go through."

"It's nothing like the fires of hell," Duncan McNabb said. "Like what awaits us if we do not repent and embrace the Lord."

I rose to my feet and looked at my watch in an ostentatious sign that it was time to leave.

The watch was a Rolex. It was a Christmas present from my wife.

Duncan McNabb gazed up at me. I kept wishing he would blink.

"You're troubled," he said.

"We're all troubled."

"I've sensed it from the moment you walked in. An unease of spirit. You have much. Possessions. But they don't make you happy."

I mumbled something about telling my clients all about our conversation. I was sure they'd be interested but there were no guarantees they'd do anything further.

"You must accept the Lord into your life. Until you do that, you're just existing."

I closed my briefcase and thanked him for talking to me. I tried to make my mind a blank. I tried not to think about Magdalena and what I now knew.

"I used to have everything. Houses. Cars. A boat. Women. I thought I was happy. But I wasn't. I began reading His Word in prison and suddenly it wasn't a prison at all because my spirit was liberated. And I found peace. True peace. The peace that comes from inside you. And that is the only true path to happiness."

I said my plane was leaving in an hour and I had to get back to the airport.

"Everything happens for a reason. There's a reason why you're here today. A reason why I'm here."

That's right, I thought. *You sold tons of crack cocaine throughout the country.*

"The Lord brought you here. A troubled spirit. To hear what I had to say."

I told him I really had to be going.

Duncan McNabb leaned across the table and I almost jumped because I thought he might be coming after me but I heard a chain rattle and I saw that his legs were bolted to his chair but his eyes went wide and I saw the street that still seethed in them as he said, "I have to get out of here."

SIXTEEN

Josette and her people had decorated the Happy Land storefronts with red and purple banners in jagged patterns that brought to mind stories I'd heard about bad acid trips from veterans of the sixties. I stopped across the road to admire her over-the-topness, then restarted the Rover and drove to an IHOP.

Only a few vehicles were in the lot and mine was easily the largest. I parked way in back, far from the others, and walked through damp air that already foreshadowed the late-afternoon rain. I chose a booth in the rear that looked as if it would be the last part of the room to fill up and took a copy of *The Herald* from my briefcase.

"You're up early."

A woman slid a menu in front of me. She looked in her fifties and was a little overweight. Cheap jewelry dangled from her ears and fingers. Her frizzy hair was a dull red and I wondered about its natural color and how many times she had changed it. Her voice echoed a time when all of Florida was still part of Dixie.

"I have a big day," I said.

"Then you'll want a big pot of coffee, won't you?"

"Please."

"We'll get along just fine."

I did not want to talk to anyone. I wanted to think about what I would say to Magdalena the next time I saw her. The rational side of my brain was telling me that I should just break it off and then call Helen and apologize for everything and tell her I would henceforth be a model husband and father-to-be. But when I thought about doing that I began to have trouble breathing and the side of me that did not care about reason or logic said I would be desperately unhappy for the rest of a life that would seem interminable.

"Here you are."

The waitress put a pot of coffee beside me and began to walk away.

"I'm ready to order."

"Are you sure? Don't you want a little more time?"

"No."

I asked for blueberry pancakes and whole wheat toast and a glass of orange juice. She asked if that was all and I said it was. I glanced at *The Herald* because I wanted a distraction but a headline and small picture attracted my attention.

The headline said "Miami Cop Linked to Drug Ring" and the small picture was of Police Officer Pilar Hurtado. The story, written in the usual breathless tones of Upright Newspapers Exposing Official Corruption, repeated allegations from members of the Internal Affairs Division that Officer Hurtado had been in the thrall of a Colombian cartel. According to the investigators, she had protected the kingpins and even helped them bring drugs into the country.

Far down in the article, two paragraphs from the end, nestled deep in a well next to a Macy's ad, the reporter shared with his readers the information that Officer Hurtado denied the charges.

"Here's your breakfast. Blueberry pancakes. You be careful now. They're piping hot."

I pushed the paper aside. An enormous platter filled with food and juice was placed in front of me. The waitress hovered for a second.

"Are you all right?"

"Fine. Thank you." Then I pointed to the paper and said, "I know her."

The waitress leaned over and looked at the picture before straightening and glancing around the room. A few people had trickled in, but they were all close to the hostess stand.

"That's what happens," she said.

"What do you mean?"

"When you let women on the police force. And those people."

"Which people?"

"Latins. And the coloreds. There's an awful lot of temptation on the police force, and only white people are strong enough to deal with it. You know what I mean."

"No, ma'am," I said in a voice that sounded too loud in my ears. "I don't know what you mean."

"They let those people on the police force."

"Those people?"

I pushed the tray to the other side of the table. Plates and flatware clattered.

"And they can't handle it. Because they're not honest enough. They're not taught how to be honest."

I grabbed my paper and told her I was no longer hungry. As I walked out, I heard a voice suddenly stripped of phony traces of warmth and honey, a harsh southern voice that was full of the days of plantations and Jim Crow and massive resistance: "They shouldn't let those people on the police force. It isn't right. They make us do so many things in this country that aren't right."

As I walked around the side of the building, I reached for the keys to the Rover and thought about what I would say when I got to Happy Land.

As soon as I saw my vehicle, my jaw went slack. At first I tried to tell myself I was seeing an optical illusion, but then I ran across asphalt that was already sticky, my loafers making an awkward clopping sound and my tie flying over my shoulder. Sweat poured down my face and back.

The Rover was damaged more badly than I thought. The windows and grille and headlights were smashed, the doors dented, the windshield cracked. When I looked inside, I saw that the CD player and stereo had been torn out and the cell phone destroyed and the seats and dashboard ripped open.

A piece of yellow paper fluttered in the shards that remained on the windshield. I looked in every direction and saw a few people at the other end of the lot glancing at me as they straggled toward breakfast.

I opened the paper and saw this message, scrawled in angry red ink: "THE NEXT TIME, WE'LL DO THIS TO YOU."

I ran back toward the restaurant and prayed for a phone in the foyer, prayed it would be working, prayed I could remember my caller ID number.

The AT&T gods answered my pleas. When I called Information, an automated voice asked what city I wanted.

"I think it's Davie. I'm looking for the police department."

Another disembodied voice came on, reciting numerals that I wrote on the back of my hand. I punched in that number, thinking it would go through immediately, but AT&T demanded a caller ID.

And suddenly I remembered it. Our home phone, plus 120968. Helen's birthday. I once told her I wanted a number I'd never forget.

I got through to the Davie Police Department and yet another voice that belonged to no one started to run through a menu. The last option, as always, was for an operator.

"Can I help you?"

The voice belonged to an African-American woman who sounded as if she had long passed the point of being bored by everything.

"My car," I said. "Actually, it's an SUV."

I spoke quickly, hoping to convey urgency and desperation.

"What about it?"

"It's been trashed. Totally."

"Where are you, sir?"

I said I was at an IHOP, but was unsure of the address. She said she'd check it while she put me on hold. A recorded voice said the Davie Police Department was proud to serve and protect its citizens.

"Sir? The address you're at? It's in unincorporated Broward County."

"What does that mean?"

"It means it's not in our jurisdiction. You'll have to call the sheriff's office."

I asked her to give me that number, but before my question was completed I heard the telltale click that indicated she had hung up.

Information again. The number for the sheriff's office was given in the same disconnected voice as before. I used my caller ID to get through and ran through a menu and checked my watch.

"What is it?"

The voice was flat, transplanted from the Midwest, no doubt lured to Florida by the prospect of a snowless life. I told it of my predicament and described my location as quickly as I could.

"That sounds like it's in Davie, sir. You'll have to try their police department."

"Wait a minute!"

"There's no reason to snap at me, sir."

"I just called Davie's so-called police department—"

"Sir—"

"And they told me it was in your jurisdiction—"

"Excuse me, sir—"

"And you're not going to hang up on me and you're going to give me an answer!"

"I'm going to put you on hold, sir."

"No!"

I heard a click, followed by a tape recording that said the Broward County Sheriff's Office was proud to protect and serve its citizens.

I was not expecting what I heard next—a gruff male voice that I assumed belonged to a cop consigned to desk duty because his preferred method of dealing with members of the public was hitting them.

"Yes, Officer, as I was—"

"That's 'Sergeant.'"

"Well, Sergeant, as I was trying to explain—"

"Sarah says you were rude to her."

"If somebody would just listen to me—"

"We don't tolerate that kind of behavior."

"My car's been trashed! Aren't you supposed to care?"

A pause from the sergeant, who finally said, "Sarah was right. You are rude."

"My Rover is in a parking lot. At an IHOP. Somebody wrecked it and nobody seems interested in looking into it or even taking down the most basic information."

"That location you described," the sergeant said. "It's unclear from our maps if that's actually in our jurisdiction."

"The Davie police certainly think it is."

"Maybe your problem is with them, not us."

"*I just want somebody to take a look at it! Send a squad car out and make a report! What's so hard about that?*"

"You're trying my patience, sir."

I leaned my head against the wall, which in the classic style of Sun Belt construction felt as if it was made from the cheapest kind of plaster imaginable. For a second I imagined I was doomed to spend eternity at this place, ping-ponging between two police forces vigorously asserting their lack of authority.

"My name is Garrett Doherty," I said quietly into the phone, making sure to pronounce my last name the way I preferred. "I'm an executive at Cooperman and Associates, the public relations firm. I have extensive contacts in the media. Let me assure you, Sergeant, that if you don't dispatch a squad car here immediately, I'll make sure that this story is mentioned prominently in tomorrow's editions of the *Sun-Sentinel* and *Miami Herald*. I'll also give interviews to all the local TV stations, and maybe even CNN."

I thought I heard him gulp. "There's no reason to talk to me like that, sir."

"Just send a squad car here."

"I'll see what I can do."

The Happy Land kickoff was only a half hour away. Outside, traffic was congealed in the typical weekday morning ritual of the exurbs, although to cheer myself up I imagined they were all heading to the strip mall after falling under the spell of my promotional genius.

I had no way of getting to the rally.

This thought entered my head suddenly, as if I'd just realized that I'd forgotten to buy Christmas presents.

I called Red White & Blew. Teresa answered. I told her I needed to talk to Josette.

"She's not here. She's never here anymore."

"Did she leave already?"

"A while ago. I bet she's already at Happy Land. She likes going there."

"Does she have a cell phone?"

"No. She hates them."

I hung up and tried Information again and got the number of the lamp store, which I called immediately. A woman picked up. I thought I recognized the voice and asked if this was Cary/Corey, deliberately slurring the word so it sounded something like Curry.

"Yes." She sounded wary, as if she were afraid I was calling from a charity.

"It's Garrett."

"Where are you?"

"Up the road. Is Josette there?"

Phone fumbling. And then I heard Josette's voice, airy and giddy, saying in a tone that was lighter than ether, "We're all waiting. Where the fuck are you?"

I described my situation as briefly as I could and asked if she could pick me up.

"Be happy to. I love IHOPs."

The squad car and Josette arrived at the same time. By then I had shoved the note in my pocket. I did not show it to the police.

It was ten minutes after the scheduled start of the rally and the photographers and camera operators were getting fidgety as they and their equipment wilted in the humidity. A large platform had been raised in front of the stores. It was plastered with streamers and patriotic bunting. Off to the side, cordoned off behind a few cops who looked as if they wouldn't need much of an excuse to start using nightsticks, were two dozen people with signs that said "Save Our Green Space," "Strip Malls Are Poison" and, my favorite, "Sprawl Sucks."

An image of Magdalena, on the deck of a boat as the sun went down, my lover's hair and face framed by the orange glow of golden hour.

"They're too orderly," I said to Josette as I pointed to the protesters. "We need a little drama. Somebody should go over there. Get them started on a chant."

She asked if I had any suggestions.

"'Hey-hey, Ho-ho, Strip malls, Gotta go.'"

"That's stupid. I like it."

I asked if Cary/Corey knew any of the protesters. Josette shook her head. She said none of the store owners had any idea where these people had come from.

"Then she should infiltrate them," I said. "Get the chant going. I'm sure they'll be easily led."

On the platform, unsupervised members of the media had surged in close to the players. The actor whom Josette had recruited was smiling and nodding and looking around, as if hoping Spielberg would suddenly materialize. Winston and Evan Copley had also drawn the attention of several reporters and camera crews. Winston was talking earnestly into the camera, applying his handkerchief around his forehead the way a Zamboni smooths the ice, while Evan stood off to the side, looking like a man who wished he had just stayed in bed.

I clambered up the steps and told myself to straighten my back, look everyone in the eye, walk quickly and smile broadly and shake hands firmly while constantly talking loudly and keeping my feet moving.

I recognized many of the people in the media and thanked them individually for coming and made a point of getting the names of the ones I didn't know. I kept hearing questions, the same questions, as I told myself to nod and smile and pretend I couldn't make out anything because of the din.

"Do you think you should be encouraging sprawl?"

"What about the protesters?"

"Isn't this whole thing just hype?"

I walked up to the actor and clapped my hand on his back and steered him away from a young woman with the local cable news station.

"You were late," the actor said softly but firmly, as if all the world's problems could be traced to my tardiness.

"It was out of my control."

"We're just milling around. Nobody's sure what to do."

"Relax. In two minutes, you'll be launching your shtick. You know what it is, don't you?"

"Of course I do. What kind of an actor do you think I am?"

One who has to do gigs like this.

I grinned at him and headed toward the Copleys before remembering that there was one more thing. There's always one more thing.

"By the way," I told the actor, "they're gonna heckle you."

He looked as if I'd just changed all his lines to iambic pentameter.

"Heckle me? Who? Why?"

"Them." I pointed to the edge of the crowd, where a few more people had joined the group. I smiled to myself when I saw Cary/Corey bobbing around among the signs. "Because I want them to."

"What!?"

"It'll make great TV. You'll be on every newscast in South Florida. Maybe even CNN, if it's a slow day."

"But what should I say?"

"Call them un-American. That always works. Say that they're pampered, tree-hugging elitists who are trying to deprive common folks of a chance to make money."

"But I don't believe that. Not for a second."

"You're an actor. Act."

I made my way to the edge of a circle in which Winston Copley was surrounded by several reporters backed by camera-toting goons. My client was saying, "We want to share this opportunity with anyone who might be interested."

I slipped in next to him and put my arm around his shoulder and said, much more loudly than necessary so there was no chance it would get on TV, "Winston, my friend, you're gonna give away all the good stuff."

We shook hands. As always, I was surprised by how soft and moist his palm was. Winston once again mopped his face with a handkerchief.

I turned to the reporter he'd been talking to. She was a young woman who did mostly crime stories. Almost all the reporters in South Florida did mostly crime stories.

"You're Juanita Lopez," I said. "I recognize you from TV. You're terrific. Love your stuff."

I grinned as I stuck out my hand. She looked as if she knew I was bullshitting her, but didn't mind because she didn't get complimented on her work too often. She took my hand and I told her my name and she asked how I was connected to this project.

"I'm the creative."

"Creative what?"

"Muse, I guess." I grinned again. I hadn't smiled so much since my wedding day.

When I finally reached the microphone, I felt like embracing it. The actor was to my right and the Copleys to my left. Cameras were on either side of me. At the far edge of the crowd, the protesters were stirring, as if they suspected something was about to happen.

I removed my Ray-Bans and took in the audience. Hundreds of people, perhaps a thousand, were crammed in the lot. I saw gray heads and a few blue ones. Cars were parked by the side of the road and near the stores across 84. The cars created a sea of sensible American sedans—Dodges and Fords and Chevys, all shining under a sun that was only inches above my brow. The humidity was beginning to stick like Velcro. I took a deep breath and remembered what Lisa had once told me: "Sure you'll be nervous. It's normal to be nervous. Just don't show it."

"How are you today?"

Down below, a few people turned to look at me.

"Hot," called back an elderly voice straight out of Brooklyn.

The people who were listening laughed. I grinned again.

Lisa's words in my ears. First mentor. First betrayal. "Always let them know you don't take yourself too seriously. Even if you do."

"I'll tell you what's hotter, my friend." I tapped the lectern a couple of times for effect. The microphone's amplification made it sound as if I was calling in artillery fire. "This offer. We're going to show you a whole new way of thinking about real estate. And it's all due to a revolutionary idea by the Copley brothers. That, my friends, is why strip malls are beautiful."

I introduced the actor and stepped away, to tepid applause. He raised himself to his full height (like many actors, he was a bit on the short side) and began to speak in tones resembling a revivalist: "It's another hot day in Florida and I know you could have stayed home with your air conditioners but you chose to come here, and from the bottom of my heart, I thank you."

This produced a more forceful round of clapping. People will always cheer themselves.

"But I know you didn't come here just to make me happy." He smiled like a teacher who was determined to make everyone understand the lesson. "You came here to make yourselves happy, and I don't blame you. You're standing out here, braving oppressive heat and humidity, because you know, in your heart of hearts, that strip malls are beautiful."

From the edge of the crowd came a tinny chant: "Hey-hey, Ho-ho, Strip malls, Gotta go."

The Copleys stood in a corner of the platform with their eyes locked on the Dunkin' Donuts across the road. I clapped both of them on the back, just in case any cameras were on us.

"Helluva crowd," I said.

Winston mopped more sweat from his forehead. His face was beet red. He said it was invigorating. So many people.

I turned to Evan, whose face had the dark expression of a man who had seen the future, and did not like it. "What's the matter, Evan? Can't stand success?"

"I would have preferred to remain anonymous," he said.

I told them I was going to walk through the crowd to see how the event was playing and make sure everybody who arrived was getting a copy of the glossy brochure we'd prepared extolling the Copleys' product. The brothers nodded distractedly, their eyes roaming back to the Dunkin' Donuts.

It was steamier on the ground. I was glad to see that everyone was clutching a brochure, and made a mental note to praise the high school girls we'd hired to hand them out.

Off to the side, I once again heard the chant I'd suggested about strip malls. It was more vigorous this time, and some people in the crowd turned to look at the protesters.

A large woman in a floppy hat pressed close to the police barricade and screamed, so loudly I was sure the news crews picked it up: "You should be ashamed of yourselves! You're raping the environment!"

This produced gasps and grumbles from the people in the crowd. I couldn't tell if they were mad at her, or thought she had a point.

On the platform, the actor stopped talking. Suddenly the only sounds came from the protesters, who had the momentum and were shouting, "Sprawl sucks! Sprawl sucks! Sprawl sucks!"

The actor's face was blank, as if he'd just received a prompt he hadn't been expecting.

Don't screw it up. Don't say you agree with them.

The actor threw out his arms. "I don't want to disparage the environmental movement," he said.

I was ready to rush the stage and throw him to the ground.

"It's done a lot of great things for this country."

I took my first steps back toward the platform.

"But I want to point something out."

I stopped.

"Those people can afford to take the time to be here," he said. "And do you know why? It's because they have financial freedom. And that's all we're trying to give to you."

Applause.

"If you invest with the Copley brothers, someday you'll have the time to protest things you don't like!"

Laughter and cheers drowned out the protesters, who tried to yell louder.

"This is a good old-fashioned debate, my friends, but let me tell you something else." The actor was rolling now. He had figured out his improv and he also knew he was the only one with a microphone.

"This is America."

Most members of the crowd nodded in agreement.

"And there is nothing more un-American than denying hardworking people the chance to make a little money. Or, even better, a lot of money!"

Whoops, cheers, whistles, massive applause. The protesters swayed back, like trees bearing the brunt of a gale. If no national tragedies occurred, I could see this going on TV from coast to coast.

"Hey, Garry, how ya doing?"

The voice came from behind me and the twang sounded familiar but I couldn't quite place it so I turned and grinned and stuck out my hand, ready to accept greetings and congratulations from someone I barely knew.

Frank Hedges grabbed my outstretched palm.

I let him pump it and tried to think of something to say. Fortunately he was talking at me, and although most of the words were indistinct because of the noise from the platform and the crowd, I did make out a few things: " . . . awesome . . . fucking great . . . clever idea . . . best goddamn thing . . ."

I nodded and smiled and felt more stupid than I had in years. "Thanks, Frank. Appreciate it. Thanks."

I have to call Magdalena.

Frank Hedges draped his arm around me and said it had been too long. He'd been out of touch for a while but it was great to have this chance to get back together. He gripped me tightly, both by the arm and the shoulder.

"Did you miss me?" he asked.

"Of course I did, Frank. Not a day went by when I didn't think of you."

"You're a goddamn liar, Garry. But you're really good at it. That's why I like you."

He steered me out of the crowd and I could see where we were heading—behind all the stores, where we would join the company of trash cans and Dumpsters. Although he was thin, he was taller than me and his grip was strong.

"I have to talk to you, Garry. In private. You don't mind, do you?"

"Why would I mind?"

We passed by stragglers and hangers-on. The sound from the platform became vague, like background noise that had been turned up too loud.

"What have you been up to, Frank?"

"A little of this, a little of that. Some bidness to attend to."

He nodded to someone off to the side and I glanced to see who it was. I recognized him right away: ponytailed Latino, burly with creatine, somewhere in his twenties, barely concealed rage. And suddenly I knew what was about to happen. We'd go around to the back and the Latino would ask if this was the guy and Frank Hedges would say it was and soon I'd feel hard, practiced fists pounding into my face and gut.

I would not ask why they were doing this and I would not deny the affair, although I'd be tempted to ask about the *puta* at the Orlando. Of course that would enrage Hedges. I imagined him standing off to the side while the Latino worked me over but when I asked my question he'd storm over and toss the goon aside and finish the job himself, punching me hard in the nose and the kidneys and smashing my face against the plaster walls of the mall until I was left helpless and bleeding amid the garbage from the place we'd selected as an icon of America.

We turned the corner, slowed, then stopped. Sweat bound my shirt to my skin. I kept looking around, but no one had followed us. Hedges let me go and we stood face-to-face, only inches from each other. All the breath left my body and there was no breeze and the air was damp and I had the sensation that this must be what the first few seconds of death are like.

"The Copleys," Frank Hedges said at last.

"What about them?"

"I've had my eye on their bidness for a while. You know that, don't you?"

My face must have gone blank.

"Maggie was at one of their seminars."

"Right. Of course. How is she?"

"Fine, fine. Listen"—here he brought his lips close to my ear and now I was ready for it, the rabbit punch that would double me over, followed by a kick to the jaw with the heavy heel of his cowboy boots— "are they looking for a partner? Would they be willing to sell?"

"I don't know," I said as I fought an urge to break into the loud, unreasoning peals of laughter that I hadn't enjoyed since I last smoked marijuana. "Why don't you ask them?"

"I wanted to get a feel for it. From someone who might be familiar with the situation. Do you have any idea?"

I felt my self-control returning. "I know this, Frank." And here I patted him on the shoulder, like an avuncular doctor about to give a patient the worst possible news. "They really like their business. Even if—just between us—they aren't very good at it. So I don't think they're looking to sell. But there's no harm in asking."

Frank Hedges nodded. "Thanks, Garry. Thanks a lot. I'll think about what you just said."

I had a sharp, sudden thought: *He knows where Ernesto is. He's come back to provoke a final confrontation and he's come by here to keep me close at hand.*

"So you've, uh, you've given up on Tierra Grande?"

Hedges' face grew red for a second. "Ernesto Rodriguez is the most ungrateful fucker I've ever met in my life." Then he punched me a little too hard in the shoulder and said, "But I'm sure you're getting along with him just fine."

"Ducky," I said.

"I'm not surprised. And now, Garry, I'm gonna be honest with you—I've gotta take a leak, and this looks like the best place for it."

"Go right ahead, Frank."

He stepped toward the wall and I walked away, as light-headed and giddy as a teenager who's made out for the first time. Back in the parking lot, the crowd was cheering and the actor was saying "Thank you very much" in an Elvis-like voice as the protesters slunk away, although the woman in the floppy hat was still pressed close to the barricade, screaming at anything that might be willing to listen.

I asked Juanita Lopez what she thought. She said that if she rushed it out, she could get it on the news at noon.

Up on stage the actor was cheek-kissing Josette and Cary/Corey. I walked up to them and shook hands and said, "Great job, everybody."

In an anxious voice, the actor asked how he'd gone over with the audience.

"Fantastic," I said. "They loved it. Especially the ladies." I adopted my elderly-Jewish-woman-from-Queens voice and said, "'What a nice young man. So good-looking.'"

As the actor's chest swelled, Frank Hedges mounted the stage.

"I thought it over, Garry. I'm gonna take you up on it."

"Fantastic, Frank. Glad to hear it."

I guided him toward the Copleys, who were straining the railing in their desire to get even a few millimeters closer to the Dunkin' Donuts. I called out their names but they did not respond. I called again, louder, and this time Winston turned his head.

When he saw us, his face registered an expression that I could not interpret because I'd never seen it before. At the time I thought it was annoyance because we'd interrupted a sugary reverie, but now I think it was the face of a man who had just seen the thing he feared most.

Within a second, he regained his pudgy blandness. He poked Evan in the side and pointed toward us.

His brother raised his eyebrows.

I greeted them and said I'd run into Hedges while I was working the crowd and he'd been impressed with the rally and wanted to talk to them and when you got right down to it, networking was what business was all about, wasn't it?

I have to call Magdalena.

"Frank says he's met you before but he's not sure if you'd remember—"

"We remember him," Winston said. "How are you, Mr. Hedges?"

He insisted they call him Frank.

I saw a pay phone outside the bagel place. I could walk right over. It would take only seconds.

"How'd you ever dream this up?" Frank Hedges asked the Copley brothers.

I could not make the call from a public place. What if we got a bad connection or the ambient noise got too loud and I had to start yelling?

"It was Garrett's idea," Winston Copley said. His tone was as frosty as a New England winter.

"I should have guessed," Frank Hedges said as he clapped me on the back again—a little too hard, as if he wouldn't be upset if he damaged my spine. "He's a sharp guy. Everybody says so."

I grinned and looked at my watch, although I didn't care what time it was, and announced I had to make an important call. The Copleys looked as if I'd just said I was deserting them to promote tax-free municipals. I assured my clients I'd be gone for only a couple of minutes. The Copleys mumbled a few words to each other that I could not decipher.

"Are you all right?" I asked.

"Fine," Evan said in his most clipped voice. "We'll be fine, Garrett. The toothpaste is out of the tube anyway."

I slipped away. Down on the asphalt, retirees gawked as Josette nuzzled Cary/Corey.

"Hey, guys," I said as I approached.

"Guys?" Josette said. She and her lover started to laugh and I told Cary/Corey that I needed a favor. I had to make a call; my cell phone was unavailable; perhaps Josette had told her what had happened to my Rover. The woman said of course I could use the phone in her store; it was right behind the counter; I didn't even have to ask.

I thanked her and grinned and resisted the urge to run.

The air-conditioning brought relief even though the place was stale with the smell of plastic and boxes. The counter was surrounded on

three sides by shades, Styrofoam and bubble wrap. I squeezed through
the only opening and looked around for the phone.

I wondered what I would say if Frank Hedges walked in and overheard me talking to his wife.

At last I saw a cordless receiver sticking out from underneath the
cash register. I grabbed it and pressed the talk button and put it to my
ear and was never so happy to get a dial tone.

As a reaction to my years of Catholic school, I rarely if ever find myself
engaged in the practice of praying. Religion requires faith, which is something I've always regarded as foolish. But on this day, at this moment,
under these circumstances, I found myself asking a God I barely believed
in to please make sure that Magdalena was around to answer my call.

"*Hola.*"

I expected the boxes and lamps to transform themselves into loaves
and fishes.

"It's me. I have to tell you something."

"I can barely hear you. If you're going to talk to me, speak up."

"I can't. I'm at the rally."

"Your big project. How did it go?" Her voice sounded bored, as if I
were talking about a television program that did not interest her.

"Your husband is here."

Her voice rose sharply as she fired a series of one-word questions in
Spanish.

"I saw Frank," I said. I kept looking in the direction of the door. "I
talked to him."

She started swearing in her native language.

"He's talking to the Copleys right now," I said.

Her voice became desperate and out of control as she started speaking in Spanglish and again I made out only parts of it, but the thrust of
what she was saying was this: It cannot be. Frank Hedges cannot be
alive and at the rally and talking with my clients.

"I asked him how you were," I said. "He told me you were fine."

"He has no idea. I haven't seen him in weeks. He didn't even call me.
Bastardo."

"What are you going to do?"

"I can't stay here. Can you help me? Can you pick me up? Right now?"

I was about to agree when I realized I was in no position to help anybody.

"I can't," I said. "I'm sorry."

"You can't leave? Not even for me?"

I told her what had happened with my Rover. I wasn't even sure how I was going to get back to Miami.

"He did it," she said.

I had no reason to disbelieve her.

"I'm going to do what he did," she said. "Disappear. Perhaps this is our chance."

I knew what she meant. Frank Hedges had reappeared and although our initial response was panic, perhaps this was the impetus we needed to flee into the rain forest and never return.

Before I could say anything, Magdalena said she would call me.

Outside the humidity made my spine and shoulders sag. I told myself to straighten up. Keep the facade intact. Let no one know what was happening to me.

The parking lot had cleared out and the only people who remained were on the platform, which the workers from the construction company were beginning to take apart. Frank Hedges had the Copleys cornered, and from the expressions on their faces I believed they were ready to surrender just about everything they owned if he'd just let them get some doughnuts. The burly Latino stood only a few feet away. His arms were folded across his chest and he looked as if he'd need only a minor excuse to start punching people.

I smiled at the Copleys and gave them a thumbs-up and made the obligatory inquiry about how they were doing.

"We're fine, Garrett," Winston said. "Aren't we, Evan?"

His brother nodded. The heat and humidity seemed to have sucked everything out of him.

I stood between Frank Hedges and Winston Copley and put my arms around both men's shoulders.

"You guys finish making your multibillion-dollar deal yet?" I asked.

Frank Hedges looked at me as if I had committed the worst form of blasphemy. Some people regard money as sacred, and recoil whenever somebody talks about it in a manner that is less than reverential.

"Nothing like that, Garrett," Winston Copley said.

"Maybe we can pursue this later," Frank Hedges said. His tone sounded ever-hopeful, as if he were the host of a late-night infomercial. But there was something behind it, something with iron that suggested he could be delayed, but not denied.

"We can," Winston said in his most noncommital voice.

"But our position isn't going to change." This came from Evan. I was surprised he was speaking and even more surprised by his vehemence. "We're not going to sell. And we're not interested in having a partner." He was not looking at his brother or Frank Hedges or me as he said this. Instead his eyes were fixed on the Dunkin' Donuts, and I had the feeling he was angry at all of us for keeping him away from what he truly wanted.

He shook his head and lowered his voice. His next words were for my benefit, although he did not look at me. "I can't believe we let you talk us into this," he said. "My God, what have we done?"

"Am I a shit?" Josette shouted as she drove me back to the IHOP. She had lowered the top of her Mustang and was blasting a Beach Boys tape. I still had to get the Rover towed and arrange for a car service back to Miami. I wasn't sure my company would pay for it.

"Why do you say that?" I shouted back.

She said it was because of Cary or Corey or whatever her name was. I still couldn't hear it clearly.

I shrugged. "People do what they have to."

An image of Magdalena, writhing with pleasure as I buried my face between her legs.

"I've been with Teresa a long time," Josette said. "I never thought about leaving her. Christ, I don't know what to do. I almost wish somebody would tell me."

"I'm not the person to do that. But I want you to know something."
I turned to her and adopted my sensitive-man-of-the-new-millennium
voice. "You'll always be one of my favorite lesbians."

Josette burst out laughing and I wondered why my wife and colleagues couldn't share her appreciation of my sense of humor.

Occasionally I made Magdalena laugh. Those were some of my happiest moments.

"*You* are a shit," she said.

I did not tell her how correct she was.

"And what do you mean—'one of'? How many lesbians do you know?"

"Lisa," I said softly, reflexively.

"Huh?"

"Lisa Shapiro." I was back to shouting. "My mentor. Years ago. Back
in New York."

"That name sounds familiar. You've mentioned her to me."

"Downtown type."

"Big bull dyke?"

"I never thought of her that way. But I guess she was."

"It's coming back to me. Lisa. PR muck-a-muck. High on the food
chain. Back then I was just a kid off the bus."

"She might have liked you."

"Whatever happened to her?"

I'd been dreading the question although Lisa crashed into my
thoughts all the time, a constant reminder of who and what I had sur-
rendered.

"She left the company," I said. "We lost touch. I don't know where
she is."

Josette shrugged. "It happens."

This is what happens: People help us and we stab them in the back,
and to avoid living in a state of constant self-loathing we tell ourselves,
"That's how the world works."

Sometimes in the early morning, when I can't sleep and I'm trying to
stop thinking about the way my life has turned out, I watch documentaries
on the Nature Channel. An animal's existence is elemental. It sleeps and

mates and spends most of its time searching for food or hiding from predators. And I now realize that there are only two fundamental differences between animals and humans: our ability to talk, and their lack of deceit.

When I walked into my office after paying the driver from the car service fifty dollars, including tip, my coworkers applauded and shouted my name. My boss came out of his glass cage and pumped my hand. Champagne, cookies and finger sandwiches were set on top of a long row of file cabinets, and the entire place had been decorated with balloons. As the cheers continued, I kept shaking my head and looking down at the floor and smiling shyly, like a political candidate who's so far ahead he can afford to be gracious.

An image of Magdalena walking into a crowded room, her dress cut low, pearls clinging to her skin.

My boss talked about shifting the paradigm and thinking outside the box and staying ahead of the curve and then he said he was sure I had a few words of wisdom to offer. I said I always had things to say, but I didn't know how wise they were. Everybody laughed. I thanked my colleagues for all the help I'd received in developing the campaign (although I couldn't remember much) and said everything we did in this office was a team effort. I told them how much I enjoyed working with all of them and I believed we'd shown headquarters exactly what the Miami office could do (whoops and hollers of agreement), and I concluded by saying I could go on and on praising all of us, but I was sure everybody would rather start drinking.

Corks were popped. Champagne was poured into plastic cups. I took one and started toward my office. People kept congratulating me and I kept thanking them and nodding and grinning and engaging in chitchat and resisting the urge to look at my watch.

As Isabel applied a new coat of nail polish, I asked if she had taken any messages. Without looking up she handed me several pink "While You Were Out" slips. Most were from people in the local media. One was from the head office in New York.

There was nothing from Magdalena.

I phoned New York. According to the note, the call had come from Mr. Cooperman himself, although I was sure the message actually originated from one of his underlings who had invoked his name to impress me and my secretary. The tactic would fail, of course. I was alert to the ploy and Isabel was never impressed by anything.

"Mr. Cooperman's office."

"Garrett Doherty. I'm returning his call."

"One minute, Mr. Doherty." She mispronounced my name. I expected to wait on hold awhile before being informed that Mr. Cooperman was out. If I was lucky, I might get voicemail.

"Garry, how are you?"

It was the voice of the company's founder and president, a voice smoothed and honed by thousands of dealings with the media, a voice that would remain unruffled if it was spinning Armageddon. Scott Cooperman was the man we all aspired to be.

"I'm fine, Mr. Cooperman. How are you?"

"Great. Thanks for asking. I'm feeling better after I saw that segment on CNN."

"I haven't watched it yet. I just got back to the office."

What if Magdalena is trying to reach me?

"Have you ever thought of coming back to New York?"

Cooperman asked the question idly, as if he were wondering about my picks in the Final Four pool.

"I'm really focused on what I'm doing down here."

"That's good. But that's not what I asked."

I was tempted to inquire about Ogilvie. I assumed he'd have to sign off on something like this. And then I saw it all before me: the downtown office with a view of the bridges and rivers, a four-bedroom house in Westchester or Long Island, taking the train every day and gradually getting gray and fat and telling myself I was happy.

Helen would be thrilled about this, if I ever talked to her again.

"New York is where the action is," I said. "It's my hometown."

"It is?"

"If you count New Jersey."

Cooperman chuckled. Like his voice, his laugh had the gloss of well-aged scotch.

"Why don't you come up here someday?" he said. "Someday soon. So we can talk. How does next Wednesday sound?"

On Lisa's last day at the company I walked into her office and tried to maneuver around the boxes that held the contents of the last twenty years of her professional life. I stood in the middle of the room for a long time, with what must have been a hangdog look, while she shoved the last of her stuff into a carton that looked ready to burst.

"Help me out here, Garry."

Lisa ripped off a long strip of packing tape while I pushed down on the box. She slapped the tape across it while I held everything in.

"I never thought it would end this way, Garry."

I felt I should say something. If this had occurred a year or two earlier I would have been stalking about in what little empty space there was, loudly objecting to this monstrous act of corporate injustice and proclaiming my loyalty to Lisa and telling her I had angrily submitted my resignation.

But I was married now. I had obligations that extended beyond myself. Everybody told me so.

"There are times to stand up and be counted," Lisa said. She still had not turned to face me. "And then there are times when you should crouch down in your foxhole and wait for the shooting to stop."

The only noises that came from my throat were a croak and gurgle.

"There's an opening in Miami," she said.

I had no words at all.

"I think you should get out of New York," she said. "It's not gonna be comfortable here for my people. Not for a while."

I would have left for another company, but my credentials were still meager.

"You like Miami, don't you?"

Helen and I had spent a few days at one of the Deco hotels on South Beach. We stayed out until dawn and made love as the sun rose.

"In a couple of years, Ogilvie will forget. If he's around. I still don't think he's smart enough to last."

I had just passed a gathering at the watercooler where fifteen people were listening to Ogilvie talk about his place in Amagansett. He said it needed work.

Lisa's shoulders heaved and the sound that came out of her resembled the death rattle of a wounded animal. "Oh, God, I can't believe this is happening," she said.

I stood there frozen, as if nails had been driven into my feet. Lisa was a proud woman but I imagined putting my arms around her. I imagined telling her everything would work out.

The door was open. I wondered what would happen if someone saw us.

And this is what I did: I withdrew. I left Lisa's office and went back to my desk and pretended to work. I overheard Ogilvie talking about how much a new roof would cost.

That night I propped my pillow against the headboard while Helen douched.

"What do you think of Miami?" I called out.

"You wanna go back?"

"Maybe yes. Maybe permanently."

She came out of the bathroom and looked at me incredulously, as if I'd just announced I wanted to convert to Islam.

"What brought this on?"

I told her. I told her with a certain amount of fear because I felt I still didn't know her and I was unsure how she'd react. It was possible she'd blame me for my predicament and rail at the Fates for marrying a loser.

My wife crawled into bed and rested her head on my chest.

"Thank you," she said.

"For what?"

"For being honest." She said Miami was nice and she was sure she could get a job there and if I thought this was the best way to deal with my problems at work, then I should do it.

I should have fallen in love with her then.

The next day I had a one-on-one with Ogilvie in which we were supposed to discuss my role in the company. It was part of an officewide performance review. Many of Lisa's allies had let him talk first and they'd been told he wasn't sure if there was a place for them as Cooperman and Associates restructured.

I entered the room briskly and shook hands with the man and congratulated him on his appointment as senior executive vice president for operations.

He nodded. He was about to say something.

I asked how his house in Amagansett was doing.

He said he wanted to replace the shingles. The place was right on the beach and always got battered during nor'easters.

I said I respected him and the work he had done for the company. I told him that I regarded myself as a team player and wanted to apply for the opening in the Miami office.

He asked me why.

I said I was looking for an opportunity to grow.

He said he was happy to hear me say that. He was always looking to cultivate talented individuals.

Magdalena did not call and I assumed the worst. For some reason she had been unable to get away and Hedges had come crashing in, full of anger and bile as he screamed obscenities and came closer, ever closer, until finally he grabbed her, all the while yelling about what he was going to do—

I kept the radio in my office on low, tuned to the all-news station, waiting to hear about police responding to a domestic dispute and finding a husband or wife or possibly both dead.

It was shortly before five when Isabel rose from her desk and strolled toward my office. Her bag was slung over her shoulder and zipped tightly, in the manner of a secretary who was ready to go home no matter what her boss thought of the idea.

She announced, loudly enough for everyone within earshot to hear, that a woman was calling me on Line Two.

I replied, in equally loud tones, that it was probably my wife.

Isabel said she doubted it, and walked out.

I knew who it was, of course, and my first instinct was to close the door so no one could hear us. But as I looked around the office I saw people who were intent only on getting out and I did not want to draw the attention that a sudden, sharp slam would bring.

"Hola," I said. *"Dónde estás?"* My voice was low but intense as I spoke in the urgent whispers favored by conspirators in low-budget movies.

Magdalena said she was at a pay phone on Collins Avenue. It was on the sidewalk outside her hotel.

"Are you crazy? You know Frank goes to the Orlando all the time."

"When he goes there, the only thing he's interested in is that *puta.*"

"Why can't you call from your room?"

"I don't trust hotel phones. You never know who's listening."

"You're taking a helluva chance."

"If he looks for me, it won't be here. I always told him how much I hate South Beach."

Despite the stories in the fad-obsessed press, the Art Deco hotels in Miami Beach were not constructed for the fashion-entertainment-media elites. Behind the sleekly lined exteriors are plain rooms, small and spare, with bathrooms like the ones people my age remember from our grandparents' houses.

But the lure is irresistible. The lure makes the reality seem better than it is.

Magdalena was staying at a small, two-story place with a courtyard that was almost overgrown by bushes and plants. I had rented another Taurus, which I parked in a garage a few blocks away. I made my way through knots of tourists and trendoids and wondered what they thought of this man in jacket and tie and suspenders. Or if they even saw me at all.

When I stopped at the hotel desk, the woman behind it did not look up from her copy of *Le Monde*. I told myself that perhaps she had not heard me even though my heels had clicked loudly as I crossed the tile floor.

I cleared my throat.

"We have no more rooms," she said as she turned a page.

I said I was looking for a guest.

"Who is it?" She deigned to look up. I saw ice blue behind harlequin glasses.

I almost blurted Magdalena's name but an emergency synapse must have kicked in because I remembered the alias she told me she was using.

"Ma-Maria Romero."

The woman glanced down at the ledger in front of her. "Two-eleven," she said before giving a wave that indicated I had already consumed enough of her attention.

I walked into the courtyard, where I was surrounded by heavy greenery. I imagined someone leaping out at me—Frank Hedges or Ernesto Rodriguez or one of those psychotic serial killers South Florida seems to attract—and I tensed, waiting for the rustle behind me. I imagined myself whirling around to confront whoever it was as he came toward me with a knife or machete.

But the only sounds were my footsteps, and my own breathing.

It was growing dark and I climbed to the second floor on a staircase that was not yet lit. The hall was dim and I slowed as I passed by each door. From behind a few I heard the sounds of television, and from one the frantic pants of lovemaking. At the end of the hall, so dark against the door I could barely read it, was the number 211.

I knocked softly.

Nothing happened.

I knocked more loudly.

Still no response.

And then I realized that Magdalena was waiting for a sign that the knock had come from the person she was expecting.

"It's me," I said.

I heard the soft padding of bare feet and the sharp snaps of a chain being pulled and locks undone. The door opened and I saw no one but I stepped through anyway and heard it close quietly but quickly.

The room was dark.

She's not here. She has lured me to this spot and now somebody is going to hit me over the head and somebody else is going to start working a few punches to my body and somebody else will put a knife to my throat and by the time they're done I'll be naked and bleeding and they'll stuff me in the tub and my body won't be discovered for days.

But then I felt the familiar arms around me and I smelled the perfume that always reminded me of hyacinth and I heard her saying in a voice that was barely audible, "I'm so glad, Garrett, I'm so glad to see you."

I felt her lips against my cheek. I kissed the top of her head and ran my hands through her hair.

"*Cómo estás?*" I asked. My voice was so low I could barely hear myself.

"Scared."

"You must be hungry too."

She nodded.

I said I'd like to eat but the hotel didn't seem like the kind of place that delivered room service. I said this jokingly and she smiled. Her hands kept running up my arms, as if she were trying to make sure I was not an apparition.

"Let's go somewhere," I said. "Let's get something to eat. We have a lot to talk about."

She told me she wasn't going to leave the room.

"You went outside before."

"A calculated risk. Besides, I wore a disguise."

"Then wear it again."

She started muttering in Spanish and the gist of it was that she couldn't believe she was involved with such a crazy person although she swiftly reached into a bag at the bottom of the closet and removed a few things I could not see clearly.

Magdalena told me to wait and to keep the room dark and above all else to remain quiet. She slipped into the bathroom while I lay on the bed and propped a pillow against the headboard. The next thing I remember is a rough shaking on my left shoulder. I was disoriented for a second because it was dark and I wasn't aware I'd fallen asleep.

When I looked up, I saw something I would not have expected even if I'd remained awake.

The woman standing over me was blond, with short curly hair. She wore dark wraparound glasses and a high-collared black dress with buttons and long sleeves. She had applied layers of blush to her cheeks and her lips were painted a metallic shade of crimson.

I tried to find a sign of Magdalena, but even her height seemed different. I looked at the floor and saw she was wearing platforms that added two inches.

"What do you think?" she asked. The voice, at least, was familiar.

"Who are you?"

She smiled. The teeth, too, were familiar.

"I can't believe you," she said as I swung my legs to the floor and tried to stand before I was ready. "I was in there less than ten minutes and you're sound asleep."

"I've had a long day."

"So have I."

"What about here?" I asked as we walked along Lincoln Road.

"I can't even read the menu. It's these glasses."

"Mexican food. Hometown cooking for you."

Magdalena shrugged as I led her in. The hostess asked in a paper-or-plastic tone where we'd like to eat and I said outside. She took us to a table and dropped two menus on it. I slid out a chair for Magdalena and sat down and spread a napkin on my lap and opened the menu and asked my lover if she could see any of it. She said she could make out only a few words but she had a good idea of what she wanted, and what she wanted most was a margarita. I ordered one too and when it came I lifted it to my mouth and enjoyed the way the salt left my tongue dry and wanting more.

Magdalena put her glass down. She had taken half her drink in her first attempt.

"Where's Ernesto?" I asked.

"*No sé.*"

"Have you talked to him?"

"*Cuándo?*"

"*Hoy.*"

"*Sí.*"

"You told him Frank was back?"

"Of course."

I glanced around. Dozens of people were looking in the windows of stores that were already closed for the night and although we were in a public place, surrounded by potential witnesses, I had a vision of gunmen walking up to us out of the shadows. When they opened fire passersby would scream and scatter as Magdalena and I slumped to the ground, blood and life oozing from us. Afterward the descriptions of our killers would conflict.

"Where has Ernesto been?" I asked.

"In a different place every night. Mostly in the Everglades."

"Why did he disappear?"

"It wasn't because of you. Sorry."

Magdalena lowered her glasses. I could see the playful glint that always appeared whenever she was teasing me.

"I never thought it was. Did he disappear because of Frank?"

Magdalena tossed her menu to the side of the table. "Where's our waiter? I'm starving."

The man who had brought our drinks was leaning against the bar, his hands thrust deep in his pockets. I raised my arm and signaled. We could hear him sighing as he trudged toward us.

"What do you want?" he asked in the surly tone New York cab drivers used back when they spoke English.

I said we'd like to order. Sighing again, with the kind of effect that labeled him an out-of-work actor, the waiter rummaged for an order form.

Magdalena spoke sharply. Even with my imperfect Spanish, I understood she was telling him to change his attitude.

His back straightened. He asked in Spanish what we would like. As soon as he was out of earshot, I told Magdalena that I didn't think Ernesto was afraid of anyone.

"Frank is a scary individual," Magdalena said.

"Frank wanted to invest in Tierra Grande. Ernesto didn't want him to. Am I right about this so far?"

Magdalena nodded.

"Why was Ernesto opposed?"

"He wanted to forget Frank. He wanted to forget that part of his life."

"But he didn't want to forget you."

She lit one of her slim cigars. "Ernesto and I have a relationship. You think that means we must be sleeping together." She turned her head to the side, blew out a plume of smoke, and said, "We're *simpático*. We always have been. We tell each other things we tell nobody else. But I have never made love to him. I've never wanted to. He's a handsome man, but he's so old."

I ran my fingers up the sides of my head. I rarely get headaches but I felt a dull throb in my temples and I was beginning to regret the margarita. I needed to ask Magdalena about Duncan McNabb and what she had done for Ernesto in California way back when.

But I could not find the words and Magdalena was talking. Usually I hung on everything she said but now it was like background noise and all I could make out was how nice Costa Rica was and how much I would enjoy it.

I had to say something and what came out of my mouth was this: "Why was Frank so gung ho on investing with Ernesto?"

"Frank needed a place to put his money."

"To launder it?"

Magdalena nodded, and I laughed.

"But Ernesto was probably using Tierra Grande to launder his own money. He didn't need something dirty from somebody else."

Magdalena nodded again. "I'm not sure exactly. But that's a good guess." She laughed too. "Frank spent all that time fighting the Communists. Do you know who he's been working with the past couple of years? Before he came here? Russians."

I smiled at the irony but I also thought of Ernesto Rodriguez and Frank Hedges, once warriors in the twilight struggle against Communism, now reduced to arguing over a real-estate deal. For some people, the triumph of capitalism has proved unexpectedly difficult.

And then I remembered Magdalena hovering at the back of the Copleys' seminar at a small hotel conference room in Miramar.

"If Ernesto's out of the picture, Frank still needs to put his money somewhere."

Magdalena emitted another plume of smoke. "He's probably been trying to figure that out. While he's been out of sight. *Bastardo.*"

"He keeps coming back to the Copleys. He thinks they can make his money clean."

Magdalena nodded vigorously. "That promotion of yours—now the Copleys will bring in lots of cash. Frank will be able to hide his."

"He wants to be their partner. Or buy them out."

"It makes sense. He'll have total control."

"But they're not interested."

Magdalena shook her head. "Frank took 'no' from Ernesto, but he was very unhappy about it. He won't take it from them."

I walked over to the pay phone near the bar and called the Copleys. They weren't home, which surprised me. So I left a message on their machine telling them to get out of town until the matter of Frank Hedges and Ernesto Rodriguez was resolved.

As we walked back to her hotel, Magdalena told me the plan: With false identities ready, complete with passports, we'd pay cash and fly first to JFK under assumed names, then change planes and catch a flight under the names on our passports to the Cayman Islands. From there we'd fly elsewhere in the hemisphere. We'd be on the move for a month before finally stopping in Costa Rica.

When we stopped outside her room, she grabbed my arm and pulled me toward her. I thought she wanted to kiss me but instead she put her palm against my chest and stood on her toes and murmured this into my right ear: "I'm afraid."

"We'll be okay. It's a good plan."

"*Ahora mismo.* What if they know we're here? What if they're waiting for us in the room?"

It was dark in the hall but I could see the fear in her eyes so I took her key and slipped it into the lock and turned the knob and pushed open the door. We both stayed in the hall for a minute.

No sounds. No movement.

I went in first and turned on the light and for a second the brightness was blinding; I squinted and blinked until everything came into focus—the TV only a few inches from the foot of the bed, the faux Moderne chair wedged into the corner, the indentation in the pillow where I'd fallen asleep before.

I opened the closet suddenly, hoping the quick motion would immobilize, at least for a second, anybody who was in there.

The closet was empty except for a small suitcase.

I dropped to the floor and lifted the skirt of the bed and saw nothing except dust. I moved toward the bathroom. The door was closed and I tried to remember if we'd left it that way. When I put my hand on the knob I felt my breath getting short.

This door I opened slowly. I wanted a chance to get away. I wanted to shout a warning to Magdalena.

The hinges made a horrible squeaking sound.

I waited.

Nothing happened.

I turned on the light and as the switch flicked upward the sound reminded me of a bullet being fired. I jumped a bit but everything seemed in order—towels neatly folded, medicine cabinet closed, toilet seat down.

The shower curtain was pulled taut. It had not struck me at first but now it seemed obvious that something was hidden there and I felt my mouth go dry as I swallowed a few times and shifted my weight to the balls of my feet. I was ready to tear open the curtain and then jump away, yelling to Magdalena to run to safety and get help while I grappled with whoever it was.

I yanked the curtain aside and leaned away from it. I started to cry out but the words stuck in my throat.

A six-inch-long black bug with a glistening shell scurried across the bottom of the tub. I looked around for something to kill it with while I muttered about the size of tropical insects.

And then, with no warning whatsoever, the thing sprouted wings, spread them and flew right toward my head.

"*Jesus Christ!*"

"What is it?"

Magdalena rushed in. I hopped around and waved my arms in every direction and invoked the names of various deities.

"What happened? *Qué? Cómo?*"

Perhaps she thought I was having a seizure. All I could do was spit out the words, "That . . . *insect.*"

She spotted it on one of the light fixtures. I asked what it was.

"A palmetto bug."

"What's that?"

"A huge flying *cucaracha* that stings."

I backed away while Magdalena grabbed a guidebook from the Chamber of Commerce and began swatting at the thing, which became airborne again and started buzzing around her head.

"Open the door!"

I did. Magdalena came out of the bathroom brandishing the guidebook like a sword as the big angry bug buzzed around her head.

"*Vamonos! Vamonos!*"

For a second I thought it was heading right for my face, so I shielded my eyes and swatted at where I thought it was with my hand, but the only thing I felt was heavy, sticky air.

"Close the door!"

I slammed it shut.

Magdalena sat at the edge of the bed and her breath came in short bursts, as if her lungs would allow only a little air each time she inhaled.

She took off her wig and shook her head but her hair had become sweaty and it clung to her scalp. She closed her eyes and leaned back and for a moment it seemed as if a lifetime on the edge had left her overpowered by weariness.

I realized I could not go with her.

The thought occurred to me suddenly but it seemed obvious, as if somebody had pointed out an irritating habit I should have known about for years. I was unsuited by training or temperament for the kind of life I would have with her—constant suspicion of my surroundings, the perpetual glance over the shoulder, moving every few months despite our protestations that this time we had found a place where we could stay forever.

New identities.

New stories to remember.

Never making friends.

I knew where I was going: back to Helen and New York. Soccer dad. Little League coach. Member of the PTA. The other parents would ask me to do publicity for fund-raising drives and school plays.

Of course I might wind up in the parallel universe: Divorced father. Downtown loft. Mailing child-support checks once a month for a kid I rarely saw and bitching about my ex-wife to the twentysomethings I dated. Always comparing any woman in my life to the one I was with at this moment.

But I had been too successful with my questions. I now knew too much about her.

"Relax for a bit," she said. "This may be our only chance. The flight's at six in the morning."

"I can't," I said.

"Yes, you can. Just kick off your shoes and lie down."

"I can't go with you."

She opened her eyes and turned her head toward me. At first she had a small smile but it disappeared as soon as she looked in my eyes.

"I talked to Duncan McNabb," I said. "I know all about what you and Frank and Ernesto did in California."

"No, you don't. Because he doesn't."

"I know enough."

"He's an *idiota*. Flashing all that money around, with the cars and the boat and the houses. It got to the point where the police had to arrest him. If he'd stayed low-key, he could have retired by now."

"Then why hasn't Ernesto retired? Why hasn't Frank?"

"Most of what they made went to The Cause. Frank and Ernesto were fighting the Communists, remember?"

"Who were you fighting?"

"Nobody. I wanted excitement."

"You certainly found it. McNabb told me about that night you were ready to shoot him."

Magdalena shook her head. If she hadn't been so tired and nervous, she might have laughed.

"The gun wasn't loaded. The *idiota* and his *amigos* were so stoned they didn't notice." She turned away from me and seemed to be studying a pattern on the wall that only she could see. "Everything we did was because we were asked to. Everything."

"You were just following orders?"

I could not keep the sarcasm out of my voice. Magdalena looked sharply at me.

"We did what we had to. Ernesto is a businessman. So was my father, and I learned a few things. Were we tough? Certainly. Ruthless? Absolutely. But that's the only way to succeed, Garrett. Nobody ever got ahead by being nice. So stop being a child."

As I put my hand on her shoulder, I realized this would be the last time I touched her.

"And whatever you do, don't judge me. You don't have the right."

She pushed me away and rolled over. I could see only her back.

"Go," she said. "Just go."

SEVENTEEN

The bodies of Winston and Evan Copley were discovered early the next morning in the small house they were renting in Hallandale. The police said the place had been ransacked and there was no telling how much had been taken, although the brothers didn't have much worth stealing. Maybe a CD player. The Copleys had been bound and gagged and their throats were slashed and cigarette burns covered much of their bodies.

"The Copleys were in the news only twenty-four hours earlier," the announcer on the all-news station said, "when one of their properties was the centerpiece of a campaign titled 'Strip Malls Are Beautiful'—"

I snapped off the radio and stumbled into the hall. Everything in the world was upside down. Winston and Evan Copley were more than a little eccentric, but they were earnest and well-meaning and I kept telling myself that the only thing I was trying to do was help them.

I wanted to talk to someone and suddenly I realized what was disorienting me most of all: I missed Helen. I needed a sounding board and some sympathy and most of all reassurance; I wanted my wife to tell me that this wasn't my fault. That none of what had happened was my fault.

I knew I should call her but I had no idea where she was. I looked at my watch. She wouldn't be at her desk until nine.

When the phone rang I took an involuntary step toward it, as if somehow I had willed her into calling me. But something made me stop. My inborn wariness told me it was best to start screening all my calls.

Juanita Lopez said she was sorry to tell me this, but in case I hadn't heard, the Copley brothers had been found murdered at their house. She was wondering if I had any comment.

Cameras, microphones and news vans lapped against the front of my office building and I knew what would happen if I plunged ahead: I'd shield my face and shout, "No comment," while reporters bellowed questions that could not be distinguished from each other. The footage would run on the news at noon and perhaps CNN.

I turned sharply to my left, headed down the alley that led to the freight entrance and skirted past a mound of garbage that was already giving off a stench that lingered in the humidity. I heard a rustle and jumped a bit, imagining for a second that whoever had killed the Copleys was now lunging at me.

The only thing I saw was a rat, long and gray and hairy, moving listlessly from one bag to another.

When I reached the rear of the building I pressed the button for the freight elevator. It was big and boxy and large enough to hold a dozen people and all the office supplies they'd ever need. One man was in it, a burly Cuban in his fifties. His shirt was hanging out and there were bags under his eyes and although he was tall, his back and shoulders were slumped in the manner of a man doing graveyard hours who was, mercifully, at the end of his shift.

He looked at me—suit and tie, leather briefcase, newly showered and shaved and scented with expensive cologne—as if he knew I was trying to hide from something.

"What do you want?" he asked.

I grinned and wished the man a good morning and tried to step inside the elevator. He stuck a beefy hand in my chest and said I wasn't allowed.

"I work here," I said.

"For freight only. Can't you read?"

He pointed to a sign above the entrance that said, *"CARGA SOLA-MENTE."*

"I have to use this elevator."

He shook his head.

"What's your supervisor's name? I'm gonna tell him—"

"He won't care."

I shoved his hand away from my chest and stepped right up to him.

He was inches taller than I was. Pounds heavier. I could see the grime and smell the sweat from a night of hard work.

"Goddamnit what's wrong with you?"

He backed away.

"I just wanna use the fucking elevator. What's so fucking hard about that?"

He was retreating into the corner and his whole body was sagging and I stood on my toes while my veins bulged almost to the point of bursting and suddenly I knew I had power, I would overcome this man, if I showed enough force I could overwhelm anything that got in my way.

"I just wanna go up to the tenth fucking floor so I can do my fucking job. And if you don't let me do that, I'm gonna kick your fucking ass back to Cuba and let fucking Fidel take care of you."

He could have crushed me. Just picked me up by my Armani suspenders and tossed me on top of the boxes and packages and plastic bags leaking sticky day-old coffee.

Instead he slunk toward the controls and pushed the button for Number Ten.

I slowed as I approached Isabel, who was focusing on her nails and the phone. She kept glancing over her right shoulder, which was toward the way I had entered the office from the day I began working in Miami.

I told myself to be as quiet as possible.

She was talking in Spanish, I assumed to a girlfriend, and in the rough translation I was able to make she was saying something like:

"The creep's in big trouble now. It's about time. He thinks he's so much smarter than everyone else."

I coughed, more loudly than necessary. Isabel looked at me as if my existence made no difference to her.

"*Buenos días,*" I said, as coldly as I could.

She tilted her head in a manner that could be construed as a nod and said my boss wanted to see me in his office. *Inmediatamente.*

I put my briefcase under my desk and reached for the phone. I had to call Helen and whatever my boss wanted to talk about could wait.

Isabel must have seen me because she cupped her hand over the receiver and said, loudly enough so the entire office could hear: "You have to go now. There's a man with him. He's from the FBI. They both want to talk to you."

I glanced at my colleagues, the people with whom I worked and shared idle chatter. They were all looking into my office, and from the expressions they wore I could see that they all assumed I was guilty of something.

We will always believe the worst about people we know.

When I entered my boss's office he did not rise or extend his hand or make any other gesture of greeting. All he said was, "We've been expecting you."

"It's a shock," I said. "A terrible shock."

My boss pointed toward the corner sofa.

"This is Agent Lang, with the FBI. He says you've met before."

The man sat ramrod straight, both feet firmly on the teal carpet. Resting in his lap was a small black pad with a silver pen clipped to it. He was shaved and his hair was slicked back and he wore an off-the-rack suit and it was hard to reconcile this remorseless-looking man with the guy who kept chugging cans of Bud on Virginia Key.

From the way he stared, I could tell that he had always expected to be facing me in a situation like this.

His name was Richard. Not Rich or Rick or any of the diminutives one could attach. Richard.

"We went sailing once," I said. "Our wives work together."

My boss nodded slightly, as if he had to acknowledge this information but had no interest in it.

"Agent Lang called me at home early this morning," my boss said. "Got me out of bed, in fact."

I cringed. If there was one thing my boss prized, it was his eight hours a night.

"I'd just returned from a crime scene," Richard Lang said. "I don't sleep after I go to one."

Neither one of them had asked me to sit. Whenever I stand for a long time, my lower back aches.

"Why is the FBI interested in the Copleys?" I asked.

"For openers," Lang said, "their names aren't Copley."

At first I suspected a macabre joke and looked at my boss in the expectation of receiving a wink or knowing chuckle that would relieve me of the responsibility of taking this man seriously. But my boss avoided eye contact, and his attention was absorbed by the yellow legal pad in front of him, on which he drew a series of ever-expanding concentric circles.

"Then what are their names?"

"Winston Copley's real name is—or was—Jack D'Agostino."

"And Evan is—or was—Somethingelse D'Agostino," I said. "And I really don't see how important it is, or how it concerns me."

FBI Agent Richard Lang flipped through his notepad—for effect, I thought, because he began speaking the nanosecond he reached a particular page, without bothering to look at the information that was written on it.

"Evan Copley's name was Paul Calabrese. And believe me, my friend, this does concern you."

I looked from Lang to my boss and back again. They looked like guardians of a riddle who were reluctant to divulge the answer.

"They were in the Witness Protection Program," Lang said at last. "When something like this happens, it's bad for business."

I found myself taking a chair.

In the mid-eighties, Jack D'Agostino and Paul Calabrese had opened a restaurant together in Providence, Rhode Island. They loved food, loved to cook, loved each other, and within a couple of years their place was regarded as one of the best in New England. But business fell when the economy turned down. Matters were made worse by Jack D'Agostino's gambling debts. The two of them owed money to banks and loan sharks and there was no way to pay them.

Then Paul Calabrese had an inspired idea: honesty. He told the local mobsters about the financial problems he and D'Agostino were having, but he also proposed a solution—have somebody torch the restaurant, so the two of them could get the insurance money and repay their creditors.

It was a good plan. The only flaw was that the FBI knew all about it. The restaurant had become a hangout for wiseguys and wannabes, so the feds had the place wired. They let the fire proceed, then arrested D'Agostino and Calabrese when they filed their insurance claim.

"We threw the book at them," Lang said. "Conspiracy, arson, intent to defraud, double parking." He laughed and my boss joined in.

Jack D'Agostino and Paul Calabrese were not gangsters. They were just a couple of closeted, overweight, middle-aged gay men who were staring at twenty years in prison.

Unless they made a deal.

Which they did.

They testified against the guys who had helped them burn down their restaurant. Those men, in turn, testified against their superiors— the capos and bosses of southern New England's leading organized crime family.

There were convictions all around; the media praised a great victory for law enforcement.

As part of their deal, the government gave D'Agostino and Calabrese new identities. The two of them told agents they felt as close as brothers, so the feds made that bond seem real. D'Agostino and Calabrese said they were tired of northern winters. The feds sent them to Florida.

"Why Florida?" I asked.

"We send a lot of people to Florida," Lang said.

"You're crazy. There are a million criminals down here."

"That's why it's perfect. They blend in."

Jack D'Agostino and Paul Calabrese became Winston and Evan Copley. At first the government gave them jobs in the Social Security Administration, but the two of them were used to working for themselves and hated the bureaucratic routine. So they quit to start their own business. They promised to be strictly legitimate.

"They'd dabbled in real estate in Providence," Lang said. "They probably figured this was a fucking gold mine."

The Copleys' investment business, with its emphasis on REITs, was no more or less successful than hundreds of others like it. But it was low-key until the federal marshal assigned to keep track of them was transferred to Seattle. Nobody else was told to monitor them, leaving the Copleys unsupervised.

"And that's where you come in, my friend," Lang said. "You raised their profile. And it got them killed."

"How was I supposed to know?" I said. "I'm not a mind reader."

"How did they seem to you?"

"'Seem?' They 'seemed' weird. But if I threw out everybody who acted a little strange, I wouldn't have many clients."

"Maybe Garrett went a little over the top on the campaign," my boss said.

"How did they feel about it?" Lang asked.

"I sensed reluctance," my boss said. "They were quiet guys. Kept to themselves. They made it clear they didn't want to be out front on this."

"Didn't that tell you something?"

"This is a public relations firm," I said. "When people come to us, it's because they want publicity."

"Or want us to manage it," my boss said.

"You're gonna get a lot now," Lang said. "I hope you're ready."

He snapped his notepad shut and rose to leave and suddenly I understood that this visit was about placing blame, not obtaining information. Within a few hours the media would know the true identities of the men I still thought of as Winston and Evan Copley, and questions would arise as to why this had happened, and the FBI would say the two could have lived a long and secret life if it weren't for the intervention of a certain PR campaign.

Above all else, this double murder was not the fault of anyone in the government. If there's one thing civil servants believe in protecting, it's themselves.

"How do you know?" I asked.

Lang stopped at the door. "Huh?"

"How do you know that what we did led to their deaths?"

"Because I don't believe in the fucking Easter Bunny."

He reached for the knob.

"You haven't offered any proof," I said.

He looked at me as if I were a disease-bearing tick.

"I'm using my common sense," he said. "This stunt of yours was all over the news yesterday. Somebody in the Mob saw it, tracked them down and whacked them."

"In less than one day?"

"How else could it have happened?"

I found myself standing. I found myself walking slowly toward him. I found myself staring straight into his eyes.

"I don't know," I said. "And I don't think you know, either. You have a hunch. A theory. That's great. I'm not saying you're wrong. But I am saying you should do a little more investigating before you lay all this on us."

He looked over my shoulder. My boss was still behind his desk and Lang's next words, although directed at me, were clearly intended for my superior.

"How many angles are you playing, Doherty?"

He mispronounced my name. Deliberately, I thought.

"Fewer than you are, Dick."

Lang left. The door rattled behind him.

I whirled around and started to speak but the words died in my throat as I saw my boss reach for the telephone. It was a sign that my presence was no longer required—not now, and perhaps never. In less than a day, I had gone from golden boy to pariah.

"A preemptive strike," I said. I was surprised the words escaped.

My boss did not look up. He continued to punch in a number, and from the amount of keys he was pressing I guessed he was calling overseas.

"Why don't you write a memo, Garrett, and give it to my secretary?"

I walked over to my boss's desk and put my hands on it and leaned over him in a manner I hoped he found vaguely intimidating.

"We don't have time for a memo," I said. I kept my voice low and steady although I was struggling not to shout. "The shit's gonna hit the fan in a couple of hours and we need to get something out right now. To give the media our side first so they train their fire on the FBI, not us."

My boss stopped hitting the keys on his phone and put the receiver back in its cradle and drummed his fingers on his desktop.

"Something up your sleeve?"

"I'm gonna draft a statement we can give to the media. There's a bunch of them outside the building."

"What do we say?"

"We talk about how distressed we are. We emphasize that we didn't know anything about the Copleys' past. That they were wonderful clients. That they never said anything about their past. We end it by saying how distressed we are."

"Make sure you run the ball by me, Garrett."

"You'll have it in fifteen minutes. Those FBI assholes won't know what hit them."

I felt as if I had just discovered a path through quicksand but when I reached for the knob I said, under my breath, more for my own benefit than my boss's, "I still don't believe the Mob tracked them down in less than a day."

And then I remembered something I should have said to Richard Lang. It was a point I would have made if he'd asked me any questions, or if I hadn't been so rattled by his inquisition.

"Talking to yourself, Garrett?" my boss said. "At least then some-body's listening, right?"

"Right," I said before grinning quickly.

And then I was out of his glass cage and running across the floor of the Miami office of Cooperman and Associates at a no-doubt-about-it sprint, my jacket threatening to rip at its seams and my colleagues throwing not-so-idle glances in my direction. As I approached the eleva-tor bank I began shouting Lang's name with what I hoped was a proper mixture of respect and desperation. One of the elevators was open and I rushed toward it even though I couldn't see if anyone was inside.

I thrust my hands in just as the doors began to slide together. When I stepped inside, I saw Lang standing by the panel. The light for the lobby was lit.

"I just remembered something," I said. The words came out in gasps. "I should have said it before."

"How's your wife?" Lang asked.

"She's fine. Thanks for asking."

Lang shook his head, as if he'd just found some vermin in the kitchen at a three-star restaurant. "I took it easy on you in there. I didn't tell your boss about that scene with Helen the other night."

I waited a second before replying. "That's none of your business."

"It is when she winds up at my house. She was hysterical. Diana's letting her sleep in the guest room."

He looked at his watch and turned away from me.

"You didn't ask me about the message I left on the Copleys' machine last night."

"I didn't hear anything."

"I called them between eight and nine and told them to lay low. You must have heard it."

He shook his head. I thought he was on the verge of smiling.

"It was on their tape. The local cops must have it. You should track it down and—"

"I checked that house thoroughly. Top to bottom. I didn't hear any-thing."

He said these words slowly, as if I was having trouble grasping a particularly easy lesson.

I had dissembled enough over the years to recognize when a man was lying. At first I couldn't figure out why Lang was being so bald-faced, but then I had a realization: He's protecting Ernesto.

Lang glared at me as the elevator opened. I leaned back and closed my eyes, ready for the ride back to the tenth floor.

"There he is! Omigod! He's there!"

I recognized Juanita Lopez's voice, even though it was cast in a higher pitch than the usual somber tones she used for the nightly slaughter. She was in the front line of a regiment of reporters who were backed by a battalion of still and video cameras. They must have overrun the security outside the building, and now they swarmed toward me.

My first instinct was to flee. Just press Ten and the Close Door button and ascend to a place that offered dubious sanctuary. But then I thought of the footage they'd get and how it would look—an expensively dressed yup trying to run away from reasonable questions. The image would outweigh whatever words I ended up putting in my statement.

I stepped out of the elevator while Lang slid around the media rush. Reporters and photographers jostled to get close to me and the din of questions drowned out everything, including my own thoughts. I breathed deeply and reminded myself to look serious. Two men were dead after all.

I began this way: "Speaking on behalf of everyone at Cooperman and Associates, I want to say how saddened and distressed we all were to hear about the deaths of Winston and Evan Copley. We certainly hope that the perpetrators of this grisly crime are apprehended, and brought to justice. In the meantime, we intend to cooperate fully with the authorities in their investigation."

From inches away, the reporters shouted their questions. Most of them were variations on a theme—were the Copleys' murders somehow related to the strip-mall campaign?

I tried not to laugh as I raised my hands, narrowed my eyes, shook my head. "Please," I said softly. "Please, please." I hoped this would make the broadcasts. Nothing arouses public sympathy like enduring a siege by the media.

"I'll have a statement for you in fifteen minutes," I said. "As a matter of fact, I was in the middle of drafting it when I came down here. If you'll just be patient—"

Clamor. Din. Asking reporters to wait always sends them into a frenzy.

I started to shout: "I just want to say, on a personal level, that I regarded Winston and Evan Copley as more than clients. They were my friends, and I'm grieving for them. Thank you."

I stepped away and headed back to the elevator as security tried to herd the media out of the lobby. Behind me I could hear questions (most of them along the lines of "Do you know who did it?") but the savviest one belonged to a voice I identified as Juanita Lopez: "Why did you come down here in the first place?"

The statement took me five minutes to write. My biggest problem was dealing with a paper jam in the printer. I brought the draft to my boss, who read it and nodded and handed it back. I ran off a hundred copies and rode down to the lobby.

It was empty, except for a businessman and businesswoman who had the nasty and impatient air of a couple blaming each other for being late.

"If you'd just been on time—"

"If you'd just ask for directions—"

I told myself it was possible the guards had shoved the media outside. But on the street and sidewalk the sights were the normal activity of a workday morning—cars and buses cruising by while well-dressed men and women with cell phones walked quickly, bags and briefcases held tightly against their bodies.

"Looking for someone?"

I turned around as Juanita Lopez emerged from behind the column that was hiding her.

"Where is everybody?"

"You gave them some quotes, and they left. What do you expect? Nobody wants a statement."

I threw my shoulders back and grinned. "But you stayed. Good girl. I'll give this to you first."

I handed her a sheet of paper, which she barely glanced at. "I stayed because I thought you were hiding something. Everybody else went to a triple murder in Hialeah."

"Read it, Juanita. Then ask your questions. This statement is not your usual PR bullshit." I grinned again. "Not so much of it, anyway."

She gave me a look that indicated she knew better than to believe any of my assurances, but she started to read. After thirty seconds, she stopped and went back to the top and traced some words with a well-manicured finger.

"Holy shit," she said. "The Witness Protection Program. Holy shit." She grabbed my wrist. "You have to give this to me exclusively, Garrett. Exclusively. What can I do for you?"

"When I get back to my office, I'm gonna fax a copy of this to *The Herald*. I won't send this to the other broadcast outlets for a half-hour, and it'll probably take at least that long for *The Herald* to update its Website. That should give you time to put a special report on the air."

Juanita Lopez nodded vigorously.

"One other thing," I said.

She froze. The way she was panting, sexual favors were not out of the question.

"I want to read the second paragraph of this statement for the camera. And I want you to run it, in full, in your report."

"You know the rules. No guarantees."

"This is very important to me."

A young man toting a video camera and a cell phone ran from around the corner, crying out in Spanish that the news director had just called and wanted to know why they weren't on their way to Hialeah.

"I'm sorry to play hardball like this," I told Juanita Lopez. "But if you don't do it my way, I'm gonna fax this to the other stations. Call them up, too. You know how it goes."

She grabbed the cameraman's cell phone and punched in a number while directing the guy to get ready to shoot. I heard her say, "I'm still downtown . . . I know, I know . . . Listen . . . Listen . . . *Will you listen to me for a minute?*" She looked jazzed by the energy from the tension we'd created.

"I have something on the Copleys. Exclusively." A short pause. The tone of the voice on the other end went from hectoring to quizzical. "They were in the Witness Protection Program." An explosion of noise from the cell. "I'll have something ready in fifteen minutes. We're gonna kick everybody's ass. Don't worry about Hialeah. People get murdered there every day."

She put the phone in her purse and pointed to the cameraman, who immediately began filming. I looked down at my statement and began reading the second paragraph, in which I emphasized three different ways that I had no idea the Copleys were under government protection and would have stopped the campaign immediately if only someone had informed me.

Back in the office I switched my TV from CNBC to Channel Seven. Within minutes *The View* was interrupted by a news bulletin. I later learned that this produced more than two hundred calls of protest.

About ninety seconds into the report, Juanita Lopez looked directly into the camera and said, "Cooperman and Associates executive Garrett Doherty"—she pronounced my name correctly, God bless her—"who masterminded the strip-mall campaign, issued a statement in which he expressed his shock and dismay over the murders. He also said this."

And there I was, my body language and voice conveying the proper tone of regret and solemnity as I emphasized that I knew nothing about my clients' past.

My phone rang. I picked it up immediately.

"Slick, Garry," my boss said. "Really slick."

I held the receiver in my hands for a long time before I finally punched in Helen's number. I wondered what I would do if I got her voicemail but on the second ring I heard the familiar voice, crisp and deep, sexy in a professional way: "This is Helen."

Why do I not love this woman? Perhaps I can learn to do it. Perhaps I can teach myself.

Of course I noticed that she did not use her married name. "Helen who?" I had asked when I called her at work a few weeks after our wedding. She had laughed and I threw out a few pickup lines and she laughed again and said she was really interested but unfortunately she'd just gotten married.

After that, she had always identified herself as Helen Doherty, always pronouncing it the way I preferred.

"It's me."

She could have screamed at me or slammed down the phone or informed me in her iciest manner that any communication between us would have to be conducted through lawyers. But instead, after a few seconds, in a voice that indicated she regarded me as merely one level above a telemarketer, she asked, "How are you, Garrett?"

I decided, for once, to be honest. "Not so good."

And then it began to creep in, the warm tone that always suffused her voice whenever she was talking to someone she cared about. "I know," she said. "I heard about the Copleys on the news. Those poor guys."

It was a mundane yet powerful thing to say, and it echoed my feelings. Whatever sins they had committed, Winston and Evan Copley had not deserved their fate.

"I know you're staying with the Langs."

"How'd you find out?"

"Richard told me. I think you should get out of there. It could get uncomfortable." I let her know about the Copleys' background and the way Lang had tried to intimidate me and the press release I had just issued. She said she hadn't heard any of this. She'd been in meetings all morning.

She also told me she had talked to Ernesto Rodriguez.

I almost dropped the phone. "When?"

"Last night. Richard said there was someone on the phone who wanted to talk to me. At first I thought it was you. I don't know why. I just did."

"Where is he?"

"I didn't ask him, Garrett. I didn't really care. He said he'd heard that we'd split and he offered to help in any way he could."

Solicitous, I thought. *Ernesto is still solicitous.*

"I think you should come home," I said.

"I'm not ready."

"Please, Helen. The house seems empty without you."

"You're good, you know that? You're really good. But I've known you awhile, and I'm not going to succumb to the charming soundbites of Garrett Doherty."

I was not sure how to react. Charming soundbites were the best weapons in my arsenal.

"Why don't you come back to the house tonight? We should talk. About Ernesto and other things. And if you're still uncomfortable, I'll check into a motel."

She paused for a few seconds before agreeing. My wife said I was right: we had things to discuss. She said she'd had a sonogram the day before and the embryo wasn't developing as quickly as it should. The doctor detected a heartbeat, but she was concerned about the baby's development and now so was Helen.

"I'm sorry," I said. "I didn't know."

"You had no way of knowing."

"It's not that. I'm sorry about everything. This is all my fault."

"That's good, Garry," my wife said. "That's a start."

Although the armies of therapists now in charge of our emotional lives constantly preach about the value of closure, I am dubious about its necessity. Life is a messy business and you cannot heal all your wounds and often the best course of action is to just move on and learn to live with your pain.

I realize this now. Back then I felt the need to talk to Magdalena one more time. I did not want "Just go" to be my last memory of her.

I called the hotel where she was staying and congratulated myself for remembering to ask for Maria Romero in Room 211.

"Ms. Romero is no longer here," said a woman with a plummy British accent.

My body drooped. Although I was no longer part of her plan, most likely she had proceeded with it on her own. That meant she had checked out at daybreak and gone to the airport. At this moment she was probably at JFK, waiting for a plane to the Caymans.

I said I was sorry to hear that. There was something important I'd wanted to say to her. And then, in a tone of idle wonderment, I asked if Señor Rodriguez had helped her depart.

"The gentleman did not tell me his name," the woman said. She was clipping her words. The Empire is gone but its tone remains.

"A middle-aged man. About six feet, with graying hair and a thick mustache. Handsome, but gaining a little weight."

"No," she said. "This gentleman was thin."

It can't be.

"With sandy hair."

It isn't.

"And a prominent nose."

Somehow I found a way to ask a question. I'm not sure if my voice was quavering but I managed to say, in what I hoped was a tone of informed guessing, "Did the man speak with a twang? An accent that could come from Texas or the South?"

The woman said American accents all sounded the same to her ear, although now that she thought about it, his voice came across as a bit hillbillyish.

I swiveled around in my chair and looked out at the bay and the ocean beyond it. My first thought was that he had managed to find her and was taking her someplace against her will.

I have to find them. I have to save her.

And then I realized it had not happened that way at all. I had spent years spinning people, telling them that black was white or at least a shade of gray, but in this matter—the most important one of my life—I had allowed myself to be manipulated.

I have to find Ernesto. They're going to kill him.

EIGHTEEN

I f you're registered to vote, all sorts of information about you is available to anyone with a decent search engine. So a trip to the Miami-Dade election rolls revealed that Pilar Hurtado was a Republican who was born on September 12, 1974. I also learned her address.

Hurtado's apartment was in a low-slung stucco affair several miles out on Tamiami Trail. The building consisted of boxlike one-bedrooms that fronted a gas station and a 7-Eleven. I walked up to the second floor on an outdoor stairway littered with candy wrappers and condoms. After I found the number I was looking for, I pressed the button right under the peephole and heard a tinny ring echo inside.

I heard nothing. Saw nothing. The blinds were drawn shut, but I sensed a presence within.

I leaned close to the door.

"Officer Hurtado?"

Nothing. Not even the stirring of molecules. I was suddenly aware of how humid it was and of how tired I felt, as if the air itself was sucking all the energy out of me.

"It's Garrett Doherty. I don't believe what they're saying about you."

I heard slow scraping, as if an overstuffed chair was being pushed along the floor while its occupant decided if she really wanted to stand and move. Footsteps sounded heavy at first and then softer, even though they were getting closer. I imagined a rug bought at a second-hand store, frayed at the edges and dulled by sunlight.

I saw a finger push up a blind and then let it fall. The footsteps came close to the door. I stood back, ready to grin.

And then it occurred to me: She wasn't here. The door would open and Frank Hedges would be standing there, inviting me to come inside. In the background I'd hear Magdalena laughing.

My back was against the railing. I was ready to leap over it and plunge to the ground and start running for the Taurus.

The door slid open until it was stopped by the safety chain. A slice of Pilar Hurtado's tearstained face appeared, then withdrew. The chain came undone, and the door opened enough to let me through.

She said I was the last person she expected to see.

Pilar Hurtado owned a couch that would have fit in perfectly at a Salvation Army thrift store, as well as chairs and a table that reminded me of the furniture my parents had purchased when I was in grade school. I looked down at the floor. The rug was even tattier than I'd imagined.

"I can help you," I said. "I know people. I know how to get a story out. Don't worry about paying me."

Pilar Hurtado walked toward her dining table, where a big handbag leaned precariously to the left.

"You should think about what you're going to do," I said. "They're trashing your name and you shouldn't let them get away with it."

She reached into the bag and removed something with her right hand.

"I could organize a press conference and—"

Pilar Hurtado turned around and pointed a gun at me. It was not her service revolver, which *The Herald* said she'd had to surrender. It looked like a semiautomatic, although I don't know enough about weapons to give the precise make, model and caliber.

She asked what I wanted. I said I wanted to help. She said she didn't believe me and shut her left eye and cocked her head to the right.

"I want information," I said. "About Ernesto."

"That's better."

"I know the charges against you aren't true."

"How?"

"Because crooked cops live a lot better than this."

She opened her eye and straightened her head, then blinked a few times before her body seemed to collapse on itself. Her shoulders shook and her head snapped forward and the gun dangled from her hand. Between sobs she said, "It's so unfair."

I put my arms around her in a light embrace.

"*Yo sé,*" I said. "*Yo sé.*"

I reached down for the gun. It slipped out of her hand and into mine. I had never held one before and was surprised by how cold it felt.

I put the gun on the dining table and wrapped my arms more firmly around Pilar Hurtado.

"Even *mi familia,*" she said. "Even they believe what the papers are saying."

Everybody always believes what they read in the paper. They say they don't, but they do.

I told her that I had meant what I said. I was ready to help.

She stepped out of my arms and slapped me hard across the face. The ring on her middle finger sliced the corner of my mouth, and I felt blood trickling toward my chin.

"*Bastardo,*" she said. "I wish I'd never met you. I wish you'd never told me about Ernesto Rodriguez."

"You could have let it go," I said. "Why didn't you?"

"He's a bad man."

"Ernesto's not a bad man. But he's done some bad things."

"He's a leader in the community," she said. "People respect him. Because they don't know the truth. You know that stuff about him being at the Bay of Pigs? Bullshit. He was in high school in Homestead."

I shrugged. Everybody inflates his résumé.

"And then there's the drugs," she said.

"He has protection," I said. "All the way up."

"You should have told me."

She said she talked to the man who had owned the land where Ernesto was building Tierra Grande. She intimidated him with her badge and he told her that Ernesto had paid him in cash. So she began watching Ernesto's vans. She watched them for days. They had returned to their old spot behind the storefront in Hialeah and several nights ago she followed one of them to Coconut Grove. The driver parked by a pier and went to a boat that had just docked.

"You can probably figure out what I found," she said.

"How much?"

"Ten kilos."

She said she questioned the driver at headquarters. He was a Caucasian with blue-green hair and rings in each ear and an attitude. He said he was just the bagman. He implied that the guy in charge was wealthy. Powerful. She asked if it was Ernesto. He didn't say no. She thought she was ready to break him when, out of nowhere, a lawyer barged in even though the driver hadn't asked for an attorney.

"Somebody leaked to Ernesto," I said. "Somebody you work with."

"The lawyer got him to shut up. Next day, he's out on bail. I tried to find him. No luck."

I said he was dead or underground or out of the country. Pilar Hurtado agreed.

"Then do you know what they did?" she asked, her voice both rising and breaking. "They took those kilos that I found, that I had seen in Ernesto Rodriguez's van, and they planted them in my locker. I recognized their markings but before I could say anything IAD had swooped in and—"

Her resolve cracked. The words came out in weepy spurts.

"—and they wouldn't listen."

"Why did Ernesto disappear?" I asked.

"It's not because of me or you," she said. Her voice regained some of its I'm-a-cop-and-you're-not toughness. "He's afraid of someone. But not us."

"Where is he?"

She shook her head.

"I have to find him. His life is in danger."

"Good."

I picked up the gun and placed it inside my jacket. I told her I didn't like the idea of leaving her alone with a weapon and her thoughts.

"You have no idea how to handle it, do you?" she said.

"Only from watching movies and TV."

"It's different in real life. It jumps in your hand. Brace yourself before you shoot."

I headed for the door.

"There's one other thing I should tell you," she said.

I turned to face her.

"If you're going to use it, take off the safety catch."

As I stepped into the furnace of a South Florida summer afternoon, I heard Pilar Hurtado laughing.

I parked the Taurus behind the building where Ernesto and I once drank Cuban coffee. I crouched behind the wheel, told myself no one would see me, and turned on the radio to listen for reports about Winston and Evan Copley.

The FBI had announced it was involved in the investigation. Beyond that it refused to comment. The radio then played some of the comments I had made in the morning. I smiled and pushed the driver's seat back and lowered myself until I could barely see over the dashboard.

I was fighting the urge to doze when the back door of the building opened. I almost sat straight up before reminding myself to stay out of sight. The chiseled figure that emerged was familiar. Aquamarine hair, six rings in each ear, a body swelled by weightlifting and creatine. He kept the door open and looked in every direction, as if he was ready to stop what he was doing if he thought he was being watched.

I slid even lower. The Taurus was on the far end of a row of parking spaces, separated from him by several other cars and a couple of Dumpsters.

He closed the door and walked toward one of Ernesto's vans. As he drove past me I shrank down as far as I could. When he turned right, I started the ignition.

He drove west and I followed. He did not change lanes or speed up. In fact he seemed unaware of my presence and in no particular hurry to get where he was going. He drove far enough west for traffic to thin out and I began to think I was now quite conspicuous, but could not turn away.

The van merged onto the turnpike and headed south. I followed easily. At the top of the hour, I discovered that the murders had gone national. The Gay and Lesbian Anti-Violence Project was demanding that the FBI investigate the Copleys' deaths as a possible hate crime. I smiled when I heard the voice of the group's publicity director. Lisa Shapiro had taken a big pay cut when she went to work for a nonprofit, but I'd heard she was happy.

I knew where the van was heading as soon as it turned off the turnpike. I recognized the piney scrubland, as well as the sudden jagged expanse where bulldozers had leveled every piece of vegetation. The sign announced that this was the future site of Tierra Grande, a luxury development by Ernesto Rodriguez and Company.

A green Chrysler (another obvious rental) was waiting by a brown mound of plowed-up earth. No one else was around—no traffic, no pedestrians, not even wildlife, as if Ernesto had banished all animals from his kingdom. I stopped as far away as I could while still keeping the car and the van in sight. I found it impossible to believe that the van's driver hadn't seen me, but perhaps he was so intent on his mission he didn't have time to lose or confront me.

The guy with aquamarine hair got out of the van. He carried two suitcases.

Ernesto Rodriguez emerged from the Chrysler, walked behind it and opened the trunk. His associate put the two suitcases in there. Ernesto pawed through their contents and nodded, as if he were a quality control inspector approving an item that had just rolled off the assembly line.

He snapped the suitcases shut and closed the trunk.

I was ready to follow him. My plan was simple: signal him when he was alone and get him to pull over and say I had important information that I would relay only if he promised to somehow make everything right with Pilar Hurtado. Then I would tell him what I thought: Frank Hedges was trying to kill him and Magdalena had been keeping both of us close at hand while he perfected his plot.

I crouched below the dashboard while the van pulled away. I saw its top cruise by and heard a second vehicle go past although I did not see it. I waited for the sound to fade. I raised myself and reached for the ignition.

Suddenly a noise as loud as an explosion filled my left ear and at first I thought someone was shooting at me and I braced for an impact, for some hard thing to crash into my head or neck. But there was no pain. Nothing whizzed past my ear. There was no blood or shattered glass.

I heard the noise again and this time I recognized it as the rapping of something hard against glass.

I turned slowly. I did not want to look.

FBI Agent Richard Lang had his left hand, wedding ring at the forefront, resting against the driver's side window.

I tried to locate his car but could not. It was as if he had materialized from an upturned root.

I considered pulling out and leaving him behind in a swirl of mud and dust.

The Chrysler was fading.

Instead I lowered the window and grinned.

"Richard, how are you?"

"What the fuck are you doing here?"

"The same as you. Watching."

"We have to talk. Right now."

"To tell you the truth, I'm kinda busy."

He reached into the car and put a rough firm hand on my wrist.

"I don't think you're in a position to refuse a reasonable request."

"Of course I'm not." I grinned again. "But if you're gonna question me in a formal way, I need to find an attorney. Because there's no way I'm talking to you, or anybody else in authority, without having a lawyer beside me."

I grew up with cops. Signs of intelligence from an opponent always flustered them.

"We don't need to go through that," Lang said.

"Good. Why don't you call me at home tonight? But make it late—Helen's coming by."

"We have to do it now."

And then an idea occurred to me—an idea so clear and simple I had to resist the urge to grin.

"It's a gazillion degrees," I said to Richard Lang. "The bugs will eat us alive if we do it here. There's a bar down the road. The last outpost of civilization. Why don't we go there?"

When I walked in I felt the surge of stillness that always passes through a room whenever somebody unexpected enters. I certainly looked out of place—a non-Hispanic white in a suit and tie and Kenneth Cole shoes, surrounded by brown-skinned men in jeans and sneakers and short-sleeve shirts.

Lang came in a few seconds later. He was the biggest man in the bar and he stood ramrod straight and his no-nonsense attitude told everyone that he did not want to be disturbed while he drank.

I motioned toward a table in the farthest and darkest corner, then told Lang I insisted on buying the first round. His eyes brightened. I headed to the bar and after a minute a bearded Cuban with a hard stare strolled over as he dried out a shot glass. I help up two fingers and said, *"Dos cervezas, por favor."* He drew two Buds and I handed him a five and said, *"Gracias."*

"You're welcome," he replied.

When I put the drinks on the table, Lang reached for the one that had slightly more beer in it. I took a sip of mine while he chugged back half his glass.

"That's good," he said. "Very good. Or should I say *'muy bueno'?"* He took another chug. "It's my own damn country and I get shit for speaking my own language."

I raised my glass to him and took another sip. I was beginning to like this place. It had sawdust on the floor.

"What do you want to talk about, Richard?"

"Why were you there?"

"I've told you. Ernesto owes my company money."

Lang downed the rest of his beer and said he wanted another. I made no attempt to stop him. As I waited for him to return, one of Lisa's aphorisms crashed into my head: *Only losers play defense.*

"Where's the tape?" I asked Lang before he had a chance to sit down.

He looked genuinely puzzled, as if I'd tested his sports knowledge by asking a question about cricket.

"C'mon," I said. "The tape from the answering machine. The one that has the message I left for the Copleys last night."

Lang shook his head. "There is no tape," he said.

"You destroyed it."

"There never was a tape."

"Why did you destroy it? Because I mentioned Ernesto's name?"

Lang knocked down about two-thirds of his glass and said, "Let me advise you very strongly to keep your goddamn mouth shut."

"I used to work at a newspaper. This sounds like a story to me."

"Ernesto is taking care of some business. It should be concluded tonight."

"Is that what he told you when you spoke with him last night?"

"All of that is privileged, my friend. But I will say this: as far as I'm concerned, twenty-four hours from now, the two of you can go back to conning people into buying mansions in the swamps."

"His business is with Hedges, isn't it?"

Lang finished his beer.

"They're going to kill him," I said. "Hedges murdered the Copleys. He probably ripped them off. Now he'll do the same to Ernesto before he disappears. Aren't you supposed to arrest guys like that?"

Lang's left hand struck the table with the force of a rock slamming into a windshield, and the cracking sound his ring made against the fake wood caused everyone in the room to look at the two gringos.

"Don't tell me how to do my job."

Each word was uttered slowly and distinctly. Each syllable contained its own threat.

"That's the last thing I'd do," I said, sipping my beer as a sign of good faith.

Lang stood up again and pointed at my glass. I shook my head. He asked if I was sure. I said I was. Within seconds, the FBI agent had returned with another Bud. I had yet to come up with another question, and this time Lang took the initiative.

"What were you doing at Tierra Grande, Garry? And don't give me that bullshit about Ernesto owing you money."

I leaned back and sipped my beer. By now it had turned flat and warm and I told myself it was good that I'd lost all desire to drink it.

"I was looking for a woman."

I'm not sure why I said that. Perhaps it was because I wanted to say something Lang would believe. Or perhaps it was the truth, and subconsciously I'd been hoping that somehow Magdalena would materialize from Ernesto's car.

Lang took a few gulps. "That girl you've been seeing on the side? I hear she's hot."

I wondered how much Richard Lang knew about me.

"I bet she fucks great."

I wanted to toss what was left of my beer in his eyes and then smash my glass in his face. Instead I drummed my fingers on the tabletop.

"I know what you think," he said. "You think you're in love with her. Because she's everything your wife isn't." He shook his head vigorously, as if I were a rookie who had just violated the most basic elements of police procedure. Then he drank some more. "Love," he said, spitting out the word as if it were a bad piece of fish. "Shit. What the fuck is it? You're supposed to love your wife and your kids but what does that mean? They're always around and after a while you just stop thinking about it. About how you feel. Because what you mostly feel is aggravation." He finished his beer. "They're always around."

He got up and walked to the bar.

An image of Magdalena, her belly swelled to bursting, asking me what we should name our child.

Lang returned with a beer that he began drinking before he sat down. Then he looked at his watch. "It's a good thing that we're here like this," he said.

"Why is that?"

"I can keep an eye on you while I wait for Ernesto to call and let me know the deal's gone down."

"You'll never hear from him."

"They're not going to kill him. Hedges and that girl you've been fucking? They just want the money. And then they'll *vamonos.*"

"Ernesto got the money by running drugs, didn't he?"

"I have no idea." Lang was in government-official-denying-the-obvious mode.

"And you're just gonna let him continue?"

"Ernesto gets a pass, my friend. That comes directly from Washington. My superiors have made it clear that from now on, a big part of my job is baby-sitting him."

"Why? What does he do?"

Lang laughed with the kind of derision that's reserved for a question that will never be answered truthfully.

"Let me put it this way: He gives us good information."

"He's being rewarded, isn't he? I know what he did in the eighties. I've talked to Duncan McNabb."

Lang brought his glass down hard on the table. The sound was like chalk breaking. Or a rifle shot.

"Your goddamn mouth, Garry. Just watch it."

That seemed to consume most of his energy. His head drooped toward his chest.

"Fuck it," he said. "I'm gonna have another."

He left me there and my beer was almost gone and I wondered how long I could continue nursing it. I thought of Ernesto getting further away and considered bolting. Just getting up and running for the door and then for the Taurus and relying on my sobriety to get me away. I figured Ernesto was on the other side of the Everglades by now.

I pushed myself from the table.

I was ready to spring up.

Lang was walking back with another full glass of beer, which he brought to his lips.

There was a patch of wet sawdust on the floor and I saw his heel ready to strike it and I was about to cry out before stifling the words. His shoe settled onto the damp spot and his feet slipped out and he landed on his back as the glass crashed onto the floor and shattered.

Everyone in the bar rushed toward his prone form. I squatted beside him. Lang was surrounded by blood and alcohol. His eyes were closed.

I asked if he was all right.

Around me I heard questions and statements that I could translate even with my imperfect Spanish: "What happened?" "Is he okay?" "What an asshole."

I bent closer and asked again if he was all right.

"Fuck," he said.

"Can you move?"

"Fuck." He raised his right knee, then his left.

"Can you get up?"

I extended my right hand and put my left arm behind his back. Lang swore a few more times as I helped him to his feet. He was bleeding from his hands and the beer had soaked his tie and shirt and jacket. He wobbled a little as I braced my arm behind him.

"Fuck," he said again.

"You need to wash up," I said. "Get yourself clean."

The bartender stepped in beside me. Perhaps he was also the owner. Doubtless he was considering the prospect of defending a lawsuit. He said he had a first-aid kit in back.

We guided Lang to a small room that had a medicine cabinet, mirror and sink. He stripped down to his boxers as the bartender began applying iodine and bandages. Lang winced. He said it hurt. He said he didn't think the bartender was doing it right.

I filled the sink with soap and water and soaked Lang's shirt and tie in it. The jacket was best left to dry cleaning.

Lang sat on a small wooden folding chair and looked at his hands, which were swaddled in white and tinged with red. He looked dazed, as if he didn't know what month it was, let alone the day of the week.

"I'm okay, guys."

That was it. No expression of thanks or gratitude.

"I'm okay. Just leave me."

He waved at us weakly, and the bartender and I returned to the main room.

I looked ostentatiously at my Rolex. "I'm late," I said. "For an important appointment. I have to go."

"What about your friend?"

"He's not my friend."

"He's in no condition to drive."

"I understand that."

"I thought you'd leave together. I thought you were the designated driver."

"I can't wait for him."

"I can't let him drive in his condition."

"I know. Legal issues." I looked around like a man scanning the heavens for a sign although I knew exactly what I was going to do. Slowly, with seeming reluctance, I reached for my wallet and put a fifty on the bar. "When he's ready, call a cab for him. Keep what's left for yourself."

The bartender slid the bill under the tray in the cash register.

"There's something you should know about him," I said.

I put my elbow on the bar and leaned close to the bartender, as if I were drawing him into a conspiracy from which both of us would profit.

"When he's had a few drinks, he likes to claim he's an FBI agent. He even has fake ID that he'll wave around. Usually it's to impress women. But sometimes he just does it."

"Isn't that illegal? Impersonating an agent?"

"He means no harm."

* * *

As I drove through the Everglades the radio stations faded and after a while I was alone on a two-lane road that cut through dying cypress and sycamore. I had no company except for my thoughts and I wondered if there was anybody left to betray.

What Magdalena had done to me was only fitting. As I made my way south and west a voice within me said it would be best to turn around. Perhaps I still had time to get back to the house before Helen arrived. I could get some takeout and set up for dinner and light the tapered candles we rarely used. Perhaps I'd even open a bottle of wine.

Of course my wife wouldn't be drinking. I had to keep reminding myself of that.

But as I drove on I realized what was luring me; why I had to keep going.

There was a chance I might see Magdalena again. If I could say just a few words, everything might work out.

By the time I reached the far end of the Everglades, the sun had slipped below the horizon and the sky had turned gold. The brightest stars were already out, and the moon was full.

I parked the Taurus and got out slowly. The place was familiar to me—asphalt parking lot, convenience store with neon signs in the window, concrete dock for the tourist boats, and above all the profound and overwhelming sound of quiet.

The green Chrysler was parked at the foot of the dock. At the far end, bathing in the glow of the brief South Florida twilight, I saw a lone figure with a fishing pole.

I walked up to him slowly. I could not escape the feeling that someone was watching me.

When I sat beside him, I let my legs dangle toward the water.

"Qué pasa, Ernesto?"

He drew back his arm and cast his line again.

"Do you fish, Garrett?"

"No. Never saw the point."

"That's what you're missing. Every man needs at least one pointless activity. What is it in your case? Women?"

He looked older. Patches of gray flecked his mustache, and there were lines around his mouth and eyes that had formed only recently.

"Chasing you around is the only pointless activity I've had recently."

"I'm sorry you had to do that."

"If you'd just paid us the money you owed, I would have dropped everything. And then none of this would have happened."

"No, my friend. It all would have happened."

"Sebastian Overstreet?"

"A nosy young man who pried into other people's affairs. But his death was an accident, wasn't it?"

"Solomon Weinstein?"

"My old friend Señor Weinstein. His time was up. In fact, it had passed long ago."

He bowed his head, as if in prayer.

"Even the Copleys?"

Ernesto nodded. "You should have let it go, my friend. In fact, you still have time. Just drive away from here. Go home to your wife. The lovely Helen. I've talked to her."

"I know."

He looked surprised for a second, as if I'd applauded at the wrong time in a speech he'd carefully rehearsed. But then he smiled, like an actor who was confident about the rest of his lines.

"I believe she will take you back. Before you know it, you'll have a child. And you'll forget all this."

"I can't do that."

"Why not?"

"You know why."

Ernesto Rodriguez cast his line again. He didn't seem interested in catching fish, just in doing something repetitive while he waited.

"I think your life is in danger, Ernesto."

A deep rumble came from somewhere within him. It was the sound of a man who does not laugh much, although he would like to.

"The only life that's in danger is yours. If you leave *inmediatamente*, you'll have nothing to worry about."

"Frank Hedges killed the Copleys and ripped them off. There's no reason to think he won't do the same thing to you. No matter what arrangements you've made."

"Go on. I find this interesting."

"I think Magdalena knew he was going to do it. I think she's been in on it from the beginning. So she kept me busy. You too."

"Rest assured, my friend, you've been much busier with her than I have. And I'm sure you found her attentions . . . soothing."

"I still love her."

"Don't. I'm quite fond of Magdalena, but she made her decision a long time ago. When she mistook excitement for love."

"Is that it? You make a mistake when you're young and you're stuck with it forever?"

"We're Catholics, Garrett. In marriage, there are no do-overs."

The dark arrived suddenly. I could barely make out Ernesto's features although he was only a few feet away. Something tugged at his line and he played with the rod and reel for a minute, shifting to his left and then his right, before bringing in an eel that was four inches long.

"That's the problem with fishing," I said. "Great effort and little reward."

Ernesto tossed the eel back into the water.

"It teaches a man patience," he said. "It would do you some good."

"Hedges is coming, isn't he? With her?"

Ernesto nodded.

"Why?"

"For the suitcases."

"What's in them?"

"You're an intelligent man. Guess."

"Ten million in cash?"

"You're close."

I grinned and meant it. "Christ, Ernesto, you've been stiffing us for thirty thousand."

The deep rumble again came from Ernesto Rodriguez. He punched me in the thigh—playfully, I like to think—and said my company

278

would have the money, with whatever interest he owed, within forty-eight hours. He said we should continue working together. He wanted to take a few days off but within a week he would be back at his office and Tierra Grande would resume. The completed project would be magnificent.

He said he still needed my help. He needed someone who knew how to deal with the Anglo media.

"I don't like that word," I said.

"What word?"

"Anglo. The Anglo-Saxons were the ones who oppressed the Irish. That's why I insist on pronouncing my name the way my ancestors did, not the way the English forced them to."

Ernesto shrugged. He said all of this was news to him.

"That's the problem with the world," I said. "Nobody is interested in anybody else's problems."

Ernesto tossed out his line again. "It's funny, though," he said.

"What's funny?"

"Your access to the Anglos—it's the only reason you're still alive. Some people wanted to kill you, but I said, 'He's only a minor nuisance. He will help me greatly when this unpleasantness is over.'"

"Is it really over?"

"What do you mean?"

"I've heard this is what you do."

"That blundering police officer," he said, with the steel his voice acquired whenever he encountered someone who was trying to thwart him. "She told you things that were not true."

"Such as?"

"I have not been in that business for many years."

"Then why did you go back?"

"I did not want Mr. Hedges involved in my life. In any way, shape or form."

"So you're paying him off?"

It was difficult to tell in the darkness, but I believe Ernesto Rodriguez nodded.

"You don't strike me as the type," I said.

"For what?"

"To give in to extortion."

"I'm helping Magdalena."

Solicitous, I thought. *Ernesto is still solicitous.*

"What happens next?" I asked.

"A boat comes in. It will take them to a seaplane, which I believe will fly them to the Caymans. From there . . ." He shrugged. "They're adults. They can take care of themselves."

Behind me I heard a car slow down and then drive away.

"Magdalena said she wanted me to go with her. To JFK, and then to the Caymans."

"At that moment, she might have meant it. But Mr. Hedges would have intervened."

"Did she help him kill the Copleys?"

"No sé."

I stood to leave. But then something occurred to me as Ernesto Rodriguez cast his line once more into nothingness.

"You still have friends in the government. Why didn't you explain the situation? Ask them for help?"

I believe Ernesto smiled. "Austerity is in vogue. Fiscal discipline. They were sympathetic, but could not help."

"So you disappeared while you made your arrangements?"

"I dealt with a lot of people I had not talked to in years. And had not missed. It took all of my time and energy."

"Have you talked to Duncan McNabb recently?"

"Señor McNabb has found Jesus. I'm sure he will be rewarded."

"You've ruined a lot of lives, Ernesto. My own isn't in such great shape."

He put his fishing line down and stood up and walked close to me. I detected a trace of cologne and wondered if he was wearing it for her.

"Let me tell you something, my friend. I did not ruin the life of anyone who would not have been destroyed anyway. That includes you."

"You're right about one thing—my problems are my own fault." I found myself jabbing my forefinger at him, like a prosecutor trying to break down a recalcitrant witness. "But you ran drugs into the country and sold them to Duncan McNabb. Millions of people got addicted. A lot of them went to prison or died. Communities were turned into war zones."

"It all would have happened anyway. The time was ripe. If it had not been me, it would have been somebody else. And we did things with the money. Positive things. We sent it to Nicaragua . . . Guatemala . . . El Salvador. Even some to the freedom fighters for my homeland. It's easy now to condemn what we did. But you weren't in the war. We contained Castro. We stopped the Communists everywhere else. What we achieved—it was magnificent, and no one thought it was possible."

"And the government knew?"

He laughed again. I began to think he was enjoying himself. "Your government recruited me. My one regret—"

And here he turned and walked away, and for a second I thought it was because he might cry and if there was one thing Ernesto Rodriguez would not show, it was weakness.

"—is that Luisa will no longer stay under the same roof with me. She did not approve. Even though the cause was just."

Ernesto Rodriguez looked at his watch.

"You have lingered too long, my friend. They will be here in five minutes. So will the boat. They might see you if you try to leave."

There was a restaurant at the motel where the tourists stayed. Ernesto suggested I go to the bar and have a drink. Within an hour, he told me, everyone would be gone.

The place was stuffed with overweight Midwesterners in T-shirts and Bermuda shorts. I sat at the bar and tried to avoid thinking about a life without her, or how she had fooled me.

I asked for a glass of merlot and slid a ten toward the bartender.

Soon I would be home with Helen.

"What kind of Irishman drinks merlot, for Christ's sake?"

I turned sharply in the direction of a familiar voice that was as dusty and ragged as tumbleweed.

Frank Hedges was smiling.

"One who's evolved past stout and Jameson. Cheers." I took a sip and blanched. It tasted almost like grape juice.

"Why don't we go someplace where you can get a real drink?"

"That's okay, Frank. I'll just stay here until you're gone. Don't you have a boat to catch?"

And then I saw the gun. He had on a light jacket, which made sense in the air-conditioning. The barrel nosed out of his right-hand pocket.

I thought of the result if he shot me right there: confusion, screaming, hysteria, conflicting accounts about the assailant.

Hedges drew closer to me. I recoiled when he slapped his hand on my shoulder. "Maggie wants to say good-bye."

I thought about reaching for his gun but I realized he'd shoot me before my fingers were halfway to his pocket.

I took another sip of the alleged merlot.

"Then let's not keep the lady waiting."

We walked into the humid night. Insects swirled around us. The only thought I had was to stay alive for the next thirty seconds, and the thirty seconds after that.

"Where are we going, Frank?"

"To the dock."

"It's a long walk. Let's take my car."

"That's awfully nice of you, Garry."

Sweat ran down my chest and back. My shirt was fused to my skin, as if they'd been melted together.

Pilar Hurtado's gun was still in the glove compartment.

When we got into the car I asked Hedges how he knew where I was and he said that he and Maggie—he still called her Maggie, I hated the harsh way it came off his tongue—had arrived a little early because you can never be too careful and they noticed the out-of-place Taurus in the parking lot and then they saw me talking to Ernesto. They figured I wouldn't leave because I'd be afraid of being seen. Hedges said Irishmen always headed for a bar when they had time to kill so Magdalena suggested he go there to greet me.

"I don't intend to say anything to anybody."

"I'm sure you mean that, Garry. I'm sure you do. But I've been engaged in high-risk opportunities for a long time now. And I've learned that, well, sometimes people don't carry through on their promises. No matter how much they mean them at the time."

"Was it necessary to kill the Copleys?"

"Maybe I got a little carried away." He paused and shook his head, as if he were considering some deeper truth. "Faggots. God, I hate them."

"Did Magdalena help you?"

"She got there late, Garry. To tell you the truth, she thought I'd gone overboard, but they were dead by that point."

"How did those burns get on their bodies?"

"I put them there."

"With one of her cigars?"

He nodded.

"That's one of your calling cards, isn't it? Like that reporter in San Francisco."

"You're smart, Garry. Nobody else thinks you're dangerous, but I do."

"Why did you even talk to the Copleys? Didn't you know Ernesto was going to deliver?"

"I didn't know for sure until this morning. When word got out about the Copleys, that lit a fire under Ernesto. Maggie'd gone back to the hotel and he called her there. My old friend Ernesto said he was tired of playing cat-and-mouse. He said, 'This must end now.'" Hedges smiled mirthlessly. "He said he'd give us a nice payout if we relocated."

I decided that Hedges had knocked down a few drinks himself, or else he wouldn't be talking so much.

"You were never really gone, were you?"

"After I saw Ernesto at the hotel, I decided it'd be good to disappear for a while." Hedges laughed. There was no humor behind it. "It's funny that my old friend had the same idea. Must be that government training. When the shit hits the fan, keep a low profile. We did that a lot when we worked together."

"You're going to kill him, aren't you?"

"To tell you the truth, Garry, I haven't decided yet."

I stopped the Taurus near the dock. A boat was swaying in the water as Ernesto talked to the guy with aquamarine hair. Magdalena stood off to the side. Two suitcases were beside her.

Hedges watched me as I got out of the car. I could not reach for the gun.

I greeted Ernesto and his associate before nodding to Magdalena. She motioned toward me but I stayed where I was and finally she said, "There's something I want to tell you," in a tone that indicated I had to listen to her, no matter what.

I walked over to the woman who'd once been my lover. She strained to put her mouth against my right ear so I found myself bending slightly.

"I don't want to go with Frank," she said. "I want to go with you. I knew you'd try to find me. So just get on the boat. It's all arranged."

I jerked my head back and tried to look at her directly, to get confirmation that what I'd heard was accurate and not the wishful thinking of a mind that was trying to will itself into just a few minutes more of existence.

But she had turned her head away so she could light one of her slim cigars.

Ernesto clapped me on the shoulder. His hands were beefy. I wondered why I'd never noticed.

"I'm afraid this is *adiós*, my friend."

The guy with aquamarine hair had one foot in the boat and one on the dock. He motioned toward me and suddenly I understood. Hedges' plan was to take me out on the water and dump my body into the bay. But Magdalena and Ernesto and his associate had decided on something different while Hedges waited for me at the bar.

Documents were ready. I could use his. Magdalena and I would fly to the Caymans and then go wherever we wanted. Ernesto probably figured I wouldn't demand the full ten million, or however much it was. Magdalena and I could take what we needed and put the rest in the account I was sure Ernesto had in George Town to provide future funding for Tierra Grande.

An image of Magdalena, her body stretched out on all fours, beads of sweat gliding down her back, looking over her shoulder as she waited to accept me. Asking me in a low and urgent voice that indicated she was already sure of the answer, "This is what you want, isn't it?"

It was. Despite everything I knew I wanted a future with this woman. All traces of Garrett Doherty would vanish and our lives would be filled with jokes and pranks and carefree nights of lovemaking.

At that moment, I confess, I did not think of Helen. When you want something badly enough, you don't consider the consequences.

I did not hear anyone come up behind me, although there must have been footsteps. I did not hear an arm being raised or a hand wrapping itself around a hard object. What I did hear was something like a bomb going off inside my head, as if everything inside me was trying to burst open. I think I cried out, but I'm not certain. I may only have whimpered. I know I pitched forward onto the dock and my nose smashed right into it and I tasted blood and mucous as they mingled together in a free flow toward my chin.

I heard Ernesto asking in Spanish what had happened and Magdalena calling out, "Garrett? Are you all right?"

The only sound that came out of me was a faint gurgle, as if the blow to my head had disconnected my brain from my vocal cords.

A hard heavy boot crashed into my stomach and rib cage and an angry voice from hardscrabble America screamed "You think I don't know what you've been doing? You think I'm stupid? You think I don't know what all of you are up to?"

I heard Magdalena shrieking at him to stop it.

I heard boots heading toward the boat.

I raised myself to my hands and knees. The pain in my body was surging and subsiding, like water being roiled by an approaching storm.

"Put the gun away, Frank." It was Magdalena's voice, in a tone that mixed anger and anxiety.

I tried to stand but could not. Instead I bent over like a drunk about to puke. I tried to look toward the boat but the pain was so intense I had to close my eyes. I heard Magdalena and Ernesto exchanging words with Hedges in angry Spanglish.

Hedges knew they were planning to kill him.

He wanted all the money.

He had half a mind to shoot all of them right now.

He was certainly going to take care of that motherfucker who'd been screwing his wife.

Ernesto said he was leaping to conclusions.

Magdalena told her husband he was paranoid.

Hedges told Ernesto that he had never trusted him. Not from the beginning.

Pilar Hurtado's gun was still in the glove compartment. I remembered her telling me to make sure the safety catch was removed.

I stumbled toward the car and crawled along its side, waiting for the *pop-pop-pop* of Frank Hedges' gun. I figured I had five seconds, ten at the most.

I opened the Taurus and prayed prayed prayed that Hedges didn't hear me. Leaned inside. Jiggled the handle to the glove compartment and let the door swing down.

Pilar Hurtado's semiautomatic handgun lay on top of a South Florida road map.

I reached in and grabbed the gun and tried to find the safety catch, but my eyes still had trouble focusing.

I leaned against the hood of the car. On the dock I saw a blurry form that looked like a man's back. Beyond them were three other figures at the edge of darkness.

I saw one of the figures—I believe it was the guy with aquamarine hair; the bulk indicated it was a large man—lunge forward. And then I heard and saw the sight and sound I'd been expecting: *pop-pop-pop* from the blurry form in front of me and the three figures falling, although I could not tell if they'd been struck by the bullets or were trying to get out of the way.

I pulled up what I thought was the safety catch and squeezed the trigger and what happened next was my own fault because I had ignored an important part of Pilar Hurtado's advice; I had seen too many movies and TV cop shows so I was not braced and was using only one hand.

The gun jumped up, seemingly on its own, and I had the sensation I was firing wildly into the air and the force knocked me over and I fell on my side and the gun clattered to the ground a few feet away from me.

I lay there a second looking for the gun. It was just outside my arm's reach and I slid along the ground until I was able to wrap my hand around it.

The next thing I remember is Frank Hedges standing over me. He laughed. He pointed his weapon at my head.

"What's it like?" I asked.

"What's what like?"

"Killing people. Killing them and thinking nothing of it."

"I sleep at night."

Just survive. For a second more.

I rolled over and put both my hands around the handle of Pilar Hurtado's gun and fired and fired and fired again.

As long as I keep shooting, nothing bad will happen to me.

And then the place was filled with light, as if a supernova had exploded over the Everglades, and a sharp, booming voice came through a bullhorn telling me, "This is the FBI. Stop firing. Put your weapon down. This is the FBI."

I stood up slowly and raised my hands over my head.

I wanted to find Magdalena.

Richard Lang walked toward me, his body backlit as if he were a movie star. He motioned at a lump lying on the ground. I went over and looked at it; winced when I saw that half his head was blown off.

"Who's this?" Lang asked.

"Frank Hedges. At one point, he was Ernesto's Sancho Panza."

"Real name William Zolak. Former CIA asset. He was a freelance who did work that was too dirty even for the covert guys." Lang kicked at the body the way a car buyer checks out a new set of radials. "Just another cold warrior who didn't know what the fuck to do with himself when peace broke out."

By now I could see three figures lying on the dock. Lang must have seen them the instant I did, because he swore and ran toward them and I did too.

"Oh, Christ," he said. "Ernesto Rodriguez. Christ. He's dead. Christ Christ Christ. And this guy too. Oh shit."

Magdalena was still breathing, her chest moving up and down in short, shallow movements. I knelt beside her and saw blood seeping through her clothes, the stain spreading ever outward.

I looked up at Lang, who was taking in the scene with a minimum of comprehension.

"An ambulance," I said softly.

"Huh? What?"

"She needs an ambulance!"

He glanced at her, shook his head and walked away.

Magdalena's eyes were hooded and I imagined she was looking at the void on the other side—and deciding, perhaps, that it was better than what she had known.

She lifted her eyelids. Her lips turned up, as if she were trying to smile, but her breathing was short and irregular.

"It's okay," I said. "We're gonna get an ambulance. You'll be okay."

She moved her head slightly from side to side in gentle disagreement and then raised her arm. The effort seemed to take everything within her. I thought she was going to hold my hand but instead she tried to reach up, with her palm open, and I wondered if she saw some kind of light beyond me that finally gave her everything she wanted.

The house was dark although Helen's minivan was in the driveway. I parked behind it and entered the house through the front door and turned on the lamps in the living room. I wondered where my wife was and looked down the hall to the bedroom where we'd once slept together. No light leaked out from under the door and I told myself that perhaps she had already fallen asleep.

I went into the guest room and began taking off my clothes. They were dirt-covered, sweat-soaked, bloodstained. I threw them all into a heap in the corner and told myself I never wanted to wear any of them again.

I stepped into the bathroom off the hall and flicked on the light.

The white walls were streaked with red and I saw angry splotches in the sink and the tub and especially around the toilet. My breath came in painful spurts and I didn't know if I should call the police or run into the bedroom or just flee into the night, not even bother to put my clothes on, just jump in the car and speed away. I assumed Hedges had been here to commit one final act of mayhem before heading to the Everglades.

But then I heard a soft footfall in the open doorway. I jumped as I turned toward it.

"Are you happy?" Helen asked.

I had no idea what the question meant, so I stood there mute. I had the sense that my mouth was agape. Helen's face was the color of chalk and her hair was askew. She was wearing a nightgown, but it was torn and stained red.

"You were with her, weren't you?"

I said nothing. There was nothing to say. Or perhaps there was too much.

"Was it good? Tell me. Tell me if it was good."

And then she came at me, her fists balled up and her eyes ablaze and in her fury she began pummeling me on the chest and shoulders and then she started slapping my face and I, numb, all numb throughout my mind and body, just stood there and let her do it.

"I lost the baby! Are you happy now? I lost the baby!"

She stepped away from me and her body drooped, as if the weight of everything that had happened was crushing her. I thought about putting my arms around her and uttering some meaningless words of comfort but I knew that the last thing she wanted was for me to touch or talk to her.

"I got here early. I've been waiting for hours. And then I started to cramp. And then . . ."

She didn't need to go on. The evidence was all around. Helen raised her head and looked at me through water-filled eyes that were bursting with hurt and rage.

"Do you love me?" she asked. "Did you ever love me?"

I did not answer, and by doing that, I said everything.

EPILOGUE

*W*here does betrayal begin? I've had time to consider the question. I sit all day in a room that has no light, little air, few decorations; the kind of place inhabited by people with no future, but too much past. As night falls, after I've spent hours trying to make sense of the things I've done, I look across the alley into a small apartment furnished with second-hand pieces. I often see a woman there. Many times she's with a man. They talk; they make meals; they watch TV. Occasionally they kiss. I do not know the status of their relationship, but they both wear wedding rings.

But sometimes the light in the room flicks on and the woman enters, followed by a guy I don't recognize. He carries flowers, or perhaps a bottle of wine. She smiles at him in a way she never does at her companion.

I watch from the darkness. She never draws the blinds.

After a few minutes, or perhaps an hour, when the flowers have been placed in a vase or the wine finished, the woman walks over to the guy. She undoes his pants and sinks to her knees; his face contorts with pleasure.

A few days ago, in one of my rare trips to the street, I passed by the man who lives across the alley. I caught his eye, and he looked at me curiously, as if he suspected that I had knowledge of something he cared about.

I almost spoke. A word lifted into my throat.

But it died there, and I turned away, and continued to walk with my head down.

I wonder what the woman says to him about those nights when he's not there. Probably nothing. I wonder how she explains what she's doing if she ever gets introspective, and I assume she's like everyone else. We can always justify our actions to ourselves.

I am not sure where betrayal begins. But I am quite certain of this: it never ends.

ACKNOWLEDGMENTS

I want to thank Jimmy Vines, Mitchell Ivers and Amanda Ayers for their assistance and, above all, their patience. I also want to thank Melody Lawrence for her constructive critique of a manuscript that still needed work.

Two books helped frame my thinking as I wrote this novel. *Miami*, by Joan Didion, remains a penetrating look at the city, and at the conflicts that define it. *Dark Alliance*, by Gary Webb, is a well-reported account of a recent part of our history that many people would prefer to deny. Webb's original reporting in *The San Jose Mercury-News* was controversial; at the risk of wading into an argument I'd prefer to avoid, it seems to me that his stories were pretty much on the mark.

Most of all, of course, I want to thank my wife, Jill—for many things, including the title of this book.

TOM COFFEY
New York City
November 2000